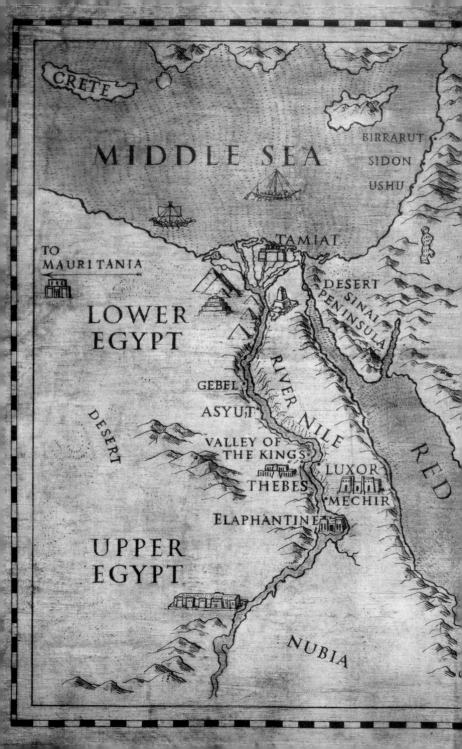

DESERT GOD

DESERT GOD

WILBUR SMITH

HarperCollins*Publishers*

HarperCollins*Publishers*
77–85 Fulham Palace Road,
Hammersmith, London W6 8JB

www.harpercollins.co.uk

Published by HarperCollins*Publishers* 2014
2 4 6 8 10 9 7 5 3 1

Map © Nicolette Caven 2014

A catalogue record for this book
is available from the British Library

ISBN: 978-0-00-759292-0

FICTION

This novel is entirely a work of fiction.
The names, characters and incidents portrayed in it are
the work of the author's imagination. Any resemblance to
actual persons, living or dead, events or localities is
entirely coincidental.

Set in Minion by Palimpsest Book Production Ltd,
Falkirk, Stirlingshire

Printed and bound in India by Thomson Press India Ltd.

I dedicate this novel to my precious wife and cherished companion, Niso. I never really knew what happiness was until I met you. Now you fill every day of mine with love, laughter and happiness

With you by my side I scorn to change my state with Kings

Aton blinked his little eyes that were set deep in their rolls of fat, and then raised them from the bao board laid out between us. He turned his gaze on the two young princesses of the royal house of Tamose who were disporting themselves naked in the limpid water of the lagoon.

'They are no longer children,' he remarked casually, without a trace of lascivious interest in the subject. We sat facing each other under an open barrazza thatched with palm fronds beside one of the lagoons in the backwaters of the great Nile River.

I knew that his reference to the girls was an attempt to distract my attention from his next move of the bao stones. Aton does not enjoy losing, so he is not overly scrupulous about how he wins.

Aton has always been high on the list of my oldest and dearest friends. Like me he is a eunuch and was once a slave. During the period of his slavery, and long before he reached puberty, his master had singled him out for his exceptional intellect and his acute mental powers. He wished to nurture and concentrate these gifts; and prevent them from being diluted by the distractions of his libido. Aton was an extremely valuable property and so his master employed the most renowned physician in Egypt to perform the castration. His master is long dead, but Aton has risen high above his slave status. He is now the chamberlain of the royal palace of Pharaoh at Thebes, but he is also a master of spies who administers a network of informers and clandestine agents across the civilized world. There is only one organization that exceeds his, and that is my own. In this, as in most things, we are in friendly competition with each other and very little gives us greater pleasure and satisfaction than to score a coup, the one over the other.

I enjoy his company immensely. He amuses and often surprises me with his good advice and perception. On occasion he can test my skill on the bao board. He is usually generous with his praise. But mostly he acts as a foil to my own genius.

Now both of us studied Bekatha, who was the younger of the royal princesses by almost two years, although you might not have guessed that fact, for she was tall for her age and already her breasts were beginning to swell and in the cool lagoon waters her nipples perked out jauntily. She was lithe, agile and she laughed readily. On the other hand she was possessed of a mercurial temper. Her features were nobly chis-elled, her nose narrow and straight, her jaw strong and rounded and her lips finely arched. Her hair was thick and sparkled with glints of copper in the sunlight. She had inherited that from her father. Although she had not yet shown the red flower of womanhood, I knew that her time was not far off.

I love her, but truth to tell I love her elder sister a shade better.

Tehuti was the senior and the more beautiful of the two

sisters. Whenever I looked upon her it seemed to me that I was seeing again her mother. Queen Lostris had been the one great love of my life. Yes, I had loved her as a man loves a woman. For unlike my friend Aton, I was gelded only after I had grown to full manhood and known the joy of a woman's body. True it is that my love for Queen Lostris was never consummated for I was castrated before she was born, but it was all the more intense for never having been assuaged. I had nursed her as a child and had shepherded her through her long and joyous life, counselling her and guiding her, giving all of myself to her without stinting. In the end I held her in my arms as she died.

Before she went on into the underworld Lostris whispered to me something which I will never forget: 'I have loved only two men in my life. You, Taita, were one of them.'

Those were the sweetest words I have ever heard spoken.

I planned and supervised the building of her royal tomb and laid her once beautiful but then wasted body in it, and I wished that I could go with her into the nether world. However, I knew that I could not; for I had to stay and take care of her children as I had cared for her. Truly, this has not been an onerous burden, for my life has been enriched by this sacred charge.

At sixteen years of age Tehuti was already a woman fully fledged. Her skin was lustrous and unblemished. Her arms and her legs were slim and elegant as those of a dancer, or the limbs of her father's great war bow which I had carved for him, and which I had placed on the lid of his sarcophagus before I sealed his tomb.

Tehuti's hips were full but her waist was narrow as the neck of a wine jug. Her breasts were round and taut. The dense golden curls that covered her head were a gleaming glory. Her eyes were as green as her mother's had been. She was lovely beyond the telling of it; and her smile wrung my heart whenever

3

she turned it upon me. Her nature was gentle, slow to anger but fearless and strong-willed once she was roused.

I love her almost as much as I still love her mother.

'You have done well with them, Taita.' Aton gave praise unstintingly. 'They are the treasures which may yet save our very Egypt from the barbarian.'

In this, as with many other things, Aton and I were in full accord. This was the true reason why the two of us had come to this remote and secluded location; although everyone else in the palace, including Pharaoh himself, was convinced that we had met here to continue our endless rivalry across the bao board.

I did not respond at once to his remark, but I dropped my eyes to the board. Aton had made his latest move while I was still watching the girls. He was the most skilled player of this sublime game in Egypt, which was as good as saying 'in the civilized world'. That is excepting for me, of course. I can usually best him in three games out of four.

Now, at a glance, I saw that this game would be one of my three. His last move had been ill considered. The layout of his stones was now unbalanced. It was one of the few flaws in his game that often, when he had convinced himself that victory was within his grasp, he threw caution to the winds and disregarded the rule of seven stones. Then he tended to concentrate his full attack from his south castle and allowed me to wrest control of either the east or the west from him. This time it was the east. I did not need a second invitation. I struck like a cobra.

He rocked back on his stool as he evaluated my surprise move, and when at last the sheer genius of it struck him, his face darkened with outrage and his voice choked, 'I think that I hate you, Taita. And if I don't, then I certainly ought to do so.'

'I was lucky, old friend.' I tried not to gloat. 'Anyway, it's only a game.'

He puffed out his cheeks with indignation. 'Of all the inane things I have ever heard you say, Taita, that is the most crass. It is not only a game. It is the veritable reason for living.' He really was angry.

I reached down under the table for the copper wine jug and I refilled his cup. It was a superb wine, the very best in all of Egypt, which I had taken directly from the cellars beneath Pharaoh's palace. Aton puffed out his cheeks again and tried to bolster his anger and affront, but as of their own accord his plump fingers closed around the handle of his cup and he raised it to his lips. He swallowed twice, his eyes closed with pleasure. When he lowered the vessel he sighed.

'Perhaps you are right, Taita. There are other good reasons for living.' He began to pack the bao stones into their leather drawstring bags. 'So what do you hear from the north? Astonish me once again with the extent of your intelligence.'

We had come at last to the true purpose of this meeting. The north was always the danger.

Over one hundred years ago mighty Egypt was split by treason and rebellion. The Red Pretender, the false Pharaoh – I deliberately do not speak his name; rather may it be cursed through all eternity – this traitor rebelled against the true Pharaoh and seized all the land to the north of Asyut. Our very Egypt was plunged into a century of civil war.

Then in his turn the Red Pretender's heir was overwhelmed by a savage and warlike tribe that emerged from the northern steppes beyond the Sinai. These barbarians swept through Egypt conquering all of it by means of a weapon which we had never known existed: the horse and chariot. Once they had defeated the Red Pretender and captured the northern part of Egypt, from the Middle Sea to Asyut, these Hyksos turned upon us in the south.

We true Egyptians had no defence against them. We were driven from our own lands, and were forced to retreat southwards beyond the cataracts of the Nile at Elephantine and into the wilderness at the end of the world. We languished there while my mistress Queen Lostris rebuilt our army.

My part in this regeneration was not altogether insignificant. I am not by nature a boastful man; however, in this instance I can state without fear of contradiction that without me to guide and counsel my mistress and her son, the Crown Prince Memnon, who is now the Pharaoh Tamose, they would never have achieved their purpose.

Among my numerous other services to her I built the first chariots with spoked wheels that were lighter and faster than those of the Hyksos, which had only solid wooden wheels. Then I found the horses to draw them. When we were ready Pharaoh Tamose, who had now grown to manhood, led our new army down again through the cataracts, northwards into Egypt.

The leader of the Hyksos invaders called himself King Salitis, but he was no king. He was at the best only a robber baron, and an outlaw. However, the army he commanded still outnumbered us Egyptians almost two to one, and it was well equipped and ferocious.

But we caught them off guard and, at Thebes, fought a mighty battle with them. We smashed their chariots and slaughtered their men. We sent them scurrying, in rout, back northwards. They left ten thousand corpses and two thousand wrecked chariots on the battlefield.

However, they inflicted heavy losses upon our gallant troops, so that we were unable to pursue and completely destroy them. Since then the Hyksos have been skulking in the delta of the Nile.

King Salitis, that old plunderer, is dead now. He did not die on the battlefield from a blow by a good Egyptian sword, as would have been just and proper. He died in bed of old age, surrounded by a horde of his hideous wives and their ghastly offspring. Amongst them was Beon, his eldest son. This Beon now calls himself King Beon, Pharaoh of the Upper and Lower Kingdoms of Egypt. The truth is that he is nothing but a freebooting killer, worse even than his evil father. My spies regularly report to me how Beon is steadily rebuilding the Hyksos army which we so grievously wounded at the battle of Thebes.

These reports are disturbing because we are having great difficulty procuring the raw materials to make good the losses that we suffered in that same battle. Our land-locked southern kingdom is cut off from the great Middle Sea and from trade with the other civilized nations and city states of the world, which are rich in leather, timber, copper, antimony, tin and the other sinews of war which we lack. We are also short of manpower. We need allies.

On the other hand our enemies, the Hyksos, have fine harbours in the delta where the Nile enters the Middle Sea. Trade flows into these uninterrupted. I also know through my spies that the Hyksos are seeking to forge alliances with other warlike nations.

Aton and I were meeting in this isolated spot to discuss and ponder these problems. The survival of our very Egypt was being held on the point of a dagger. Aton and I had on many occasions discussed all this at length, but now we were ready to make the final decisions to lay before Pharaoh.

The royal princesses had other plans. They had seen Aton pick up the bao stones and they took this as a signal that they were now able to command my full attention. I am devoted to them both but they are very demanding. They charged out of the lagoon splashing water in all directions and raced each other to get to me first. Bekatha is the baby but she is very quick and determined. She will do almost anything to obtain what she wants. She beat Tehuti by a length and dived into my lap, cold and wet from the lagoon.

'I love you, Tata,' she cried as she threw her arms around

my neck and pressed her sodden mop of red hair to my cheek. 'Tell us a story, Tata.'

Bested in the race to reach me, Tehuti had to accept the less desirable position at my feet. Gracefully she lowered her naked and dripping body to the ground, and hugged my legs to her breast while she rested her chin on my knees and looked up into my face. 'Yes please, Tata. Tell us about our mama and how beautiful and clever she was.'

'I must speak to Uncle Aton first,' I protested.

'Oh. All right then. But don't be too long,' Bekatha chipped in. 'It's so boring.'

'Not too long, I promise.' I looked back at Aton and switched smoothly into Hyksosian. Both of us are fluent in the language of our deadly enemy.

I make it my business to know my enemy. I have a way with words and languages. I have had many years since the return to Thebes to learn. Aton had not joined the exodus to Nubia. He was not an adventurous soul. So he had remained in Egypt and he had suffered under the Hyksos. However, he had learned everything they had to teach, including their language. Neither of the princesses understood a word of it

'Oh, I hate you when you speak that dreadful jargon.' Bekatha pouted, and Tehuti agreed with her.

'If you love us you will speak Egyptian, Taita.'

I hugged Bekatha and stroked Tehuti's lovely head. Nevertheless I continued speaking to Aton in the language that the girls so bitterly deplored. 'Ignore the babbling of infants. Proceed, old friend.'

Aton smothered his grin and went on, 'So we are agreed then, Taita. We need allies and we need trade with them. At the same time we have to deny both of these to the Hyksos.'

I was tempted to make a sarcastic reply, but I had already annoyed him enough across the bao board. So I nodded seriously. 'As usual you have come to the point unerringly and you have stated the problem succinctly. Allies and trade. Very well, what do we have to trade, Aton?'

'We have the gold from our mines in Nubia which we discovered while we were in exile beyond the cataracts.' Aton had never left Egypt, but to hear him tell it he might have been the one who led the exodus. I smiled inwardly but maintained a serious expression as he went on, 'Although the yellow metal is not as valuable as silver, yet men also lust for it. With the quantities that Pharaoh has piled in his treasury we can readily buy friends and allies.'

I nodded in agreement, although I knew that the amount of Pharaoh's treasure was greatly over-estimated by Aton and many like him who are not as close to the throne as I am. I went on to enlarge on the subject. 'However, do not forget the produce of the rich black loam that Mother Nile casts up upon her banks with every annual inundation. Men must eat, Aton. The Cretans, the Sumerians and the Hellenic city states have little arable land. They are always hard pressed to find corn to feed their people. We have corn in abundance,' I reminded him.

'Aye, Taita. We have corn, and we also have horses to trade; we breed the finest warhorses in the world. And we have other things even more rare and precious.' Aton paused delicately, and he glanced at the lovely child I was cuddling and the other who sat at my knee.

Nothing else needed to be said on this subject. The Cretans and the Sumerians of the land between the Tigris and the Euphrates Rivers were our nearest and most powerful neighbours. Both of these peoples tended to be swarthy and sable-haired. Their rulers find the fair-haired and light-skinned women of the Aegean tribes and of the royal house of Egypt desirable. However, the pale and insipid Hellenic women cannot stand comparison with our glowing Nilotic jewels.

The parents of my two princesses were Tanus, he of the fiery red curls, and the bright blonde Queen Lostris. They had bred true and the beauty of their two girls was becoming renowned across the entire world. Ambassadors from afar had already made the onerous journeys across wide deserts and deep waters to the palace of Thebes to convey delicately to Pharaoh Tamose the interests of their masters in making a marital and martial alliance with the House of Tamose. The Sumerian King Nimrod and the Supreme Minos of Crete were two of those who had sent envoys.

At my behest, Pharaoh had received both these ambassadors kindly. He had accepted the handsome gifts of silver and cedar wood that they presented. Then he had listened sympathetically to their offers of marriage to one or both of Tamose's sisters, but then Pharaoh had explained that the two girls were still too young to contract a marriage and that they should speak again on this subject after both girls had reached maturity. That had been some time ago, and now circumstances had changed.

At the time Pharaoh had discussed with me the possible alliance between Egypt and Sumeria or Crete. I had tactfully pointed out to him that Crete would make a more desirable ally than would the Sumerians.

Firstly the Sumerians were not a seafaring race and, although they could field a powerful army well equipped with cavalry and chariots, they did not possess a navy of any distinction. I reminded Pharaoh that our southern Egypt had no access to the Middle Sea. Our Hyksos enemies controlled the northern reaches of the Nile and we were essentially a landlocked country.

The Sumerians also had limited access to the sea and their fleet was puny compared to those of other nations, such as the Cretans or even the Mauretanian people in the west. The Sumerians were always reluctant to risk the sea passage with heavily laden ships. They feared both the pirates and the turbulent weather. The overland route between our countries was also fraught with difficulties.

The Hyksos controlled the isthmus that runs between the Middle and Red Seas and connects Egypt to the Sinai Desert in the north. The Sumerians would be forced to march across the Sinai Desert much further south and then take ship across the Red Sea to reach us. This route would present so many problems to their army, not least the lack of water and the dearth of shipping on the Red Sea, that it might prove to be impossible.

What I had previously proposed to Pharaoh, and which I now outlined for Aton, was a treaty between our very Egypt and the Supreme Minos of Crete. 'The Supreme Minos' was the title of the Cretan hereditary ruler. He was the equivalent of our Pharaoh. To suggest that he was more powerful than our own Pharaoh would be treason. Suffice it to say that his fleet was reputed to comprise over ten thousand fighting and trading galleys of such an advanced design that no other ship could outrun them or outfight them.

We have what the Cretans want: corn, gold and lovely brides. The Cretans have what we need: the most formidable fleet of fighting ships in existence with which to blockade the Hyksos ports in the mouth of the Nile Delta; and in which to convoy the Sumerian army down the southern shores of the Middle Sea and thus catch the Hyksos in a deadly pincer movement which would crush their army between our forces.

'A fine plan!' Aton applauded me. 'An almost an infallible plan. Except for one small almost insignificant detail which you have overlooked, Taita my old darling.' He was grinning slyly, savouring his revenge for the drubbing I had just given him on the bao board. I have never been a vindictive person, but in this instance I could not restrain myself from having a little bit more innocent fun at Aton's expense. I contrived an expression of dismay.

'Oh, don't tell me that, please! I have thought it all out so carefully. Where is the fault in my plan?'

'You are too late. The Supreme Minos of Crete has already contracted a secret alliance with King Beon of the Hyksos.' Aton smacked his lips, and slapped one of his own elephantine thighs gleefully. He had confuted my proposition decisively, or so he believed.

'Oh yes!' I replied. 'I presume that you are referring to the trading fort to deal with Beon that the Cretans opened five moons ago at Tamiat, the most easterly mouth of Mother Nile in the delta.'

Now it was Aton's turn to look crestfallen. 'When did you learn about that? How did you know?'

'Please, Aton!' I spread my hands in a gesture of appeal. 'You do not expect me to reveal all my sources, do you?'

Aton recovered his poise swiftly. 'The Supreme Minos and Beon already have an understanding, if not a war alliance. Clever as we all know you are, Taita, there is very little you can do about it.'

'What if Beon is planning treachery,' I asked mysteriously, and he gawked at me.

'Treachery? I do not understand, Taita. What form would this treachery take?'

'Do you have any inkling of how much silver the Supreme Minos of Crete is hoarding in this new fortress at Tamiat in Hyksos territory, Aton?'

'I imagine it must be substantial. If the Supreme Minos proposes to buy the greater part of next season's corn crop from Beon, then he would need to have a heavy weight of silver on hand,' Aton hazarded carefully. 'Perhaps as much as ten or even twenty lakhs.'

'You are very perceptive, my dear friend; however, you have stated but a small part of the problems that face the Supreme Minos. He dare not risk sending his heavily laden treasure ships to cross the open seas during the season of storms. So for five months of the year he cannot send bullion to the southern shores of the Middle Sea which in winter entails a voyage of more than five hundred leagues from his island.'

Aton broke in quickly, trying to beat me to my conclusion. 'Ah, yes indeed! I take your point. So that means that for all that period of time the Supreme Minos is unable to trade with the states and nations that lie upon this African shore of the Great Sea!'

'During the whole of winter half the world is closed to him,' I agreed. 'But if he could obtain a secure base upon the Egyptian coast, his fleet would be protected from the winter gales. Then all year around his ships would be able to ply their trade from Mesopotamia to Mauretania under the protecting lee of the land.' I paused to let him see the full magnitude of what the Supreme Minos was planning, then I went on remorselessly, 'Twenty lakhs of silver would not be sufficient to fund a hundredth part of this activity. Five hundred lakhs is a more likely amount that he will have to hoard in his new fortress at Tamiat to carry his trade through the winter. Do you not agree that amount of silver would make any man contemplate treachery, more especially such a naturally perfidious and rapacious rogue as Beon?'

For fifty heartbeats Aton was struck dumb by the magnitude of the vision that I had presented him with. When at last he stirred again his voice croaked as he asked, 'So you have proof that Beon, in defiance of his incipient treaty with the Supreme Minos, is planning to storm the Tamiat fortress and seize the Supreme Minos' treasure? Is that what you are telling me, Taita?'

'I did not say that I have proof that it is Beon's intention to do so. I merely asked you a question. I did not make a statement.' I chuckled at his confusion. It was unkind of me, but I could not restrain myself. Never in our long acquaintance have I seen him so lost for rebuttal or repartee. Then I took pity upon him.

'You and I both know that Beon is a savage oaf, Aton. He can drive a chariot, swing a sword, draw a bow or sack a city. However, I doubt he is able to plan a visit to the privy without ponderous and painful deliberation.'

'Then who is it that is planning this raid upon the Supreme Minos' treasury?' Aton demanded. Instead of answering him immediately I merely sat back on my stool and smiled. He stared at me. Then his expression cleared. 'You? Surely not, Taita! How can you plan to rob the Supreme Minos of five hundred lakhs of silver and then court the Cretan for his support and alliance?'

'In the darkness it is difficult to tell a Hyksos from an Egyptian, especially if the Egyptian is dressed in Hyksos war array, and carrying Hyksos weapons and speaking Hyksosian,' I pointed out, and he shook his head, once again at a loss for words. But I pressed him further. 'You do agree that such a treacherous attack would destroy for ever any chances of Crete and the Hyksos ever forming an alliance against us?'

Aton smiled at last. 'You are so full of guile, Taita, that I wonder how I can ever trust you!' Then he demanded, 'Just how large is the Cretan garrison at Tamiat?'

'At the present time it comprises nearly two thousand soldiers and archers. Although almost all of these are mercenaries.'

'So!' He was impressed. He paused again and then continued: 'How many men would you need, or should I ask rather how many men would Beon need to carry through this dastardly plan?'

'Enough,' I hedged. I would not reveal all my plans to Aton. He accepted that and did not press me directly. However, he asked another oblique question.

'You would leave no Cretan survivors in the Tamiat fort? You would slaughter them all?'

'Of course I would allow the great majority of them to

escape,' I contradicted him firmly. 'I want as many of them as possible to make their way back to Crete to warn the Supreme Minos of King Beon's treachery.'

'The Cretan treasure?' Aton demanded. 'These five hundred lakhs of silver? What will become of that?'

'Pharaoh's coffers are almost empty. We cannot save Egypt without treasure.'

'Who will command this raid?' he demanded. 'Will you do it, Taita?'

I looked aghast. 'You know that I am no warrior, Aton. I am a physician, a poet and a gentle philosopher. However, if Pharaoh urges me to do so, I am willing to accompany the expedition as an adviser to the commanding officer.'

'Who will command then? Will it be Kratas?'

'I love Kratas and he is a fine soldier, but he is old, bull-headed and not amenable to reason or suggestion.' I shrugged and Aton chuckled.

'You have described General Kratas perfectly, O gentle bard. If not him, then whom will Pharaoh appoint?'

'He will probably appoint Zaras.'

'Ah! The famous Captain Zaras of the Blue Crocodile division of the Royal Guards? One of your favourites, Taita. Not so?'

I ignored the taunt. 'I have no favourites.' On occasion even I can stretch the truth just a little. 'But Zaras is simply the best man for the job,' I responded mildly.

When I laid before Pharaoh my plan to discredit King Beon with the Supreme Minos of Crete and to drive a wedge of steel between the two powers which were potentially the most dangerous enemies we had in all the world he was amazed at the brilliant simplicity of my design.

I had begged for a private interview with Pharaoh and of

course he had granted it without a quibble. He and I were alone on the wide palm-lined terrace which encircled his throne room, overlooking the Nile at its widest point in southern Egypt. Of course beyond Asyut the river becomes wider and the current slower as it passes through the territory that the Hyksos have seized from us, and flows down into the delta before debouching into the Middle Sea.

There were sentries at both ends of the terrace to ensure that we could not be overlooked or overheard by either friend or enemy. The guards were under the direct command of reliable officers, but they kept discreetly out of sight so Pharaoh and I were not distracted. We paced along the marble paving. Only now that we were alone was it permissible for me to walk shoulder to shoulder with him, even though I had been intimately involved with him from the minute of his birth.

In truth it was I who had delivered him into this world. I had been the one who caught his infant body in my hands as Queen Lostris propelled him from her royal womb with the force of a stone from a sling shot. The very first act the prince ever performed was to empty his bladder over me. I smiled now at the memory.

I have been his tutor and his mentor since that day. I was the one who taught him to wipe his own arse, to read and write; to shoot a bow and drive a war chariot. From me he has learned how to rule a nation. Now at last he has grown into a fine young man, a doughty warrior and the seasoned ruler of this very Egypt. But we are still the very best of friends. I would go so far as to say that Pharaoh loves me like the father he never knew, and I love him like the son I never had.

Now, as he listened to the stratagem that I was proposing, he stopped walking and turned to face me with mounting wonder. When I reached the denouement of my plan he seized my shoulders in hands that were hard and strong as bronze

16

from swinging a sword, drawing a bow and driving a team of four horses in the traces of a chariot.

'Tata, you old scallywag!' he shouted into my face, 'you never fail to amaze me. Only you could have dreamed up such an outrageous plot. We must begin at once to plan the finer details. Well I remember how I hated it when you forced me to learn to speak Hyksosian; now I would be lost without it. I could never have commanded this expedition without being able to pass as one of our enemies.'

It took me several hours of tactful manipulation before I could convince him that the danger of leaving Egypt without a leader at such a crucial point in our history far outweighed the glory or other benefit that he could hope to win from a successful capture of the Minoan fortress at Tamiat and the treasure it contained. I gave thanks to Horus that he is young enough to be flexible in his thinking and old enough to have learned a modicum of good sense. Long ago I learned how to sway him to my purpose without allowing him to realize that I was doing so. In the end I usually have my own way.

At my suggestion Pharaoh appointed Zaras to command the expedition. Even though Zaras was young, only twenty-five years of age – almost the same age as Pharaoh himself – he had already made a considerable name for himself, as his military rank attested. I had worked with him many times before and I knew that his reputation was well founded. Most important was the fact that he revered me.

However, before he dismissed me Pharaoh Tamose placed in my hands the royal hawk seal. This was Pharaoh's means of delegating all of his powers to the bearer. The bearer of the seal answered only to Pharaoh. On pain of death no man could question or hinder him in the course or commission of the royal duties.

It was customary for Pharaoh to bestow the hawk seal upon his chosen emissary with solemn ceremony in the presence of

17

the senior members of his court, but I realized that in such a sensitive matter as this he had decided to do so in total secrecy. Nevertheless I was humbled by the trust he had shown in me.

I fell to my knees and touched my forehead to the ground before him. But Pharaoh stooped and lifted me to my feet.

'You have never failed me, Taita.' He embraced me. 'I know you will not do so now.'

I went directly to find Zaras. I impressed upon him the importance of our mission and the opportunity it presented to him to establish himself in Pharaoh's esteem. Success in this mission would set his feet firmly on the high road to advancement and royal favour. He tried unconvincingly to hide his awe from me.

The two of us drew up a list of 220 men to make up the raiding party. At first Zaras was adamant that this number was insufficient to take on the Cretan garrison of almost two thousand. When I explained the particular circumstances which I had not shared with Aton or even with Pharaoh he accepted my plan in its entirety.

I allowed him to choose his own men. I insisted only that the single attribute all the men he selected must possess was the ability to speak Hyksosian fluently. Zaras was too young to have been part of the exodus to Nubia when the Hyksos overwhelmed southern Egypt. In fact he had been pressed into the Hyksos legions at the age of sixteen. The result was that he could speak the language as though born to it, and he could pass for one of them in any circumstances. However, he was a loyal Egyptian and had been amongst the very first to revert to his true race when Pharaoh Tamose led us down through the cataracts to thrash the Hyksos at the battle of Thebes and drive their survivors in panic and confusion back into the north.

The men Zaras selected to make up the raiding party were highly trained and drilled, mostly under Zaras himself. They were all sailors as well as soldiers and had spent most of their time as fighting crews on board the river galleys, when they were not handling the war chariots. There was nothing more that Zaras needed to teach them.

I told him to divide this force into small detachments each of fifteen or twenty men so that they would not draw too much attention to themselves when they left the city of Thebes.

When I showed the royal hawk seal to the captain of the guard at the city gates he did not question me. Over three successive nights these small bands of Zaras' men slipped out of the city during the hours of darkness and headed out into the eastern wilderness. They reassembled in the ruins of the ancient city of Akita, where I was waiting for them.

I had with me wagons laden with authentic Hyksos helmets, armour, uniforms and weapons. This was just a small part of the booty we had captured from the enemy at the battle of Thebes.

From Akita we marched on eastwards to the shores of the Gulf of Suez at the northern end of the Red Sea. The men wore Bedouin robes over their uniforms and weapons.

Zaras and I had ridden ahead of the main party. We were waiting at the little fishing village of Al Nadas on the shore of the gulf when they caught up with us.

Zaras had hired a guide whom he had employed before, and whom he recommended highly. His name was Al Namjoo. He was a tall silent man with one eye. He was waiting for us at Al Nadas.

Al Namjoo had chartered all the available fishing vessels from the villagers to ferry us across to the eastern shore. The gulf was less than twenty leagues wide at this point and we could see the low hills of the Sinai on the far side.

We crossed in the night, with only the stars to light our way.

We disembarked on the eastern shore of the gulf near another tiny fishing village. This was Zuba, where one of Al Namjoo's sons was waiting for us. He had a string of over a hundred donkeys which he had hired to carry our heavy gear. We still faced a march of almost two hundred leagues northwards to reach the Middle Sea, but the men were trained to peak condition and we moved fast.

Al Namjoo kept well to the east of the Sinai isthmus which links Africa to Asia to minimize the risk of us encountering any Hyksos troops. Finally we came out on the rocky southern coast of the Middle Sea near the Phoenician port of Ushu. This was approximately midway between the Sumerian border and that part of northern Egypt still in the hands of the Hyksos invaders.

I left Zaras and his men encamped outside the port and went ahead with two donkeys loaded with gold ingots concealed in leather sacks of corn and four picked men to help me. After three days of bargaining with the merchants of the port I had three medium-sized galleys drawn up on the beach below the Phoenician Temple of Melkart. Each of these ships was capable of carrying a hundred men. They had cost me dearly, and there was very little gold remaining in the corn sacks we had brought with us from Thebes.

I let it be known in the port that we were a band of mercenaries travelling eastwards to sell our services to the Assyrian King Al Haturr who was laying siege to the city of Birrayut. As soon as the men were embarked we shoved off from the beach. When we reached deep water and while we were still visible to the watchers in Ushu we turned and rowed eastwards towards Lebanon. However, once we were out of sight of land I reversed our course and headed back towards Egypt and the delta of the Nile.

There was a light offshore breeze blowing that favoured us. We hoisted the mainsails, and relieved the rowers at the long oars at regular intervals. We passed Ushu once again, but heading in the opposite direction. I kept our ships below the horizon, and out of sight of the port.

Although each galley was crowded with seventy men or more, we made good speed and there was curling white water under the bows of every vessel. By late afternoon of the second day I calculated that the Cretan fortress of Tamiat lay less than a hundred leagues ahead of us.

Of course I was in the leading galley with Zaras and I suggested to him that as we had left Ushu far behind us, we could now close in and keep within sight of the shore. It was much easier for me to navigate and judge our position when I had sight of solid land to guide me. At last, as the sun touched the surface of the sea ahead of us and darkness gathered behind us, I pointed out to the helmsman a sheltered but deserted bay with sandy beaches. We ran in until our keels grounded and then the men jumped overboard and dragged the boats up the sand.

The journey from Thebes to where we now lay had been long and gruelling but we were within a few leagues of our goal. There was a contagious sense of excitement and anticipation in our camp that evening, tempered by the foreboding which even the bravest men feel on the eve of battle.

Zaras had selected two of his best men to command our other galleys. The first of these was named Dilbar. He was a tall and handsome man, with muscled forearms and powerful hands. From our first meeting he had particularly engaged my attention and earned my approval. His eyes were dark and piercing, but he had a glossy pink scar from a sword-cut across his right cheek. This detracted not in the least from his good looks. When he gave an order the men responded to him readily and swiftly.

The commander of the third galley was a stocky man with broad shoulders and a bull neck. His name was Akemi. He was a jovial man with a bull voice and an infectious laugh. His weapon of choice was a long-handled axe. Akemi was the one who came to me after the men had eaten.

'My Lord Taita.' He saluted me. When first the men had used that title I had protested mildly that I was not entitled to it. They had ignored my protestations and I did not persist. 'The men have asked me if you will do them the honour of singing for them tonight.'

I have an exceptional voice and under my fingers the lute becomes a celestial object. I can seldom find it within me to deny entreaties of this kind.

That night before the Battle of Tamiat I chose for them 'The Lament for Queen Lostris'. This is one of my most famous compositions. They gathered around me at the camp-fire and I sang for them all 150 verses. The best singers amongst them joined in the chorus while the others hummed the refrain. At the end there were very few dry eyes amongst my audience. My own tears did not detract in any way from the power and beauty of my performance.

With the first glimmering of dawn the next day our camp was astir. Now the men could strip off their Bedouin robes and head-dresses and open the sacks that contained their Hyksos body armour and weapons. The armour was for the most part made of padded leather, but the helmets were bronze skull-caps with a metal nose-piece. Every man was armed with a powerful recurved bow and a quiver of flint-headed arrows, which were fletched with coloured feathers in the Hyksos style. Their swords were carried in a scabbard strapped to their backs, so the handle stood up behind their left shoulder, ready to hand. The bronze blades were not straight-edged as those of regular Egyptian weapons, but were curved in the eastern fashion.

The armour and weapons were too heavy and too hot to

wear while they worked the oars in the direct sunlight. So the men stripped to their loin-cloths and laid their battle gear on the deck beneath the rowing benches between their feet.

Most of my men were of light complexion and many of them had fair hair. I ordered them to use soot from the cooking fires to darken their beards and skin, until they were all as swarthy as any Hyksos legionnaire.

When our three crowded galleys pushed off from the beach and rowed out of the bay, I was once again in the leading ship with Zaras. I stood beside the helmsman who wielded the long steering-oar in the stern. From the same merchant in the port of Ushu who had sold me the boats I had also purchased a papyrus map which purported to set out the details of the southern shore of the Middle Sea between Gebel and Wadi al Nilam. He claimed to have drawn this map with his own hand from his own observations. Now I spread it on the deck between my feet and anchored the corners with pebbles that I had picked up on the beach. Almost at once I was able to identify some of the features on the shore. It seemed that my chart was gratifyingly accurate.

Twice during the morning we spotted the sails of other vessels on the horizon, but we sheered off and gave them a wide berth. Then, when the sun was directly overhead, the lookout in the bows shouted another warning and pointed ahead. I shaded my eyes and peered in the direction he was indicating. I was astonished to see the surface of the sea along the entire horizon was churning white water as though a heavy squall were bearing down on us. This was not the season of storms.

'Get the sails down!' I snapped at Zaras. 'Ship oars and have the sea anchors rigged by the bows and ready for streaming.'

The furious waters raced towards us and we braced ourselves for the onslaught of the wind. The white water emitted a mounting roar as it approached.

I took a firm grip on the wooden coaming of the hatch in front of me and braced myself. Then the seething water enveloped the hull. The uproar became deafening, with men shouting orders and oaths, and the waters dashing against the ships' sides. However, to my astonishment there was no wind. I knew at once that this storm without wind was a supernatural phenomenon. I closed my eyes and began to chant a prayer to the great god Horus for his protection, and I clung to the coaming with both hands.

Then there was a hand upon my shoulder shaking me rudely and a voice shouting in my ear. I knew it was Zaras but I refused to open my eyes. I waited for the gods to dispose of me as they saw fit. But Zaras kept shaking me and I remained alive. I opened my eyes cautiously. But I kept on praying under my breath. Now I realized what Zaras was saying to me, and I risked a quick glance over the side.

The sea was alive with enormous gleaming bodies that were shaped like arrowheads. Again it took me a moment to realize that they were living creatures, and that each of them was at least the size of a horse. However, these were gigantic fish. They were packed so densely that those below were forcing the others to the surface in a tumult of waves and spray. Their multitudes stretched to the limit of the eye.

'Tuna!' Zaras was yelling at me. 'These are tuna fish.'

Upper Egypt is a landlocked country so I have never had the opportunity to spend enough time on the open sea to have witnessed a tuna migration of this magnitude. I had read so much about the subject that I should have known what was happening. I realized that I was in danger of looking ridiculous, so I opened my eyes and yelled as loudly as Zaras, 'Of course they are tuna. Get the harpoons ready!'

I had noticed the harpoons when I came aboard for the first time. They were stowed under the rowing benches. I had supposed that they were used to repel pirates and corsairs if they tried to board the ship. The shafts were about twice as long as a tall man. The heads were of razor-sharp flint. There was an eye behind the barb to which the coir line was spliced. And at the other end of the line was tied a carved wooded float.

Although I had given the order for harpoons, it was typical of Zaras that he was the first of any of them to act upon it. He always led by his own example.

He snatched one of the long weapons from where it had been strapped under the thwart, and as he ran with it to the ship's side he unwrapped the retaining line. He jumped up on to the gunwale of the galley and balanced the long harpoon easily, with the shaft resting on his shoulder and the barbed flint head pointing down at the flashing shoal of fish that was streaming past him like a river of molten silver. They looked up at him with great round eyes that seemed to be dilated with terror.

I watched him gather himself and then hurl the harpoon, point first, straight down into the water below him. The shaft of the heavy weapon shuddered as the point struck and the harpoon was whipped away below the surface by the rush of the huge fish that was impaled by the flint point.

Zaras jumped back on to the deck and seized the running line as it streamed away, blurring with speed and beginning to smoke with the friction of the coarse rope against the wood of the gunwale. Three other men of the crew leaped forward to help him and they latched on to the rope and battled to subdue the fish and bring it alongside.

Four other men had followed Zaras' example and each of them grabbed a harpoon from its place below the thwarts and ran with it to the gunwale. Soon there were knots of struggling men on each side of the boat, shouting with excitement, swearing and bellowing incoherent orders at each other as they struggled with the massive creatures.

One after another the fish were heaved on board and clubbed to death. Before the last of the harpooned fish had been killed and butchered, the rest of the mighty shoal had disappeared back into the depths as suddenly and miraculously as they had appeared.

We went ashore again that night, and by the light of the cooking fires on the beach we feasted on the succulent flesh of the tuna. It is the most highly prized delicacy in all the seas. The men seasoned the flesh with just a little salt. Some of them could not wait for it to be thrown on the coals, and they wolfed it down raw and bleeding. Then they followed it with a swallow from the wine-skins.

I knew that the next morning they would be strong and eager for the first sight of the enemy. Unlike corn or other insipid foods, meat rouses the demon in the heart of a warrior.

So that night I sang for them 'The Ballad of Tanus and the Blue Sword'. It is the battle hymn of the Blues, and it set them afire. Every man joined in the chorus, no matter how rough his voice, and afterwards I could see the light of war shining in their eyes. They were ready to meet any enemy.

We launched the galleys again the next morning as soon as it was light enough to make out the reefs below the surface, and to find a safe passage through them.

The closer we came to the many mouths of the Nile Delta the more certain I became of our position, until in the late afternoon we sailed past an estuarine mouth which was bounded on the east side by a low forested headland and on the west by an exposed mud-bank. On the headland facing the sea stood a rudimentary tower of mud-bricks that were painted with limewash. The roof of the tower had collapsed, as had most of the wall on the seaward side of the construction. However, enough of it was still standing for me to be certain that this was the navigational marker for the Tamiat channel, probably erected there by some long-dead Egyptian mariner.

I ran to the foot of the single mast and clambered up it until I reached the sloping yard of the lateen sail. I wrapped my legs around it and hugged the mainmast. From this vantage I had a clear view inland and I immediately picked up the square outline of a man-made structure which just showed above the treetops far inland. Like the channel marker it also was painted with limewash. I was in no doubt at all that this was the watch-tower of the Minoan trading fort and treasury which we were seeking. I slid back down the yard and as my feet hit the deck I shouted at the helmsman: 'Put up your helm! Turn three points to starboard!'

Zaras strode across to where I stood. 'Yes?' he asked. Usually he is genial and gregarious, but at a time such as this he becomes a man of quick decisions and even quicker reactions.

'Yes!' I agreed, and he gave a brief cold smile and a curt nod to the helm to confirm my order. We turned out towards the open sea. The other two galleys followed us around. Now we headed obliquely away from the shore. However, as soon as we passed the next headland and were screened from the surveillance of any sentry on the tower of the Tamiat fortress, I ordered another change of course. We headed back directly towards the labyrinthine swamps of the delta.

I knew from my map where to find what looked to be a secure anchorage. We lowered the masts and laid them flat on the decks while we poled our way through the dense banks of papyrus and bulrushes into the sheltered lagoon that I had chosen. Here we were completely screened by dense vegetation. We anchored a boat's length apart in the shallow murky water with our keels only just clear of the mud of the bottom. We were able to wade between the boats with the water at the deepest parts of the lagoon reaching only as high as our chins.

While we watched the sun set and the moon rise, the men

feasted on what remained of the smoked tuna steaks. Zaras waded quietly from galley to galley, selecting eight of his best men and warning them to be ready before sunrise the next morning to accompany us on a reconnaissance.

An hour before dawn we crowded into two of the skiffs that we had towed behind the galleys. We paddled across the wide lagoon to the shore nearest the headland on which I had spotted the watchtower of the fort.

I could hear the cries of swamp birds and the susurration of their wings passing over us in the darkness. As the light strengthened I could make out the long flighting lines of waterfowl and their arrowhead formations against the brightening sky. There were wild ducks and geese, storks, herons, cranes with long necks and trailing legs, ibis and egrets and fifty or more other species. They rose in huge flocks from the surface of the lagoon as we rowed through them. At last the sun pushed itself above the horizon and the vast expanses of the delta around us were revealed. It is a wild and desolate place, unfit for human habitation.

We had to drag the skiffs through the shallows and hide them in the reeds when we at last reached firmer ground. I was uncertain of the layout of the fort and its surroundings so we groped our way through the dense stands of reeds and bulrushes ever more cautiously.

Abruptly we came out upon the bank of a deep channel which cut through the papyrus beds from the south in the direction of the open waters of the Middle Sea. It was about 150 paces wide, and I could see that it was too deep to wade. On the opposite bank of the channel I was able to make out the flat roof of the watchtower we had spotted the previous day. The helmeted heads of at least three of the guards were showing above the parapet as they patrolled their beats.

Suddenly I heard the unmistakable sounds of a moving vessel coming up the channel from the seaward direction of where we lay, and I cautioned my companions to silence. The creaking of the rigging, the voice of the seaman chanting the soundings in the bows and the thud of the oars in the rowlocks increased in volume until suddenly an enormous seagoing vessel appeared around the bend in the channel.

I had never seen a ship of this type or size before; however, I knew from descriptions that my spies had sent me that this was a Cretan trireme. She was both a cargo vessel and a warship. She was triple-decked, with three banks of oars.

Her long, pointed bows were reinforced with sheets of beaten bronze for ramming enemy ships. She had two masts, which would enable her to spread a goodly area of sail, although these were now furled as she threaded the narrow channel under oars. She was a lovely vessel, with long clean lines and a high transom. Looking at her it was not difficult to understand why Crete was the pre-eminent naval power of the world. This was the fastest and most powerful ship on all the seas. Even though she was heavily burdened and low in the water no other vessel could challenge her. Nevertheless I wondered what cargo she carried in her holds.

As she drew level with where we lay hidden in the reed beds, I was able to study her officers. There were three of them in the stern, standing aside from the four crewmen who were manipulating the long steering-oar. Although the cheek-pieces of their armour masked most of their features they seemed to be taller and more robust than our average Egyptian. I could see that their kilts were of the finest linen and that their weapons were lovingly polished and engraved. These were more warriors than they were merchants.

As she passed us the breeze wafted the stench of the ship to where we lay. I knew that her upper bank of long oars was rowed by her crew, who were fighting men more than they were beasts of burden. At an order from their captain they could jump up from the rowing bench and seize their weapons which lay at their feet. They would fight like men and share in the prize money.

However, the lower banks of oars were pulled by slaves who were shackled to the deck timbers. The stench I smelled was that of these unfortunates who would live their whole lives on the benches. They would row, sleep, eat, defecate and ultimately die where they sat.

The Cretan galley swept on past us and then we heard the shouted orders of her officers. The upper bank of oars rose from the water like the wings of a silver seagull as they were shipped, and only the lower banks continued dipping and pulling delicately as the ship turned into the final bend of the channel, heading towards the glistening white walls of the fortress which showed in the distance above the nodding heads of the papyrus banks.

Then a most extraordinary event occurred; something for which I was completely unprepared. A second ship, almost identical in every respect to the first, rounded the bend of the channel and rowed past where we lay. She also was low in the water, carrying a weighty cargo.

Then to my utter astonishment and delight a third heavily burdened trireme came down the channel and sailed past us. She followed her two sister ships towards the fort.

I realized what had happened. Three months previously I had been informed by my agents that the three treasure ships were prepared to sail from the principal Cretan port of Aggafer. However, it had taken many months for this information to reach me. In the meantime the departure of the convoy must have been delayed by unforeseen circumstances, the most probable reason being unfavourable weather conditions. My agents had been unable to warn me timeously of this delay.

I had expected to reach the Tamiat fort only long after the convoy had arrived, discharged its cargo and departed again on its return voyage to Aggafer.

The chances of me arriving at Tamiat at exactly the same time as the treasure convoy was so remote that it must have been arranged by divine intervention. From an early age I have known that I am a favourite of the gods, particularly of the great god Horus to whom I pray. How else could I have been gifted from birth with so many talents and virtues? How else have I been able to survive so many terrible perils and mortal dangers that would certainly have destroyed any lesser being? How else have I been able to stay so young and handsome and my mind so sharp when all those about me wrinkle, turn grey and fade away with age? There is something about me that has set me aside from most other mortal men.

This was yet another example of Horus' favour and indulgence. I whispered my thanks to him and swore that I would make a lavish sacrifice to him at the very first opportunity. Then I crawled closer to where Zaras lay, and tugged his sleeve.

'I must cross this channel and get closer to the Cretan fort,' I told him.

There are two enigmas in our very Egypt that I have never been able to come to terms with. The first is that although we use the horse as beast of burden and the chariot as our primary weapon of war almost no Egyptian will ride astride. The second enigma is that although we live on the banks of a mighty river almost no Egyptian is able to swim. If you ask one of them why this is so, they will usually shrug and answer: 'The gods frown upon such uncouth behaviour.'

I have already asserted that I am different from most others. I hesitate to suggest that I am in any way superior. I think it is sufficient to point out that I am both an expert horseman, and a strong and tireless swimmer.

I knew that Zaras has neither of these skills, although to give him full credit I have never seen him bested when he had the reins of a chariot in his hands. Thus I had ordered him to bring with him a buoy made from the bark of the cork tree to keep him afloat. The two of us stripped to our breech clouts and entered the channel. Zaras had his sword strapped to the cork float. I carried mine on my back. Zaras blew and puffed like a bull hippo, while I swam like an otter and reached the far bank of the channel before he was halfway across.

When he managed to complete the crossing I helped him ashore. Then, when he had regained his breath, we crept stealthily through the reeds towards the Cretan fort. When we reached a position from which he had a good view of the building I realized why the Cretans had selected this site. It was on the highest point of a narrow ridge of limestone which poked up through the soft alluvial soils and provided a strong foundation on which they had anchored their fortress.

This limestone intrusion divided the flow of the main channel to form a moat around the fort. There were a number of different types of vessels anchored in the basin formed by the sweep of the river around the fortress. Most of these craft were mere barges which I presumed the Cretans had used to carry building materials. There was not a single sea-going ship amongst them. The exception to this was the squadron of three magnificent triremes which had rowed past our hiding place earlier.

These were not anchored in the basin, but were already moored to the stone wharf directly below the main gate of Tamiat fortress. The gate stood wide open, and there was a gathering of uniformed soldiers on the wharf to welcome the new arrivals. I could see by the plumed helmets and gold decoration they sported that many of these were high-ranking officers.

In the time that it had taken Zaras and me to swim across the channel and reach our present position the crews had opened the hatches of the leading trireme and a chain gang of half-naked slaves was beginning the task of unloading her cargo. The slaves were working under the charge of a number of overseers who wore half-armour and short swords on their belts. All of them wielded whips of plaited rawhide.

The slaves were carrying a succession of identical wooden chests ashore over the gangplanks. Although the chests were not very large they were obviously heavy for the slaves staggered under the weight. The whole unloading process moved too slowly for the satisfaction of the overseers who harangued and ranted at the working gang.

As we watched, one of the slaves lost his footing while stepping from the gangplank to the wharf. He fell heavily and dropped the chest he was balancing on his head. It crashed to the stone slabs and burst open.

I felt my heart jump against my ribs as I saw the brilliant flash of sunlight reflected from the metallic surfaces of the silver ingots as they spilled out in a heap on to the wharf. The bars were small and rectangular, no longer than a man's hand; however, there were twenty or more of them packed into the chest. A single chest of these bars would most likely have been sufficient to pay for the building of the great trireme which had carried it across the Middle Sea. All my hopes and expectations had been fulfilled. Here was the vast treasure that I had anticipated.

Three of the overseers gathered around the prostrate slave and wielded their whips with gusto, swinging the lashes from high above their heads to crack against his sweat-shiny skin. The man screamed and writhed and tried to cover his head with his arms. One of the lashes caught him in the face and popped his right eyeball out of its socket. It dangled on its optic cord against his cheek as he rolled his head from side to side. At last the slave lay unconscious, no longer able to protect himself. One of his tormentors stooped and grabbed his heels, dragged him on his back to the edge of the wharf, and then heaved him over the side. The body splashed into the river and sank swiftly, disappearing below the muddy surface.

On the wharf the other slaves responded at once to the shouts of the overseers and the cracking of their whiplashes. The file of half-naked men began to move again, tottering under their burdens as though the work had never been interrupted.

I tapped Zaras' shoulder to get his attention and then we both crawled back deeper into the reed beds. Once we were safely hidden I led him around to the far side of the fort and the bank of the other branch of the river. It took me an hour or so of cautious and careful manoeuvring before I could find a vantage point from which I was able to overlook the strategic layout of the fort and its surroundings. Now I was able to verify in person the reports I had received from my spies.

Although the walls of the fort were formidable and probably even impregnable, the area they enclosed was not very large. There was a severely limited amount of space on the ridge, insufficient for anything more than the treasury alone, and barracks to house a detachment of guards to beat off any attempt to land by a small raiding party coming up one of the channels from the sea.

However, the Cretans must also have realized that they required a much larger force of several thousand men on hand to oppose any larger enemy force that might land on the coast and march inland to mount a more determined attack on the fort. They had solved this problem by stringing a pontoon bridge across both channels of the river, so that the fort sitting on the island in the centre of the river could be reached swiftly by defending Cretan troops from either bank.

From where I lay I had a good view across the most easterly channel to the flat dry ground beyond. This was where the Cretans had built their fortified camp, which provided barracks for the main body of their army. They had surrounded the camp with a protective palisade of sharpened logs, which stood twice the height of a man. I calculated that this camp would be capable of housing two or three thousand soldiers.

There was a watchtower at each corner of the square

enclosure, and I could see that the roofs of the buildings within the palisade were plastered thickly with black mud from the river-bank which had dried hard. These would afford protection from the fire-arrows that an enemy might shoot over the walls.

From the gate in the wall closest to the river the Cretans had built a passageway of dried black mud-bricks to the head of the pontoon bridge. This would protect their troops from enemy arrows when they sallied forth from the camp.

They had used a series of longboats anchored side by side across both channels of the river to serve as the pontoons for their bridge. Over these they had laid a causeway of hewn planks. This bridge ensured that large numbers of troops could be rushed from the camp to wherever they were needed most.

'They have planned it all thoroughly.' Zaras gave his opinion as he surveyed the fortifications.

'That is what the Cretans are most famous for . . . thoroughness,' I agreed, but I was still studying the ground, seeking out any weakness in the Cretan defences. Search as I might I could find only one. That was the pontoon bridge itself, but I was confident that I could deal with that.

I switched my attention back to the wharf where the three great triremes still lay moored. I considered the manner in which the Cretans were unloading the cargo of the first ship. I could see that it was not very efficient. If I were presented with this task I would rig tripods and pulleys over the open hatches and hoist the chests of silver up to deck level on pallets. There I would have carts ready to trundle the chests across the wharf and into the gates of the fort.

The Cretan slaves were manhandling each chest individually up the ladder from the bottom of the hold to the main deck. At this rate it would take several days to unload each ship.

I was worried. I had not truly recognized the immensity of my own task until I saw it laid out before me. It was one thing to speak lightly of handling hundreds of lakhs of bullion, but it became entirely another matter when I was presented with the physical weight and bulk of such a treasure and the problem of seizing it and transporting it hundreds of leagues over sea and mountain and desert while being pursued by a vengeful army.

I began to worry that I had taken on an impossible task, and thought dismally that perhaps the only solution if I was ever able to get my hands on such a vast cargo was to take it out into the deep waters of the Middle Sea and to dump it overboard where it would be forever beyond the reach of both King Beon and the Supreme Minos.

Then I would flee with all my men who had survived the wrath of the Cretans back to the safety of Thebes. Perhaps the Supreme Minos could then be persuaded that King Beon was the culprit, but I doubted it.

The solution did not come to me at once, and even I had to wrestle with the problem for almost an hour while Zaras and I lay there in the papyrus beds. Then suddenly the solution struck me like a thunderbolt. It was so ingenious that even I was stunned by the beauty of it.

I thought I would explain it all to Zaras, but then I decided not to overpower him with something so simple and yet so devilishly complex.

I looked up at the sun. It had reached its zenith some time ago and was already halfway down the sky again. I looked back at the trio of treasure ships and I think I grinned. I sensed that Zaras was watching me intently. I think he knew that I was on to something at last, and he was waiting eagerly for my orders, which I was not yet ready to reveal to him.

'Enough!' I told him. 'We must go.'

'Where to, Taita?'

'Back to the boats. We have a great deal of work to do before nightfall.'

* * *

The sun was setting when at last Zaras and I managed to swim and wade back to where we had left our three small boats in the lagoon. The men were overjoyed to see us again. I think they had convinced themselves that we had been discovered and killed by the enemy, leaving them leaderless and thrown back on their own limited resources. They scrambled to obey my orders.

The first of the many challenges facing me was to get every single one of my heavily armed and armoured men, almost none of whom were able to swim, across the deep channels of the river to reach the fort.

To this end I selected the smallest and lightest of our three boats. Then I made the men strip the ropes and other useful loose items from the remaining two hulls. I thought of burning these, but the Cretans would surely have seen the smoke and sent men to investigate it. Instead I ordered my men to knock the bottoms out of them and scuttle them in the deepest part of the lagoon.

Then we dragged the single boat that I had selected through the shallow waters to the eastern bank of the lagoon, nearest the fort. From there I needed every single one of my men to manhandle it across the dry ground to the river channel. I ordered them to attach the anchor ropes that we had salvaged from the two scuttled boats to the bows of this one that we had retrieved.

With a hundred men hauling on each rope the keel of the boat acted as a skid, and the hull slid readily enough over the papyrus stalks which were flattened beneath its weight. Nevertheless we had almost half a league of dry ground to cover before we reached the main channel of the river. By that time it was close to midnight and the waxing gibbous moon was high in the sky.

I allowed the men a short time to rest on the river-bank, and to don their armour and to wolf down a cold meal. Then with muffled oars and carrying fifty men at each crossing we began to ferry them over the channel. When every one of them was across, I divided our little force into two groups.

The larger group of 150 men I sent with Zaras to creep through the reed beds until they were as close to the main gate of the fort as possible without being in danger of discovery by the sentries. They were to conceal themselves there until they received my signal.

Before we parted I explained to Zaras what I planned. I would row up the channel with a crew of fifty men. My intention was to attack and destroy the pontoon bridge which connected the main enemy camp to the island on which the treasury stood. Before we parted company I embraced Zaras briefly, and I repeated my orders to him so that there could be no misunderstanding.

Then I sent him away, while I clambered on board the waiting galley and gave the order to my rowers to ply the oars. The current was swift and strong, but my men heaved away lustily and, hugging the bank of the channel furthest from the fort, we made good speed upstream. Soon we could see the lime-washed tower of the fort gleaming in the moonlight. The sight encouraged my oarsmen to still greater effort.

We came around the final bend in the channel and the fort lay before us. The three triremes were as I had last seen them, moored against the stone wharf. The moonlight was bright enough for me to make out that two of them were still riding low in the water; still fully laden with their cargoes of bullion. The third trireme was standing a little higher. Much of her cargo must have been unloaded. Nevertheless I estimated that she still had more than half her load of treasure chests in her holds.

There were no Cretan sentries anywhere in sight. There were no lights showing aboard any of the great ships. However, there was a fire glowing at one end of the wharf and there were torches burning in brackets on each side of the gates of the fort.

I lifted the bronze helmet from my head and placed it on my lap. Then I adjusted the bright yellow cloth that was knotted around my throat to mask the lower half of my face. This is an extraordinary type of cloth known as silk. It is extremely rare and worth a hundred times its own weight in silver. It comes from a land at the edge of the world, where it is spun not by men but by worms. It is possessed of magical powers. It can turn away evil spells and such diseases as the plague and the Yellow Flowers. However, now I used it simply to hide my face.

My features are so distinctive that there is always a strong possibility that they will be recognized by either friend or foe. Beauty comes at a price. After that of Pharaoh himself my face is probably the best known in the civilized world, by which I mean Egypt. When I replaced my helmet I was faceless in the ranks of faceless men.

As we rowed closer to the wharf the torch flames threw just sufficient flickering light for me to make out the blanket-wrapped forms of the sentries crouching close to the warmth of their watch fires.

It was obvious to me that the Cretan officers had not wished to spend the night in the crowded fort with all their men. At nightfall they must have gone back across the bridge with the majority of their men to the comforts of their elaborate camp on the further bank of the channel. This suited my purpose well enough.

Still keeping as far from the wharf as the channel allowed we rowed quietly past the moored galleys and the looming walls of the fort. As we left those behind I could make out ahead of us the row of longboats that formed the pontoon bridge strung out across the channel.

We rowed on up the main channel until I judged we were

at least two hundred yards upstream of the pontoon bridge. Then I turned our boat across the current and I aimed our bows at the centre of the long narrow pontoon bridge. I gave a quiet order to the rowers to stop heaving and to ship their oars, and we let the current run us down on the centre of the bridge.

At the last moment I put the helm over and we turned broadside to the bridge and came to rest with our starboard side pressed by the current hard against the causeway.

My men were ready for this. Two small groups of three men each jumped from the bows and stern of our ship and made her fast to the bridge. The rest of them armed with axes and swords swarmed over the ship's side on to the pontoons. Without waiting for further orders they began to chop at the ropes that secured the line of longboats to each other.

The sounds of the blows had certainly carried across the channel to the camp on the far bank, for almost at once we heard the Cretan drums start to beat the call to arms. Pandemonium broke out in the camp; the shouted orders of the sergeants, the clatter and clash of arms on shields, the rattle of armour and the clamour of the drums carried back to us. Then the flare of light as the torches were lit and the reflection of their flames sparkled off the polished metal of shields and breastplates.

A long column of trotting infantry burst out of the mouth of the passageway that led from the palisade wall of the camp to the head of the pontoon bridge. Four abreast the Cretans charged out on to the narrow bridge, and it heaved and rocked under the stamping of their metal-studded sandals.

Swiftly the enemy front rank bore down upon our wrecking team, which was revealed by the glare of the torches. Still the mooring ropes between the pontoons resisted the axe-blows of my men. When only fifty paces separated them I heard one of the officers who led the charge shout an order.

I did not understand the language, but the meaning was immediately clear.

Without checking their rush along the causeway the leading Cretan infantrymen heaved back and then hurled a volley of spears. The heavy missiles fell amongst the team of my men who were still hacking at the bindings that held together the line of longboats. I saw a javelin strike one of my fellows in the back and transfix him so that the point emerged a good yard from his chest. He toppled over the side of the longboat on which he was balancing and was sucked down into the black waters. None of his comrades even glanced up from their task. Grimly they continued swinging their axes at the hempen ropes that bound the pontoons together.

I heard a sharp report as a rope parted, and then the grinding and crackling of timbers of the hulls bearing against each other as more of the lines holding the longboats together gave way.

Then at last the bridge was cleaved asunder. But the two disjointed halves were still held together by our own ship which was strung between them. I found myself screaming wildly at my axe-men to come back on board. Of course I was not troubled for my own safety. My only concern was for the safety of my brave lads.

The torrent of armoured Cretans came on unchecked over the pontoons. They rushed at us in a solid phalanx, bellowing their challenges and hurling their javelins. My own men were scrambling back into our little boat and cowering down as the missiles slammed into the timbers of our hull.

Now I was shouting for someone to sever the ropes that still locked our vessel into the centre of the bridge. In the uproar my orders were drowned out. I could not make myself heard. I grabbed an axe from one of my men who was crouching in the bilges and ran to the bows.

A Cretan came at me down the causeway. Both of us reached the bows at the same time. He had thrown his javelin and was

41

struggling to unsheathe his sword which seemed to be jammed in its scabbard. It came free as we met each other.

I could see that he was grinning under his helmet. He thought that he had me at his mercy and that he was about to kill me. He drew back his sword and aimed a thrust at my chest, but I had seen his eyes move, signalling his intention, so I was able to anticipate the blow. I twisted my body and the point of his sword flew under my armpit. I locked my arm over his elbow.

Now I had him fully extended. He tried to pull free, but the causeway heaved under him, throwing him off balance. At that critical moment I released the lock I had on his sword-arm. He was unprepared for that, and he tottered backwards, extending both arms towards me as he tried to regain his balance.

I swung my axe, aiming at the only part of his body that was not covered with metal: the wrist of his sword-hand. I was also unbalanced in the rocking and heaving boat, so it was not a perfect stroke. It did not sever his sword-hand cleanly, as I intended. But it slashed down to the bone on the inside of his wrist. I heard the tendons pop as they parted. His fingers opened involuntarily and the sword fell from them and rattled on the planks of the bridge. He reeled backwards into one of his companions who was crowding up behind him. Clinging to each other the two of them went over the side of the bridge and hit the surface of the water with a tall splash. The weight of their armour dragged them under immediately.

The axe was still in my hands and the two mooring lines that secured the bows of our ship to the pontoon bridge were stretched in front of me so tightly that the water was spurting out of the twists of the rope. I lifted the axe above my head and then swung down, aiming it at the thicker of the two ropes, putting all my weight and power into this stroke. The rope parted with a snap like a bowstring. Our boat canted over sharply as the full weight was thrown on to the single, thinner rope. I swung again and that rope jumped apart, twisting and unravelling in mid-air. The bows of our boat bobbed up as the weight and drag were taken off them, and we swung free across the current.

The effect on the bridge was far more dramatic. Each of the segments of the bridge was still firmly attached to their moorings on the river-banks. However, in the middle of the channel they were no longer bound together and the current snatched them apart swiftly. I watched as the dense pack of Cretans was thrown about by the causeway bobbing and lunging wildly under their feet.

Their shifting weight intensified the instability of the floating pontoons. Men in heavy armour lost their balance and staggered about drunkenly, barging into each other, throwing each other overboard.

I watched in horror as one of the pontoons capsized and a score of men were hurled over the side. Within minutes the greater part of the Cretan horde was struggling in the dark waters and drowning like rats in the bottom of a well.

What made it more tragic for me was that these were not even our enemies; all this destruction I had deliberately engineered to trick them into becoming our allies. It gave me very little consolation to know that I had done this for my very Egypt and for my Pharaoh. I was appalled by the consequences of my actions.

Then, with an enormous effort of will, I thrust aside my guilt and remorse. I knew what had been done could not be undone. I tried to put the drowned men out of my mind and thought instead about my own people and the losses that we had suffered. I forced myself to turn away, and pushed my way back to where I cut the line that held us attached. I was shouting at my crew, taking out my anger on them. Roaring at them to take up their oars again, shoving them back to the rowing benches, kicking and slapping those who hesitated in bewilderment.

At last I had the steering-oar in my hands again and the men were beginning to pull in unison. I put the helm over and steered us back towards the stone wharf under the main gate of the fort where the treasure ships were moored.

I jumped from our little boat as soon as the bows touched the stone steps of the wharf, and Zaras was there to meet me, sword in hand and panting with exertion but grinning like an idiot.

'We have captured all three of the treasure ships, and even the fort is ours!' he told me as he pointed with his bloodstained blade at the gates of the fort, which stood wide open. 'The uproar you created at the pontoon bridge was a fine distraction. We cut down the guards at the fort while they were still watching your performance, and totally unaware of our existence. I don't think that any of them escaped, but even if they have they won't get very far.' He paused to catch his breath and then demanded, 'How did it go with you at the bridge, Taita?' I was pleased to hear that even in the heat of battle and victory he was remembering to speak Hyksosian.

'The bridge is down and half the enemy were thrown into the river and drowned,' I told him curtly, and then I turned to Akemi, who had run up when he saw me come ashore. 'Take command of this boat and keep a dozen men with you to row.' I pointed to the cluster of small unmanned craft anchored in the basin formed by the sweep of the river. 'Take with you torches and fire-pots and burn those boats, before the Cretans can get their hands on them and use them to ferry their men across to attack us again tonight.'

'At once, my lord,' Akemi replied.

'Keep only the largest of them,' I went on. 'That big lugger at the end of the line. Don't burn that one. Bring it back here and we will leave it tied up at the wharf when we depart.'

Both Akemi and Zaras looked at me askance; however, it

was Zaras who dared to question my orders. 'Leave it for the Cretans? Why would we want to do that?'

'We want to do that so the senior Cretan officers are able to sail back to Crete with all despatch and warn their king of the treachery of his Hyksos allies. Even the mighty Minos of Crete will be sorely hurt by the loss of five hundred lakhs of his silver. When he receives the news, he will thirst for King Beon's blood.'

I waited on the wharf and watched Akemi and his crew pull away from the wharf, heading back into the basin of the river. I saw him transfer four of his men into the big lugger. They set a jib sail and brought her back to the wharf below where I stood.

Out in the basin Akemi stood in the bows of our little boat. His men rowed him along the line of anchored boats and Akemi hurled a flaming torch into each of them as he passed. Only when all of them were burning fiercely was I satisfied. I went back to find Zaras in the confusion.

'Bring these men with you, and come with me,' I told him, and I ran down the stone wharf to where the nearest Cretan trireme was moored. 'I want you to take command of this ship, Zaras. But I will sail with you.'

'Of course, master,' he answered. 'Some of my men are already aboard her.'

'Dilbar will captain that one.' I pointed at the second trireme. 'And Akemi will take the third Minoan treasure ship.'

'As you command, master.' It seemed that Zaras had promoted me from plain Taita to master. However, he was still sufficiently familiar with me to ask impudent questions. This he did immediately.

'Once we are out in the open sea, in which direction will we sail? Will we head east for Sumeria or west for the Mauretanian coast?' Then he even condescended to offer me a little fatherly advice. 'We have allies in both those countries. In the east there is King Nimrod, the ruler of the Land of the Two Rivers. In the west we have a treaty with King Shan Daki of Anfa in Mauretania. Which of them will it be, Taita?'

I did not reply to him immediately. Instead I asked my own question. 'Tell me, Zaras, which king or ruler in the entire world would you trust with a treasure of five hundred lakhs of silver?'

Zaras looked bemused. He had not thought about that. 'Perhaps . . . well, certainly not Shan Daki. His people are corsairs, and he is the King of Thieves.'

'What about Nimrod?' I suggested. 'I am not certain I would trust him with a piece of silver larger than my thumb.'

'We have to trust somebody,' he protested, 'unless we find a deserted beach and bury the silver on it, until we can return to reclaim it?'

'Five hundred lakhs!' I reminded him. 'It would take a year to dig a pit deep enough, and a mountain of sand to cover it.' I was enjoying his confusion. 'The wind favours us!' I looked up at the Minoan ensign, the golden bull of Crete, which still flew at the masthead of the trireme I had allotted to him. 'And the gods always favour the bold and the brave.'

'No, Taita,' he contradicted me. 'The wind does not favour us. It is blowing in from the sea, directly up the channel. It is pinning us against the land. It will take all our oars to get us out into the open waters of the Middle Sea. If you trust neither Shan Daki nor Nimrod whom then do you trust? To whom should we turn?'

'I trust only Pharaoh Tamose,' I told him, and he let his frustration with me show for the first time.

'So is your plan to return to Pharaoh by the same route we followed here? Shall we carry the treasure on our heads from Ushu through the Sinai Desert, and swim with it across the Red Sea? From there it will only be a short walk to reach Thebes. Pharaoh will be surprised to see you; of that you can be sure,' he scoffed at me.

'No, Zaras.' I smiled back at him indulgently. 'From here we are going to sail south down the Nile. We are going to sail all three of these Cretan monsters and the silver in their holds directly back to Thebes.'

'Have you gone mad, Taita?' He stopped laughing. 'Beon commands every yard of the Nile from here as far as Asyut. We can't sail three hundred leagues through the Hyksos hordes. That really is madness.' In his agitation he had switched back from Hyksosian into Egyptian.

'If you speak Hyksosian anything and everything is possible!' I contradicted and rebuked him. 'Anyway, we have already scuttled two of our boats and I am going to burn the third before we leave Tamiat, just to make certain that we leave no traces of our true identity behind us.'

'In the name of the great mother Osiris and her beloved son Horus, I think that you really believe what you are saying, Taita.' He started to grin again. 'And your plan is to drive me as frothing-at-the-mouth mad as you already are, so that in my madness I will agree with you. Is that it?'

'In battle, madness becomes sanity. It is the only way to survive. Follow me, Zaras. I am taking you home.' I started up the gangplank to the deck of the trireme. There were twenty of Zaras' men there before me. I saw that they already had control of the ship and every man aboard her. On the deck the Cretan crew were kneeling in a row with their heads bowed and their arms pinioned behind their backs; most of them were bleeding from fresh wounds. There were only six of them. Zaras' men stood over them with drawn swords.

'Good work, lads.' I gave them encouragement. Then I turned back to Zaras. 'Now, have your men strip the uniforms and armour from the prisoners, and send them ashore under guard.' While he gave the orders, I ran down the companion ladder to the upper rowing deck. The benches were unmanned and the long oars were shipped. But I had fifty of my own men to fill them again. With barely a pause I dived down the next companionway that led to the lower slave deck. The reek came up to meet me. It was so powerful that I gasped, but I kept on down.

There were smoky oil lamps burning in the brackets set in the low roof which gave just enough light for me to make out the ranks of almost naked bodies crouching on the rowing benches or resting their heads on the long oars in front of them as they slept. Those of them who were awake looked up at me with blank and incurious eyes. As they moved the chains on their ankles clanked.

I had thought to make a little speech to them, perhaps offering them their freedom once we reached Thebes if they would row strong and long. But I abandoned this idea as I realized that they were only partly human. They had been reduced to the level of the beasts by their vile durance and cruel treatment. My kindly words would mean nothing to them. The only thing they still understood was the lash.

Almost doubled over to save my head from striking the low upper deck I ran aft down the walkway between the slave benches until I reached the door that I was certain would lead into the cargo hold. There was a heavy brass lock on the door. Zaras followed me closely. I stood aside and let him prise the lock loose with his sword and kick the door open.

Then I lifted one of the oil lamps from its bracket and held it high as I entered the commodious cargo hold. The chests of silver bullion were stacked from deck to deck. However, there was a large and gaping hole in the centre of the pile. I made a quick estimate of the number of the precious chests that had already been taken ashore by the Cretans. I reckoned it to be a hundred at the very least.

For a craven moment I considered abandoning that small part of the treasure and sailing away with what we had on board, but then I thrust the thought aside.

While the gods are smiling, Taita, take full advantage before they frown again, I told myself, and I turned back to Zaras. 'Come with me. Bring as many men as you can spare.'

'Where are we going?'

I pointed to the empty space in the stack of chests. 'We are going to the fort to find where the Cretans have stored those missing chests. There is enough silver in those alone to equip an entire army and to place them in the battlefield. We must prevent any part of it falling into Beon's hands.'

We hurried back to the deck, and then Zaras followed me down the gangplank to the wharf. Ten of his men came behind us, bringing the captured Cretan sailors with them. They had stripped them naked. Inside the gates of the fort we found Dilbar and thirty of his men guarding the men and slaves that they had captured ashore.

I ordered Dilbar to strip these captives also. I needed as many of the Cretan uniforms and as much of their armour as we could find. The Minoan officers all wore necklaces, rings, armlets and wristlets of silver and gold and precious stones.

'Take those from the prisoners also,' I instructed Dilbar. I picked out two of the more exceptional pieces of jewellery from the pile and slipped them into my leather pouch. Like most women my two princesses do so love pretty and shiny trinkets.

I turned my attention to the captured slaves, who stood stolidly in their chains. I saw at once that although they were a mixed bag, which included Libyans, Hurrians and Sumerians, the majority were Egyptians. In all probability they had been captured by the Hyksos and handed over to the Cretans to help them build the fort. I picked out one of them, who had an intelligent face and who seemed not yet to have succumbed to despair.

'Take that one into the next chamber,' I ordered Dilbar, and he grabbed the Egyptian and dragged him into the antechamber of the fort. There I told him to leave us. When he had gone, I stared at the slave in silence for a while. His attitude was one of resignation but I saw the defiance in his eyes that he was trying to conceal.

Good! I thought. He is still a man.

At last I spoke to him softly in our own sweet language. 'You are an Egyptian.' He started and I saw he had understood me. 'What regiment?' I asked him but he shrugged, feigning incomprehension. He looked down at his own feet.

'Look at me!' I ordered him and I removed my bronze helmet and unwound the silken cloth that covered the lower half of my face. 'Look at me!' I repeated.

He lifted his head and started with surprise.

'Who am I?' I asked.

'You are Taita. I saw you at Luxor in the Temple of Hathor when I was a child. My father told me you were one of the greatest living Egyptians,' he whispered in awe, and then he threw himself at my feet. I was moved by this show of veneration, but I kept my voice stern.

'Yes, soldier. I am Taita. Who are you?'

'I am Rohim of the Twenty-sixth Charioteers. I was captured by the Hyksos swine five years ago.'

'Will you return with me to our very Egypt?' I asked, and he smiled. There was a tooth missing in his upper jaw, and his face was bruised. He had been beaten but he was still an Egyptian warrior and his reply was firm.

'I am your man to the death!'

'Where did the Cretans store the chests that they forced you to unload from the ship yesterday?'

'In the strong room at the bottom of the stairwell, but the door is locked.'

'Who has the key?'

'The fat one with the green sash. He is the master of slaves.'

I had seen the man he described kneeling with the other

prisoners. 'Does he also have the key to your chains, Rohim? You will need them, for you are a free man again.' He grinned at the thought.

'He keeps all the keys on a chain around his waist. He hides them under his sash.'

I learned from Rohim that over eighty of the slaves in the fort were captured Egyptian archers and charioteers. When we unchained them they worked with gusto to carry the silver chests back from the fort and stack them in the hold of Zaras' trireme.

While this transfer of silver chests was taking place Rohim led me to the armoury. When we broke open the door, I was delighted to see the array of uniforms, armour and weapons that were stored there.

I ordered all this equipment to be taken to the ships and packed in the main rowing deck where it could be easily reached when we needed it.

Finally we locked all the captured Cretans into their own slave barracks, and we boarded the three waiting triremes.

I had divided our available men equally between the three ships, so all the rowing benches carried their full complements. At my orders the slaves still chained in the lower decks had been given a meal of hard bread, dried fish and beer that we had found in the store-rooms of the fort. It was pathetic to watch them cramming the food into their mouths with calloused hands blackened with filth and their own dried excrement. They gulped down the beer we gave them until their shrunken bellies could hold no more. Some of them vomited it back into the bilges between their bare feet. But the food and friendly treatment had revived them. I knew they would serve me well.

As the dawn was glimmering in the eastern sky we were

ready to sail. I took my place in the bows of the leading trireme beside Zaras with the Hyksos helmet crammed down on my head and my nose and mouth covered with the silken scarf.

Zaras called the order to cast off, and the drum on each rowing deck sounded the stroke. The long oars dipped and pulled and rose again to the tempo of the drums. I passed the order to the men on the steering-oar, and we turned into the main channel of the river. The two other triremes turned in succession behind us. In line astern we headed boldly south-wards for the Hyksos capital and two hundred leagues of enemy-held river.

The smoke from the boats that were still burning drifted in a dense bank across the river, from time to time blanketing the Cretan camp on the far side. But when a gust of the north-erly wind parted the curtain of smoke I saw that my own crews were not the only ones who had been taken by surprise when I headed south.

The troops from the Cretan camp who had survived the destruction of the pontoon bridge were drawn up on the open river-bank in full battle array. The officers commanding them had chosen a point where the navigable channel ran close to the bank. The ranks of their archers were lining the edge of the water, as close as they could get to the channel. They were prepared for us to attempt to run the gauntlet towards the north to reach the open sea. Their bows were strung and every one of them had an arrow nocked and ready to draw.

Four of their senior officers, those with the tallest plumes in their helmets and the most decorations glittering on their breasts and shoulders, were mounted. They sat their horses behind the formations of archers, preparing to direct the arrows of their men at us as we passed on our way down to the Middle Sea.

Their astonishment was apparent as they watched us make the turn into the southern branch of the channel and begin to sail away from them. For a short while none of them reacted. Only when the trireme commanded by Dilbar followed our ship into the turn did they start to move. Then when Akemi, whose ship was bringing up the rear of our squadron, followed us around the voices of the Cretan officers shouting orders became frantic. They carried clearly to me across the water, and I laughed as I watched them spurring their horses back along the river-bank in a futile attempt to head us off.

The Cretan archers broke their perfectly ordered ranks and in an untidy rabble ran after their officers, but as we began remorselessly to pull away from all of them they stopped. They lifted their bows and sent volley after volley of arrows arching after us on a high trajectory. However, these all fell pitifully short and plopped into the wake of Akemi's ship.

The mounted officers refused to abandon the chase. They flogged their mounts and drove them down the towpath to try and catch up with our flotilla. When gradually they came level with Akemi's trireme they drew their swords. They stood in the stirrups shouting abuse and wild challenges across the water at Akemi's men.

Akemi had my strict orders not to shoot arrows at the Minoans. Although they would have made an easy target for his archers on the upper deck of his trireme, he and his crew ignored them. This seemed to infuriate the Minoans. They galloped up the towpath, passing first Akemi's ship and then that of Dilbar. At last they came level with where I stood in the leading ship.

On my orders our men made no attempt to conceal themselves. The quartet of Cretan officers was able to examine our authentic Hyksos uniforms and accoutrements from a distance of a mere hundred paces as they pounded along the towpath keeping pace with our ship.

By this time they had pursued us for well over three leagues, and their horses were beginning to tire rapidly. When the onshore breeze from the Middle Sea began to rise in volume, driving us southwards, we pulled away from them steadily. The towpath deteriorated into swamp. The hooves of the horses threw up clods of black mud and the struggling animals sank to their knees in the muck. They were forced to abandon the pursuit. They reined in their horses and watched forlornly as we sailed away from them.

I was well pleased with how it had all turned out. The Minoan officers had seen all that I had wanted them to see, which was three shiploads of Hyksos pirates with five hundred lakhs of the Supreme Minos' silver bullion heading southwards down the river towards the capital city of King Beon at Memphis.

N ow it was time to begin the transformation into our next role. I gave the orders for the Cretan uniforms and weapons that we had captured at the Tamiat fort to be brought up on deck. Then our men, laughing and joking, stripped off their Hyksos uniforms and gear and replaced them with the full panoply of Minoan military splendour, from gilded helmets and engraved swords to knee boots of fine soft leather.

Both Akemi and Dilbar had my strict orders not to allow their men to jettison their discarded Hyksos uniforms into the river. If these were to be washed down by the current and retrieved by the Minoan troops at Tamiat, then my deception would be discovered.

It would not take a great leap of imagination for the Cretans to realize how we had bamboozled them. So I had the discarded Hyksos equipment bundled up securely and packed away below decks.

With the wind directly behind us, our sails bulging and our banks of oars rising and falling like the silver wings of a wedge of great white swans in flight, we ran on southwards. These Minoan triremes were the largest and swiftest ships afloat.

Despite the massive burden of men and silver they carried their speed was exhilarating. Added to the speed there was an infectious excitement in knowing that we were heading homewards which put my men in high spirits.

As we left the delta and its myriad tributaries behind us and sailed out at last into the main river the three ships of our flotilla spread out into a line abreast and raced each other southwards. The crews shouted challenges and friendly abuse from one trireme to the other.

We flew past anchored fishing boats and swiftly overtook other small vessels laden with produce and trade goods. In passing I could look down into them from the height of our upper deck. I saw a few Egyptian faces amongst the crews who stared up at us in astonishment as we passed them, but most of them were Hyksos.

It is a simple matter for me to tell the difference between these two races. My Egyptians are a handsome people with lively and intelligent faces, high foreheads, large widely spaced eyes, and finely etched features. In short, one is usually able to tell at a glance that they are a superior race.

The Hyksos on the other hand have very few of these attributes. I am not in any way mindlessly prejudiced against them. However, I do have every reason to loathe them with a deep and bitter hatred. They are thieves and bandits; every one of them, with no exception whatsoever. They delight in cruelty and torture. Their coarse and guttural language offends the ears of civilized men. They worship Seth who is the foulest of all the gods. They have stolen our land from us, and enslaved our people.

But I am not a bigot. I abhor those who are. Indeed I have tried my very best to find laudable traits in the Hyksos national character. All the gods know that it is not my fault that I have discovered none.

Now as I looked down upon examples of this unfortunate

race, an idle thought occurred to me that at some time in future it might be appropriate for me to express my disapproval in a more definite and unambiguous manner. I should make a gesture that even King Beon might fully recognize as being well deserved.

That will be a joyous day indeed for all Egyptians, I mused. I smiled, and then the thought hardened in my mind: Why should that day not be sooner rather than later? The entire plan sprang into my mind almost fully formed, conception to birth taking place in moments.

I had seen a number of papyrus scrolls and a writing tablet in the captain's cabin on the lower deck. The Cretans are a literate people. They employ a variation of cuneiform not dissimilar to that of the Sumerians. I can read and recognize the symbols although I confess that at that time I was not yet conversant with the Minoan language.

As one would expect, the Hyksos are entirely illiterate. However, I had learned through my spies that they have captured and enslaved Egyptian scribes whom they force to read, write and translate our hieroglyphics for them.

I also knew that they had learned from these same scribes the use of birds in sending their messages swiftly over great distances. Like the apes the Hyksos are great imitators; although they are seldom able to solve a problem with original thought, they are often able to plagiarize the inventions of greater minds than their own.

I excused myself from Zaras with a few short words and hurried down into the cabin below the main deck. The writing equipment was where I had last seen it. It was contained in an ornate casket decorated with miniature paintings of Thoth, the ibis-headed god of writing.

I sat cross-legged on the deck and opened the writing case. To my delight I saw that apart from the papyrus scrolls of different sizes and shapes, and a selection of brushes and ink blocks, the case contained four miniature pods the size of my thumbnail, skilfully woven from strands of hair from a horse's mane. The pods could be knotted to the leg of one of the common pigeons that we breed for eating. These birds also have a strange ability to return unerringly to the same coop in which they were hatched from the egg, unwittingly carrying with them one of the tiny message pods attached to their leg.

Swiftly I chose a scrap of papyrus small enough to fit into a pigeon pod. Then I selected the finest of the writing brushes and ground a fresh batch of ink from the block of carbon.

I did not have to ponder the composition of my message for it was clear in my mind. When necessary I am able to form hieroglyphics which are not only tiny and closely painted but also lucid and legible, for I have been gifted with a fine writing hand.

'To mighty Beon, Pharaoh of Upper and Lower Egypt.' I opened with the customary salutation. Of course he was none of these things, but those attributes are amongst those to which he aspires. 'I, Supreme Minos of Crete, greet you. As an earnest of my friendship and favour I am sending to Your Grace three of my great treasure ships laden with tribute. They will sail on the second day of the month of Epiphi from my outpost at Tamiat in the delta of the Nile. I trust that they will reach your palace at Memphis on the fifth day of that same month. I have delayed informing you of these events until the final hours to prevent this intelligence falling into the hands of evil men before it comes to your noble attention. I trust in your amity to receive these gifts in the same spirit of respect and accord as that in which they are sent.'

As soon as the ink on it dried I rolled my little scroll carefully and placed it in one of the pigeon pods. This I sealed with a glue of gum arabic. Then I left the cabin and descended to the lower deck and went to the door of the cargo hold.

The lock had not been repaired since Zaras' rough treatment.

It opened readily to my hand. I closed it again behind me. The chest which I had opened to inspect its contents stood apart. The lid was not firmly secured. I prised it open again with the dagger which was part of my Cretan costume. Then I knelt beside it and took out one of the silver ingots. It was heavy but I placed it in the pouch on my belt. Then I returned to the upper deck and took my place at Zaras' side. I spoke to him quietly so that none of the crew could hear my words.

'Within the next hour we should reach the river port of Kuntus where Beon maintains a customs post to collect taxes from all passing ships—'

Zaras interrupted me with a chuckle. 'That is of no consequence, Master Taita. We will not be long delayed. I will brush them aside like mosquitoes . . .'

'No, Zaras. You will back your oars and sails to let the customs boat come alongside. When it does you will show them all respect. I must bespeak the tax collector, because I need his cooperation.' I turned away to the ship's side before he could pester me with more questions. The truth was I was uncertain of what to expect when we reached Kuntus.

We sped on up the river, taking all other shipping by complete surprise. We were the swiftest ships on the Nile. Even a man on horseback could not outrun us to give prior warning of our approach. As soon as they saw us coming up against the stream every boat tried to avoid us, either by running into the bank or by dropping their sails and turning to the north to allow the current to carry them out of our way. They did not know who we were. But in these uneasy times fraught with the smoke clouds of war looming over all the world no sensible man took chances.

When we swept around another wide bend in the river I saw the port of Kuntus lying on the east bank ahead of us. I recognized it by the tall stone-built watchtower on the hill above the town. There was a large black flag waving from a pole set on top of the tower. This was the emblem of the tax collector. I knew that he would have men posted on top of the tower to watch for any vessel that tried to slip past without paying its dues.

As we sailed closer to the port a felucca flying another black tax flag shoved off from the stone jetty of the port and set a course to intercept us in mid-river. I ordered Zaras to furl our own sails and back oars to enable the felucca to come alongside. There were a number of heavily armed Hyksos grouped on the open deck of the felucca. Zaras leaned over the side of our ship and commenced a shouted conversation with one of them, who told us that his name was Grall and that he was the provincial tax administrator.

I was greatly relieved by the fact that this conversation was in Hyksosian. If this creature Grall had addressed us in Minoan it would have been extremely awkward to try to explain how nobody on board a Minoan trireme spoke a word of the language. In that instant I determined that at the very first opportunity I would begin a study of the subject. With my ability to master foreign languages I was confident that within a mere few months I would be able to pass as a native of Crete.

From the deck of the felucca Grall was demanding in the name of King Beon to be allowed to board our ship. As I had coached him, Zaras did not demur but immediately ordered our crew to lower a rope ladder to enable Grall to come aboard. He was a wiry little man and he swarmed up the rope with the agility of an ape.

'Are you the master of this ship?' he demanded of Zaras. 'It is my duty to inspect your ship's manifest.'

'Certainly, sir,' Zaras agreed. 'But first let me invite you to my cabin to partake of a glass of our excellent Minoan wine and then you shall have whatever else you require.' He took the little man by the arm in a friendly grip and ushered him down the companionway to the master's cabin.

Up until this time I had kept myself well in the background. Now I waited until I heard Zaras slam the door of the cabin beneath my feet. Then I followed them quietly below deck.

Zaras and I had planned this meeting carefully, and I had taken the precaution of drilling a peephole in the bulkhead through which I could watch and hear everything that took place within the cabin. Now I saw that Zaras had seated the visitor facing my peephole. Grall bore more than a passing resemblance to a poisonous giant toad. He had the same wide mouth and beady eyes. In addition his face was decorated with large warts. When he swallowed a mouthful of the wine which Zaras had poured for him his entire throat contracted as though he were gulping down a water rat, which is the favourite fare of the giant toad. I found myself fascinated by this exhibition, which was so true to nature.

'Of course you are aware that King Beon has accorded our shipping diplomatic exemption from taxation.' Zaras was speaking respectfully and reasonably.

'It is for me to determine whether or not you qualify for that exemption, Captain.' Grall lowered his wine mug. 'However, even if you do qualify I may have to charge you for my expenses.' His smile was sly and knowing. 'But it will be a paltry sum, I do assure you.'

'Of course.' Zaras nodded. 'All of us must live. However, I am grateful for this opportunity to speak to you in private. I need to send a message to Memphis informing King Beon of our imminent arrival. I am conveying to him a large amount of silver bars as tribute from our Supreme Minos.' Zaras reached under the table and produced the silver ingot which I had given him earlier. He placed this on the table top between them. 'Here is a sample.'

Grall set aside his mug slowly and fastened his gaze on the ingot. His eyes seemed to bulge from their sockets. His toad's mouth hung open slackly so the wine dribbled over his lips and ran down into his scraggly beard. He seemed bereft of the power of speech. Probably he had never laid eyes on such a treasure in his entire lifetime.

'I wondered if you have carrier birds here at Kuntus; birds that can fly to Memphis and take my message to your king to alert him ahead of our arrival at his capital city?' Zaras continued.

Grall croaked and nodded his head. He was unable to answer coherently or to take his eyes off the glistening bar of silver.

'Perhaps we should look upon this ingot as the payment for your invaluable services.' Zaras nudged the silver bar an inch towards him. 'A token of the accord that exists between our two great nations.' Zaras placed the pigeon pod containing my missive beside the ingot. 'This is the message that must be sent to your King Beon, if it so pleases you.'

One of Grall's hands crawled across the table like a great hairy spider and spread itself over the silver ingot. He lifted it reverently and pushed it down the front of the stained leather jerkin that he wore, and knotted the fastenings. His hands were trembling with emotion. The ingot made a considerable bulge under his jerkin, but he clasped it to his breast as tenderly as a mother giving suck to her infant.

He came unsteadily to his feet and with his free hand picked up the pigeon pod. 'I understand now that you are involved in affairs of high state, Your Honour.' He bowed deeply to Zaras. 'Please forgive my intrusion. Of course I consider myself to be privileged to be given the honour of flying your message to King Beon with one of my birds. The king will have your message in his hands before sunset this very evening. Even in this magnificent ship of yours you will not be able to reach Memphis before noon the day after tomorrow.'

'You are extremely kind. Now I will escort you safely back on board your felucca,' Zaras offered, but Grall was already halfway up the companion ladder to the upper deck.

Zaras and I watched the felucca racing back to Kuntus. We delayed long enough to see Grall scramble from the felucca to the jetty and then hurry into the village. Only then did I nod at Zaras. We spread our sails and ran out our banks of oars to resume our southerly course.

I looked back over our stern and saw a horseman leave the scattered buildings of Kuntus and gallop up the track to the watchtower on the headland. I shaded my eyes against the sun and watched him pull up at the base of the tower and toss his reins to a waiting groom, then drop to the ground and hurry into the tall building.

A short time later the same man reappeared on the top platform of the tower. He was silhouetted against the sky as he lifted both his arms above his head. A purple pigeon fluttered from his cupped hands and whirled aloft on swift wing-beats.

The bird circled the tower three times and then settled on to a determined southerly heading. It came down the middle of the river, climbing swiftly. But as it passed directly over our ship it was still low enough for me to imagine that I could see the shape of the tiny pod fastened to one of the legs that was tucked in under its tail fan.

We sailed on into the south for the rest of the afternoon. Then, as soon as the sun sank below the hills on the west bank, I ordered Zaras to find a safe anchorage for the night. He chose a stretch of shallow water in a bend of the Nile out of the main current.

I knew that Grall had been correct in his estimate, and that we were still a day and a half's sailing north of Memphis. Zaras set an anchor watch on board each of our vessels. Then he posted additional sentries ashore to ensure that no bandits could creep up on us under cover of darkness.

As we ate our dinner around one of the camp-fires I discussed with my three captains the tactics of ramming an enemy ship. I had studied the theory of this manoeuvre during the writing of my celebrated treatise on naval warfare. I detailed for them how to inflict the greatest amount of damage on an enemy ship and its crew, without destroying your own vessel and murdering your own men in the process. I reiterated that the most important fundamental is to teach your men the brace position that they must adopt before collision with an enemy ship.

In all other respects it was a quiet and uneventful night. We were astir again before daybreak and as soon as it was light enough to discern the channel we hoisted the anchors and set sail again. The wind had strengthened during the night, blowing strongly out of the north-east. It drove us onwards so briskly that the spray splattered in over the bows to wet our faces as we stared ahead. The men were in high spirits. Even the slaves who were still chained in the lower decks had responded well to the increase in their rations and to my promise of manumission once we reached Thebes. I could hear them singing even where I stood at the helm.

I think that I was probably the only one on board who had misgivings about our enterprise. All had gone so well since we left Thebes that the men were beginning to believe that I was infallible and that they were invincible. I knew well enough that both these assumptions were false. Even I did not know what we would find when we reached Memphis. I began to regret bitterly that I had been so bold as to alert Beon to our arrival. In retrospect I thought that it would have been so much better and safer to creep by his capital with muffled oars during the night. It did nothing for my peace of mind when Zaras came to where I was brooding at the ship's side and slapped me on the back with such bonhomie that the blow staggered me.

'Despite your reputation, I never realized that you are such a reckless daredevil, Taita. I know no other who would have dreamed up any of these escapades of yours. You should compose a ballad to celebrate your own heroics. If you don't then I may be obliged to do so on your behalf.' He guffawed and slapped me again. It hurt even more than the first blow.

Although this was Egyptian territory that we were sailing through, it had been seized by our enemies many years ago. I had not revisited this part of the river since my boyhood. This was all unfamiliar territory to me, as it was to every other man aboard, with one exception.

That was Rohim of the Twenty-sixth Charioteers, the Egyptian slave that I had found and freed in the fort at Tamiat. He had been a captive of the Hyksos for five years and half that time he had been chained on the rowing benches of a galley that patrolled this section of the Nile.

He stood behind Zaras and me as we navigated the trireme southwards with sails straining and every oar driving hard. He was able to point out the twists and turns in the navigable channel long before we reached them, and to warn us of hidden obstacles below the surface.

When night fell we anchored for the night. But at sunrise the next morning we were once again under sail and boring on up the Nile. This was the fifth day of the month of Epiphi, the day which I had warned Beon to expect our arrival at Memphis.

We sailed on for four hours until eventually we entered a narrow dog-leg bend that ran between low bluffs. We emerged from this into a straight run of calm water that stretched out for a good two leagues ahead of us.

'This is the last run before we reach Memphis,' Rohim told us. 'The channel turns to the left hand at the end of this strait and the city of Memphis is spread out over both banks directly beyond the turn.'

'Avast heaving!' I ordered Zaras. 'Let the men at the oars rest until we reach the turn. Let them drink from the water-skins. They must be ready to bring us up to ramming speed as soon as I call for it.' The other two triremes followed our example as soon as we shipped our oars. The three of us continued down the strait under sails alone.

The river was alive with shipping of every type and size; from galleys to luggers and longboats. These behaved in a completely different manner from any boats we had encountered up until this time. Although they gave way to us respectfully, they did not try to run from us. The crews waved and shouted friendly greetings as we passed.

'They are expecting us,' I told Zaras complacently, trying to hide my relief. 'It seems that our pigeon found its way back to its loft.'

Zaras looked at me with unconcealed astonishment. 'Isn't that what you planned? Were you expecting anything less, master?' he demanded and I shook my head and turned away. I find it daunting that men expect me to perform miracles as a matter of routine. I know that I am more astute and wily than most other men, but to my mind luck is preferable to brains and luck is a fickle mistress. I am never sure when she will desert me.

I walked down the rows of benches and here I met the same childlike trust and limitless expectations. The men greeted me with smiles and silly little jests, which I returned as guilelessly. However, my true purpose was to check that the bows that lay hidden under the benches were strung and the quivers beside them were filled with arrows.

With the wind blustering in from dead astern we were tearing through the water and the final bend in the river seemed to race to meet us. Without any semblance of urgency, still smiling and exchanging repartee with the men, I made my way back to my station at the helm.

I glanced over each side of our hull to make certain that the triremes of Dilbar and Akemi were in their arrowhead attack formation flanking us. Both Dilbar and Akemi raised their right arms to salute me, and to signal their readiness for battle.

I nodded at Zaras as we swept into the bend and called out one word: 'Oars!'

We spread our wings, the feathered blades of the oars skimming the surface.

'Pull!' I gave the command and the blades dipped and caught the water and shot us forward, almost doubling our speed. The drummers set the stroke rate, increasing it as our speed built up.

Suddenly we were through the bend. The banks of the river opened on each side of us and the city of Memphis lay ahead of us. The dazzling sunlight reflected from the marble walls and towers, from the domes and towers clad in gold leaf. The splendour of the palaces and temples spread before us almost rivalled those of my beloved Thebes.

Each bank of the river was lined three and four deep with small craft, and every craft was packed with humanity. Their multitudes were beyond counting. Most of the boats were draped with bunting of white and red; these I knew were the Hyksos colours of rejoicing and happiness. The crowds were waving palm fronds in greeting. Their voices rose in a tumult of song and wild ululation.

The wide lane down the centre of the Nile had been left completely devoid of shipping to welcome us. At the far end of this watery highway was anchored a cluster of magnificently painted barges and river galleys. In their centre was the royal barge that dwarfed anything else on the river, with the exception of our trio of triremes.

'Increase the stroke to ramming speed.' I raised my voice above the uproar to shout at Zaras. 'The red barge in the centre of their line must be that of Beon. Aim for it.'

I reached up with both hands and made certain that my silk mask covered my lower face to just below my eyes, and then I jammed my bronze helmet down firmly on my skull. I wanted to be entirely certain that no member of Beon's court would ever be able to recognize me at some awkward time in the future.

The two men on the steering-oar kept the bronze ram on the bows of our trireme aimed unwaveringly at the centre of King Beon's state barge. The other two triremes of our squadron held their station half a ship's length on either side of us and slightly behind us, so that we would be first to strike. Our drummer pounded out the rowing stroke for ramming speed, and I listened to my own heartbeat matching it almost exactly.

The distance between us and the red barge closed swiftly from four hundred paces to two hundred. I could see that the barge was anchored by the bows and by the stern, so that it was broadside to the current. In the centre of the upper deck was a high-stepped pyramid, surmounted by a tented canopy. Under the canopy I could make out the throne and on it sat a large human form. But it was still too distant for me to be sure of any details.

Surrounding the throne was drawn up an honour guard of pikemen, all of them fully armed and armoured. Their helmets and breastplates made a warlike and glittering show.

On each side of the royal barge was anchored a line of smaller vessels. These were crowded with the courtiers who made up Beon's entourage. It seemed to me that there were several hundreds of them, but it was impossible to judge their numbers with any accuracy because they were packed so closely, and most of the women were hidden behind the taller men. All of them were laughing, cheering and waving. Some of the men were in ceremonial armour and ornate metal helmets. The others, male and females both, were dressed in lustrous and exotic materials of every conceivable colour. They were as fantastic and multi-hued as a cloud of freshly hatched butterflies, fluttering, whirling and dancing in the wind.

In a smaller vessel, which was moored alongside the great royal barge, a band of musicians played barbaric Hyksos music. This was a cacophony of drums and lutes, of animal horn trumpets, woodwinds and reed pipes.

We were racing down so swiftly on the royal barge that I was now able to make out the details that had been previously been obscured by distance. On the summit of the pyramid-shaped dais, under the painted canopy, on his throne of beaten silver sat King Beon. He had taken that throne after the death of King Salitis, his father.

I recognized him on sight. I had seen him before on the battlefield of Thebes. He had been the commander of the Hyksos left flank, with forty thousand infantry and archers under him. He was not the kind of man that one would readily forget.

He was colossal. His white robes were voluminous as a tent, billowing around his protuberant belly. His beard was curling black and plaited into thick ropes, some of which hung to his waist while others were thrown back over his shoulders. Woven into the plaits were chains and ornaments of bright silver and gold. He wore a high-crowned helmet of polished silver that was studded with ornate patterns of glittering jewels. His aspect was magnificent, almost godlike. Even I, who loathe all things Hyksos, was impressed.

King Beon had one hand raised, with the open palm turned towards us in greeting or in blessing; I was uncertain which he intended, but he was smiling.

In a few terse words I pointed out to Zaras the most vulnerable point in the hull of the royal barge where the strain on the ship's main timbers was centred. This was slightly forward of the high podium.

'Take that as your mark, Zaras, and hold true on it right up to the moment of impact.'

By now we were so close that I could see that King Beon was no longer smiling. His lower jaw was hanging open, exposing his brown-stained front teeth. Abruptly he closed his mouth. At this late juncture he had realized that our intentions were hostile. He dropped his hairy paws on to the armrests of his throne and tried to push himself to his feet. But he was ungainly and slow.

The courtiers packed into the barges on each side of his royal vessel suddenly became aware of the menace of our racing triremes bearing directly down on them. The wild screams of the women carried clearly to where I stood. The men were struggling to reach the sides of the anchored barges, unsheathing their weapons and challenging us with futile war cries and bellows of rage. I saw many of their women knocked down and trampled. Others were carried forward to the ship's side. They jumped or they were shoved overboard into the Nile. We came down on this confusion like a mountain avalanche.

'Oars!' Zaras shouted the command loudly enough to be heard above the wailing and shrieking of the Hyksos. The rowers on each side of our trireme lifted their oars to the vertical position and clamped them in their buckets so they would not be sheared off by the impact. Our speed was undiminished as we covered the last few yards of open water.

At the last moment before impact I dropped to my knees on the deck and braced myself against the rowing bench in front of me. I saw that the men around me were at last taking my instruction seriously. Every one of them was doubled over with his arms locked around his thighs and his face pressed to his knees.

We struck the royal barge precisely on the point of aim that I had given Zaras. The massive bronze ram on our bows sheared through her timbers with a crackling roar. Most of our own men were thrown from the rowing benches to the deck by the collision, but I managed to keep my grip on the sturdy hardwood bench. I was able to see everything that was happening around me.

I watched as the full force and weight of our trireme was concentrated on one small area of the royal barge's side. Like the blade of a heavy axe striking a log of kindling, we cut through her cleanly. The severed halves of her hull rolled under our bows as we trod her under.

As she went over I saw the Hyksos guardsmen flung from the steps of the royal pyramid in swirling profusion, like the autumn leaves from the high branches of sycamore tree in the gale winds of winter. King Beon was thrown highest of them all. His white robes billowed about his gross body, and the tangled braids of his beard lashed his face. He dropped back into the river with his arms and legs flailing. The air trapped in his robes floated him on the surface not thirty paces from where I was dragging myself upright, using the rowing bench as a support.

On either side of me the other triremes of our squadron smashed into the smaller barges of the Hyksos formation. They rolled them over effortlessly, ripping through their hulls, catapulting the panic-stricken passengers from the decks into the river.

The wreckage of the royal barge scraped down the sides of our trireme, to an uproar of tearing sails, snapping ropes, splintering timbers and the agonized shrieks of men being crushed between the grinding hulls. Our own deck was canted over at a severe angle, men and loose equipment sliding towards the port side.

Then our lovely ship shook herself free of the wreckage, and with almost feminine grace she regained her equilibrium and came upright in the water.

Zaras was yelling again for 'Oars!', and the men responded quickly enough. They heaved the heavy oars from the buckets and settled them in their rowlocks.

'Reverse the stroke!' Zaras shouted again. Only the rowers on the rear benches were able to reach the water with their oars. The men in the forward benches were blocked by the wreckage of the floundering royal barge.

Those who were able to do so dug in their blades and with a few powerful strokes pulled us free. Within seconds the severed sections of the royal barge filled with water. They rolled over and went down. An eruption of trapped air roared up to the surface.

I glanced over at the other two triremes. Dilbar and Akemi were bellowing orders at their men. Their crews clambered swiftly back on to the rowing benches, set their oars and picked up the stroke from the beat of the drums. The helmsmen were steering them back into formation on our leading ship.

Between us the surface of the river was covered with bobbing human heads, splashing and struggling bodies and shattered wreckage. The cries of drowning men and women were as piteous as the bleating of sheep being driven through the gates of the abattoir when they smell the blood.

For a long minute I watched the carnage in horror. I was almost overwhelmed by guilt and remorse. I could no longer force myself to look upon these doomed creatures as merely Hyksos animals. They were human beings struggling for life itself. My heart went out to them.

Then I saw King Beon again and my feelings changed in an instant. My wayward heart returned to me as swiftly and unerr-ingly as a pigeon to its loft. I remembered what Beon had done to two hundred of our finest and bravest archers when his Hyksos brutes had captured them during the battle of Naquada. He had barricaded them in the Temple of Seth on the hill above the battlefield and burned them alive as a sacrifice to his monstrous god.

Now Beon was clinging to a shattered plank from his royal barge with one hand; while in his other hand he was wielding his bejewelled sword, using it to chop at the heads of the women of his harem who were trying to take refuge on his plank with him. He drove them away ruthlessly, unwilling to share his perch with a single one of them. I watched him strike at a girl child who was no older than my darling little Bekatha. His blade split her skull down to her chin as though it were a ripe pomegranate. While her bright blood spurted out to incarnadine the water around her, Beon called her a filthy name, and struck her again.

I stooped quickly and picked up the recurved war bow from under the rowing bench in front of me. The arrows had spilled from the quiver around my feet. I nocked one of them as I straightened up and drew to full stretch. Like any expert archer I always loose as the bowstring touches my lips. However, this time my hands were shaking with fury and the arrow flew wide.

Instead of taking Beon in the throat where I had aimed, my arrow pinned his forearm to the plank on which he lay; the plank for which he had killed his own child bride.

Zaras and the others who were watching me howled with glee. They know how well I can shoot and they thought I had deliberately winged Beon. I nocked another arrow, and this time I admit that I was playing to my audience. I deliberately nailed Beon's sword-arm to the plank, so he was stretched out on the timber baulk in the attitude of crucifixion. He howled like the cringing jackal he was.

I am by nature a compassionate man, so I did not allow him to suffer much longer than he richly deserved. My third arrow went into the precise centre of his throat.

The crews of all three of my triremes followed my example. They seized their bows and crowded to the sides of our vessels to shower arrows on the floundering wretches in the water below them.

I was powerless to prevent it happening, or perhaps I lacked the motivation and inclination to do so. Many of my men had lost their fathers and brothers to these unwholesome wretches. Their sisters and mothers had been ravished and their homes burned to the ground by them.

So I stood by and watched the flower of Hyksos nobility being pruned down to the very quick. When the last floating corpse, bristling with arrows, was carried away on the current I regained control of my men and cursed them back to their seats on the rowing benches.

Totally unrepentant, still howling with bloodthirsty glee, they hoisted the sails and heaved back on the oars. We left the Hyksos to the mercy of their foul god Seth, and we raced on southwards towards Thebes and the true Kingdom of Egypt.

T he border between our very Egypt and the territory that the Hyksos hordes had overrun was never clearly demarcated. The fighting seemed to fluctuate on a daily basis as attack followed counter-attack, and the fortunes of war ebbed and flowed across the land.

We had left from Thebes on the fifth day of the month of Payni. At that time Lord Kratas had driven the Hyksos invaders back twenty leagues north of the town of Sheik Abada. However, we were now well into the month of Epiphi, so much could have changed in our absence. But we still had the element of surprise on our side.

Neither the Hyksos front-line troops nor our own men fighting under Lord Kratas would be expecting the miraculous appearance of a fleet of Minoan warships in our Nile, over four hundred leagues from the shores of the Middle Sea.

There were no ships on the southern stretches of the Nile, either Hyksos or Egyptian, that could oppose our triremes. We had just proven that we were unstoppable. Of course, the Hyksos might fly pigeons to try and warn their troops who stood between us and Egypt. But pigeons are free spirits and fly only to where they were hatched, and not to any other destination that their handlers might prefer.

We did not anchor at nightfall; because we were now in familiar waters and we knew every bend and sandbar, every channel and every obstacle in this section of the river.

Six day and nights after we left Memphis, a few hours before midnight, just as the moon in its first quarter was rising, we passed through the encamped armies.

The watch fires of the opposing legions were spread out for several leagues along both banks of the Nile. There was merely a narrow strip of darkness between them, which demarcated no-man's-land.

Our own ships showed no lights, except a tiny shaded lamp on the stern so we could keep contact with each other in the darkness. These dim lights were not visible from the river-banks. I did not wish to be recognized by either army so we kept to the middle of the river. We sailed through unchallenged, until at last we were back in our very Egypt.

In the dawn we ran into a small flotilla of eight river galleys coming towards us from the direction of Thebes. Even at a distance I could see that they were laden with Egyptian troops, and they were flying the blue colours of Pharaoh Tamose. I knew that these must be Egyptian supply vessels bringing up reinforcements for Lord Kratas' army.

As soon as they saw our strange squadron bearing down on them every one of them put over the helm and tried to fly from us in panic. During the previous few days I had ordered my men to stitch together crude but effective blue pennants in preparation for just such an encounter. Each of our triremes hoisted one of these at the masthead and the galleys pulled into the bank and let us pass. The crews stared after us in astonishment as we sailed on towards Thebes with only a passing salutation. I am certain none of them had ever seen ships like our triremes.

This was a meeting that I would have avoided if it were at all possible. It was far better that the fate of the treasure triremes remain forever a mystery to the Supreme Minos in Crete. He must never doubt that the Hyksos were the false allies that robbed him of his hoard of silver bullion. To achieve this I had to ensure that our captured prizes, colossal and conspicuous as they might be, disappeared without trace. This was a task that might have daunted a lesser man, but I had already devised the solution.

I n the time before our people were driven from their homeland by the Hyksos, before the exodus, our ruler had been Pharaoh Mamose. At that time I, Taita, was the slave of Lord Intef who was the Nomarch of Karnak and grand vizier of all the twenty-two nomes of Upper Egypt. However, amongst his numerous other titles and honorifics my master was also the Lord of the Necropolis and the Keeper of the Royal Tombs.

He was responsible for the upkeep of the tombs of all the pharaohs past and present, living and dead. But much more importantly he was also the official architect of the tomb of Pharaoh Mamose.

My Lord Intef had never been gifted with any creative skills. His talents were vested more in havoc and destruction. I doubt that he could have designed a cattle pen or even a pigeon coop, let alone an elaborate royal tomb fit for a pharaoh. While retaining for himself the royal gratitude and favours that went with the title, he left the arduous work, that which was not to his liking or which was beyond his limited abilities and skills, for me to attend to.

My memories of Lord Intef are not happy ones. It was he who commanded one of his minions to take the gelding knife to me. He was a cruel man and utterly ruthless. But, in the end, I had decisively settled the score between us.

Long before that happy day it was I who designed every chamber and tunnel and funerary hall of Pharaoh Mamose's magnificent tomb. Then I supervised and directed the builders, the masons, the artists and all the artisans that were called upon to labour in this enterprise.

Pharaoh Mamose's outer sarcophagus was carved from a gigantic single block of granite. It was sufficiently commodious to encompass a nest of seven silver coffins, which fitted neatly one within the other. The innermost of these was intended to contain Pharaoh's embalmed corpse. All this added up to a burden of massive bulk and weight. This had to be transported in great reverence two thousand yards from the funerary temple on the banks of the Nile River to the tomb in the foothills of the Valley of the Kings.

To accomplish this transit I surveyed and built a canal that ran as straight as any arrow from the bank of the Nile across the riparian plain of black soil to the entrance of the royal tomb. This canal was wide enough and deep enough to accept Pharaoh's funeral barge.

Pharaoh Mamose had been overtaken by destiny and had never lain a single day in his tomb before the Hyksos drove us out of our land. When we embarked on the long exodus we were commanded by his wife, Queen Lostris, to carry his embalmed body with us.

Many years later, Queen Lostris ordered me to design and build another tomb in the savage Nubian wilderness thousands of leagues further south. That was where Mamose now lay.

The original tomb in the Valley of the Kings had stood empty all these years. More importantly for my plans, the canal that I had built from the funerary temple on the bank of the Nile to the royal tomb was still in an excellent state of repair. I knew this because only a short while previously I had ridden along the bank with my two little princesses to show them their father's empty tomb. I must admit that neither of them showed much interest in this lesson in the history of their own family.

Even after all these years I was able to recall the precise dimensions of Mamose's funeral barge. My memory is infallible. I never forget a fact, a figure or a face.

Now I measured the overall dimensions of our requisitioned Minoan treasure triremes. Then I ordered Zaras to anchor briefly in calm water, while I swam down to the trireme's keel and measured the amount of water she drew with her full cargo of bullion in the hold. These measurements varied somewhat from ship to ship.

I returned to the surface well pleased with the results of my investigations. Now I was able to compare the dimensions of Pharaoh Mamose's funeral barge with those of the captured triremes. The funerary canal would accommodate the transit of the largest of my triremes with ten cubits to spare on each side of the hull, and with clearance of fifteen cubits of water under the keel. What was even more encouraging was that all those years ago I had lined the canal with granite blocks and I had designed a system of locks and shadoofs to keep it always filled with Nile water.

It has been my experience that if you defer to the gods with the full reverence and respect that they deserve and expect, they are often inclined to return the compliment. Although they can be capricious, this time they had remembered me.

I planned the last leg of our journey to arrive at the entrance to the funerary canal shortly after the setting of the sun. In darkness we tied up at the stone jetty below Pharaoh Mamose's funerary temple. Of course Mamose is now a god and has his own temple overlooking the Nile. It is but a short walk from the jetty on which Zaras and I landed.

It is not a very imposing temple. I must accept the responsibility for that. When we returned to Thebes after the exodus and we defeated the Hyksos at the battle of Thebes, my mistress

Queen Lostris was determined to dedicate a temple to her husband, the long-dead Pharaoh. She wanted to honour him and at the same time render up thanks for our safe return from the wilderness.

Of course she summoned me to build the temple. When I saw the extent and sumptuousness of the edifice she had in mind I was shocked and alarmed. It would have overshadowed and outshone the grand palace of the Pharaohs which would face it from the opposite bank of the river. Pharaoh Mamose had almost reduced this very Egypt to penury with the erection of his two tombs: the one here at the entrance to the Valley of the Kings and the other even more complex and expensive tomb in Nubia.

Now my mistress, whom I adored and worshipped, planned to bring the nation low yet again with the erection of another astonishing building in his memory.

Fortunately I have considerable sway over her only son, the present Pharaoh Tamose, who is a sensible lad. To a much lesser extent I had learned from long and bitter experience how to control the wilder excesses of my queen. The dimensions of the temple to Mamose that we eventually settled upon were half the size of the tax collector's building in Thebes, and I even managed to do away with the marble floors.

An establishment of this size no longer required the services of as many priests as my queen had in mind. I whittled away at her resolve until finally she threw up her hands in resignation and agreed to my counter-proposal of four priests, as opposed to her original estimate of four hundred.

Now when Zaras and I made our way up from the river to the rear entrance of the temple and walked into the nave without announcing our arrival we discovered the four religious gentlemen rather more than moderately inebriated on cheap palm wine. They were in the company of two young ladies who for some arcane and obscure reason were without clothing.

They were engrossed in a prayer ritual with two of the priests of Mamose, which seemed to consist of rolling around on the floor of baked mud-bricks, clinging together and uttering cries of wild abandon. The two unoccupied priests stood over them clapping their hands and extorting the worshippers to a more strenuous display of religious devotion.

It was some little time before any of them became aware of our presence. At that point the ladies hurriedly retrieved their apparel and disappeared through the secret door behind the statue of the god Mamose. We did not see them again, nor were they mentioned in our subsequent conversation with the priests.

The priests of Mamose are well disposed towards me. Since the death of Queen Lostris I have made myself responsible for the payment of their monthly stipends. The four of them knelt in front of me, genuflecting vigorously and in the name of the god calling down blessings on my head.

As they knelt at my feet I produced the hawk seal of Pharaoh from under my cloak. They were struck dumb with awe. The high priest crawled to my feet and tried to kiss them. He smelled overpoweringly of sweat, cheap wine and cheaper femininity. I stepped back and Zaras dissuaded him from further demonstrations of piety with the flat of his sword across his bare buttocks.

Then I addressed the four of them briefly but firmly, warning them strictly that the presence of three large warships moored at the wharf outside their front door must never be mentioned or admitted to anybody but Pharaoh Tamose in person. In addition armed guards would be placed over their temple and the empty tomb at the far end of the canal both day and night. Only those men under the command of Captain Zaras were in future allowed to enter the sacred precincts. These same guards would ensure that the four priests themselves would remain strictly incarcerated within these precincts.

Finally I commanded the high priest to hand over to me the large bunch of keys to the tomb and all the other monuments under his charge. We left them still protesting their duty and devotion to me and Pharaoh, and their strict obedience to my orders. Zaras and I returned to our ships.

The fall in the ground from the entrance to the Valley of the Kings to the dock on the river was less than twenty cubits but it required four separate locks to lift each of our triremes that height before we could bring them to the tomb. We rowed the first ship into the lock below the temple and then closed the gates on it. The water level in the lock was five cubits lower than that in the canal.

I demonstrated to my three captains how to open the ground paddles. Water from the upper canal then drained down into the lock and slowly lifted the enormous ship up to the same level as the upper canal. Once the gates were closed behind her, fifty men on the tow lines were standing ready to drag the great trireme down the canal to the next lock, while behind her the process was being repeated to raise the second trireme.

None of my men had ever seen anything to match this, which was not surprising because I had invented the system myself. There was not another like it in all the world. They were elated and excited by what they perceived to be witchcraft. But there was usually hard work involved in my kind of magic.

Fortunately I had over two hundred men to apply to this labour. These included the slaves that had been chained below by the Minoans. They were now freed men but they were obliged to work for their freedom.

The water that was drained from the higher canal to lift the boat had to be replaced. I achieved this by pumping up fresh water from the river by means of a battery of shadoofs. These were counterweighted bucket chains each served by two men. It was an involved and laborious business that had to be repeated four times with each trireme.

Before each boat was lifted through the first lock the sails and masts were lowered flat on the upper deck. Then the hull was covered by woven reed mats until it resembled a shapeless mound of trash. When the citizens of Thebes awoke the following morning and looked across the river they would see nothing untoward on the far bank. The three great triremes had disappeared as though they had never existed.

It was almost sunrise the next day before we had towed the ships across the plain and moored them at the entrance to Mamose's tomb. The men were exhausted so I ordered Zaras to issue them with extra rations of dried fish, beer and bread, and let them rest through the hot hours of the day.

I walked back along the towpath of the canal to the temple. The priests seemed to have recovered from the strenuous rituals, devotions and prayers of the previous evening. They rowed me across the river in the temple skiff. I was on my way to report on the success of our expedition to Pharaoh.

This was a pleasant duty to which I was looking forward immensely. My devotion to Pharaoh is exceeded only by that I had for his mother, Queen Lostris. Of course, it is futile to compare superlatives so I deliberately do not mention my royal princesses in this equation. Let it suffice to say that my devotion to the royal family extends to all its members.

My tame priests landed me on the steps below the bazaars of the waterfront of the city, which were already thronged despite the early hour. I set off through the narrow streets towards the palace gates. Under my battered helmet and filthy face mask nobody recognized me, although a gang of small ragamuffins danced around me calling me vile names and throwing stones at me. I caught one of their missiles in mid-air and returned it with considerably more force than I received it. The urchin who was clearly leader of the gang screamed with pain and clutched at the wound in his scalp, which was fountaining copiously, and he led his followers in the flight for safety.

When I reached the palace gates I removed my disguise, and the captain of the household guards recognized me at once. He saluted me respectfully.

'I must see Pharaoh!' I told him. 'Send a messenger to tell him I am waiting on his pleasure.'

'I offer you my apologies, Lord Taita.' I did not correct him. I was becoming accustomed to my new title. 'Pharaoh is not in Thebes, and we do not expect his imminent return.'

I nodded. This came as a disappointment, but as no real surprise to me. Pharaoh spends the greater part of his time and energy in prosecuting the interminable campaign against the Hyksos in the north. 'Then take me to the chamberlain, Lord Aton.'

When I reached his private rooms Aton rushed to embrace me at the door. 'What tidings, old friend?' he demanded. 'How went our venture?'

'Grave tidings indeed.' I assumed a gloomy expression. 'The treasury of the Supreme Minos in his fort at Tamiat has been plundered, and King Beon has been murdered.'

He held me at arm's length and stared into my face. 'You jest with me, good Taita,' he accused me. 'All honest men must weep to hear it told! Who would commit such heinous crimes?'

'Alas! Both committed by the same hand, Aton. One that you might recognize, mayhap?' And I held up my right hand before his face. He stared at it with cleverly feigned mystification. To have survived so long in the role of royal chamberlain one had to be a gifted thespian.

Then he shook his head and began to chuckle, softly at first, but the volume of his mirth built up swiftly until he was snorting and hooting with glee. He staggered around the room bumping into the furniture and laughing. His belly and every other part of him were shaking with laughter. Then abruptly he stopped laughing and fled to the adjoining closet. There was a moment of silence, but before I could follow him there came a sound like the flooding of the Nile through the cataracts. It went on for some considerable time before Aton returned to where I waited. Now his expression was once more serious as he adjusted his robes.

'You are fortunate, my dear friend, that I reached the pot in time, or you might have been drowned like King Beon.'

'How do you know Beon was drowned?'

'I have ears and eyes other than those you see in my face.'

'If you know so much, then tell me about the treasure of the Minos.'

'I have heard nothing of that.' He shook his head ruefully. 'Is there aught you might have learned about it?'

'Only that you were wrong.'

'In what way was I wrong?'

'You told me that the treasure might amount to a hundred lakhs, did you not?' He nodded and I went on:

'You sadly miscalculated.'

'Can you prove it to me?' he demanded.

'I can do better than that, Aton. I can let you weigh it,' I assured him. 'However, I must get a message to Pharaoh before we leave the palace.'

Aton pointed to his writing case, which lay open in a corner of the room. 'Write your message and Pharaoh will have it in his hand before nightfall,' he assured me.

My message was short and cryptic. 'Please be patient with me,' I begged Aton as I handed it to him, 'but I have not bathed or worn fresh apparel for almost two moons. I must visit my own quarters here in the palace before I return with you to the tomb of Mamose.' I did not think it worth mentioning that neither had I seen my two little princesses since my return.

As soon as I reached my quarters I sent one of my slaves to the quarters of the royal women to convey a message to Their Highnesses.

The two of them arrived with the force and fury of the

khamsin wind out of the desert just as I was stepping into my hot tub. They are the only ones in all the world that I allow to see me unclad, except for my slaves. However, my slaves are all eunuchs as am I, so they are of no account.

Now Tehuti and Bekatha perched on the marble surround of my tub and pestered me with questions. They took no notice of my nudity. Once many years ago Bekatha had spoken for both of them on the subject: 'You are just like me and Tehuti; all three of us look so much neater without all those dangly things hanging in front of us.'

Now she paddled both her neat little feet in my tub and complained, 'It's been so boring since you went away. Whatever were you doing that took you so long? You must swear that next time you will take us with you.' I poured a pitcher of hot water over my head to avoid taking the oath she had set for me.

'Did you bring us a present, Taita? Or did you forget?' Tehuti took over the interrogation. As the elder sister she has a firmer grasp on the intrinsic value of things.

'Of course I brought you both something. How could I ever forget you two little pests?' I replied, and they clapped their hands with delight.

'Show us!' Bekatha chirruped.

'Oh yes, darling Taita,' Tehuti agreed. 'Please show us. We do so love you.'

'Then fetch me my pouch.' I pointed to where it lay on my couch in the adjoining room, and as always Bekatha was first to reach it. She came dancing back to me, brandishing the leather pouch. Then she flopped down on to the marble slabs with her legs crossed under her, and the pouch in her lap.

'Open it!' I told her. With my princesses firmly in mind, I had selected two pieces of jewellery from the loot we collected from the Minoan officers whom we captured at Tamiat.

'Is there something in there wrapped in red cloth?' I asked and Bekatha squealed with excitement.

'Yes, my best and most lovely Taita. Is it mine? Is the red one mine?'

'Of course it is.'

Her hands were shaking with excitement as she unwrapped the small parcel. As she held up the golden necklace her eyes filled with tears of delight. 'It is the most beautiful thing I have ever seen!' she whispered.

Suspended from the chain were two golden figures. Although they were tiny they were complete in every exquisite detail. The largest was an image of a charging bull. Its head was lowered ready to butt with its viciously curved horns. Its eyes were tiny green stones that glittered angrily. Its humped shoulders epitomized brute strength and fury. It was attacking the other figure: the slender form of a beautiful girl. She seemed to dance just beyond the reach of those deadly horns. There was a garland of flowers around her head, and the nipples of her breasts were red rubies. Her head was thrown back as she laughed at the raging bull.

'She is so quick that the bull will never catch her.' Bekatha bounced the necklace between her hands to make the figures dance.

'You are quite right, Bekatha. She is the charm against danger. While you wear it danger can never catch you. The bull dancer will keep you safe from all harm.' I took the necklace from her hands and fastened the clasp behind her neck. She looked down at it and shook her shoulders to make the figurine dance against the lustrous skin of her boyish chest. She was lovely when she laughed.

Tehuti had waited quietly for me to give her my attention, and I felt a little guilty as I turned to her. I don't like to show favourites. 'Your present is in the blue cloth, Your Royal Highness.'

She unwrapped it carefully and gasped as the ring sparkled. 'I have never seen anything shine so bright,' Tehuti cried.

'Place it on your middle finger,' I told her.

'It's too big. It just slides around.'

'That's because it's a very special stone. You must never show it to a man, except . . .'

'Except what?'

'Except if you want him to fall in love with you. Otherwise you must keep it concealed in the palm of your hand. Remember that the magic will only work once. So be very careful to whom you show the ring.'

She wrapped her fingers tightly around it. 'I don't want any man to fall in love with me,' she replied firmly.

'Why not, my sweetling?'

'Because if they do, then they try to put a baby inside you. When the baby is in, it does not want to come out again. I have heard the women in the harem scream, and I don't want that.'

'One day you may change your mind.' I smiled. 'But the stone has other qualities that make it special.'

'Tell us. Why is it so special, Taita?' Bekatha was not deterred by her sister's silly scruples.

'One reason is because it is the hardest thing in the entire world. Nothing can cut it, and nothing can scratch it, not even the sharpest bronze dagger. That's why they call it diamond: "the Hard One". Water cannot wet it. But it sticks to the skin of the woman who owns it like magic.'

'I don't believe you, Taita.' Tehuti looked dubious. 'It's another of your made-up stories.'

'You just wait and see if what I tell you is true. But remember . . .' I wagged my finger at her sternly. '. . . don't ever show it to a man unless you love him very much, and you want him to love you forever.' I will never know why I told her that, except that the girls love my stories and I never like to disappoint them.

I stood up from the tub and called for Rustie, my head slave, to bring a towel to dry me.

'You are going away again, Taita,' Tehuti accused me. She has a grown woman's instincts. 'You come back for just an hour, and then you are gone again. Perhaps this time it will be forever.' She was close to tears.

'No! No!' I dropped the towel and embraced her. 'That is not true. I am going only as far as your father's empty tomb on the east bank.'

'If you are telling the truth, then let us come with you,' Bekatha suggested.

'Oh, yes please! Let us come with you, dear Taita,' Tehuti insisted.

I paused to consider the suggestion, and I found that it appealed to me as much as it seemed to do to my girls.

'There is just one problem with that idea.' I feigned reluctance. 'What we are going to do is a big secret and you will have to swear not to tell anyone else about what you see and what we do there.'

'A secret!' Bekatha cried and her eyes sparkled at the thought. 'I swear, Taita. I swear by all the gods I shall never say a word to another living soul.'

T he three treasure ships were still moored alongside the wharf at the entrance to Pharaoh Mamose's tomb when the princesses, Aton and I arrived there.

Zaras and his men had worked well in my absence. Following my instructions they had rigged screens of reed matting around the tomb precincts to prevent us being overlooked from the surrounding hills. I was determined to work all night to get the triremes offloaded. However, Hyksos spies might creep in closer under cover of darkness, and of course we would have to work by torchlight. The screens would be vital in maintaining our secrecy.

Using the experience I had garnered at Tamiat, I had worked out in detail how I should best proceed with the offloading. Now I supervised and instructed Dilbar and a gang of his men as they fashioned heavy pallets of dressed timber which they prised up from the deck of the first trireme. These were eight cubits square and would fit into the hatches of the holds. Then on the upper deck of each ship I rigged tripods and pulleys over the hatches. From these my men lowered the pallets into the hold, where other teams of workers packed the chests of bullion on to them.

Then the chests were hoisted up to the deck in batches of twenty, swung outboard and lowered to the wharf.

'What is in those chests, Taita?' demanded Tehuti. I touched the side of my nose in a conspiratorial gesture.

'That is the big secret. But very soon I will show you what it is. You will just have to be patient for a little longer.'

'I never like having to be patient,' Bekatha reminded me. 'Even for a little longer.'

A long line of men received the chests as they were unloaded from the pallets. The line stretched from the wharf through the entrance to the tomb, down four flights of stairs, and then along the painted and decorated tunnels, through the three vast antechambers until they reached the four treasuries. The treasuries were sited closely around Pharaoh's burial chamber with its empty sarcophagus awaiting the embalmed corpse which never arrived. This vast complex had been hewn from the living rock, an endeavour which had taken me and two thousand labourers twenty years to accomplish, and of which I am still rightfully proud.

'You girls can be of great help to Uncle Aton and me,' I told the princesses. 'You can count and you are able to write, something that only one in a hundred of these other dolts are able to do.' I jerked my head at the line of toiling half-naked men.

The two girls entered into the roles of bookkeepers as though it were a game. They were delighted to show off their schooling.

I had left instructions with Zaras and in my absence he had set up two heavy balance bars in the first treasury. Now Aton and I each manned one of these. As the chests were suspended from the arm of the apparatus we called the weight to the girls. Bekatha worked with Aton while I had Tehuti as my assistant. They wrote down each weight on a long roll of papyrus and kept a running total after every tenth chest.

When the first treasury was filled it contained 233 lakhs of pure silver. I sent the men up to the surface and gave them an hour to rest, eat and drink. When we were alone in the treasury I took the respite to make good my promise to the girls to show them what the chests contained. I prised open the lid of one and took out an ingot, which I allowed them to handle and admire.

'It isn't as pretty as my necklace,' Bekatha remarked as she stroked the charm at her throat.

'Does all of it belong to you, Taita?' Tehuti asked thoughtfully as she looked around at the stacks of chests.

'It belongs to Pharaoh,' I replied and she nodded seriously. I watched her making the calculation. She is good with figures. At last she smiled as she reached a total.

'We are very pleased with you, Taita.' She used the royal plural as if by right.

W hen the men returned I put them back to work. They moved the balance bars to the second treasury chamber which was slightly smaller than the first. In this we found space to store a further 216 lakhs of silver.

At this stage Zaras came in from the wharf to report that the first two triremes had been completely unloaded, but that there was still a substantial weight of treasure in the third and last ship to be brought ashore.

'The dawn is close, Lord Taita,' he warned me, for I had lost all track of the passage of the night, 'and the men are almost exhausted.' There was a trace of censure in his tone, and his expression was lugubrious. I thought to give him the sharp end of my tongue, for I am not accustomed to being criticized by my underlings, and I was myself tired, but not exhausted. Despite my willowy physique, my stamina is greater than that of most men, but I restrained myself.

'Your men have worked well, Zaras, as have you. But I am going to call upon your indulgence a little longer. I will come to the wharf with you to assess how much remains to be done.'

At this point I made a fateful mistake.

I glanced around at Tehuti as she squatted on her stool behind me with her head bowed over her papyrus scroll. Her hair had flooded down in a dense golden wave to screen her face. She had not found the time from her labours to comb it up again.

'Tehuti, you have worked like a slave girl,' I told her. 'Come with me to the surface. A breath of cool night air will revive you.'

Tehuti stood up. She tossed her head and threw the hair back from her face and she looked at Zaras. He looked back at her.

I saw the pupils of Tehuti's green eyes dilate in the lamplight, and at the same time I heard the dark gods laugh. It was a far-off and mocking sound, but I knew instinctively that our little world had changed dramatically.

The couple stood as still as a pair of marble statues, staring at each other.

I tried to look at Zaras through her eyes. Although I am a better judge of feminine rather than masculine beauty I saw for the first time that he was handsome far past the normal. Even though I knew his lineage was unremarkable, there was an imposing aura that surrounded him. He had noble poise and bearing.

I knew that his father was a merchant in Thebes who had built up a large fortune by his own efforts. He had seen to it that his son had received the finest education that silver could buy. Zaras was clever and quick-witted, and as fine a soldier as his military rank attested. However, his antecedents were lowly and he was certainly no match for a princess of the royal House of Tamose. In any event Pharaoh would decide who would make that match, with a little advice from me.

Quickly I stepped between the couple, breaking their eye contact. Tehuti looked at me as though I were a stranger whom she had never seen before. I touched her hand, and she shuddered slightly and her gaze refocused on me.

'Come with me, Tehuti,' I commanded. I watched her face. With a huge effort she regained control of herself.

'Yes, of course. Forgive me. My thoughts were elsewhere, Taita. Of course I will go with you.'

I ushered her towards the door of the treasury. Zaras fell in behind her. There was elasticity in his step and an expression of awe mingled with elation suffused his features. I knew him well, yet I had never seen him in this state.

Once again I interposed myself between the young couple. 'Not you, Captain Zaras. See to it that the balance bars are transferred to the next treasury, and then the men can take another short rest.' These were trivial orders to give to an officer of his rank, but he had to be distracted from his present dangerous fascination.

Only now I realized that Tehuti and Zaras could never have met before. She lived in the little world of the palace harem, from which she was only allowed to emerge with a strict system of chaperonage surrounding her. I was perhaps the most important link in that protective chain.

As a beautiful princess her virginity was of inestimable value to the Crown and the State. It was possible, of course, that Zaras might have seen her from a distance during one of the royal processions or in the pageantry of the religious festivals. However, he had never served in the household guards. All his military service had been at the battlefront or in the training and exercise of his troops. I was certain that until this day he had never been close enough to her to have any inkling of her extraordinary presence and beauty.

I snapped a quick instruction to Zaras: 'Feed the men and give an extra noggin of beer to each of them. Let them rest until I give the word to resume.' Then I led the two princesses up to the surface, leaving Zaras staring after us.

When we emerged from the gates to the tomb I paused to glance into the east, and I saw that the roseate harbingers of the dawn were already staining the eastern sky. Then I looked down the ranks of men and realized that many of them were reeling with exhaustion. Zaras had been correct in both respects.

I hurried up the gangplank of the third trireme and as I reached the deck there was the sound of trumpets and of chariot wheels fast approaching from the direction of the river and the city on its far bank. I hurried to the ship's rail and peered into the darkness across the plain.

There was torchlight and such commotion out there that could mean only one thing: Pharaoh had received my message and had returned to Thebes. My heart beat faster as it always does when I know that the royal presence is near. I ran back down the gangplank, shouting for additional torches and for an honour guard to assemble, but Pharaoh was too quick for me.

His chariot came thundering out of the night with the rest

of his squadron strung out behind him. Pharaoh had the reins wrapped around his wrists and when he saw me he shouted a joyous greeting and leaned back on the reins.

'Well met, Taita. We have missed you.' He threw the reins to his co-driver and jumped down to the ground while the wheels were still turning. He kept his footing like the skilled charioteer he is, and he reached me in a dozen swift strides. He seized me in a crushing embrace and swung me off my feet in front of all my men, oblivious to my dignity. But I can forgive him anything and I laughed with him.

'Indeed, Majesty. It has been far too long. An hour without your presence is like a week without sunshine.'

He set me on my feet and looked about him with an enquiring expression. I saw now that he was filthy with the dust and grime of a hard campaign, but that he was invested also with the grace and nobility of a true pharaoh. He saw his sisters waiting to greet him and pay their respects. He embraced them both in turn, and then he came back to me.

He pointed out the three great triremes lying at the wharf. 'What ships are these? Even with their masts unstepped and their oars shipped they are twice the size of any other I have ever seen before. Where did you find them, Taita?' The message I had sent him was cryptic and devoid of details. However, he did not wait to receive my answers to his questions, but he went on immediately, 'And who are all these ruffians? I sent you off with a handful of men and you return with your own little army, Taita.'

He swept his gaze along the ranks of men that reached from the wharf down into the depths of the royal tomb. Those closest to us dropped the chests of bullion they were passing and threw themselves to the ground in obeisance.

'Please do not let appearances deceive you, Mighty Majesty. No ruffians here. All brave men and true warriors of your Egypt.'

'But what of these ships?' He turned back to study the triremes with intense interest. 'How do you account for them?'

'Pharaoh, let me take you to a place where we can talk more freely,' I implored him.

'Oh, very well, Taita. You have always loved your little secrets, have you not?' He strode away towards the gates of the tomb without looking back at me. I followed Pharaoh Tamose down into his putative father's tomb.

He paused as he entered the first treasury chamber, and he studied the stacks of wooden chests that filled the capacious room. I thought he might enquire again about the contents of the chests, but I should have known better that he would not lower his dignity to do so.

'It is strange that each of these chests should be branded with the emblem of the Supreme Minos,' was all he said before he walked on into the next chamber, then into the third where Aton knelt before him.

'And it is odder still that my dignified chamberlain should be party to this monkey business of yours, Taita.' Pharaoh lowered himself on to an uncompleted stack of the chests, stretched his legs out in front of him and regarded the two of us with an expression of intense curiosity. 'Now tell me, Taita. Tell me everything!'

'Perhaps it is better that I show it to you, Pharaoh,' I demurred, and went to the chest I had opened for his sisters. I set the lid aside and I lifted out the same shining ingot that I had shown to the princesses. I went down on one knee to offer it to him. He took it from my hands and turned it slowly in his own. With his fingertip he traced the hallmark that was stamped into the metal. Again this was the rampaging bull of Crete.

At last he asked softly, 'It has the weight and feel of veritable silver. Surely it cannot be so?'

'Surely it can be and it is, Pharaoh. Every chest you see here is full of the same ingots.'

He was silent again for a long time, and under the dust and sun-bronzing of his face I saw him flush with intense emotion. When he spoke again his voice was hoarse.

'How much is there, Tata?' He used my familiar name, which was always an expression of his gratitude and affection towards me.

'Every one of these chests is full, Mem.' In return I used his baby name. I was the only one to whom he ever granted that liberty.

'Stop your silly games. Tell me how much silver you have brought back to me? I am struggling to encompass the magnitude of it.' His tone was still awed.

'Aton and I have weighed the greater part of it,' I replied.

'That does not answer my question, Tata.'

'We have weighed only the bullion from the first two Minoan ships, and a part of that from the third and last. So far the total is four hundred and forty-nine lakhs, Pharaoh. There is probably another one hundred lakhs still to be weighed, although it might be as much as one hundred and fifty.'

Again he was silent, shaking his head and frowning. At last he spoke once more. 'Almost six hundred lakhs. That is enough to erect a city twice the size of Thebes with all its temples and palaces.'

'And then to build ten thousand ships and still have sufficient left over to fight a dozen wars, my Pharaoh,' I agreed softly. 'Enough to win back all of your very Egypt from the Hyksos barbarian.'

'You have given me the wherewithal to cut down and destroy Beon and all his multitudes,' Pharaoh agreed; his voice quickened and rose with the vision of it.

'You are too late, Pharaoh.' Aton came to his feet and moved in front of me to get the attention of Pharaoh. 'Beon of the

Hyksos is dead and drowned already.' He stepped back and pointed at me with a flourish. 'Taita has killed him,' he declaimed.

Pharaoh's gaze swivelled back to me. 'Is this which Aton avows true? Have you killed Beon in addition to all your other services to my Crown?' Pharaoh demanded.

I bowed my head in acquiescence. I find boastfulness abhorrent in any man, more especially in myself.

'Tell me about it, Taita. I want every detail of the death of that monstrous animal.'

Before I could reply Aton cut me off. 'Please give me your royal attention once more, my Pharaoh.' He bowed to the king. 'This is a tale that deserves all your royal attention. After our final triumph over the Hyksos tyrant it will become part of our glorious military history. Future generations will sing of it to their sons, and the sons to their sons. I beg Your Majesty to allow me to arrange a triumph this evening which will be attended by every member of the high council of state and all your royal family. It will be a triumph during which we will be able to pay due honour to a feat of arms which has probably never been equalled in our history.'

'You are right, Lord Aton. Taita has laid before me a feast that cannot be swallowed at a single gulp. We must savour every mouthful. I must inform my council of this incredible stroke of fortune. Eight of my councillors are ensconced in my palace in Thebes, near at hand. Lord Kratas follows close behind me from the north and you, Taita, and Lord Aton are already here. We can assemble the full council within three or four hours.'

'Ample time for you to bathe and rest, my Pharaoh.' I glanced down at his attire.

'It is good honest dirt, Taita, and paid for in Hyksos blood.' Pharaoh grinned at me. 'But as so often is the case, you are right. Have my slaves heat the water for my bath.'

* * *

By the time the high council of Egypt was fully assembled the third and last trireme had been unloaded and the bullion from its hold weighed on the balance. The formal triumph had been prepared and the sun was setting.

I went to inform Pharaoh, expecting him to be resting. To relieve him of the necessity of travelling to his palace and returning again before nightfall, I had ordered that his father's burial chamber be set aside as his temporary lodging. It had never contained a corpse and so the chamber was not tainted with death. It was a quiet cool place and well aired by vents drilled through the rock to the surface. His servants had set up his cot and all his portable campaign furniture here.

Far from resting I found Pharaoh very much awake and alert, pacing the chamber and dictating despatches to three of his secretaries. He was dressed in a clean uniform, over which he wore a polished bronze breastplate embossed with gold. His hair was freshly washed and curled. He was as handsome as his mother had been beautiful.

When I went down on one knee before him, he stopped me with a hand on my shoulder. 'No, Taita,' he chided me. 'It is my fast intent to make you a nobleman and a member of my inner council before much longer. You must no longer kneel to me.'

'Pharaoh is too gracious. I do not deserve such honour.' I adopted my self-effacing role.

'Of course you don't,' he agreed. 'I do it only to prevent you from endlessly bobbing up and down in front of me. By Seth's in-growing toenails, as Kratas might say, I swear you make me giddy. Stand up tall and tell me the full tally of the treasure you have garnered for me.'

'I promised you 600 lakhs, my Pharaoh, but we are twenty lakhs short of that amount.'

'That is enough and more than enough to win me back my kingdom, and for you to keep your head atop your shoulders.'

At times the royal sense of humour tends towards the ghoulish. 'Are the other members of my council assembled?'

'Every single one of them, including Lord Kratas. He arrived an hour ago.'

'Take me to them.'

When we came out through the gates of the tomb I realized at once the magnitude and extent of what Aton had contrived in my honour. Pharaoh led me down between the ranks of royal guardsmen in full ceremonial uniform to the great tent that had been set up on the bank of the canal.

When we entered his entire court was already there, waiting to greet us. This included the royal family: his two sisters and his twenty-two wives and his 112 concubines. Then there were the noble lords, his military generals and the state councillors and their high-ranking staff; every man and woman in all of Egypt that Pharaoh dared trust with the secret of the Minoan millions was gathered here to greet me.

They rose to their feet in unison as we entered and the men drew their swords to form an arch for Pharaoh and me to pass beneath. At the same time a massed band of lutes and wind horns in the desert outside the tent burst into a heroic march.

It took Pharaoh and me some time to reach the seats that had been prepared for us. Every person in the assembly wanted to touch me, to grip both my hands and to shower me with compliments and salutations.

At close intervals around the wall of the tent stood enormous jars of wine, each of them taller than a man. When at last the entire company was seated the servants filled large goblets with red wine from the jars and set one in front of Pharaoh. He waved it away.

'Taita is the one we are here to honour. Serve him the good red wine and let him be first to drink of it.'

Every eye in the great tent was on me as I came to my feet and raised the goblet towards Pharaoh.

'All honour towards Pharaoh. He is our very Egypt. Without Pharaoh and Egypt we are but dust. All our petty strivings are nothing.' I brought the goblet to my lips and I drank a deep draught while all those lords and ladies came to their feet and shouted my name. Even Pharaoh smiled.

I sensed that the less I said the more they would love me, so I bowed to Pharaoh and sat down again.

Pharaoh stood over me and laid his right hand on my shoulder. Then he spoke out in a strong clear voice that carried to every corner of the great tent.

'Lord Taita has met with my favour,' he began simply. 'He has performed for me and for Egypt a service as great, or greater even, than any man before him. He deserves to be honoured by me and by every Egyptian born and yet to be born.

'I have elevated him to the nobility. From henceforth he shall be known as Lord Taita of Mechir.' Pharaoh paused and there was a polite silence in which most of the illustrious company tried to conceal expressions of mystification. Mechir is a village on the east bank of the Nile, thirty leagues south of Thebes. It is a cluster of nondescript mud huts, and a population made up of an equally nondescript assortment of specimens of the human race. Pharaoh let us ponder this conundrum for a short while.

'I have also granted to him, to have and to hold for all time, all the royal estate situated on the east bank of the River Nile between the southern wall of the city of Thebes and the town of Mechir.'

A gasp of astonishment went up from the assembly. The river-bank from Mechir down to Thebes is thirty leagues of the richest irrigable land in the entire royal estates.

In a single breath Pharaoh had made me one of the ten richest men in Egypt.

I looked suitably stunned and delighted by his magnanimity. However, as I kissed his right hand the naughty thought did occur to me that since I had made him one of the richest kings in the world neither of us had suffered too bitterly by this exchange of favours.

Now Pharaoh lifted his silver goblet of wine and smiled around the assembled company. 'My queens, my princes and princesses, my lords and ladies, I give you the toast. Here are gratitude, honour and long life to my Lord Taita.'

They came to their feet with cups held high, and they shouted out together, 'Here are gratitude, honour and long life to Lord Taita.'

It was probably the first time in our history that an Egyptian pharaoh had toasted one of his own subjects. But now he resumed his seat and gestured for the rest of the company to do the same.

'Lord Aton!' he called down the length of the table. 'The wine is excellent. I know that the banquet will be no less.' Aton has the reputation of being the greatest connoisseur in the land. Some say that this is the main reason he had reached the exalted status of Master of the Royal Household.

Reputations are not always deserved. Aton is good but not the best. The fillets of Nile perch he served had been insufficiently salted, and the desert bustard was a trifle overdone. In addition he had allowed the palace chef too liberal a hand with the Baharat spice. If I had been given the task I suspect that the fare would have been better prepared, but the wine was good enough to dilute these trivial shortcomings.

The company was in fine and boisterous fettle by the time Aton rose to introduce the eulogy. I had given passing thought as to which poet I might have chosen if I had been in his sandals. Naturally I was disqualified from selection by the fact that I was the subject of the composition. So I expected it would probably be either Reza or Thoiak that Aton had selected for this great honour.

In the event Aton stunned us all. Although he gave credit

and praise to the recognized bards of Egypt, he tried to justify his final decision by emphasizing the fact that the one he had chosen had been an eyewitness to the actual events. Of course, this was a preposterous idea. Since when have the facts been of any great importance to a good story?

'Great Pharaoh and royal ladies, please draw close and lend your ear to a valiant officer of the Blue Crocodile Guards who sailed with Lord Taita.' He paused dramatically. 'I give you Captain Zaras.'

The assembly was unmoving and unmoved as Zaras stepped in through the curtains of the tent and bent the knee to Pharaoh, who looked as surprised as any person present. I thought that I was probably the only one in the assembly who had ever heard of Captain Zaras of the Blue Crocodile Guards. Then something snicked into place in my mind as neatly as a blade into its scabbard.

I glanced quickly at Princess Tehuti where she was placed between Lord Kratas and Lord Madalek, who was Pharaoh's treasurer. Now she was sitting forward on her stool with her face aglow and her expression rapt, staring at Zaras. She was not so blatant as to draw attention to herself by applauding or in any other manner signifying her approval of Aton's choice; but I knew she had done it. Somehow she had forced Aton to make this ridiculous decision.

I have never underestimated the diplomatic skills of my two princesses but this seemed to smack of witchcraft. I switched my attention to Bekatha and I saw instantly that she was part of the conspiracy.

From the opposite end of the banquet table she was rolling her eyes and pulling inane faces, trying to catch her elder sister's attention. Tehuti was studiously ignoring her.

I was as angry as I have ever been. But also I was filled with compassion for Zaras. He was a fine young man and a good officer and I had come to love him as a father might love a son. Now he was standing up before all the world to make himself into a laughing stock. These two heartless royal vixens had contrived this terrible cruelty.

I looked back at Zaras. He seemed to be oblivious to the disaster that was rushing down on him. He stood tall and handsome and composed in his uniform. I wished that there was something I could do to save him, but I was helpless. Perhaps he might be able to stumble his way through an awkward recitation like a schoolboy, but forever his efforts would be compared by these strict judges to those of Reza and Thoiak or even, the gods and goddesses forbid it, to the acclaimed masterpieces penned by my very own hand.

Then I was aware of a soft susurration of female voices, a sound like bees on a bed of spring flowers in my garden as they sucked up the nectar. I looked back at the company and I saw that Tehuti was not the only woman who was appraising Zaras. Some of the older women were even more blatant in their interest. They were smiling and whispering behind their fans. Zaras had never been at court and thus they had never laid their lascivious eyes upon him before.

Then Zaras made a commanding gesture and the tent went still and quiet so I could hear a distant jackal wailing out in the desert.

Zaras started to speak. I had heard his voice giving orders to his men, commanding them in the din of battle or encouraging them when they faltered, but I had never realized the timbre and depth of it. His voice rang like a bell and soared like the khamsin over the dunes of the desert. It thundered like the storm sea on the reef, and soughed like wind in the high branches of the cedar.

Within the first few stanzas he had captivated the entire company.

His choice of words was exquisite. Even I could probably not have greatly improved upon them. His timing was almost hypnotic, and his narrative was irresistible. He swept them along like debris caught in the floodwaters of the Nile.

When he described the flight of the three arrows with which I slew the Hyksos impostor Beon, all the lords of Egypt leaped to their feet and shouted their acclamation, while Pharaoh seized my upper arm in a grip so fierce that the bruises it left on my flesh persisted for many days thereafter.

I found myself laughing and weeping along with the rest of the audience and in the end I stood up with them to applaud him.

As Zaras uttered the final stanza he turned towards the entrance of the great tent and spread his arms.

'Then cried aloud noble Taita to all the gods of Egypt and to his Pharaoh Tamose, *This is but a token of the prize I have won for you. This is but a thousandth part of the treasure I lay before you. This is the proof and testimony of the love and duty I bear towards you, Pharaoh Tamose.*'

Out in the desert a solemn drum began to beat and through the entrance of the tent paced ten armoured and helmeted warriors. They bore between them a pallet on which was piled a glittering pyramid of silver bars.

As one person, the entire audience came to its feet in a tumult of praise and exaltation.

'All hail to royal Pharaoh!' they cried, and then, 'All honour to Lord Taita!'

When he had finished speaking they would not let Zaras go. Pharaoh spoke with him for several minutes, the men shook his hands or pounded his back, while a few of those women who had taken wine giggled and rubbed themselves against him as a cat will do.

When he came to me we embraced briefly and I commended him, 'Well written and well spoken, Zaras. You are both a warrior and a poet.'

'From a bard of your renown, Lord Taita, I rejoice to hear

it said,' he replied and I was touched to see that he meant it. He left me and moved on through the company. He did not make his ultimate destination obvious, but finally he bowed in front of Princess Tehuti.

The two of them were on the far side of the tent from where I sat; however, I am able to read the meaning of words on the lips of others without having heard the sound, as readily as I can read the hieroglyphics on a roll of papyrus.

'Shame on you, Captain Zaras! Your poetry made me weep!' Those were her first words to him, and they brought him down on one knee before her. His face was turned away from me so I was unable to see his reply. However it made Tehuti laugh.

'You are gallant, Captain. But I will only forgive you on one condition. That is if you will promise to sing for us again one day soon.' Zaras must have acquiesced, for she went on, 'I shall hold you to that promise.' He came to his feet and backed away from her respectfully.

Good! I thought. Come away from there, you silly boy. You are out-matched. You are in deeper danger right now than you will ever be on the field of battle. But Tehuti stopped him with a graceful gesture.

'How clumsy of me!' I read her lips again. 'I seem to have dropped one of my rings. I had it on my finger but an instant ago. Will you find it for me, please, Captain Zaras?'

He was as eager as a puppy. He went down at her feet again, searching the ground in front of her. Almost immediately he picked up something; and when he came upright he was facing half towards me so I was able to read his lips.

'Is this the ring you lost, Your Highness?'

'Yes indeed. That is it. It was given to me by a very special person; the man whom you eulogized so beautifully this very evening.' She made no immediate move to take the trinket back from him.

'You speak of Lord Taita?'

'Indeed!' She nodded. 'But look at the stone in the ring you are holding. See how clear it is.'

'It is as clear as water,' he agreed, holding the ring to the light of the nearest lantern. She had forced him to examine it minutely, so now she was satisfied and she held out her hand to him.

'Thank you, Captain.' He placed the ring in her cupped hand, and she smiled up at him.

I thought to myself, Even if there is no magic in the ring itself, there is sufficient magic in your smile, Princess Tehuti, to bring the walls of both Memphis and Thebes crashing down. How can a callow youth like Zaras possibly resist your wiles?

The first and most urgent task that faced me was to make the three great Cretan triremes disappear without trace. I had to leave no doubt whatsoever in the mind of the Supreme Minos of Crete that Beon of the Hyksos was responsible for the theft of his treasure. His rage would be exacerbated by the knowledge that the culprit was a supposed ally of his.

My first thought was to burn the three ships, and to throw the ashes into the Nile so that the mystery of their disappearance would be perpetuated for all time. But then I considered the huge amount of timber that I would have to destroy.

Egypt is a land almost without substantial forests. For us timber is almost as valuable as gold and silver. I thought about the warships and chariots I could build from the three trireme hulls, and I could not bring myself to put a torch to such hard-won booty.

I discussed this with Pharaoh and Lord Kratas as the supreme commanders of our army.

'But where in all of Egypt would you hide that amount of timber, Taita, you old rapscallion?' Kratas demanded. 'You have not thought about that, have you?'

Pharaoh rallied to my side. 'One thing you can be absolutely certain of, my Lord Kratas, is that Taita has thought about it. Taita thinks of everything.'

'Pharaoh is too kind to me. But I do try my humble best,' I murmured, and Kratas roared with mirth at my protestations.

'There is nothing humble about you, Taita. Even the smell of your farts is conceited and ostentatious.' Lord Kratas is my favourite lout; in all of Egypt there is no one who can outdo him in sheer unmitigated boorishness. I ignored him and addressed myself to Pharaoh.

'Pharaoh is right, as ever. I did have a few ideas on the subject. The fact of the matter is that we will have to station a full regiment at the tomb of your deified father, the god Mamose, to guard the silver bullion stored there. The regiment can be made to serve a dual purpose.'

Even Kratas was listening with attention now.

'Proceed, Taita!' Pharaoh urged me.

'Well, Pharaoh, I have remeasured the ante-chambers to the tomb. If we were to strip the hulls of the triremes down to individual planks, there is space to repack them in those underground chambers where they would be hidden until we had call to use them in some other warlike endeavour.' I turned to challenge Kratas. 'No doubt Lord Kratas has a better plan. Perhaps we could take the hulls out into the deep waters of the Red Sea and my Lord Kratas could sink them for us under the sheer weight of the excrement that issues so profusely from between his noble lips?'

'By the nits in Seth's matted pubic hairs, Taita, that's one of your best quips yet. I must remember it!' Kratas bellowed with laughter. He can take a joke against himself. That's one of the many things about him that I admire.

It took many weeks and half a regiment of men to break the triremes down into their individual planks and then to number each plank and stack them away in the subterranean ante-chambers. But at last I had completed my disappearing trick and the great ships had vanished completely.

For myself there was an extra benefit in the subterfuge. I was able to manoeuvre Pharaoh into placing Zaras in charge of the task of dismantling and storing the ships, with strict orders to remain within the precincts of the tomb until the task was completed. So when both the princesses, Tehuti and Bekatha separately and in concert, enquired after his where-abouts I was able in all honesty to inform them that Pharaoh had sent him on a very secret military mission from which he was unlikely to return for some considerable time.

The palace of Thebes was for Zaras a far more dangerous place than any Hyksos battlefield. I lay at night sweating in terror for my protégé. Quite apart from the fact that I looked upon him as a loyal friend who had risked his life for me, he was an intrepid soldier, a scholar and now he had revealed himself to be a poet. We had much in common. However, like all men of his age he had an overriding weakness which was in no way mitigated by the fact that most of the time he kept it out of sight, tucked up under his kilt.

I also know just how ruthless and reckless young women can be when their ovaries overheat. My darling little Tehuti's gonads had caught fire at the first sight of him. I could think of no feasible way to quench the flames.

I n the days that followed my return to Thebes I found myself overwhelmed by circumstances that assailed me from every direction I turned.

Pharaoh demanded my attendance at all hours to discuss the political storm that was boiling up between the Hyksos and the Supreme Minos.

Aton and I had agreed that in view of the urgency and danger of the situation we should declare a truce between our rival intelligence operations and that for the time being we should pool our resources and cooperate with each other for the safety and perhaps the ultimate survival of our very Egypt.

Strange and nameless men and women appeared and disappeared at our separate doors at all hours of the night, bearing messages and information from the north. Their numbers were only exceeded by those of the carrier pigeons making the same journey. I sometimes fancied that there were so many of our birds aloft at the same time that the sky might actually turn as purple as the colour of their plumage.

Aton and I had to examine and discuss every word we received, evaluating it carefully before we relayed it on to Pharaoh and his general staff.

One critical piece of intelligence was a report of the cremation of King Beon whom I had arrowed to death in the Nile before Memphis. The Hyksos have the barbaric custom of burning the bodies of their slain heroes to ashes rather than embalming them as we more advanced and civilized peoples do.

At the same time they also make human sacrifices to placate their monstrous gods, of which Seth is the chief. Aton and I learned that one hundred of our own Egyptian warriors who had been captured by the Hyksos were thrown into the flames of Beon's funeral pyre while they still lived, and that these had been followed by one hundred virgins to serve Beon's pleasure in the other world. Some of these virgins were as young as five years of age, just old enough to know what was happening to them as they entered the flames. After hearing this account how can any sensible person try to argue that the Hyksos are not the basest form of animal life?

I was the first person in Thebes to learn that after the cremation of Beon his younger brother Gorrab was crowned as the new King of the Hyksos.

Gorrab's first concern seemed to have been to avenge the death of his elder brother. He pulled ten thousand of his first-line troops out of the line of battle that faced our Egyptian forces on the border between Sheik Abada and Asyut. Gorrab's decision was a happy one for Egypt. Pharaoh was being bitterly engaged along this entire front. The Hyksos are never parsimonious with the lives of their own troops, and are always prepared to engage in a battle of attrition if the opportunity presents itself. Up until that point Pharaoh was inflicting heavy losses on Beon's army, but his own men were taking bitter punishment in return.

Now at a stroke the pressure was lifted and Pharaoh was given the opportunity to reconsolidate and make good his position as Gorrab ordered almost a quarter of his army northwards to attack the Cretan force which I had left intact at Tamiat.

Gorrab had been a witness to his brother's death. He had been the commander of the guards on board the royal barge. He had watched the three Cretan triremes bearing down upon them and he had seen the Minoan uniforms of the officers and crew as they launched that unprovoked and treacherous attack.

Gorrab had seen one of the Cretan archers deliberately shoot three arrows at his unarmed brother as he struggled in the water. Later he had retrieved King Beon's arrow-riddled corpse from the river, and wept for him as he set the lighted torch to his cremation pyre. Then he had placed the Hyksos crown on his head with his own hands, and declared a full-scale war on Crete.

Aton and I followed Gorrab's campaign against the Minoans with glee. We learned from our spies that the senior Minoan commanders had sailed back to Crete from Tamiat in the galley that I had left for them. The small galley could accommodate only forty men, the others were left at the fort. When the galley reached Crete the commander reported to the Supreme Minos the shameful and dastardly attack by the Hyksos on the fort, and the capture of the Cretan treasure ships. He informed the Minos that the pirates had made no attempt to disguise their identity, but that they had worn full Hyksos uniforms and he had heard them conversing in that language.

The Supreme Minos immediately despatched a squadron of his war galleys to Tamiat to rescue the two thousand Cretan troops that were stranded there. However, his ships arrived too late.

King Gorrab had been there before them with his ten thousand. The Cretans put up a gallant resistance, but Gorrab slaughtered most of them. The survivors surrendered. Gorrab beheaded all of these and made a pyramid of their heads on the wharf below the fort. The relieving squadron arrived from Crete only after King Gorrab had returned to Memphis, leaving the pile of human heads rotting in the sun and the vultures devouring what was left of the Minos' men. The relieving squadron sailed back to Crete to inform the Minos of the massacre.

The Supreme Minos swore an oath of vengeance at the altar of his bizarre gods and sent his fleet to ravage the Hyksos ports and bases along the entire northern African coastline.

King Gorrab retaliated by conducting a pogrom on all those Minoans living under his sway in northern Egypt. The Minoans are a clever and industrious people. They are highly skilled in all the crafts and trades. However, they are above all traders and entrepreneurs. Wherever there is the sweet smell of silver and profit, there you will find the Minoans.

How else could the inhabitants of such a small island as Crete have become the dominant power in all the lands surrounding the Middle Sea?

There were several thousands of these Minoans living in northern Egypt. King Gorrab fell upon this local population with all the cruelty and animal ferocity for which the Hyksos are notorious. They dragged the Minoans from their homes and raped the women and children of even the most tender age. Then they herded them, men women and infants, into the temples which the Minoans had erected to their Gods and burned the roofs down over their heads.

Although they tried to flee the country, very few of the Minoans were able to escape. The ships of the Supreme Minos rescued some of the more fortunate ones who lived in the towns and ports along the coast of the Middle Sea. Others who lived further inland escaped into the deserts that enclose our very Egypt. There they died from thirst and from the attentions of the Bedouin, who are also a cruel and rapacious people.

However, a few hundred Minoans fled with their families southwards from Memphis and Asyut and some of these were able to evade the pursuing Hyksos chariots and reach our battle lines. Lord Kratas ordered our men to give the refugees shelter and protection and to treat them kindly.

As soon as I heard of this I mounted up and rode as swiftly as I was able to the front lines of our legions facing the Hyksos.

There were some of our senior commanders in these legions whom I had known as striplings. I had tutored them in the science and art of war, and my influence had helped to lift them to their present exalted military ranks.

Lord Remrem had been ennobled by Pharaoh on the battle-field at Thebes and now he commanded a regiment under General Kratas, the supreme commander.

Hui, who had been an outlaw when I captured him, was now a senior officer commanding five hundred chariots. All these old friends and acquaintances were delighted to welcome me into their camp, including even that reprehensible old reprobate Kratas, who was commander-in-chief under Pharaoh. On the evening of my arrival Lord Kratas attempted to drink me insensible. Later I was one of those who carried him to his cot, and I held his head while he puked it all up.

The next morning he thanked me brusquely and sent his orderly officer to parade before me the Minoan refugees who had managed to escape the wrath of King Gorrab and reach our lines.

There were some forty or so of these unfortunates. They were a sorry lot, having fled with only meagre possessions and with their families decimated by the Hyksos.

I moved slowly down their ranks, treating the fugitives with respect and kindness, but also questioning them shrewdly.

There was one family group of three huddled together at the furthest end of the line whom I came to at last. The father spoke passable, but heavily accented, Egyptian. His name was Amythaon. Up until three weeks previously he had been a merchant in Memphis, trading in corn, wine and leather. He was so successful that even I had heard of him through my agents in that city. The Hyksos had burned his home and warehouse, and raped his wife in front of him until she bled to death.

His son was nineteen years old. His name was Icarion. I liked him immediately. He was tall and strongly built. He had a mop of thick curling dark hair, and a cheerful face. He had not been overwhelmed and crushed by misfortune as seemed to be the case with his father.

'Of course, you flew from Memphis on wings that you made for yourself?' I asked him.

'Of course,' replied Icarion, 'but I kept well clear of the sun, lord.' He had picked up my allusion to his name immediately.

'Can you read and write, Icarion?'

'Yes, lord. Although I do not enjoy it as much as my sister does.'

I looked at his sister, who stood behind the two men of her family, and I studied her face. She was rather pretty, with long dark hair and a bright intelligent face, but not as pretty as either of my two princesses. Then again there are very few who are.

'My name is Loxias and I am fifteen years old.' She anticipated my questions. She was almost the same age as my darling Tehuti. Her Egyptian was perfect, as though she had been born to it.

'Can you write, Loxias?'

'Yes, lord. I am able to do so in all three systems: hieroglyphics, cuneiform and Minoan script.'

'She keeps my accounts and writes all my correspondence,' Amythaon, her father, interjected. 'She is a clever girl.'

'Can you teach me to speak Minoan and write with Linear A?' I asked her.

She thought about that for a few moments then she replied, 'Maybe, but it will depend on your ability, Lord Taita. Minoan is not an easy language.' I noted her use of my full name and title. It indicated to me that she was as clever as her father boasted she was.

'Test me. Say something in Minoan,' I invited her.

'Very well,' she agreed and then uttered a long sequence of lisping and exotic phrases.

I repeated them. I have a musician's ear for sounds; both instrumental and spoken. I am able to replicate the cadence and accent of any human speech faultlessly. In this case I had no idea what I was saying but I said it perfectly. All three of them looked startled and Loxias flushed with annoyance.

'You are mocking me, Lord Taita. You do not need my tutelage. You speak it almost as well as I do,' she accused me. 'Where did you learn?' I smiled mysteriously, and left her guessing.

I commandeered horses from Hui's regiment and the four of us rode south to Thebes that same day. I found comfortable accommodation for the little lost family a short walk outside the city walls, in one of the small villages on my newly granted Mechir estate.

I spent several hours every day with Loxias learning to speak and write in Minoan. Within a very few months Loxias admitted that there was nothing more she could teach me.

'The pupil has outstripped the teacher. I think that probably there is much you can teach me, Lord Taita.'

My two princesses were not such eager or adept students as I was. In the beginning they were both adamant that they wanted nothing to do with such a stupid and uncouth language as Minoan. Nor did they wish any truck with a Minoan peasant girl of humble birth. They informed me that this was their joint decision, and that it was absolutely final and irreversible, and there was nothing that I could do about it. Tehuti did all the talking and her little sister stood by and nodded her head in concurrence.

I went to speak with their big brother, Pharaoh Tamose. I outlined for him the necessity of us Egyptians developing and exploiting our burgeoning relationship with Crete, and how this depended in a large measure upon the ability of the two girls to communicate with the Supreme Minos and his courtiers. Then I set out in detail the plans I had for his sisters.

Pharaoh sent for the two little rebels and remonstrated with them. He ended this one-sided discourse with such dire and convincing threats that even I was worried that he might carry them out. The princesses forthwith reversed their absolutely final decision. But for several days thereafter they sulked at me with a practised intensity.

Their rancour was rapidly set aside when I set up a prize for the student who showed the most improvement over the previous week as judged by their new language teacher, Loxias. The prize was always a piece of highly desirable feminine frippery which Amythaon found for me in the bazaars of the city.

Soon they were able to chatter, argue and emote in fluent Minoan, and Loxias exceeded her brief by teaching them a number of words and expressions that were better suited to the taverns and brothels of the city slums than to the palace. Over the following months these three little hellions delighted in shocking me with these utterances.

They soon became such a closely knit trio that the princesses took Loxias to live with them in the royal harem.

O wnership of Mechir estate provided me with an excuse to escape from the palace whenever the fancy took me and to ride free and unfettered over my own lands, usually with my princesses and the ubiquitous Loxias for company. I had taught them to ride astride, which is a remarkable achievement for any Egyptian man or woman, and even more so for the sisters of Pharaoh.

In addition I made special bows for the three girls which I carefully matched to their strength. With practice they were able to draw the bowstring to their lips and place two arrows out of three in the target I set up for them at a hundred paces. I kept alive their enthusiasm for this sport by awarding prizes and super-abundant praise for the best lady archer of the day.

When my people were sowing my fields with corn, the wild birds descended on us in flocks to steal the seed. I paid the girls an extravagant bounty for every bird which they brought down with an arrow. Each of them soon became a formidable huntress, able to hit the plumed pests high on the wing.

Riding and shooting were skills that I knew would stand the girls in very good stead in later life.

I truly revelled in the time I was able to spend with my charges, because once I was back in the palace I was firmly under Pharaoh's dominion once more. There was seldom a day that passed without him calling me to his presence at least once in order for me to solve a problem or to give him my advice or my opinion. I learned not to be put out of countenance when he rejected my counsel, only to resurrect it some little time later as his very own idea.

One of the other problems that I was faced with at this time was the disposal of the treasure that I had brought to Pharaoh Tamose from the Minoan fort at Tamiat.

Pharaoh was impatient to begin utilizing it for the welfare of his subjects. I had to restrain him from paying the nation's debts with silver ingots bearing the hallmark of the Supreme Minos of Crete.

'Great Pharaoh, you and I are both aware that the Minos has his spies in every city of our very Egypt,' I pointed out to him. 'It would take but a short time for one of them to send a message back to Crete to inform him that every souk and tavern in Thebes was awash with silver ingots bearing the hallmark of the bull of Crete.'

'Is what you are telling me I can never spend the bullion I have packed into my treasury over there?' He pointed with his chin at his father's tomb on the far side of the Nile. 'In case the Minos is alerted to its existence?' His tone was bitter and his expression angry.

'I beg your forgiveness, Royal Egypt. You are the father of the nation. The treasure belongs to you to use in any way you wish. However we must alter its appearance so that no man alive, and in particular not the Supreme Minos, will ever be able to recognize it.'

'How will we achieve that, Taita?' He was only slightly molli-fied. At least he was looking into my face with an expression which was once more friendly and interested.

'We must break the ingots down into much smaller frag-ments, each weighing the same amount; say half a deben. Each of these could bear the image of your royal head.'

'Hmm!' he murmured. I had known that he would like the

idea of his own head on the fragments. 'What would we call them, these silver fragments of mine, Tata?'

'Pharaoh will surely think of a better name, but I had the idle notion that they should be known as silver mem.'

He smiled with pleasure. 'I think that is very appropriate, Tata. Now what image are we going to stamp on the reverse side of my silver mems, opposite my head?'

'Of course, Pharaoh will decide that.' I bowed my head and avoided his gaze.

'Of course I will decide that,' he agreed, 'but you would like to make a suggestion, I can see that.'

I shrugged. 'We have been together since the moment of your birth, Majesty.'

'Yes. Horus knows I have heard about it from you often enough. When you relate how my first act was to piss on you, I always think I should have pissed harder and longer.'

I pretended that I had not heard the last part of his remark. 'I have always been close behind you, loyally and faithfully. It might be propitious to continue that tradition.' I paused, but he urged me on.

'Continue! However, I think I can see in which direction we are headed.'

'Perhaps — and I say perhaps with all humility — perhaps Pharaoh might see fit to order that the image of the wounded falcon should decorate the reverse side of his silver mem,' I suggested and he let out a shout of laughter.

'You never let me down, Tata. You had it all worked out from the very beginning!' The wounded falcon with a broken wing is my personal hieroglyph.

Under the royal auspice and in terms of strict secrecy I set up a mint within the precincts of the tomb of Mamose to manufacture this coinage. *Coin* was the new word I had conceived to describe these pieces of silver. Pharaoh accepted it without argument.

This coinage was another of my achievements which proved an extraordinary boost to the progress and prosperity of our very Egypt. Nowadays a smoothly functioning monetary system is an essential instrument of government and commerce. It was one of my gifts to my Egypt, and one of the principal reasons why we will always be the pre-eminent nation of the world. Although other nations have since imitated us, the silver mem is now the coin that is recognized and accepted joyfully in every country in the world.

With a nudge from me Pharaoh changed the name of his father's tomb to 'the Royal Mint'; thereby expunging the deleterious taint of death and interment from the place. When this was done Pharaoh appointed me to be the governor of this institution; thereby adding substantially to all my other duties and responsibilities. However, when duty calls I never complain.

One of my first acts in my new capacity of governor was to appoint Zaras to be the Guardian of the Royal Mint and Treasury. I prevailed on Pharaoh to give him the command of a battalion of guards to assist him in carrying out these duties. Of course this placed Zaras completely under my authority.

Since Princess Tehuti had contrived her stratagem to force him to inspect her diamond ring, and thereby making her intentions clear to me, I had been very careful to keep Zaras isolated on the western bank of the Nile. I knew that when my darling had fixed her mind on a certain course of action it was extremely difficult, if not impossible, to distract and dissuade her.

The only way that I could think of was to sever any contact between her and Zaras until I was able to work out her manifest destiny for her. Clearly this destiny was for her to become the queen and consort of the most powerful military figure in the world and not the plaything and camp-follower of some common soldier, however pleasant and congenial that soldier might be.

One of the few facts that I knew about the enigmatic figure of the Supreme Minos was his predilection for beautiful women of royal blood. To be entirely truthful, even this was not a proven fact. It was merely a rumour which by frequent repetition had become hard fact.

Nonetheless I was confident that this shadowy but omnipotent figure would find both my little princesses irresistible, and that through them I would be able to manipulate the Minoan to my will, and the greater good of our very Egypt. I consoled myself that Tehuti could hope for no greater honour and higher duty than to occupy a throne and to save her homeland from the Barbarian. When she realized this she would soon set aside her trivial infatuation with Zaras.

But in the meantime I would have to keep that worthy young man confined in the Royal Mint with little or no opportunity to cross the river; there to sniff around the royal harem like a dog with the scent in his nostrils of a little overheated bitch.

U p until this time Pharaoh and we members of his royal council had followed the mounting conflict between the Supreme Minos and the Hyksos King Gorrab with utmost attention. And we had done whatever lay within our power to intensify their hostility towards each other. Unfortunately this was not much. Crete was far away and we had no contact with its ruler.

While I waited for the time to come when I could put my plan for Tehuti and Bekatha into effect I set out to learn what I could about Crete and the Supreme Minos. This was where both Amythaon and his daughter Loxias provided me with invaluable information about the island state, its history and population, its resources and most importantly its rulers.

I use the plural 'rulers' deliberately; for it seems that Crete has four kings. The Supreme Minos, as his title suggests, dominates the other three lesser kings. They live in separate palaces, but these are linked to the grand palace at Knossos by roads magnificently paved with marble slabs. In Egypt we would refer to these as satraps or governors, and not kings.

When I questioned him closely I learned that Amythaon had been born in a small village only three leagues outside the walls of Knossos, the citadel of the Supreme Minos. His father had been an officer in the palace and as a child Amythaon had been a spectator at many of the festivals and processions of the Minos. He was the first person that I had ever spoken to who had actually laid eyes on the Minos.

According to Amythaon he is a splendid and imposing figure who is always masked when he appears in public. The mask he wears is in the shape of a bull's head fashioned out of pure silver. None of his subjects have ever seen his face.

'He is immortal,' Amythaon declared. 'He has ruled since the birth of the nation, back in the mists of time.'

I nodded wisely, but it did occur to me that if none of his subjects had ever seen his face how did they know that it was the same man who had ruled forever? To me it seemed likely enough that when the incumbent Supreme Minos died his successor simply donned the silver bull mask and continued the reign.

'He has a hundred wives,' Amythaon went on and looked at me to be impressed. I adopted an expression of awe. 'The Supreme Minos receives wives from all the other kings of the city states across the islands that dot the Aegean Sea. Four times a year, on the festivals which mark the changing of the seasons, they are sent to him as a form of tribute.'

'How many vassal kings does the Supreme Minos have, Amythaon?'

'He is a mighty monarch. He has twenty-six vassals in all, my lord,' he told me, 'including the three on the island of Crete itself.'

'How many wives do they send him?'

'Every year each vassal king sends him seven wives.'

'That adds up to 182 each year. Do you agree with my figures, Amythaon?' I watched him count on his fingers and at last he nodded.

'That is correct, my lord.'

'Then can you explain to me how the number of his wives remains at one hundred, as you asserted at first?'

'I am not sure, lord. That is what I was told by my father when I was a child.' He looked perplexed, and I asked another question to relieve his embarrassment.

Amythaon was even more helpful to me in describing the topography of the island of Crete and its population. I had accumulated a number of allegedly accurate maps of the island that all differed widely from each other. Amythaon went over these with me, laboriously correcting the substance and details and in the end consolidating these into a master map which he guaranteed was perfect. This map showed all the cities and villages, the ports and the anchorages, the roads and the passes through the Cretan mountain ranges.

Because of his family connections Amythaon was also able to give me reliable figures for the Minoan army and navy.

The number of foot-soldiers was substantial. However these were mainly mercenaries recruited from the other Hellenic islands or from amongst the Medes and Aryans of eastern Asia. Because of the mountainous nature of Crete itself, he told me that the Minoans possessed relatively few chariots, compared to the Hyksos or to our own Pharaoh.

It seems that the Supreme Minos makes up for this by the strength of his navy which far exceeds any other in the Middle Sea. Amythaon was able to give me estimates of the numbers and types of ships that it comprises.

The numbers that Amythaon quoted were so large that I knew they were exaggerated. I thought that if I was mistaken and Amythaon's figures were accurate, then the Supreme Minos was a mighty man indeed.

Armed with all this information, I at last deemed that the time had come when we Egyptians should actively intervene on the side of Crete in the war between the Minoans and the Hyksos, and that we might be able to exert the critical impetus that was necessary to finally defeat the barbarian Hyksos and drive them from our homeland.

Aton and I pooled all the information and intelligence that we had gathered from our agents and he was impressed with the magnitude of my accumulated research, which was much greater than his own, but I did not disparage his efforts.

After long debate we were agreed that the most feasible plan was for us to initiate friendly overtures with the Minoans directly, and work towards an alliance with them which would make our two nations the dominant power on earth; a power which the Hyksos could never hope to challenge.

This was when, in my enthusiasm, I made an error. I told Aton, 'I recall that in the time before the Hyksos incursion into Egypt we always maintained tenuous but mutually rewarding diplomatic contact with Crete. However, the invasion of Upper Egypt by the Hyksos has isolated our southern portion of the country. This has rendered it almost impossible for us to continue this contact with Crete. Our two countries have diverged; separated by the wedge that the Hyksos have driven between us.'

Aton listened to me with an expression of wonder slowly dawning on his chubby features. When I paused to hear his reply he went on staring at me in silence. I was obliged to press him.

'So what is your opinion, Aton? Does my plan not appeal to you?'

He did not address my question, but reverted sharply to what I had said at the beginning. 'Did I hear you correctly, Taita? Did you say that you actually remember the time before the Hyksos invasion of our land?'

I am usually extremely reticent about my age. Even those like Aton who know me well take me to be several decades younger than I truly am. If I were to tell them the correct figure they would think me a madman at the best, or a liar at the worst. The Hyksos invasion took place almost ninety years ago, and yes I do remember it well. But now I had to cover up my error.

I dismissed his question with a chuckle. 'I expressed myself clumsily. What I meant was that from all I have read and heard related about the time before the Hyksos invasion, when Egypt was on friendly terms with Crete.' Then I hurried on, 'If we are going to attempt to restore those friendly relations and enter into another treaty of mutual defence between our two countries it will be extremely difficult to do so directly. Do you not agree, Aton?'

He did not reply at once. He still had that odd expression on his face, and I saw his eyes flicker down over my neck to my hands which lay on the cedar-wood writing desk in front of me. Aton knows as I do that the ravages of time are always more apparent on those parts of the human body.

However, I am an exception. The skin that covers my entire body is smooth and unblemished as that of a lad who has not yet grown a hair on his chin. Aton could not find the evidence of my true age that he was seeking there. So he nodded thoughtfully and brought his full attention back to the subject I had broached.

'Of course what you say about the present situation is the truth, Taita. It would be almost impossible to make direct contact with the Minos. You have correctly identified the problem; now tell me what you believe to be the solution.' He softened his challenge with a mild tone of voice.

'Of course you know that the Supreme Minos maintains a diplomatic mission at the court of King Nimrod of Akkad and Sumer in his capital city of Babylon.'

'Of course!' Aton agreed. 'But even if we send an envoy to Babylon to make contact with the Cretan ambassador it would entail a journey even more arduous than the one you made to attack the fort at Tamiat.'

'Indeed, Aton, it would be almost twice as far and decidedly more dangerous and uncertain. Our envoy would have to travel east to the shores of the Red Sea. He would then have to cross not only that sea, but also the vast and hostile Arabian Desert which lies beyond that sea. That is a land forsaken by all the benevolent gods, and inhabited only by hostile Bedouin tribes and every cut-throat and outcast that ever escaped justice. The distance is well over one thousand five hundred leagues from Thebes to Babylon, and that would not be the end of it either.'

'Why not, Taita? I thought we agreed that the Minos has an ambassador in Babylon?'

'Yes, that is so; but that ambassador would not have the power or authority to negotiate an alliance between Crete and Egypt. He would be obliged to send our envoy with his message to the court of the Supreme Minos in Crete. Our man would be forced to find a ship in the port of Tyre or that of Sidon on the easterly extremity of the Middle Sea. After he had agreed a passage with the captain of the vessel, he must then sail with him halfway down the length of the Middle Sea, avoiding the storms of winter and the attention of pirates and Hyksos war galleys, to reach the Supreme Minos in his citadel of Knossos on the island of Crete.'

'How long do you think that journey might take him, Taita?'

'It would probably take a year if he were lucky and if the gods favoured him, twice as long if they did not.'

'A great deal can change in two years,' Aton mused.

'Again that would not be the end of it,' I pointed out, 'because after the Supreme Minos had studied the message from Pharaoh, and discussed it with his council, their response would have to be carried back here to Thebes by the same route. The round journey might take as long as three or four years.'

'No!' Aton exclaimed with finality. 'We cannot afford to wait that long. King Gorrab could be in Thebes by then with a hundred thousand of his murderous ruffians. There must be some other solution.'

'I am sure you are right, my dear Aton. What did you have in mind?' I passed the problem back to him. Sometimes even my patience can be taxed by having to spoon-feed ideas to those around me as though they were my infants.

'I have not had a chance to consider the problem as you have. Perhaps you have already come to some kind of solution?' He smiled ingratiatingly, and of course I relented. I often think that I am too forbearing with those who are not as sharp-witted as I am. The great Horus knows well that I get very little thanks for it.

'What if an Egyptian ambassador appointed by Pharaoh was given such a powerful escort that he could travel safely and swiftly across the Red Sea and the desert beyond it without fear of bandits or Bedouin? What if this ambassador was given sufficient silver to charter a ship in Tyre; a ship that was large and fast enough to out-run or out-fight any pirate or Hyksos war galley?'

'Ah!' Aton's eyes gleamed.

'What if this fine ship sailed directly to Knossos in Crete? And what if this ambassador was bearing gifts that were much sought after and valued by the Supreme Minos?' I cocked my head on one side and slanted my eyes at him knowingly. 'Do you have any idea at all what gifts the Minos might find most acceptable?'

'I think so, my old friend.' Aton laughed. 'If all that I have heard be true, the Minos has such a weighty pair of testicles

125

that he makes up several times over for those that you and I were deprived of. He has an insatiable appetite for those things that we do not particularly care about.'

I laughed with him dutifully, although I do not find that my physical deficiency is particularly amusing.

'But tell me, Taita, what would we have gained by all this? How would it help us to coordinate the offensive against the legions of King Gorrab? The command of the Egyptian army would still reside with Pharaoh in Thebes. Every one of his orders would have to be relayed over the long distances that you and I have already discussed and bemoaned.'

'Once again, you have put your finger squarely on the crux of the matter,' I commended him. 'However, I have also given this some thought. If Pharaoh's ambassador were bearing the royal hawk seal he would be able to make battle decisions in concert with the Minos and his staff in Crete without incurring those long delays. Swift reaction to changing circumstances very often wins battles.'

Aton shook his head so violently that his jowls flapped like the wings of a pelican. 'Never! Pharaoh would never hand over the command of his armies and the conduct of the war to anyone he did not trust implicitly.'

'Ah so, Aton! Do you believe that there is nobody in Egypt whom Pharaoh Tamose trusts unreservedly?'

'No, I do not believe—' He broke off and stared at me indignantly. 'You, Taita? Surely you are not suggesting that you be given complete command of the northern wing of the Egyptian army under the hawk seal? You are not a soldier, Taita! What do you know about warfare?'

'If you have not read my scrolls entitled "The Art of War" then I question your right to judge me on that count. Every candidate at the army college is made to study my treatise as the ultimate authority.'

'I admit that I have never read them. Your famous scrolls

are too long-winded and it is a subject that does not particularly engage my interest as I am unlikely ever to command a legion,' Aton admitted. 'But what I meant was that scribbling on parchment is not the same as making decisions in the heat of battle. What direct and practical knowledge do you have of commanding an army?'

'Poor Aton, you know so little about me.' I made my tone pitying. 'I might just mention before we quit the subject that I designed the first chariots for our army, and I was the driver of the chariot that carried Pharaoh Tamose into the battle of Thebes. Pharaoh relied on me to counsel him on making instant decisions in the heat of the battle. My part in the battle was such that after we emerged victorious Pharaoh rewarded me with the Gold of Valour and the Gold of Praise. Pharaoh trusted me with his life on that day. He may choose to do so again.'

'I did not know any of that, Taita. Forgive my presumption, old friend. You are a man of many parts.'

I find it necessary from time to time to remind Aton of his place and standing in the order of things. However, I found his assistance extremely useful in drawing up the submission that I was preparing for Pharaoh Tamose regarding the mission to Crete. Once he is pointed in the right direction Aton has a good eye for details.

P haraoh was not so quick to disparage my abilities as Aton had been, especially in view of the success that I had so recently enjoyed at the fort of Tamiat. He was favourably disposed to give my plans to make contact with the Minos his full attention and consideration. He sat with me for two full days going over every detail, searching for a flaw in my construction or for an angle that I might have overlooked. At the end of that time he conceded simply, 'I can see no obvious faults in your designs, Tata. However, it is possible that Lord Kratas and his general staff might have some objections.'

In the presence of Pharaoh and the full council I laid my plans before Lord Kratas. Kratas leaped to his feet and stamped around the council chamber growing purple-faced with outrage as he listened to me. He shook his finger under my nose, and slammed his huge hairy fists on the council table as he bellowed his misgivings and his premonitions of disaster to all the gods, both good and evil. Kratas is a ruffian at heart and has the manners of an oaf. However, he is a fine warrior, if not a great one.

I waited him out until his voice was hoarse and he had used up every oath, expletive and malediction in his extensive vocabulary and was gulping open-mouthed and wordless like a fish that had just been hauled out of the river. Then I interposed in a mild and reasonable tone, 'There is one thing I failed to mention, my lord. I will need to take Hui and Remrem to Crete with me. I am sure you will be able to find adequate replacements for both of them on your staff.'

Kratas stared at me in speechless horror, and then suddenly he began to laugh. His mirth began as a reluctant and muted chuckle and then rose in volume to fill the chamber more amply than his curses had done just a short while previously. His legs appeared to become weakened with mirth, to the point that they were unable to bear his great weight. He staggered backwards and crashed into his chair. This piece of furniture has been especially designed to resist his bulk, and it travels everywhere with him. But now its joints squeaked in protest at the weight, and its legs buckled almost to their breaking point.

He stopped laughing as suddenly as he had begun, and lifted the skirts of his tunic with both hands to wipe the tears of mirth from his face, in the process exposing his abundant manhood. Then he dropped his skirts around his knees, and addressed Pharaoh in his normal speaking voice: 'Majesty, on sober reflection Taita's plan does appear to have certain merits. Only he could have thought of it, and only he could have had the balls to lay it before the council.' He clutched his own forehead in mock contrition. 'Forgive me, gentlemen, I think I may have chosen an inappropriate metaphor.' He spoke seriously and then he was off again in bellows of laughter.

'May I take that to mean that Hui and Remrem can accompany me to Crete?' I managed to keep a neutral expression, despite his unfortunate allusion to my missing parts.

'Take them, Taita. Your aspirations to martial glory deserve to be rewarded. Take two of my best men with my blessing. Perhaps they might be able to save you from yourself, balls or no balls; although I seriously doubt that anybody is capable of doing that.'

The preparations for the journey to Babylon took almost two months to complete.

My overriding concern was for the safety and comfort of the princesses and their entourage. They required eighty-three slaves and servants to see to their immediate needs. These included cooks, kitchen maids, chamber maids, wardrobe mistresses, beauticians, hairdressers, masseuses, musicians and other entertainers. In addition the girls insisted on taking with them a fortune teller and three priestesses of Hathor, the goddess of joy, love and motherhood, to take care of their spiritual needs. Their big brother indulged their extravagances, against my best advice, denying them nothing.

Pharaoh's treasury was awash with treasure and he poured out his coinage without stinting a silver coin of it. After the many enforced parsimonious years of his reign I think he was enjoying this wild extravagance even more than his sisters were.

Thus encouraged my girls decided that they also needed

handlers for the assortment of pet cats and monkeys and birds, hunting dogs and falcons which they were taking with them. These were over and above the grooms and stable hands they needed to tend to the twenty horses which they had selected from the royal stables.

From my point of view it was essential that the girls be superbly dressed and looking their very best while we were in Crete, under the scrutiny of the Supreme Minos and his court. Pharaoh concurred with me, and the finest seamstresses in Egypt were put to work cutting and sewing the magnificent wardrobes that I had designed for each of the princesses.

The girls and I trawled the shops in the souks of Thebes and were able to fill several large cabinets with dazzling jewellery, the better to beguile the Minos and impress him and his ministers with the wealth and importance of our kingdom. A week before we were due to depart from Thebes, Tehuti and Bekatha decked themselves out in all this finery and paraded themselves for Pharaoh and me to admire and approve. I was satisfied that no man, be he king or commoner, would be able to resist their beauty.

By this stage in the preparations the two girls had been rendered almost hysterical with excitement by the preparations and by the descriptions that Loxias had given them of the island of Crete. Neither of them had ever seen the sea or sailed upon it. They had never seen tall mountains and dense groves of tall trees. They had never seen mountains that poured out smoke and flame. They kept Loxias and me up late on most nights, questioning us and demanding detailed description of these wonders.

The Royal Mint on the west bank worked through the final days and nights, converting a hundred of the large Cretan ingots into wagonloads of the silver mem coinage that would cover the expenses of the journey and sustain us while we were in Crete, and in the other foreign lands which we would visit along the way.

The military escort that was to accompany our caravan as far as Babylon was made up of two mounted battalions of the Blue Crocodile Guards. This was the most renowned formation in the Egyptian army. Pharaoh had every man decked out in a newly forged suit of full armour, with crested helmet, cuirass and greaves. They carried recurved war bows, spears, swords and shields. The cost of producing all these weapons and armour exceeded two thousand deben of silver. However their splendid appearance must impress all who looked upon them.

'It's a small price to pay for the survival of our very Egypt.' He shrugged when I taxed him with the cost. 'It is no good complaining to me now. All this was your idea, Tata.' I could not argue with him.

The preparations for the journey were going so smoothly that I should have known they would not continue the same way, especially not if Princess Tehuti was so deeply involved in them, as she made herself.

I had planned on leaving Thebes on the last day of the month of Epiphi; which has always been a fortunate month for me. However, when I presented a pot of my fresh stools to my favourite soothsayer for divination, she inspected my offering and then cautioned me that the date I had chosen was inauspicious and that I should avoid it assiduously.

She advised me to delay the commencement of the journey to the first day of Mesore. I have always found her divinations to be trustworthy. Reluctantly I accepted this advice and posted a warning to all those who were to accompany the caravan, including of course the princesses, of the delay in our departure.

Within the hour the two of them came storming into my

quarters in the palace without invitation or warning. Tehuti was leading the onslaught, but as usual Bekatha was resolutely backing up her big sister.

'Oh, you promised, Tata! How can you be so cruel as to spoil our fun, Tata? We have been looking forward to this for ages. Don't you love us any more?'

I am no weakling; at most times I am able to exert my iron will, but not against my princesses. When they attack in concert no man dare withstand them, not even me.

The following morning, early, I crossed the Nile in the dawn and rode along the canal to the Royal Mint. I was going there to warn Zaras of the revised date of our departure as demanded by the royal princesses, and to make certain that Zaras would deliver the last ten sacks of silver mem coins to the royal store-house at the palace before we left.

The total amount of the silver that we were carrying with us exceeded ten lakhs, enough to build a fleet of warships and pay for an army of mercenaries. I still had misgivings about ignoring the advice of my soothsayer and placing such a huge treasure in jeopardy.

When I entered the Royal Mint it was as hot and noisy as a smithy. The flames of the forges were roaring, and the din of the hammers numbed my ears.

I spotted Zaras across the workshop floor. He was stripped to his tunic and swinging a bronze hammer from high above his own head. His muscled arms were glossy with sweat, and sweat ran down his cheeks and dripped from his chin. It was typical of the lad that he would not stand by idle while there was work to be done. Despite his exalted military rank he had thrown himself wholeheartedly into the menial labour of minting coinage.

I watched him with pleasure. I had not seen him for some weeks and I had almost forgotten how fond I had grown of him during our shared expedition to Tamiat. I even experienced a sharp pang of regret that I dared not have him at my right hand on the long journey that lay ahead of us to Babylon and Knossos.

Zaras must have sensed my gaze upon him. He looked up and saw me. He threw the hammer ringing to the stone paved floor, and with arms akimbo he grinned at me through the smoke and fumes of the forge.

Despite our friendship I was surprised by the warmth of his greeting as he came striding across the floor to meet me. 'I thought that you had forgotten me and left me to rot, but I should have known better. A man like you never deserts a friend. I have polished my armour and sharpened my sword. I am ready to go along with you as soon as you give the order to march.'

I was nonplussed, and it took all my self-control not to blurt out my denial or in some other crass manner to reveal my confusion.

'I expected no less of you,' I told him and I hoped my smile was convincing. 'But how did you know . . .' I let my voice trail off, before I disclosed the fact that I had not the vaguest idea what he was talking about.

'This very morning an orderly from the war council brought the order to me. But of course I knew that you must have asked for me.' He laughed again, and I was reminded of what a pleasant and unforced sound it was. 'I have no other friend in high places.'

'Whose seal was on the order, Zaras?'

'I hesitate to speak the name aloud, but . . .' He glanced around in a secretive manner before he reached into the pouch that hung on his hip and brought out a small scroll of papyrus; handling it with care and deep respect he passed it to me.

I started as I recognized the royal cartouche with which the scroll was sealed. 'Pharaoh?' I was astonished that Pharaoh would concern himself with such a trivial matter.

'None other.' Zaras watched solemnly as I unrolled the scroll. The order was curt and explicit.

Immediately place yourself under the direct command of Lord Taita. He will issue you further orders which you will obey unquestioningly on peril of death.

'Where are we going, Taita?' Zaras dropped his voice to an eager whisper. 'And what are we going to do when we get there? I am sure there will be some hard fighting. Am I not right?'

'I will answer that question when the time is right to do so. At this moment I can say no more.' I shook my head sternly. 'But hold yourself in readiness.'

He gave me the clenched-fist salute, but although he had managed to extinguish his grin his eyes still sparkled.

I dealt with the matter of the coinage which I had come to discuss with him in a perfunctory manner and then hurried back to the palace. I wanted desperately to speak to Pharaoh and have him rescind his order to Zaras; however, even I cannot burst in upon the royal presence unannounced or uninvited. There is a strict royal protocol to be observed if one requires an audience.

I went directly to the ante-chamber of the royal apartments where several dozen of the royal scribes squatted cross-legged before their writing easels dashing away busily with their brushes, writing out his messages and commands. The head scribe recognized me at once and hurried to my bidding. But he was unable to help me.

'Pharaoh departed from the palace at dawn this morning. He left no word of when he might return. I know he would want to speak to you if he were here. Perhaps you might wish to wait on his return, Lord Taita?'

I was about to refuse this suggestion, when suddenly I heard the unmistakable pharaonical tones echoing down the corridors of power. Pharaoh marched into the ante-chamber, followed by a swarm of officials and dignitaries. As soon as he saw me he turned aside and clapped a hand on my shoulder.

'I am glad that you are here. Once again you have anticipated my wishes, Tata. I was about to send for you. Come along with me.' With his hand still on my shoulder he led me into his inner chamber and immediately involved me in deep discussion of a number of complicated issues. Then as abruptly as he had welcomed me he dismissed me, and switched his attention to the scrolls that were spread out on the low table in front of him.

'I beg one moment more of your time, Mem.' He lifted his head and scowled enquiringly at me. 'The matter of Captain Zaras and his orders . . .'

'Who?' Pharaoh looked slightly bemused. 'What orders?'

'Zaras. Captain Zaras who went with me to Tamiat.'

'Oh, him!' he responded. 'Yes, you want him to accompany you on the mission to Crete. I do not understand why you needed my permission to appoint him, or why you did not speak to me directly if you thought it was necessary. It is not like you at all to ask my sister to intercede for you.' He looked down at his scrolls. 'Anyway, it's done now and I hope you are satisfied, Tata?'

Of course I had had my suspicions as to who was at the bottom of the business, but I had under-estimated the gall and deviousness of my princess. This was the first time she had interfered directly in the workings of the military chain of command. Now I was faced with making an instantaneous decision: to capitulate cravenly or to find myself forced into a confrontation with Princess Tehuti, who never had any qualms about employing all her superior royal force and any other subterfuge in order to have her own way. I bowed my head.

'You are magnanimous, Royal Egypt, and I am grateful.' I accepted the inevitable.

O nce all our preparations were completed, and our caravan was ready to set out from Thebes, I asked Lord Aton to release a carrier pigeon. This bird had been hatched in the loft maintained by the Egyptian ambassador in Babylon, and it knew where its nest was. In the message that the bird carried I asked our ambassador to inform King Nimrod of Akkad and Sumer that the royal princesses were on a diplomatic mission to his capital city and that Pharaoh Tamose would be extremely grateful if His Majesty King Nimrod would extend a cordial welcome to the royal ladies.

Four days later another pigeon arrived in the royal loft in Thebes having made the return journey from Babylon, with a message from King Nimrod relayed by the Egyptian ambassador in that city.

The king reaffirmed his commitment to the alliance between the two nations, and expressed his pleasure at the prospect of welcoming the royal ladies to his palace where he hoped they would enjoy his hospitality during an extended visit.

As soon as we received this message, I sent Zaras ahead of the royal caravan with a strong military escort to sweep the caravan road that led from Thebes down to the nearest shores of the Red Sea. My excuse was that I wanted him to make certain that there were no brigands or footpads laying in ambuscade along the way. My true motive was to keep him well out of the reach of my darling Tehuti.

I am not certain how Tehuti came to learn about my attempt to circumvent her. She has her spies everywhere, and the royal harem is a hotbed of intrigue and rumour-mongering.

I had given Zaras his orders to take command of the vanguard that very morning, and now I was sitting in my garden beside the fish pool, enjoying the cup of wine with which I am wont to greet the fall of night and to celebrate the passing of the day with all its achievements and successes and its occasional failures. She came up behind me as silently as a shadow and covered my eyes with her cool smooth hands and she whispered in my ear, 'Guess who it is!'

'I have no idea who it is, Your Royal Highness.'

'Oh! You must have peeped!' she protested and slipped into my lap. She placed her arms around my neck. 'I love you so much, darling Tata. I will do anything you ask of me. Will you do anything I ask of you?' She hugged me.

'Of course, Your Royal Highness. I will do anything that does not endanger your safety or run counter to the security and best interests of our very Egypt.'

'I would never ask anything like that of you.' She looked horrified by my insinuation. 'However, it's going to be a long journey across that awful desert to Sumer and Akkad. My sister and I will surely be bored and starved for entertainment. It would be so delightful if there was a bard who could sing for us and recite his poetry.'

'Is that why you asked your brother, Pharaoh Tamose, to assign Captain Zaras to the caravan that is taking us all to Babylon?'

'Captain Zaras!' she exclaimed with wide-eyed surprise. 'Is he going with us? Isn't that wonderful. He is a gifted poet and he has such a wonderful voice. I know that you like him. He can ride with Bekatha and me during the day and keep us entertained.'

'Captain Zaras is first and foremost an officer and a warrior, not a wandering minstrel. We already have with us a company of professional musicians, actors and actresses, jesters, jugglers, dancers, acrobats and trained animals including a performing bear. Zaras will be in command of the vanguard at the head of our caravan. He will be sweeping the route, and providing protection for all of us; in particular for you and your little sister.'

The ingratiating smile slipped from Tehuti's lips. She leaned back and regarded me frostily. 'Why are you being so mean to me, Taita?' she demanded. I was Taita now, the sure warning of royal disapproval. 'It's such a little thing I am asking.'

137

'This is my reason, Your Highness.' I took her right hand and turned it palm-down to display the diamond ring which she had not removed from her finger since I had given it to her, except to make Zaras find it for her.

She snatched her hand away from me and placed it behind her back. We regarded each other in silence.

She had laid out the battle lines, and drawn her metaphorical dagger. She stood up and walked away from me, gracefully swinging her hips, without looking back or uttering another word.

O n the first day of the month of Mesore, Zaras, at the head of his advance guards, reached the port of Sagafa on the near shore of the Red Sea. He released a pigeon with a message to me that he had found the flotilla of dhows and barges assembled and lying offshore ready to take our entire caravan on board for the crossing. With this reassurance I gave the order to march.

Pharaoh rode with me at the head of the caravan as we climbed the escarpment of the Nile. When we reached the high ground we all dismounted.

The princesses were seated on cushioned stools, one on each side of Pharaoh. All the councillors and senior officers present formed a circle around the royal trio. Then Pharaoh summoned me forward and I knelt at his feet. He stood over me and addressed the audience.

'I call upon all my well-beloved and loyal subjects here gathered to bear witness to these proceedings.'

Every one of them, including Tehuti and Bekatha, responded with a shout of 'Hail, Pharaoh! May his will be honoured and obeyed!'

With both hands Pharaoh lifted the tiny gold statuette of a falcon above his head.

'This is my hawk seal, my sign and my signet. The bearer speaks with all my god-given authority. Let the beholder take due notice and beware my power and my wrath.'

Still kneeling I cupped my hands and Pharaoh stooped over me and placed the hawk seal in my hands.

'Use it wisely, Lord Taita, and return it to me when next we meet.'

'To hear your command is to obey, Royal Egypt,' I cried out in a loud clear voice.

He raised me to my feet and embraced me. 'May Horus and all the gods of Egypt look favourably upon your endeavours.'

He turned away to bid his sisters farewell. Then he mounted his horse and his retinue formed around him. He touched the stallion with his spurs and rode at a gallop down the escarpment towards the gleaming walls of Thebes on the banks of Mother Nile. He passed the tail end of our caravan, which was climbing the escarpment in the opposite direction.

The slaves spread an awning of woven camel hair for us to sit beneath, and shade us from the sun which was hot and high. We sat and watched Pharaoh and his escort disappear in the shimmering distance below us. The head of the caravan reached our position and began to file past us.

In the van rode a battalion of the Crocodile Guards. These were followed immediately by fifty camels and their Arab drivers. Each of these ungainly animals carried four enormous leather water bags, two on each side of their humped backs. We would be forced to rely upon these to see us across the long wastes which separated the waterholes and oases in the burning expanses of Arabia.

Behind the camels and the precious water rode a second battalion of the Blue Crocodile Guards. They were ideally placed to guard our water supply or to fall back to protect the princesses and our soft centre if we were set upon by enemies.

Although I had planned our route to pass well south and

east of the Sinai Peninsula which the Hyksos claimed as their territory; I was taking no chances that Gorrab might not have learned of our plans and sent a battalion of his chariots to intercept us.

Behind the tight formation of guards came another fifty of the lanky, long-striding camels. They carried the tents, furniture and the other elaborate camp paraphernalia which would be set up at every rest stop during the journey.

Following them on foot came the rabble of camp-followers and the servants and slaves. Next in the procession strode another twenty dromedaries. These carried the heavy sacks of silver coinage.

The rearguard comprised the third battalion of Crocodile Guards, and the loose horses, camels and the baggage waggons. As they came level with where we were resting I gave the order to strike the tent under which we sat.

We rode forward until we reached our place in the centre of the long winding procession that stretched out for almost a league across the desert. This unwieldy and slow moving agglomeration of men and animals took ten full days to reach the western shore of the Red Sea.

Zaras rode up from the port of Sagafa to meet us. He and his honour guard came galloping back along our caravan, and he reined in when he reached the royal party and jumped down from the saddle to greet the two princesses.

He went down on one knee in front of Tehuti and gave her the clenched-fist salute. She rewarded him with a vivacious smile.

'Captain Zaras, I am very pleased that we shall have your company for the rest of the journey to Babylon. I well remember your declamation on the storming of the fortress at Tamiat when you and Lord Taita returned from that mission. It would give me great pleasure if you were to dine with us this evening and afterwards entertain us with another recitation. As regards the remainder of the journey to Babylon, it is my wish and my command that you relinquish your place in the vanguard of this caravan to another officer and that you place yourself in a position to provide direct protection to my sister Princess Bekatha and myself.'

I exhaled sharply and loudly enough for her to hear me, but she ignored my smothered protest and concentrated all her attention on Zaras. He looked uncomfortable and stuttered slightly as he replied to her: the first time ever that I had heard him do so.

'Your Royal Highness, to hear your command is to obey. However, please forgive me. I must immediately report to Lord Taita whom Pharaoh has placed in command of this caravan and to whom he has entrusted the royal hawk seal.'

I was impressed by Zaras' loyalty to me, and by his attempt to remind Tehuti who held ultimate authority. The poor fellow was trying desperately to wriggle out from under the conflict of interest with which she was attempting to saddle him.

I steeled myself to come to his rescue when the royal thunderstorm broke over his head. Tehuti was unaccustomed to having even her lightest orders questioned. She surprised me yet again. Instead of cutting Zaras down she smiled and nodded.

'Do so at once, Captain Zaras. Your duty as a soldier comes before all other considerations.'

Zaras fell in beside me, and I deliberately hung back to keep us just out of earshot of the princesses while we rode down towards the rim of the escarpment, below which lay the straggling buildings of Sagafa at the edge of the sea.

Taking his cue from me Zaras lowered his voice as he told me that while he was awaiting our arrival he had taken the opportunity to sail across the sea in a fast dhow to the little fishing harbour of El Kumm on the far shore. He had gone there in order to make certain that our Bedouin guide had received our orders, and that he and his men were waiting there to lead us across the Arabian Desert.

This was Al Namjoo, the same guide who had led us across the Sinai Peninsula on our journey to the shores of the Middle Sea and the fort of Tamiat.

'I am pleased to be able to tell you that Al Namjoo has been awaiting our arrival for well over two months, ever since he first received my message that we were coming.' Zaras looked pleased with himself. 'His two sons are with him, but he has sent them on ahead to reconnoitre the waterholes and the oases along the caravan route. So far the reports they have sent back to him are that there is good water in all of them, as we might expect in this season of the year.'

'I am relieved to hear this,' I told him, but then I glanced sideways at him. 'Continue, Zaras. You were going to say more,' I prompted him, and he looked startled.

'How did you . . .' he began, and I completed the sentence for him.

'How did I know? I knew because you are not very adept at concealing anything from me. I mean that as a compliment rather than a rebuke.'

He shook his head and laughed ruefully. 'We have been separated far too long, my lord. I had forgotten how you are able to read a man's thoughts. But you are right, my lord. I was just going to mention one thing more, but I hesitated lest you think me an alarmist.'

'Nothing you can tell me will make me believe that,' I assured him.

'Then I must tell you that while I was in Al Namjoo's encampment three refugees were brought in from the desert. They were in a sorry state, almost dead from thirst and from their wounds. Truth to tell one of them died within a very short time of

142

reaching the safety of Al Namjoo's tents, and the other was unable to speak.'

'Why not, Zaras?' I demanded. 'What fate had befallen these unfortunates?'

'My lord, the first one had been flayed with heated sword-blades so that most of the skin was burned away from his body. His death can only have been a happy release from his agonies. As for the other man, his tongue had been hacked from his throat most brutally. He was only able to grunt and bellow like an animal.'

'In the name of Horus the merciful, what had befallen them?' I demanded of Zaras.

'The third man had escaped such brutal injuries. He was able to tell us that he had been the leader of a caravan of fifty camels and as many men and women carrying salt and copper ingots down from the town of Turok when they were set upon by Jaber al Hawsawi. This is the one that men call the Jackal.'

'I know of him by reputation only,' I admitted. 'He is one of the most feared men in Arabia.'

'There is every reason to fear him, my lord. He emasculated and disembowelled all the other men and woman of the caravan merely for the sport of it. Of course the Jackal and his men coupled with their captives, both men and women, before massacring them.'

'Where is the Jackal now? Did this man know where they have gone?'

'No, my lord. He has disappeared back into the desert. But one thing is certain, and that is that he will be lurking along the caravan routes like the animal he is named for.'

At that moment Tehuti turned in the saddle and called back to us over her shoulder: 'What are you two discussing so earnestly? Come up here and ride with Bekatha and me. If you and Zaras are telling stories to each other then we want to share them with you.'

Even I dared not flout her orders twice in quick succession. The two of us pushed our mounts up level with the princesses. Skilfully Tehuti interposed her own mount between Zaras and me to prevent us continuing to discuss matters that did not interest her particularly. At that moment the rugged and rocky track we were following came out on the crest of the hills and Tehuti reined in her horse and let out a cry of astonishment and delight.

'Look! Oh, won't you look at that! Have you ever seen a river so wide and blue? By the horned head of Hathor it must be a hundred times wider than our Nile. I cannot even see across to the other side.'

'That's no river, Your Highness,' Zaras told her. 'That is the sea; the Red Sea.'

'It is enormous,' Tehuti enthused, and Zaras did not know her well enough to realize that she was putting on an act for his benefit. 'It must be the biggest sea in the entire world!'

'No, Your Royal Highness,' Zaras corrected her respectfully. 'It's the smallest of all the seas. The Middle Sea is the largest, but wise men have calculated that the Great Dark Ocean on which this world floats is even larger.'

Tehuti turned to him, opening her eyes wide with admiration. 'Captain Zaras, you know such a great deal; perhaps almost as much as Lord Taita. You must ride with me and my sister Bekatha for at least a few hours every day to instruct us in these matters.'

Tehuti is not easily turned aside from her purpose.

The crossing to Arabia was infinitely more difficult and demanding than had been our voyage to Tamiat the previous year. On that occasion we had been a company of less than two hundred men, travelling swiftly and lightly; and it had only been necessary for us to cross the Gulf of Suez, that narrow westerly finger of water that pokes up between Egypt and the Sinai Peninsula. It is less than fifty leagues wide.

Now we had to keep much further south, to avoid at all costs entering the Sinai Peninsula where the Hyksosian chariots that Gorrab might send to intercept us could be lurking.

We were forced to cross the main body of the Red Sea at its widest point. This entailed a voyage of more than two hundred leagues; transporting over a thousand men and animals in fifty open-decked dhows. One of these small boats was only capable of carrying ten of the camels at a time. Each of them would have to make multiple crossings.

Taking into account all these factors I had to allow at the very least two full months for us to bring our caravan across to Arabia.

I kept the royal party encamped on the Egyptian shore while the main elements were being ferried over the narrow sea. I knew from hard experience that it was not wise to let the princesses become bored, or allow them to have too much spare time on their hands.

The royal enclosure was carefully segregated from the rest of the encampment. Although it was the size of a small village, it surpassed even a large city in the sumptuousness of its appointments and the plethora of comfort and luxury which surrounded the inhabitants.

Every few days the princesses rode out with a hunting party which I led. Either we pursued the fleet-footed desert gazelle that flitted as lightly as moths across the salt flats, or we climbed into the hills where the curling-horned ibex haunted the crags and cliff faces. When this hunting palled the girls flew their trained falcons at the wild duck and geese that swarmed along the seashore.

At other times I arranged picnics on the offshore islands where the girls could swim in the translucent waters, or spear the swordfish and giant sea bass which swarmed on the under-water coral forests.

One thing I did insist on was that most of their mornings were filled with their studies. I had brought with us two erudite scribes to coach them in their writing, mathematics and geometry. I also enjoyed acting as their tutor. Our classes were made up of solemn hard work, interspersed with bouts of merriment and girlish giggles. These were my favourite times of the day. They chatted away to Loxias in Minoan, excluding me from the conversation as though I could not understand a word of the language. They discussed the most intimate subjects in salacious detail. Loxias was the eldest of the trio, so she had set herself up as the leading authority on all matters carnal and erotic. However, listening to her it was clear that she was totally devoid of practical experience. She relied entirely on a vivid and fertile imagination for the details.

During these sessions I could truly get to know them better and find out what was really going on in those beautiful and busy little heads.

Each of them professed to having discovered the love of their lives. Loxias had decided on Lord Remrem. However, she was transmuted to stone in his presence: deprived of the power of speech and unable to do more than blush and cast down her eyes. I think she was most awed by the fact that he was a Lord of the Royal Council while she was a commoner and a foreigner. She seemed not at all deterred by the fact that Remrem was almost twice her age, already had three wives and was blithely unaware of her existence.

Bekatha had become enchanted with Hui, the famous horseman and charioteer. Little did she know that he had been a blood brother of the infamous criminal Basti the Cruel when I captured him. I had done my best to tame and civilize him, but he still had a wide streak of the barbarian in him, particularly when it came to his sense of humour. Bekatha enjoyed nothing better than being pounded over the roughest ground that Hui could find in his chariot, clinging to him with both arms around his waist and shrieking like a lost soul in Hades. The two of them exchanged jokes and insults which were totally obscure to any other listener, but which doubled them both up with laughter. As a mark of her special approbation Bekatha took to pelting him with pieces of bread and fruit across the table when he accepted her invitation to dine with us.

Tehuti kept aloof from these discussions and displays of affection. None of us pressed her on the subject.

Our evenings were passed in setting each other riddles; in storytelling and rhyming; in singing and playing musical instruments; or in playacting and reciting poetry.

By these means and with careful planning I was able to keep my three charges out of dangerous mischief, and the days fled by as swiftly as migrating birds. Finally the main part of our convoy was across to the eastern shore of the sea, and it was time for us to follow them.

Before sunrise on the morning of the fifteenth day of the month of Athyr we all assembled on the beach while the three priestesses of Hathor, ably assisted by both Tehuti and Bekatha, sacrificed a fine white ram to the goddess.

We promised the goddess that we would sacrifice a camel to her if she treated us kindly when we were on the water and guided us safely to the far shore. Then we embarked and pushed off from the beach.

The goddess must have been listening for she sent a brisk warm breeze out of Egypt to fill our sails and send our flotilla scurrying through the choppy waters. Before the setting of the sun Africa sank beneath the waves behind us.

As darkness fell every ship hoisted an oil lamp to the top of her mast, to enable us to keep each other in sight. Steering by the stars we maintained our easterly course. As the dawn broke we raised the distant shoreline of Arabia like a row of rotten shark's teeth, brooding black against the fresh blue sky of the morning sky. We steered for them all day, and the sun was still a hand's breadth above the horizon when fifty men of the Crocodile Guards waded out to seize the hulls of our dhows and drag them high and dry up the beach. The girls were able to step out on to Asian soil without wetting their dainty little feet. The royal encampment with all its delights was already laid out above the high watermark, ready to receive them. I had ordered it so.

However, we dared not dally here; for every day we used up huge quantities of the precious sweet water.

The main convoy and the baggage train had left many days ahead of us. By this time they must have covered more than a hundred leagues. On the second day after our arrival in Arabia we mounted the horses and riding camels and set out after them.

As soon as we moved away from the moderating influence of the sea, the high sun soon became too fierce to allow us to travel during the middle of the day. From then onwards we began each march in the late afternoon when the sun had lost a little of its stinging malice. We travelled on through the night, stopping only for an hour around midnight to water the horses and the camels from the cache that the main caravan had left for us to find. Then we journeyed on after the sunrise. When the heat became unbearable we erected the tents and lay sweating in their shade, until the sun sank low enough to allow us to repeat the cycle.

After fifteen days and nights we finally caught up with the main column of the caravan. By this time the leather water bags were more than half empty, with merely a few gallons of slimy green and foul-tasting water sloshing about in the bottom of them. I was forced to cut the daily ration down to four mugs a day a man.

We had now entered the desert proper. The dunes rolled

148

away before us in endless profusion. Our horses were showing signs of distress. When they were carrying even a lightweight rider the soft sand made the going extremely onerous for them. I turned them loose to join the herd of remounts at the head of the caravan, and I selected the finest racing camels as replacements for the girls and the rest of our party.

Al Namjoo assured me that the next water lay only a few days' march ahead of us. So I took the girls, together with Zaras and his escort of picked men, and we rode ahead of the main column to find the promised waterhole.

Al Namjoo gave me Haroun, his eldest son, to guide us. We were able to travel much faster than the main body. We rode hard through the night, and in the first flush of dawn Haroun reined in on the top of another monstrous dune of brick-red-coloured sand and he pointed ahead.

Before us stretched a high cliff of striated rock. The horizontal layers were of contrasting but vivid colours, varying from honey gold and chalky white to shades of red and blue and black. Some of the softer layers had been wind eroded more deeply than those above and below them. These formed overhanging galleries and deep elongated caverns almost as though they had been designed by a demented architect.

'This place is called the Miyah Keiv,' Haroun told us. I was able to translate this from the Arabic as meaning 'the Water Cave'.

Haroun led us up under the vertical rock wall, at the base of which opened a low-roofed lateral fissure. It was just high enough for a tall man to enter without bending, but it was more than a hundred paces wide and so deep and shaded that I could not see how far it undercut the cliff.

'The water lies in the depths of this cave,' Haroun told us. The princesses and Loxias urged their camels to kneel, and then they jumped down from the carved wooden saddles. I led the three of them into the opening, while Zaras held his men back to give us space to ourselves.

The stone floor dropped away gradually under our feet, and as we descended the daylight faded and the air grew cooler, until the contrast in temperature to that of the direct heat of the sun outside made us shiver.

By now I could smell the water, and hear it dripping somewhere ahead of us. My throat clenched with thirst. I tried to swallow but there was little saliva in my mouth. The girls tugged at my hands and dragged me down to the bottom of the incline.

A large pool lay before us, the surface gleaming with reflected light from the cave entrance. That same light created the illusion that the water itself was black as cuttlefish ink. None of us hesitated but with gleeful cries we plunged in to it, still wearing our tunics and sandals. I knelt until the water reached to my chin. I looked down at my own body and saw that the water, far from being black, was clear as the diamond I had given to Tehuti. I filled my mouth and sighed with pleasure.

I have drunk the finest wine from the cellars of Pharaoh's palace in Thebes, but none of it could match this divine and arcane spring.

The girls were in the centre of the pool; splashing me and one another; gasping and squealing at the cold. Encouraged by the uproar Zaras and his men came charging down the sloping floor. They were shouting and laughing, as they too flung themselves into the dark water.

When we had drunk all that our bellies could hold, the men filled the water-skins we had brought with us and carried them out to the camels. Zaras could not allow them to take the draught animals down to the pool. The rock roof was too low for them to pass beneath it; and the risk of them fouling that sublime water with their droppings was too great.

Haroun confirmed my own estimate that the main caravan was at least three days behind us at this stage. This did not worry me unduly, for the girls were tired out by the journey and this would give them a chance to rest and fully regain their strength.

What really concerned me was our vulnerability in this place. The location of the waterhole would be well known to all the Bedouin tribes for hundreds of leagues around. We were a small party, but our animals, weapons and armour were highly valued by the tribes and would be attractive to the lawless elements amongst them. If they learned of our presence at the waterhole and knew how few there were in our party we would be in grave danger. We must keep alert and make certain that we were not taken off guard.

As soon as Zaras and his men had refreshed themselves, I brought them out of the cavern and I posted our sentries and organized our defences to secure the area.

Then I took Zaras and Haroun with me to explore our immediate surroundings and search for any signs that other human beings might have been here recently.

All three of us were fully armed. I carried my longbow slung over one shoulder and a quiver of thirty arrows over the other. In addition my bronze sword hung in its scabbard on my right hip.

When we reached the top of the nearest dune we separated. But before we parted we agreed to meet back at the Miyah Keiv before the sun reached its zenith, which would happen in about an hour. I sent Zaras to make a circle out in a northerly direction, and Haroun to investigate what appeared to be a caravan trail in the valley below us. I followed the high dune towards the south.

It was difficult to remain unobserved for there was almost no cover in this terrain, but I took pains to keep off the skyline where an enemy could spot me from a great distance.

I soon found myself enchanted by this landscape that was barren and bleak, but at the same time was hauntingly beautiful.

It was an infinity of dunes that were as mutable as the swells of a tranquil sea; smooth and pliant as the body of a beautiful woman, devoid of hard edges, malleable and sculptured. The peaks of these waves of sand were being gnawed at by the wind, changing shape before my eyes. Footprints and hoof prints would become indistinguishable from each very quickly, and would disappear completely soon after that.

As I moved through it I found nothing in this other world to indicate to me that man or beast had ever existed here; until suddenly I noticed a small piece of sun-bleached bone protruding from the sand at my feet. I knelt to dig it loose, and was surprised to find that it was the skull and short gaping beak of a nightjar. The bird must have been blown so far from its usual haunts by unseasonable winds.

I turned back and slid down the face of the dune. When I reached the bottom I headed towards the entrance of the subterranean pool. As I approached it I heard the shrieks of feminine laughter and the splashing of water from within.

Zaras had returned before me. He and his men had unsaddled the camels and moved them in under the overhang of the entrance to the cavern, to kneel where they were shaded from the direct sunlight. The men were grooming them and feeding them their rations of corn in leather nosebags. I called to Zaras.

'Did you find anything?'

'No, my lord. Nothing.'

'Where is Haroun? Has he returned yet?'

'Not yet, but he will be back shortly,' he answered. I hesitated at the mouth of the cavern. Everything seemed perfectly normal and commonplace. I could not understand the reason for the sense of anxiety that was nagging at me; but I knew enough not to dismiss it.

Instead of entering the cavern I turned aside and followed the wall of rock in the opposite direction. I was out of sight of the cavern entrance when I reached a point where a narrow fissure cleft the vertical face of the rock. I had not noticed this fault before, and I studied it for a moment and decided that I might be able to climb up to the top of the cliff and see what lay beyond. I reached out and tentatively placed my hand on the exposed rock.

The sun had heated the surface so that it burned me like a live coal. I jerked my hand away so sharply that I dropped the bird skull I was still carrying. I sucked my scalded finger until the pain eased, and then I stooped to retrieve the skull. I paused before my fingers touched it.

Close up against the rock wall where the wind had not yet eroded it was a single human footprint in the packed sand. As I stared at it one side of the footprint collapsed in a soft slither of sand, demonstrating how recently it had been made.

It had certainly not been made by one of my girls. This was the print of a large masculine foot wearing a sandal with a smooth leather sole. I could still hear faintly the voices and occasional laughter of Zaras and his men behind me. I returned quickly to a point from where I could see the cavern entrance and the group of men standing in front of it. One quick glance was enough for me to make absolutely certain of what I knew already. All the men were wearing regulation military sandals with brass-studded soles.

There was a stranger amongst us.

My next thought was for the safety of my girls. I cocked my head to listen to the voices that were still issuing from deep in the cavern. I recognized two of them immediately, but I was unable to distinguish the third. Trying to conceal my perturbation from the men I strode back past them and entered the cavern. I went quickly down the sloping stone floor to the edge of the pool. I paused for a moment to allow my eyes to adapt to the gloom, and I stared at the pale and nubile bodies that were tumbling and swirling in the dark waters like frolicking otters. But there were only two of them.

'Bekatha!' I yelled at her, my voice rising with the onset of panic. 'Where is Tehuti?' Her head bobbed up with the red-gold hair smeared wetly over her face.

'She went outside to make an offering to Seth, Tata!' This was their girlish euphemism for the culmination of the human digestive process.

'Which way did she go?'

'I didn't watch her. She just said she was going out to do it.'

Tehuti was a fastidious child. I knew she would have hidden herself away before she performed any intimate bodily functions. She would not have stayed in the cavern. She would have gone out into the desert. I ran back to the entrance of the cave. Zaras and his men were still where I had last seen them grouped at the left-hand side of the entrance. Once more I shouted at Zaras.

'Did you see Princess Tehuti leave the cave?'

'No, my lord.'

'What about the rest of you men? Did any of you see her?' They shook their heads dumbly.

Tehuti would have avoided them. Perhaps she had found another exit from the cavern, I told myself. I turned and ran back past the cleft in the rock face where I had seen the alien print.

'Horus, hear me!' I entreated my god, praying with the full force of my psyche, unleashing the strange power within me that I have learned to call upon in times of deep and desperate need. 'Open my eyes, O Horus. Let me see. O my sweet God, let me see!'

I closed my eyes tightly for ten beats of my heart, and when I opened them again my vision had taken on a lucent lustre. The great god Horus had heard me. I was seeing with my inner eye. Around me colours were more vivid, shapes were starker and with sharper edges to them.

I looked along the bottom of the rock wall, and I saw her. It was not Tehuti but it was the memory of where she had recently been, like an echo or a shadow of herself. It was a smudge against the brightness, a tiny intangible cloud. It was not even human in shape or outline but I knew it was her. She was dancing away from me, keeping parallel to the striated wall of rock.

I knew instinctively that she was being pursued, and that she was trying to escape from danger. I could feel her fear resonating in my own heart and tasted the terror of it on the back of my tongue.

'To arms, Zaras!' I roared. I did not realize that my voice was capable of such power. 'Leave five men to guard Bekatha and Loxias. The rest of you mount up and follow me!'

Knowing that Zaras had heard me, I ran on without looking back, concentrating my everything on the evanescent cloud that was not Tehuti, but that was her very essence.

Suddenly I had wings under my feet. I ran faster and still faster, but the little cloud matched my speed sucking me along as though I was caught in its wake. Then abruptly it dissolved into nothingness at the point ahead of me where the striated rock wall turned back upon itself.

The lucent glow faded from my eyes, and my vision returned to normal. My feet slowed and became heavier, bereft of their god-given grace. I forced myself onwards until I reached the spot where she had faded away. I stopped with my breath sawing hoarsely in my lungs.

I looked around me wildly, but there was nothing. She had gone.

Then I looked down at the earth beneath me and I saw that although my vision of her had faded away, she had left the veritable prints of her bare feet in the sand where they were protected from the wind. I raised my eyes to follow them and I saw that only a short distance ahead they had been obliterated once again, but this time not by the wind. Rather, the sand had been churned by the feet of men wearing smooth-soled sandals. I could not tell how many there were of them but I guessed that there were a dozen or more. It was clear to me that Tehuti had been pursued by these men. When they had overtaken and seized her, she had put up a fight. I saw where and how she had struggled. Tehuti possessed the strength of a wildcat when she was aroused, but in the end they had overwhelmed her.

Between them they had dragged her to the foot of the rock wall. Here I saw there was another of the fissures in the face of the cliff. But this one was wider than and not as steep as the first one.

It was more like a staircase than a chimney. I knew that I could climb it easily but the camels would have to find another way to reach the top of the cliff. I looked back and saw Zaras leading the first camel along the base of the cliff towards me. As he reached me he shouted urgently, 'What is happening, Taita? What do you want us to do?'

'Tehuti has been taken. They must have been lying in wait for her here. She wandered off on her own and they took her.' I pointed up the cleft in the cliff. 'They have dragged her up there, where our camels can't follow.'

'Who are these men? Where did they come from?'

'I know not, Zaras. Ask no more pointless questions. Ride on along the base of the cliff until you can find a way to climb it. I am going straight up after them.'

'I'll send half my men to follow you up, and support you. Then I'll take the others around with me, and meet you at the top of the cliff.'

I did not answer him, but saved my breath for the climb that confronted me. I climbed steadily, husbanding my strength. I could hear Zaras' men coming up behind me. Although all of them were much younger than me I drew ahead of them steadily.

Halfway to the top of the wall I heard voices from above. I paused for a few seconds to listen. I do not speak the Arabian language perfectly, but I understood enough to follow the gist of it.

The men above me were Bedouin and they were urging each other to greater speed. Then faintly I heard Tehuti scream: I would know that voice anywhere and in any circumstances.

'Take courage, Tehuti,' I threw my head back and shouted up at her. 'I am coming. Zaras also is coming with all our men.'

The sound of her voice was a goad to me; I flew at the climb again with renewed strength and determination. Then above me I heard the whinny of a horse, the stamp of hooves and the jingle of harness. The men who had her were mounting up.

Tehuti cried out again but the sense of her words was lost in the shouting of the Arabs as they mounted, and then the cracking of the whiplashes as they urged their mounts into a gallop. Horses snorted, and then their hooves thudded on the soft sands.

I realized then why these bandits had left their horses at the top of the cliff. They knew that they would be able to return to them swiftly, whereas we would lose time in finding another way to bring our camels around the impassable cliff.

I hurled myself up the last few yards of the climb and tumbled over the lip of the cliff. I paused there to take in the situation.

In front of me was a rabble of some thirty or forty Arab riders, dressed in dusty burnous and keffiyeh head-dress. By this time they had all managed to mount their horses and most of them were already racing away from where I stood, urging their mounts on with wild yells, shouting at each other triumphantly.

One of the bandits was still wrestling with Tehuti. He had thrown her over the front of his saddle, and as I watched he mounted up behind her. He was a big powerful-looking brute with a curling dark beard. He answered closely to the description that I had received from Al Namjoo of the bandit Al Hawsawi, the Jackal. But I could not be certain this was him.

Tehuti was kicking out at him and screaming, but he held her down easily on the saddle with one arm pinning both of hers. I saw that her tunic and her hair were still wet from the pool. Her damp curls dangled and danced about her head.

She glanced back and saw me on the lip of the cliff, and her face lit with a pathetic gleam of hope. I could read her lips as she mouthed my name.

'Tata! Please help me!'

With his free hand on the reins her captor sawed the stallion's head around and then booted the animal into full flight out across the rock-strewn plain, speeding away from me. Once he looked back under his arm and he grinned at me jubilantly. Now I was certain that he was the Jackal. Fleetingly I wondered how he had known that we were coming to this Miyah Keiv in the striated cliff.

His gang closed up around him in a tight mass. I could not count their numbers. Watching them go I was almost overwhelmed with the wave of savage but helpless rage that swept over me and threatened to smother me.

Swiftly I gathered my numbed wits and slipped the recurved war bow from my shoulder. In three swift movements I had rebraced the bowstring, and I was reaching back to take an arrow from my quiver.

The range was opening swiftly. I knew that within seconds both Tehuti and her captor would be beyond bowshot. I took my stance, left shoulder leading the target, and I raised my eyes above the distant horizon, judging the angle of loft that I must give my arrow to reach out to the Jackal.

Battle joy engorged my heart as I realized that the body of the Jackal was interposed between Tehuti and me, and that unwittingly he was shielding her from my arrow. I could loose cleanly without fear of hitting her. I drew and the fletching of the arrow touched my lips. Every muscle in my arms and upper torso was racked by the immense weight of the tensed bow. There are very few other men who are able to draw my bow to full stretch. It is not merely a matter of brute strength. It also requires poise and balance, and achieving a sense of oneness with the bow.

When I opened my three fingers that held the bowstring it slashed back, scorching the skin of my inner forearm. I felt the blood spring brightly from the wound it inflicted. There had been no chance for me to secure the leather arm guard to protect myself from it.

I felt no pain. Instead my heart soared upwards as swiftly as the arrow I had let fly, for I saw that I had made a perfect shot. I knew that the swine who held Tehuti was dead without him yet being aware of it.

Then suddenly I shouted aloud with rage and frustration as I watched the horseman who rode hard behind my target swing his horse off the line. Horus alone knows why he did so; probably it was to avoid a hole. Whatever the reason, he blotted out my view of the target. I saw my arrow drop on him like a stooping falcon and take him high in the back, an inch to one side of his spine. He threw his head back, and writhed with agony as he tried to reach over his own shoulder to grasp the shaft of the arrow. But he was still blocking my aim.

I nocked a second arrow and let it fly again in the despairing hope that the wounded man might slip from the saddle and fall to earth while the arrow was still in flight, thus opening up Al Hawsawi's body. But the wounded Arab clung stubbornly to his saddle; only when my second arrow struck him in the back of his neck did his limp carcass flop from the saddle and roll in the loose dust kicked up by the horses in front of him.

By that time Al Hawsawi was out of range. I let another

arrow fly after him even though I knew that I had no chance of touching him. But I still cursed myself and all the dark gods who had protected Al Hawsawi when my last arrow dropped twenty paces behind the heels of his horse.

I started to run to where the body of the man was lying with two of my arrows in him. I wanted to reach him before he died so that I could beat and kick some information out of him. Perhaps if I were fortunate I might even learn for certain the name of the villain who had taken Tehuti, and where I might find him again.

It was not to be. The nameless bandit was dead when I stooped over him. His one eye was rolled up into his skull so only the white was showing, while the other eye glared up at me in dumb outrage. I kicked him anyway; more than once. Then I sat down beside him and sent up a desperate prayer to Hathor, Osiris and Horus, pleading with each of them to keep Tehuti safe until I could come to her.

The thing I hate most about the gods is the fact that they are seldom at hand when most you need them.

So while I waited for Zaras to find me I turned my hand to cutting my arrows out of the corpse of the bandit I had brought down. There is no fletcher in all of Egypt who can turn out an arrow to match one of mine.

It took Zaras almost another hour to arrive. The band of Bedouin bandits had long disappeared into the glare and dust of the horizon by that time. I am a man who usually has complete control of my emotions. I can stay calm and composed in the face of disaster and tragedy. By this I mean the sack of cities, the massacre of armies and suchlike lesser mishaps. But with the loss of Tehuti I found myself in a towering, shaking and impotent rage. The longer I had to wait the more my emotions seethed and boiled.

The men that Zaras had sent to climb the cliff after me became the target for my fury. I raved at them, excoriating them for being so tardy and ineffectual. I accused them of cowardice and deliberate procrastination when I needed their assistance.

When I finally picked out the dust of Zaras' camels approaching along the upper rim of the striated rock wall I could not contain myself an instant longer. I started to run back to meet him. I was shouting at him to hurry whilst he was still beyond earshot.

However, when he came close enough for me to read the expression on his face the realization dawned on me that his distress equalled and possibly outstripped my own. As loudly and as bitterly as I was screaming at him to hurry, even louder he was imploring me to tell him where Tehuti was and if she were still alive.

It was then I realized that it was not some casual and transient infatuation that gripped these two young people. This was the same grand and immaculate passion that I had cherished for Tehuti's mother, Queen Lostris. I could see that Zaras' anguish for the loss of Tehuti was as devastating as mine had once been for her mother.

In the moment I recognized this fact I knew also that the world had changed for all three of us.

I watched Zaras bringing his men towards me as fast as the camels could gallop. These were all magnificent beasts.

Over a short distance the Bedouin horses would be able to outrun my camels, but they could not maintain that pace for more than two or three hours. On the other hand my camels could run all day long, over sandy and treacherous ground. My camels had recently drunk their fill of water. They would not have to drink again for ten or more days. In these conditions of thirst, heat and heavy going in the sand the horses would be down by sunrise tomorrow, while my camels could still be running a week from today.

I had my orders for Zaras ready when he came up to where I stood. He had an armed man on the back of every camel. Very swiftly I had half of them dismounted and on their way back to the cavern on foot to stand guard over the other two girls. Of course Bekatha's safety outweighed that of Loxias a hundredfold, but none the less I had grown fond of the little Cretan lass.

Zaras had shown the good sense to have each of the camels loaded with full water-skins. This accounted for his delayed arrival. Now half the saddles were empty and I would be able to rotate the riders at regular intervals. I was also pleased to see that Zaras had brought our head guide Al Namjoo with him. Nobody knew the ground better than he did.

As we mounted up with each rider leading a spare camel on a guide rope behind him, and the water-skins bulging and gurgling reassuringly, I was prepared to wager a bag of silver mem that I would catch up with Al Hawsawi before noon on the morrow.

The wind had dropped to a soft breeze, but it was still too hot to give us much relief. At the very least it no longer had the strength to obliterate the Jackal's spoor until I had the chance to read it. I kept the camels moving at a pace that I judged carefully.

I calculated the passage of time by the angle of the sun, and three hours later I could already see that we had gained substantially on our quarry. We stopped briefly to rotate our mounts and I allowed the men to each drink two mugs of water before we started off again. We were not pushing hard yet; but keeping to a swinging trot that the camels made look so relaxed and easy.

Another two hours and I received proof positive that we

were wearing down the fugitives. We came upon one of the Jackal's horses broken down and limping slowly along the tracks left by its herd mates. I was grimly satisfied with our progress, and I told Zaras that I hoped we might even catch them before nightfall.

This opinion proved premature. An hour after I had expressed it we came to the first split. I held up my hand to signal my cohort to halt. Then I confirmed this with a verbal command to Zaras.

'Let the men dismount and stretch their legs. They can each drink two mugs of water. But they must stay back and take care not to confuse the tracks until I have read them.'

Splitting the chase was an old Bedouin ploy that consisted of dividing their numbers into two equal groups. Then each group would take off in a separate direction. In this instance it was doubly effective, in that it would be impossible for us to decide which of the two groups had taken Tehuti with them. We would be forced to split our own forces to follow both of theirs.

I dismounted and handed the reins of my camel to Zaras to hold for me. I went forward on foot, stepping gingerly until I reached the point at which the gang had split. I saw that they had not dismounted to do so. Thus I was unable to pick up Tehuti's footprints. I squatted down and once again called on my gods for help.

'Great Horus, let me see. Open these weak blind eyes and show me the way, I beg of you. Open my eyes, beloved Hathor, and I will make you a blood sacrifice to delight your heart.'

I closed my eyes and listened to my heart beat twenty times before I opened them again. I looked around carefully but my eyesight was unaltered. The desert was the same. There was no translucent glow lighting the brutal sands; no dancing shadows to lead me on.

Then I heard a voice, and I cocked my head to listen to it.

But it was only the wind soughing through the dunes. I turned my head slowly to allow the wind to brush my ear. I heard her then, softly but distinctly.

'Let Hathor show you the way.' It was the voice of Tehuti. I looked about me quickly expecting to find her at my shoulder. But she was not there. I closed my eyes and waited for the little miracle I knew would come. Silently I bowed my head and closed my eyes in atonement to the goddess Hathor for the recent derogatory thoughts I had directed at her.

'We need you now, sweet Hathor. Tehuti and I need you.'

Then a scene from years ago began to replay itself behind my closed eyelids. Tehuti and I were once again in the small reed boat, drifting on the sacred waters of the Nile. She was smiling with delight and holding up the gift which I had just given her to celebrate the red flowering of her womanhood. It was a lovely jewel into which I had worked all my love and all my skill. On a fine chain was suspended a tiny golden head of Hathor, the horned goddess of love and virginity.

Still smiling Tehuti passed the gold chain around her neck and with both hands secured the clasp behind her. The golden head dangled down into the valley of silken skin between her breasts, and the image of the goddess smiled at me enigmatically.

'I shall wear it always, Tata.' I recalled Tehuti's exact words. 'Every time I feel it against my skin I shall think of you and my love for you will grow stronger.' She had kept her promise. Whenever we were reunited after even a brief absence she showed me the charm, dangling it on the gold chain and then touching it to her lips.

Why I had thought of that now when time and speed were so critical, I could not fathom, and I tried to put it out of my mind. The memory persisted. Then with a sudden stab of excitement it occurred to me that the jewel would by now be imbued with Tehuti's essential ethos. I would be

164

able to detect it as unerringly as if she were here in the flesh. Then the voice in the wind confirmed what I had already sensed.

'Find Hathor and you will find me.'

When I jumped to my feet I was still standing at the point at which Al Hawsawi's gang had split. I saw that one group of ten had turned away towards the north. I decided to follow them first. I moved slowly, keeping to one side of the tracks made by the hooves of their horses.

I opened my inner senses to receive directions from either Tehuti or from Hathor. I felt nothing. I kept walking and then I felt an emotion stir within me. It was a sense of frustration and loneliness which grew stronger with every step I took.

I turned back towards the point from which I had started and the unpleasant sensation subsided gradually and then evaporated when I reached the splitting point again.

The second group of bandits had turned away towards the south. I followed their tracks.

Almost immediately I felt a lift of my spirits. I grew more elated with every few paces I took, and then I felt a small warm hand take my own hand and squeeze it. I looked down, but my hand was empty, and I knew with complete certainty that there was a presence beside me, leading me on.

I ran forward searching the surface of the parched sands. I covered another hundred paces before I saw something sparkle on the desert floor ahead of me. It was half buried in the yellow sand but I recognized it at once. I went down on one knee and brushed the loose sand aside. Then I picked up the tiny scrap of yellow gold and I touched it to my lips.

I looked back at Zaras. He was standing beside his camel watching me. I waved one hand above my head, beckoning to him. He mounted quickly and urged his camel forward, dragging my own animal behind him on its lead rein.

'How can you be certain that she went this way, and not

the other?' he demanded as he handed the reins of my camel to me.

'Do you know this trinket?' I opened my hand and showed him and goddess's head cupped in my palm. He nodded speechlessly.

'She left it for me to find, as a sign.'

'She is so wonderful.' His tone was reverent. 'There can be no other woman to compare with her in all this world.'

We rode on for two hours before we came upon another of the Bedouin horses broken down. It stood with its head hanging, unable to take another step. Its rider had flogged it mercilessly before he abandoned it. Its hindquarters were lacerated by the whiplash and the blood had congealed black and shiny on the wounds.

'Give it water,' I ordered and Zaras himself dismounted to fill a leather bucket from the water-skin that his camel carried. At the same time I also dismounted and took up a position behind the animal's shoulder. I drew my sword. Zaras placed the bucket of water in front of the unfortunate beast and it dipped its muzzle into it. I allowed it to suck a few mouthfuls before I lifted my sword with both hands above my head. The animal was still drinking when I brought the blade down with all my weight and strength behind it.

Decapitated cleanly, the head sprang from the stump of the neck. The carcass dropped to its knees with blood pumping from the severed blood vessels. Then it toppled over sideways.

'Don't waste the water,' I warned Zaras as I wiped my blade clean on the horse's shoulder, and then ran it back into its scabbard.

I watched Zaras pour the remains of the water in the bucket back into the water-skin. I needed a few moments to regain my composure. I was suffering almost as much as the horse had done before my mercy stroke. I detest unnecessary cruelty and suffering in all its forms, and the horse had been savagely abused. However, I prevented my true feeling from showing. If they had known how I felt my men would probably have thought me eccentric and lost a little of their respect for me.

By the time the sun touched the horizon we had passed another three downed horses, and I could see by the increased bite of the tracks in the sand that some of the fugitive Arabs were doubled up in the saddle behind their companions. Others were reduced to walking, clinging on to the stirrup leathers of their companions to keep themselves on their feet.

We gained more rapidly on them with every hour that passed. I kept my cohort moving after the sun had set. At last the full moon came up to light our way. It was so silvery bright that it threw a shadow in each of the hoof marks that the Arab horses had imprinted in the sand. I could pick them out from afar. Hathor is the moon goddess, so I knew that this was her answer to my prayers. We moved forward at a pace that I judged was twice that of the chase. The camels responded willingly.

We passed two more fallen horses beside the trail, but I saw that they were beyond suffering and did not waste more time attending to them. Then I came upon a human figure lying directly in our path. There was something familiar about it. This time I halted my camel and forced it to kneel.

'Take care, Taita!' Zaras called to me anxiously. 'This could be a trap. He may be playing dead. Perhaps he is holding a knife ready in his hand.'

I heeded his warning and drew my sword. But when I stood over the human form it stirred, lifted its head painfully and looked up at me. The moonlight played on the man's face and I recognized him.

I stared at him, so astonished that at first I was unable to speak.

'What is it, Taita? What ails you?' Zaras shouted at me. 'Do you know the man?' I did not reply directly to his queries.

'Send Al Namjoo to me,' I ordered without looking back at Zaras. The man at my feet was whimpering with terror as he stared up at me. Then he covered the lower half of his face with the tattered keffiyeh head-dress that was knotted around his throat, and turned his head away from me.

I heard Zaras calling Al Namjoo to come forward and then the sound of his camel being forced to kneel behind me.

'Come here to me, Al Namjoo.' My tone was harsh. I heard the crunching of his footsteps in the sand as he came to stand beside me. I did not look around at him.

'I am here, master,' he answered softly.

'Do you recognize this person?' I touched the man lying at my feet with the toe of my sandal.

'No, lord, I cannot see his face . . .' Al Namjoo murmured softly, but by the tremor in his voice I knew he was lying. I reached down and grabbed the corner of the keffiyeh head-dress and ripped it off the man's face. I heard Al Namjoo gasp.

'You see his face now,' I told him. 'Who is he?'

There was a drawn-out silence and the supine figure buried his face in the crook of his arm, and he began to sob in broken gusts. He was unable to look up at us.

'Tell me, Al Namjoo, who is this piece of stinking pig shit?' The figure of speech I had chosen to describe him was evidence of my outrage and distress.

'He is my son, Haroun,' the old man whispered.

'And why is your son weeping, Al Namjoo?'

'He is weeping because he has betrayed the trust you and I placed in him, lord.'

'How did he betray our trust, old man?'

'He told Al Hawsawi, the Jackal, where he could find us. He led him to the cavern pool to lie in wait for us.'

'What is the fitting punishment for such treachery, Al Namjoo?'

'The punishment is death. You must kill Haroun, lord.'

'No, old man.' I drew my sword. 'I will not kill him. He is your son. You must kill him.'

'I cannot kill my own son, master.' He recoiled from me. 'It would be the darkest and vilest deed imaginable. My son and I would be doomed to the dark otherworld of Seth for all eternity.'

'Kill him and I will pray for your soul. You know that I am a man of power. You know I am an intercessor with the gods. It is always possible that they will harken to my prayers. You will have to take your chances on that.'

'Please, beloved master. Spare me this terrible duty.' Now he was also weeping, but silently. I could see the tears sparkling on his beard, silver in the moonlight. He fell to his knees and kissed my feet.

'To die by his father's hand is the only fitting punishment for him.' I denied his entreaties. 'Stand up, Al Namjoo. Kill him or I will kill your two younger sons Talal and Moosa first, then I will kill Haroun and finally I will kill you. There will be no male line in your house. There will be nobody to pray for your shade.'

He came to his feet shakily and I placed the hilt of my sword in his hands. He stared into my eyes; and he saw that my determination was hard as any diamond. He dropped his eyes in resignation.

'Do it!' I insisted and with both hands he wiped the tears from his own face. Then he raised his chin determinedly, and grasped the hilt of the sword that I was offering him. He stepped past me and stood over Haroun.

'Do it!' I repeated and he lifted the sword and struck once, twice and a third time. Then he dropped my sword and collapsed on top of the corpse of his eldest son. He hugged the cloven head to his chest and the yellow brains oozed out between his fingers. He began the keening wail of mourning.

I picked up my sword and wiped the blade on the corpse. Then I went back to my camel and mounted up. I left Al Namjoo to come to terms with his loss and I took up the trail of the Jackal once more.

My sense of compassion does not encompass all of mankind. My magnanimity does not cover all the sins committed against me.

In the first light of dawn we came to the spot at which Al Hawsawi had split his troop for the second time. This was an act of desperation. By now he must be certain that his first split had not thrown me off his tail.

I dismounted and studied the tracks to make an estimate of the Bedouin numbers.

There were six horses in one group and four in the second. Every horse was carrying two riders. That added up to twenty in total. In addition there were five men walking.

I raised my eyes to follow the spoor left by the larger troop which had turned off towards the north, and my heart pounded as I saw the small and dainty footprints that I knew so well following them. They had taken Tehuti with them.

However she was now dismounted and I saw from the signs that she was being dragged along unwillingly by two of the Arabs. I ran forward to examine her footprints more closely. My relief flared up in anger as I saw that one of her bare feet was bleeding. She had cut it on the jagged chips of flint which littered the sand.

The trail was clear and unambiguous. I had not the slightest doubt that Tehuti was with the group that had gone north; and yet I knew that my anger might cloud my good judgement. I had to make certainty doubly certain.

'Stay here until I call you,' I shouted across to Zaras. I left him and I followed the string of distinctive footprints. I went only one hundred and twenty paces before her footprints disappeared completely, but I was not too concerned.

I could tell that she had been lifted off her feet by one of the mounted Arabs, probably Al Hawsawi himself. Now she was probably perched up behind his saddle again. Not only were these signs evident, but they were endorsed by the aura which emanated from the head of Hathor that I held in my right hand.

I looked back and signalled Zaras to join me. He brought up my camel. I mounted and led our cohort forward, following the tracks of the Arabs who had turned off to the north, taking Tehuti with them.

We rode up a slight undulation in the desert floor and as we topped the next rise I became aware of the fading power of the aura issuing from Tehuti's golden jewel. I reined down my mount abruptly. I looked around slowly at the vast dun landscape.

'What ails you, my lord?' Zaras brought his camel up alongside mine.

'Tehuti did not come this way, after all,' I said with certainty. 'The Jackal has tricked us.'

'That is not possible, Taita. I also saw her footprints. There could be no doubt,' he challenged me.

'Sometimes the lie is clear to see, while the truth remains hidden,' I told him as I turned my mount's head.

'I don't understand, my lord.'

'That I know full well, Zaras. There is a great deal you will never understand. So I will not waste any more time trying to explain it to you.' It was naughty of me but I had to take my frustration out on somebody.

Even though it was muted, I heard the grumbling and complaining amongst the men as they were forced to turn back and follow me. Zaras silenced them with a snarl.

I rode back to the point where I had lost Tehuti's naked footprints as she was lifted back into the saddle by Al Hawsawi. I dismounted and gave the lead rein of my camel to one of the men to hold.

I knew that there was something that I had overlooked, but it continued to elude me.

I walked back to where the two troops of Bedouin had split up, and I examined the ground minutely. Were there any tracks going in a contrary direction? I pondered. The answer was that there were not. From the point at which they had separated the two troops had kept straight on; nobody had turned back.

However I knew that I was looking at the answer to the anomaly, but I could not recognize it.

'She must have gone back,' I whispered to myself. 'She did not continue forward with the second troop, so she must have gone backwards.'

I checked myself. Why had I employed the word 'backwards'? It was incorrect in that context and my usage of words is usually flawless.

'A person does not go backwards.' I spoke aloud now. I knew how close I was to the solution. 'A person either turns back, or walks backwards . . .' I broke off again. That was it! I had it!

I ran back to where the trail of Tehuti's naked footprints ended.

Because I now knew what to look for, I picked it out immediately. There was another set of masculine footprints which seemed to be going in the same northerly direction as all the others in the troop. However, now I picked out subtle differences.

These odd footprints began where Tehuti's footprints came to an end. They trod on top of all the other prints. Whoever had made those footprints was carrying a heavy weight. Most significantly at every pace the heel of his sandals had thrown a little feather of sand backwards . . . whereas I might have expect the toe to throw the sand forwards.

'The Jackal made those footprints.' I worked it out, almost seeing it happening as I spoke. 'Firstly, he set Tehuti down at the point where the gang split. He forced her to walk forward in front of his horse, following this northerly troop. After they had covered two hundred paces he dismounted. He sent his horse on with the northerly troop. Then he picked Tehuti up bodily and carried her back to where the first group was waiting for him; but now he was walking backwards, carrying her over his shoulder. The first group had another horse waiting for him and Tehuti. On this horse he carried Tehuti away with the southerly troop, leaving us to chase off after the northerly group. All this was devilishly complicated and cunning. I smiled grimly.

'But not quite cunning enough.' I spoke aloud with satisfaction.

Zaras and his men were watching me with expressions of confusion and total mystification, which only deepened further as I turned my back on Tehuti's palpable footprints, and led them back to where the two groups of Bedouin had parted company.

As I set off in pursuit of the smaller southerly group I expected Zaras or at least one of his men to protest, and I was somewhat disappointed when none of them could summon up enough courage to challenge my decision. With every league I led them southwards the warmth radiating from the golden head of the goddess I held in my hand grew stronger.

I knew how Tehuti was suffering by this time. She had been wearing only a light cotton tunic when the Jackal captured her. This would have given her very little protection from the wooden saddle under her or the sun above her. I had seen

173

the blood from her torn feet where she had been forced to walk. The feet of an Egyptian princess are more delicate than those of a peasant girl.

One consolation for me was my conviction that the Jackal would never have allowed himself or any of his men to violate her barely mature body. She was much too valuable in her virgin state. He must be astute enough to realize that he could buy ten thousand pretty slave girls for her ransom price. Nevertheless, I was sorely tempted to increase the pace, and push the camels to their utmost to save her from even one more hour of her torment.

My usual good sense restrained me. I knew that the Jackal might have a few more desperate tricks to play, and that I had to have something in reserve to counter those. I kept the camels down to that relaxed trot, but there were no more stops to drink or rest. We rode on through the morning.

Then an hour after the sun had made its noon I led the climb up another ridge of compacted sandstone and when I reached the summit I was looking down into a wide basin of ground many leagues across. This was a valley of giant natural sculptures that had been fashioned by the winds of eternity. Ramparts and pinnacles of petrified red rock thrust their heads so high that they seemed to brush the belly of the pale blue sky, but their bases had been eaten away by the wind until they were slender pillars upon which their massive heads were balanced.

My eyes were the oldest in the cohort, but as usual they proved to be the sharpest. I was the first to pick out the fugitives. Even when I pointed them out to Zaras and the men they could not make out the cluster of humanity in the shadows at the base of one of the gigantic stone monoliths. To be fair to them the heated air rising from the sun-baked rocks trembled and quivered with mirage, disturbing their vision.

Then a pinpoint of sunlight was reflected off a blade or the tip of a lance, and this immediately focused their attention. There were shouts of triumph and bloodthirsty battle cries from the cohort behind me, but I knew that the worst was yet to come. We were now facing desperate men, and Tehuti was in greater peril than she had ever been since the Jackal had seized her.

With an abrupt gesture I silenced the men and led them back behind the ridge. I left a trustworthy sergeant and two of his men to keep the Bedouin under surveillance. Then once we were off the skyline I allowed the rest of my cohort to dismount, to rest and ready their weapons for combat.

From the pack on my camel's back I took down my war bow in its leather carrying bag and my arrow quiver. I carried these with me when I led Zaras aside. I found a seat on a slab of sandstone, and I beckoned Zaras to sit beside me.

'All their horses are down. They cannot run any further. The Jackal has chosen his ground on which to make his last stand,' I began and then I went on to explain exactly what he had to do if we were to extricate Tehuti unhurt from the Jackal's clutches. When I finished I made him repeat my instructions, so that there could be no misunderstanding.

While we were talking I rebraced my bow with a new bowstring. Then from the quiver I selected three arrows which appeared at first glance to be perfect. These I rolled between my hands to detect the slightest distortion. When they passed my stringent scrutiny I tucked them under my belt. I left the arrows which I had rejected in the quiver which I strapped to my back. It was unlikely that I would get a chance to shoot more than a single arrow, and that would have to be at extreme range. If another opportunity presented itself I would not have a moment to waste in making my arrow selection.

'I am ready, Zaras.' I stood up and slapped his shoulder. 'Are you?'

He jumped to his feet. 'Yes, Taita! I am ready to die for the princess.' It was a melodramatic declaration, but I was moved by his sincerity. Young love has a peculiar splendour all of its own.

'I think both Princess Tehuti and I would prefer you to remain alive,' I remarked drily, and I led him back to join the waiting cohort.

While Zaras was giving them their orders I appropriated the crocodile-skin cuirass and bronze helmet from one of the guardsmen and donned them to conceal my distinctive robes and long flowing hair. I did not wish to stand out from amongst my men.

When our preparations were completed we remounted, and crossing back over the ridge we started down into the valley of sandstone monoliths, walking the camels sedately towards the place where the Jackal and his men were waiting for us.

I took this last opportunity to adjust the leather guard over my left forearm to protect myself from the lash of the bowstring. The wound that I had already inflicted on myself was still open and weeping.

Zaras was leading the cohort. Our men were bunched up in close order twenty paces behind him. I was no longer riding in the van beside Zaras.

Inconspicuous in my borrowed armour, I hung back on the extreme left flank of the second rank. I concealed my war bow under the saddle-cloth of my camel, where it could not be seen by the enemy until I raised it.

Zaras rode well out in front our formation, where he could focus the Jackal's attention upon himself. He had reversed his sword, holding it high with the hilt uppermost. This was the universal sign of truce.

I knew that the Jackal would be expecting this invitation to parley, for we were locked in a stalemate. He could not escape. All his horses were down, and his men were played out.

On the other hand we could not charge in to finish it while he still had a knife to Tehuti's throat.

I had to rely on Zaras to get me within certain bowshot of the Jackal without triggering his murderous reaction. As we closed I was able to study the ground more effectively.

From my reading of their spoor I knew that the number of Al Hawsawi's men had been whittled down by splitting and by the hostile desert to fifteen survivors. I had fifty-six guardsmen, including Zaras. All of them were relatively fresh and in fighting condition. There could be only one outcome if it came down to a fight to the finish. They would all die, but then so would Princess Tehuti.

Al Hawsawi had chosen with care his final position under the towering loom of the sandstone monolith. The rock secured both his flanks, but it gave him an additional advantage. The shelving sandstone roof that extended out over his position limited the range of even my great war bow. I could not stand off at a distance and loft my arrow high enough to kill the Jackal without my arrow first striking the roof of rock above his head. I had to get into closer quarters and shoot on a much flatter trajectory.

However, the red rock was also the Jackal's prison wall. It cut off any line of retreat. He had to negotiate an exchange with us: the lives of his men and himself for that of my princess.

Led by Zaras we rode slowly towards where the Jackal was waiting at bay.

Now I was able to see that the horses of the Bedouin had all succumbed to the thirst and the harsh conditions. The Arabs had dragged the last few carcasses into a half-circle facing outwards towards us. Behind this makeshift and pathetically inadequate stockade the survivors now crouched. Just the tops of their heads were showing, together with the tips of the lances and curved scimitar blades which they presented to us.

As we closed with them I could see that there were at least three of the Arabs holding bows with arrows nocked, ready to let them fly at us. But the Bedouin are not archers of any consequence. Their bows are feeble, with half the range of the mighty recurved weapon that was clamped under the saddle-cloth beneath my knee, ready to my hand.

Now everything depended on how close to these meagre fortifications Zaras was able to bring me before Al Hawsawi called a halt to our approach. I was judging the shortening range with every pace my camel took under me.

We reached the critical point from which I knew that I could lower my trajectory and reach any of the Arabs with my arrow without fear of hitting the stone roof that hung over their heads. I grunted with relief. Every pace forward that my camel took from here onwards placed me in a stronger position.

The guardsman riding in the rank ahead of me was screening me as I reached down and took my grip on the war bow. Then without glancing down I selected an arrow from those on my belt with my free hand. I laid it across the top end of the hand grip of my bow and held it there with the forefinger of my left hand.

My camel carried me forward another five slow and stately paces, before a man came to his feet in the centre of the Bedouin line and faced us. He threw back the hood of his burnous to uncover his face, and he roared at us in Arabic.

'Stop! Come no closer.' The echoes of his voice boomed off the roof of sandstone above him.

I recognized him at once as the black-bearded brute I had last seen three days previously throwing Tehuti on to his saddle as he leered at me under his upraised arm. This was confirmed for me immediately as he shouted again.

'I am Al Hawsawi, war chief of the Bedouin. All men fear my might.'

He reached down and from behind the carcass of his horse, where he had concealed her, he lifted Tehuti to her feet.

Now he held her so that we could see and recognize her

face. His left arm was locked around her throat from behind, choking her so she dare not struggle or cry out. In his right hand he held his naked sword. Tehuti's body screened his as he glared at us over her shoulder.

Al Hawsawi had stripped Tehuti of every stitch of her clothing. I knew he had done this to humiliate her, and to demonstrate how completely he dominated her. Her limbs seemed slender and childlike when compared to the massive hairy arm which he had clamped around her throat. The skin of her naked form was opalescent as mother-of-pearl. Her eyes were so huge with fear that they seemed to fill her face.

Zaras leaped down from the back of his camel and, still proffering his reversed sword, he started walking slowly towards where Al Hawsawi was holding Tehuti. He lifted the visor of his helmet, revealing his identity just as Al Hawsawi had done.

As she recognized Zaras I saw the terror fade from Tehuti's eyes, to be replaced by the fierce light of courage and hope. Her lips moved as they formed his name, but the sound of it was throttled by the thick arm around her throat.

I was proud of her then, as proud as I had ever been of her mother. But I closed my mind to all these distracting thoughts and memories. My eyes measured the range and my mind calculated the loft and drift of my arrow in flight.

I felt the light breeze on my left shoulder, but I saw that where Al Hawsawi stood he was sheltered from it by the bulk of the great slab of sandstone. Only a master archer could be certain of that target: first the wind drift to the right and then the patch of still air as the arrow fell the last few cubits to strike its target.

Al Hawsawi was lashing himself into a fury, hurling abuse and warning Zaras to stand where he was, and to come no closer. He held his short sword in his right hand and was pressing the point of the bronze blade up under Tehuti's jaw, into the soft swell of her throat.

'Stand your ground, or I will kill this bitch and cut out her putrid and diseased ovaries,' he screamed at Zaras.

'Nobody has to die,' Zaras called back in a placatory and appeasing tone. 'We can talk.' He kept moving towards the pair. I edged my camel forward. Zaras was winning me precious ground. Every pace my mount took made my shot that much less formidable.

What was more important was that he was forcing Al Hawsawi to turn slightly to keep facing him. He was opening the target area for my arrow.

I needed only to divert the attention of the Jackal for the time it would take me to draw and loose, and for the arrow to fly to its mark.

Without moving my head I emitted the cry of a hunting falcon as it begins its stoop. My life sign is that of the wounded falcon. I have perfected the cry. Even the most experienced falconer is unable to tell my imitation from that of the actual bird. The rock walls amplified and echoed the sound so that it carried clearly above Al Hawsawi's tirade of abuse.

All Bedouin are avid falconers, and Al Hawsawi recognized that evocative call and was not able to resist it. He cut short his stream of foul abuse, and glanced up to where he thought the cry had emanated. It was a momentary distraction, but all I needed.

I brought my bow and my perfect arrow together and they nocked and fitted like the bodies of divine lovers cast in paradise for each other. I drew and as the bowstring touched my lips I loosed. I watched the arrow climb, reach its zenith. It skimmed the rock roof above the Jackal's head without touching, and then began the drop.

To me it seemed to be moving with a stately grace, but I knew that only an eye as keen as mine could follow it.

Then I saw the Jackal's eyes flicker in their sockets. Impossible as I knew it to be, he had seen or like a wild animal he had sensed my arrow dropping towards him. His head jerked up slightly, and his body began to turn. Then my arrow struck him high in the chest and a hand's breadth to one side. He had moved just enough to disturb my aim, and I knew that my arrowhead had missed his heart.

Nevertheless the weight and speed of the strike hurled him backwards. Instinctively he threw his arms open in an attempt to regain his balance, but his legs collapsed under him and he slammed into the sandstone floor.

Tehuti was sent spinning from his grip. I saw her twist her body in the air, and she landed with the agility of a cat. She rebounded to her feet, and poised, naked and lovely, momentarily bewildered by the sudden turmoil that boiled around her.

Zaras had been ready for the cry of the falcon; that we had agreed upon earlier. As I uttered it so he launched himself towards where Tehuti stood.

He was as swift as a hunting cheetah. He had to run past the Jackal's prostrate body to reach Tehuti. He saw my arrow protruding from Al Hawsawi's upper body and he thought that I had killed him. He paid him no further attention. He reached Tehuti before any of the other Bedouin realized what was happening. He grabbed her and thrust her bodily behind him, shielding her with his own bulk. He tossed up the sword he was holding reversed in his other hand, and as it dropped he caught it by the hilt and went into the on-guard position; waiting to meet the rush of Arabs that were coming at him.

'Charge!' I urged our men forward to protect the couple. 'Have at them, lads!' I goaded my camel into a lumbering gallop, and at the same time nocked another arrow. I saw one of the Arab archers check his forward run and lift his bow, aiming at Zaras.

I shot my arrow an instant before the Arab could loose his. I struck him in the throat just in time to spoil his shot.

His own arrow flew wide, and the Arab fell to his knees clutching at my shaft, which protruded from his throat, bright blood spouting from his gaping mouth.

Undaunted, one of his comrades rushed at Zaras and with his scimitar raised high launched a blow at his head. Zaras swatted the Arab's blade aside, and then used his momentum to sever the man's sword-arm cleanly at the elbow. The Arab screamed and stumbled backwards, clutching the stump of his arm. He tripped over the kneeling man with my arrow in his throat. They went down together in a heap, obstructing the charge of their comrades.

I shot my third arrow and brought down another Bedouin bandit. Zaras turned his head and flashed an approving grin at me. Incredulously I realized that the young idiot was actually enjoying himself.

'Come back here!' I shouted at him. 'Bring Tehuti to safety.'

He lifted her off her feet as though she was a small child, and he slung her over his left shoulder.

'Put me down!' she yelled at him and kicked her legs wildly to be free. He ignored her protests and started back to meet us as we raced forward to cover his retreat.

Al Hawsawi still lay where my arrow had brought him down. All of us had switched our attention from him to the charging Bedouin. I was as guilty as any of them. I knew that the Jackal had managed to duck my heart shot, and that he was probably still alive. But I thought that at the least I had crippled him, and that he was no longer a menace to any of us. His inert body was spreadeagled, and his sword was trapped under him.

Zaras had been forced to run past him to reach Tehuti. Now he was retreating and backing up towards him again. All Zaras' attention was concentrated on the Arabs who were menacing him.

Suddenly Al Hawsawi rolled over and sat up. Now he had his sword in his right hand, but he did not have the strength to come to his feet.

'On guard, Zaras!' I yelled at him as I groped for another arrow, but the closed lid of my quiver thwarted me. 'Behind you, Zaras! Beware the Jackal.'

Perhaps my voice was drowned out by the hubbub of battle; or perhaps he did not understand my warning. He took another step backwards, which brought him into range of Al Hawsawi's blade.

With an incoherent shout of despair the Jackal lunged at him. The thrust was from below and behind. The blow lacked power, but Al Hawsawi's point was sharp enough to pierce Zaras' leather skirt and go between his sturdy young legs.

Al Hawsawi tried feebly to pull his blade free of Zaras' clinging flesh, but he did not have the strength to do so. He fell backwards and supported himself on his elbows. As he panted hoarsely for breath the shaft of my arrow which protruded from his chest twitched in time to his breathing, and a trickle of blood ran from the corner of his mouth.

Zaras' entire body buckled and then stiffened into rigidity. His sword fell from his right hand and lay at his feet. Tehuti wriggled out from the grip of his left arm and landed on her feet.

'Go to Taita.' I heard him gasp to her through the pain. 'I am killed. Taita will defend you.' He doubled over and clutched at his lower belly where he could feel the sword blade deep inside him.

Tehuti ignored his instruction. She stood transfixed beside him. It seemed to me that at first she was unable to comprehend what had happened, until she looked down and saw the haft of the Jackal's sword protruding from under Zaras' skirt, and the blood dribbling down from between his legs.

Zaras fell forward on to his knees. He bowed his head until his forehead touched the ground.

Standing over him Tehuti's face twisted into a mask of anger and she screamed at Al Hawsawi, 'You have killed Zaras! You have killed my man!' She snatched up Zaras' sword from where he had dropped it. She turned on the Jackal with strength that was out of all proportion to the delicacy of her body and a fury out of keeping with her femininity. She drove the point of the sword into the Jackal's throat.

His breath hissed from his severed windpipe, and he grasped the naked blade with both hands, as though to prevent her stabbing him again. With frenzied strength Tehuti ripped the blade from his throat. As it slid through Al Hawsawi's clutching fingers the razor-sharp edge sliced them down to the bone.

Tehuti stood over him and thrust again and again into his chest, between his ribs and into his vitals.

My men swept past where Tehuti stood, driving the surviving Bedouin ahead of them, leaning out from the saddle to run them through with their long cavalry lances.

I let them go. I reined in my camel beside Tehuti and swung down from the saddle. I threw my arms around her and held her until she quietened, and then I plucked the sword from her hands.

'You have killed him ten times over,' I told her sharply. 'Now Zaras needs our help.' I knew that his name would calm her fury and focus her mind.

I did not want to move Zaras, as doing so can often aggravate such an injury as he had received. I had the men build a rude shelter over him where he lay.

While they were doing this I ordered the sergeant of the guards to collect the cleanest and least bloodstained robes from the Arab corpses and bring them to me. I used these to protect Tehuti from the sun and from the fascinated scrutiny of the men.

Then I ordered them to drag the dead Arab horses and the corpses of the Jackal and his men a league downwind and

dump them in the desert. In this heat they would begin putre-
fying within the hour. The last I ever saw of the Jackal he was
being towed naked behind a camel with a slip knot around his
ankles and his head bumping over the stony ground. His arms
extended over his head towards me were flapping as if in
farewell.

I had brought with me my medical pack, and a small supply
of herbs and drugs. These go with me always and everywhere,
almost as though they are part of my own body. But I knew
before even I began to examine Zaras' wound that they were
inadequate for the task that lay ahead of me.

I had no trained assistant to help me. The rough guardsmen
with me were all highly proficient at taking human life, but
abysmally ignorant when it came to saving and succouring it.

The only one that I had whom I could trust was Tehuti. She
had helped me care for injured horses and other domestic
animals. But I still looked upon her as a child. I did not want
her to watch Zaras die, as he was bound to do. But I had no
choice.

'You will have to help me care for him, Princess,' I told her
as I prepared a draught of the juice of the Red Sheppen flower
that was powerful enough to stun an ox.

'Yes,' she responded quietly, but with such fixed determination that I was reminded forcibly of her mother. 'Just tell me
what you want me to do and I will do it.'

'First of all make certain he drinks all of this.' I handed her
the copper cup brimming with the narcotic. She placed his
head in her lap. She held the vessel to his lips and pinched
his nostrils closed so that he was forced to gulp it down. In
the meantime I laid out my surgical instruments.

When the pupils of Zaras' eyes dilated and he fell into a
stupor induced by the drug, we removed his armour and his
under breeches. Then we laid him mother-naked on his
stomach on a bed of saddle blankets. Of course I had seen

Zaras naked before, but as always I was impressed by his magnificent physique. I felt a deep pang of regret that so soon we would have to consign this masterpiece of nature to the earth.

I separated his legs so that I could reach the entry point of the Jackal's blade. Of course the blade was still sealing the wound. I know others who claim to be surgeons who would have ripped it out without a care or a thought, sealing their patient's fate in the instant.

While I studied the angle and depth of the blade's entry, I saw that the sword thrust had missed his masculine parts entirely. This was a state of affairs about which I had mixed feelings.

I silently rejoiced for the sake of Zaras and Tehuti. However, on my own account I was not so sanguine. Perhaps it would have been preferable if these basic organs of Zaras' had been rendered harmless by the cutting edge of the sword. If that had happened then many of those problems which I foresaw looming ahead of me might have been eliminated at a single stroke. I thrust such unworthy thoughts aside and gave my full attention to the removal of the blade.

It had passed through his left buttock. If it had then struck the cradle of heavy pelvic bone it might have gone no further.

This had not happened. I could tell that it had found a pathway along which to enter the bony basin in which Zaras' entrails were contained. I have taken the opportunity to dissect and study hundreds of human cadavers. I know how the food we eat is passed down through these fleshy tubes until it is voided from the fundamental orifice set between our buttocks.

I was by now seriously alarmed. If the Jackal's blade had punctured one of these tubes in Zaras' gut the waste would have leaked into his stomach cavity. This waste that we refer to familiarly as dung is composed of evil humours which give it the characteristic unpleasant smell. These humours are also fatally poisonous, and if set free in the body will cause it to mortify. Death is the inevitable consequence.

The sword had to come out at once. I summoned six of our strongest men to restrain Zaras, for despite the powerful opiate that I had given him the pain that he must suffer would render the drug ineffectual.

Tehuti sat with his head in her lap. She stroked his hair and crooned to him like a mother to her infant. The holders took their places and pinned his limbs. I knelt between his legs and took a double-handed grip on the hilt of the sword.

'Hold him!' I gave the order, and then I leaned back and applied all my weight and strength, keeping the blade aligned to its entry channel so as avoid further damage to his flesh and innards.

Zaras' entire body stiffened. Every muscle tensed hard as marble, and he bellowed like a wounded bull with agony. The six strong men were hard put to restrain him. For a long moment nothing gave. The bronze blade was trapped in a vice-like grip; jammed against the pelvic bone and held by the suction of clinging tissue. Then the suction broke and the blade slid from the wound. I toppled over backwards.

Zaras gave one last shuddering moan and his body slumped back into unconsciousness. I had a pad of lamb's wool ready, and I placed this over the wound and ordered Tehuti, 'Hold this in place, but put all your weight on it to try and stop the blood.' Then I looked to the men who were holding him down. 'Release him!' I ordered them.

I switched my attention to the sword in my hand and with my eye measured how deeply in had penetrated.

'One and a half hand's length; half a cubit,' I estimated, with dread overshadowing hope. 'That's deep, too deep!'

Briefly I lifted the pad that Tehuti was pressing over the wound. I leaned forward to examine the wound.

It was a slit as wide as two of my fingers together. As soon as I released the pressure on it a thin trickle of blood leaked out. It looked clean and healthy. I brought my face close to it, and sniffed at the blood. There was no odour of faeces.

I felt a flicker of renewed hope; was it possible that the razor-sharp bronze had not sliced open his guts?

Tehuti was watching me intensely. 'What are you doing, Taita?'

'I am trying to estimate our chances.'

I bound the pad of lamb's wool in place to cover the entry wound and I dribbled distillate of wine over it to subdue the evil humours. Then I moved around behind Zaras and placed one of my hands on each of his buttocks. I steeled myself and then drew them apart. I let out a soft sigh of relief. His fundament was clean and tight.

There was one more test I needed to make. I placed my hand on the small of his back and pressed down hard. There was a splutter of released gas from his bowels followed by a spurt of watery excrement and bright blood from his anus. The stink made both Tehuti and me wince.

Now I knew with fatal certainty that the sword had indeed pierced his entrails. I felt devastated with sorrow and despair. Zaras was a dead man. No surgeon in this world, however skilled, could save him; not even I. He belonged to Seth now.

I did not look up at Tehuti although I could feel that she was staring at me. I was helpless, and I hated that sensation. It is not something that I could ever become accustomed to.

'Taita.' She whispered my name. Still I could not raise my eyes to her and admit my inadequacy.

'Please, Taita!' Her voice rose slightly. 'You can save his life, can't you? You can save Zaras for me?' I had to answer her; I could not allow her to suffer any longer.

I lifted my head and looked at her. I had never seen such suffering and sorrow as hers; and I have seen freshly created widows by the scores.

I formed the negative in my mind and on my tongue, and I even shook my head. But I could not utter the word 'No'. I could not abandon these two young people.

'Yes! I can save him for you, Tehuti.' I knew it was a heartless thing to say. Finality is surely better than false hope, but I could not bear her anguish and despair.

So silently I begged the good gods to pardon my lie, and I set out to do battle with Seth for Zaras' soul.

All I knew for certain was that I had to work swiftly. No human body can survive such long-drawn-out anguish.

I had no other guidelines to follow. There was no other surgeon in this world who had ever dared to go where I was preparing to venture.

I had one remaining flask of the Red Sheppen that might be sufficient to keep Zaras unconscious for an hour at the longest. I would need all of it.

I would have to open the stomach cavity and find where Zaras' entrails had been punctured. I would have to repair the sword-cuts by sewing them together. Then I would have to flush out the evil humours that had escaped from his bowels into his stomach cavity.

Fortunately, like all of us, Zaras had eaten little since leaving the Miyah Keiv. We were short of food, and I had rationed our stores strictly. His gut would not be full of waste. I had infusions of willow bark and cedar sap but insufficient quantities for the task of flushing out the poisons. The most efficacious of all was distillate of wine. I had only one small water-skin full of this. Both Tehuti and I washed our hands in a single small bowl of this precious liquid.

I had long ago discovered that heat will reduce if not destroy the humours. On my instructions two of my men set a large pot of water on the fire. When the water was boiling furiously

I dangled my bronze surgical razors, needles and catgut sutures into it.

I forced another large dose of the Red Sheppen down Zaras' gullet while Tehuti sponged his belly with the distillate of wine.

Then my hefty guardsmen pinned Zaras down once more. I placed a doubled leather pad between his teeth so that they would not crack and shatter when his jaws clamped down in a seizure of agony. All was in readiness. I could find no further excuse to delay longer.

I made the first long cut through the wall of his belly, from just below his belly button to the crest of his pubic bone. Zaras howled through his leather gag and he whipped his head from side to side.

I showed Tehuti how to hold the wound open by hooking her fingers into each side of my long incision and pulling the lips apart. I was now able to get both my hands into the cavity of his belly as deep as my wrists. I had a picture in my mind of the course that the sword blade had taken as it was driven into his belly, and I worked along this route.

Almost at once I found a perforation as long as my little finger in the slippery rope of his guts. The stinking debris of digested food was oozing from the aperture.

I sewed it closed with catgut and neat regular stitches of my curved bronze needle. Then I took the rubbery snake of the gut and squeezed it in my two hands, to make certain that there were no leaks. My suture was watertight, but the pressure forced the brown and turbid filth to squirt from three other cuts deeper in his bowels.

I sewed these smaller cuts closed, working with a delicate balance of speed to efficacy. I could see that Zaras was beginning to weaken under this extreme treatment that I was forced to inflict upon him.

By the time I was satisfied that I had not overlooked any other damage that the blade had caused, both Tehuti and I were inured to the faecal stench. Nonetheless, it was a constant reminder to me how vital it was to wash out all the humours from his body before I closed his gaping stomach cavity. Anything that stank so atrociously must be evil.

With Tehuti still holding his stomach open I took mouthfuls of the distillate of wine and squirted it through my pursed lips into the recesses and convolutions of his bowels. Then we rolled him on his side and drained the fluid out of his belly.

Then we washed out his guts again with boiled water which had cooled to body temperature, and drained that out of him.

Finally we washed him out with our own urine. This is one of the most effective recipes against the humours, but the urine must be fresh and uncontaminated by any other fluid or bodily substance. Ideally it should come directly from a healthy bladder without contacting the external sexual parts of the donor: the penis and foreskin of the male or the female labia.

With me this presented no difficulty. The removal of the emblems of my sex is such ancient history that their memory no longer causes me even a tremor. While I emptied my water into Zaras, Tehuti swabbed her own privates with a woollen pad soaked in the distilled wine; when I stood aside she squatted over Zaras and spread the lips of her vulva. Then she aimed a hissing stream into his belly cavity. When she had finished we rolled Zaras' inert form on to his side to drain for the third and last time.

Then I closed up his belly, and with each stitch I recited a verse from the prayer for the closing of a wound.

'I close your cruel red mouth, O evil thing of Seth! Leave this place. I command you: go!

'Retreat from me, jackal-headed Anubis, god of the cemeteries. Let this one live.

'Weep for him, gentle-hearted Hathor. Show him your mercy and ease his pain. Let him live!'

It was dark by the time that I had trussed up his belly with linen strips torn from the skirts of my robe and laid him on the litter in his shelter. Tehuti and I sat on each side of him ready to give whatever comfort and succour we could.

When Zaras in delirium began to rant at and struggle with the imaginary and real demons that crowded around his litter, Tehuti lay down beside him and took him in her arms. She held him tightly and sang to him.

I recognized the lullaby. It was one of those that Queen Lostris had sung to Tehuti when she was an infant. Gradually Zaras quietened.

His men built their watch fires in a circle around the shelter in which we waited with Zaras. I think they prayed for him as we did. I heard the murmur of their voices throughout the long hot night.

Towards the dawn I fell asleep. There was nothing further that I could do other than husband my reserves for the ministrations which I knew I would soon be called upon to render.

I felt a small hot hand tugging at my shoulder and I came awake instantly. I saw through the chinks in the roof of our shelter that morning was not far off. I had slept only briefly, but I felt as guilty as if I had committed murder.

'Taita, wake up. You must help me.' I could hear the effort she was making to prevent herself from weeping.

'What is it, Princess?'

'His skin is on fire. Zaras is burning up inside. He is so hot it is almost painful to touch him.'

I had a cedar-wood taper to hand. I thrust the tip of it into the dying coals of the fire and blew upon it. When it burst into flames I lit the oil lamp at the head of the litter and I bent over Zaras.

His face was flushed and shining with sweat. His eyes were open but unseeing with delirium. When we tried to hold him

192

still and quieten him he lashed out at us. He rolled his head from side to side and screamed curses at us.

I had been expecting this. I knew well the burning fever which heralds the onslaught of the evil humours. I had seen many cases that exhibited almost exactly the same symptoms. They had all ended in the death of the patient. But I had prepared my first line of defence.

I summoned my six stalwarts and between us we were able to truss Zaras in a cocoon of saddle blankets, so that he was unable to do more than move his head. Then we soaked the blankets with buckets of water and fanned them to speed up the evaporation. This reduced the temperature of Zaras' body until he was shivering with the relative chill.

We kept this up through most of the morning, but by noon Zaras' strength was fading. He was following the same course that all my previous patients with the humours had taken. He no longer had the strength to resist the treatment I was forcing upon him.

He uttered no sound but the chattering of his teeth. His skin had taken on a pale blue tinge.

We unwrapped him and Tehuti took him in her arms again and looked at me across his wet and quivering body.

'You said that you could save him, Taita. But now I understand that you cannot do so.'

The depths of her despair cut me as deeply as the Jackal's sword had wounded Zaras.

In the time of the exodus when we Egyptians were driven from our homeland by the Hyksos invaders we escaped south through the cataracts of the Nile into remotest Africa. For many wandering years we survived in the wilderness, until we grew strong enough to return and win back our birthright. During that time I learned to know and understand the black tribes. They had strengths and special skills that I envied. I was particularly attracted to the Shilluk tribe, and I made many friends amongst them.

One of these was an ancient medicine man named Umtaggas. Others of our company looked upon him as a primitive witch doctor who consorted with demons. They considered him to be barely one level above the wild animals that abounded in that far southern land. But I came to realize that he was a sage with a grasp of many things that eluded us interlopers from the north. He taught me more than I was able to teach him.

When the weight of his years finally overwhelmed him and he was only days away from dying he pressed into my hands a leather bag of sun-dried black mushrooms of a type that I had never seen before. They were covered in a thick green mould. He cautioned me not to remove this mould, as it was an essential element of the medicine's healing powers. Then he instructed me how to prepare from these fungi a draught which he warned me killed more often than it cured. I should employ it only when it was all that stood between my patient and the void.

Over the years since the return to our very Egypt I have dared to use this infusion on only seven occasions. In each case my patient was moribund, with merely the weight of a sunbird's feather preventing him from being tipped over the edge of eternity. Five of my patients expired almost as soon as the draught passed their lips. One struggled on the brink for ten days, slowly gaining ground all the time until the end came abruptly and unexpectedly.

Only my seventh patient has survived the arrow through his lung and the evil humours that followed that wounding. He has grown strong again. He still lives in Thebes and each year on the anniversary of what he refers to as my miracle he comes to visit me with all his grandchildren.

I know full well that one out of seven is hardly a score to boast about, but I could see that Zaras had about one hour of his life left to live, and Tehuti was looking at me with those huge reproachful eyes.

There was less than a handful of the mouldy mushrooms

remaining in the gazelle-skin bag. I boiled them in a copper pot of water until the juice was black and sticky. Then I allowed it to cool before I placed a wooden wedge in the corner of Zaras' jaw to keep his mouth open while I spooned the concoction into him. I have tasted a drop of this elixir on only one previous occasion. It was an experiment which I have no intention of ever repeating.

Zaras' reaction to the taste accorded with mine. He fought so wildly that it took my six helpers and Tehuti to subdue him, and then he vomited up more than half of what I had forced him to swallow. I scraped up his returns and fed them to him a second time. Then I removed the wedge from between his jaws, and held his mouth closed until I was certain that my precious mushrooms remained below decks despite his repeated attempts to offload them once more.

Then Tehuti and I wrapped him in saddle blankets and sent the others away. We sat one on each side of him and waited for him to die.

By nightfall he seemed to have achieved this state. Despite the blankets his temperature had plummeted to that of a freshly netted catfish and his breathing was almost inaudible. The two of us took turns in placing an ear to his mouth to listen for it.

A little after midnight when the moon had set Tehuti told me firmly, 'He is cold as any corpse. I have to lie with him to keep him warm.' She removed the bloodstained and ill-fitting clothes that I had collected for her from the carcasses of the Bedouin and climbed under the blanket with Zaras.

Neither of us had slept for the last three days, but we did not sleep now, and we did not talk. There was nothing left for us to say to each other. We had given up hope.

The graveyard hour came upon us: the darkest hour of the night. There was an aperture in the roof of our shelter where two blankets had been roughly joined. I looked up and saw that in it the great red wandering star, which we know is the eye of Seth, was perfectly framed.

The evil god was looking in upon us. My spirit quailed. I knew that Zaras had lost the battle and that Seth had come to take him.

Then a strange and wonderful thing happened. The light of the star was snuffed out in an instant. My heart jumped against my ribs. I could not fathom the omen, but I knew it must be good. I rose silently to my feet so as not to alarm Tehuti where she was huddled in the litter with Zaras. I ducked through the entrance to our shelter and I lifted my head to look up at the night sky.

The entire firmament blazed with the glow of countless stars – except in the spot directly above my head where a moment earlier I had seen the red eye of Seth staring down at me. Now the eye had been obscured.

A tiny dark cloud covered it. It was the only cloud in the sky. It was no larger than my fist, but the malignant god Seth had been blinded by it.

Then I heard voices. They came not from the starry sky above me, but from the rude shelter which I had just left.

'Where am I?' whispered the voice of Zaras. 'And why does my belly ache so abominably?'

Then the voice I knew so well answered him immediately, 'Don't try and stand up, Zaras, you silly man. You must lie still. You have been sorely wounded.'

'Princess Tehuti! You are in my bed.' Zaras voice rose with shock and trepidation. 'And you are without clothing. If Taita finds us like this he will kill the both of us.'

'Not this time, Zaras,' I assured him as I ducked back into the shelter with my heart singing, and knelt beside the litter on which the couple lay. 'But the next time I will do so for certain.'

A s soon as the daylight was strong enough I examined Zaras minutely. His skin had cooled so that it was the same temperature as my hand. The vivid inflammation had faded from the punctures of the stitches I had placed in the great wound in his belly. I sniffed the scabs and they were clean.

Zaras was thirsty and Tehuti brought him a large bowl of water. He drank it and asked for more. I was elated. This was a certain sign that he was on the mend. However, it was also a reminder that the water-skins were almost empty and that the nearest fresh water was at the cavern where we had left Bekatha and the rest of our company. We must start the return immediately.

Although Zaras protested that he was able to walk, or at the very least to ride a camel, I ignored this bravado and I designed and assembled a drag litter for him. This was composed of two long lances with saddle-cloth stretched between them. This I attached to each side of a camel saddle with the tips of the lance poles dragging behind the beast. We laid Zaras on this stretcher.

Tehuti insisted on riding on his camel. She sat facing backwards so she could watch over him. When the ground was uneven and rocky she jumped down and climbed into the litter with Zaras: to hold him and cushion him from being shaken too roughly.

During the course of our journey she fussed over him and bullied him shamelessly; and although he protested I could tell he was revelling in her attentions.

On the afternoon of the third day he insisted on climbing out of his litter and walking beside it for a short stretch; doubled over and hobbling along like an old man. He supported himself with one hand on the litter. Tehuti took his other arm to balance him and encourage him. She chattered to him, making silly little jokes and telling him what a clever boy he was. When she made him laugh he had to stop to clutch his belly with both hands, but that didn't seem to place a limit on his capacity for mirth.

When we stopped to rest I examined Zaras' stitches anxiously, and was relieved to find that they were intact. I administered the last mouthful of the Red Sheppen which remained in the flask and he slept like an infant.

On the following day he was stronger and he walked further and faster. I knew that for him Tehuti's company was more therapeutic than mine, so I moved forward to the vanguard of our column. Although I kept discreetly out of earshot, I was able to follow their conversation.

Both of them were still totally oblivious to my skills as a lip-reader. So they spoke to each other without restraint. Some of their humour was ribald and indelicate for a young lady of such high birth. But I let them enjoy the moment for none of us knew when they might share another.

There was one exchange between them that has stayed with me to this day, although they must have thought that they were the only persons in the world to have been party to it.

The rate of our progress had been limited by Zaras' condition, so our return to the Miyah Keiv was much slower than our pursuit of the Jackal and his gang of bandits had been. On the fifth day we had still not reached our destination. I had sent five fast camels ahead to fetch water for us, but they had still not yet returned. Almost all the water-skins were empty and we had very little food remaining. I had been obliged to reduce the daily ration to three small mugs of water and half a loaf of hard bread per man. Naturally this restriction did not apply to the princess. It was her royal right to eat and drink whatever she wished from our well-nigh exhausted stores. I kept a few items in reserve for her exclusive use: half a round of cheese and an even lesser amount of salted dry beef. However, despite my urging she refused to take advantage of my largesse, and she restricted herself to the general ration.

Then on the evening of the fourth day I saw her surreptitiously slip a thick slice of the hard cheese and another of the dry beef from the sleeve of her robe and try to persuade Zaras to accept them.

'You are wounded, Zaras. We must husband your strength.'

'I am just a common soldier, Your Highness,' he protested. 'You are too condescending towards me. I am grateful for your kindness, but I am not at all hungry.'

'Gallant Zaras.' She spoke so softly and shyly that even I had difficulty reading her lips. 'You saved my life, and almost sacrificed your own to do so. I would gladly give you anything you want from me.' If her words were suggestive, then her expression was unambiguous

My heart softened towards them. Their budding love was a beautiful thing to watch. I above all men knew that it must soon be overtaken and crushed by stern duty.

So at last we reached the striated cliffs that towered above the Miyah Keiv, and those of our company who waited for us there came thronging to meet us. They surrounded us with shouts of joy, and prostrated themselves at the feet of Princess Tehuti. Then they lifted her high and carried her to where her sister Bekatha waited with Lord Remrem and Colonel Hui to welcome her.

We feasted for three nights in succession. We killed three young camels and roasted their sweet flesh on the coals of fifty fires. Each evening Princess Tehuti ordered fifteen large amphorae of beer to be opened and distributed to all. I thought this was excessive, but nonetheless I supressed my scruples and sampled a mug or two of the brew. However, I paid more respect to the less abundant offerings of wine from the cellars of Pharaoh's palace. I justified myself with the knowledge that this nectar would have been wasted on a rabble of unsophisticated soldiers.

The court musicians played for us and the company danced

and sang around the fires until the moon set. Then the royal princesses prevailed on me to sing, but I called upon Zaras to join me. I had been coaching him when I had the opportunity. I had been able to give his natural ability a lustre and sophistication which was only excelled by my own. When the two of us sang a duet the audience hardly dared breathe lest they miss a single exquisite note of it.

I went to bed feeling rather pleased with myself. Within a very short space of time I had fallen asleep. I seldom sleep very deeply. My mind is too active and alert to allow for that form of indulgence.

I awoke with the certainty that somebody had entered my tent with elaborate stealth, and in the complete darkness was hovering over my cot. I could hear his breathing, and I knew that for him to have evaded the sentries at the gates to the royal enclosure his intentions were evil and he must be a serious threat and menace.

Without altering the pace of my own breathing or uttering the faintest untoward sound I reached for the dagger which always hangs in its special sheath at the head of my cot.

The starlight was filtering through the cloth of my tent, and I have excellent night vision so I was able to make out the shape of the assassin's head above me. I drew my dagger from its sheath with my right hand and at the same time I whipped my left arm around the villain's neck in a strangle hold.

'If you move I will kill you!' I warned him and he squeaked like a young girl. Then I smelled the sweet milky odour of his breath and felt the unmistakable swells and hollows of his body that I had locked against my own.

'Don't kill me, Taita. It's me, Bekatha! And I am already dying. I came to you to save me. I am bleeding to death. Please don't let me die.'

I released her with alacrity and jumped up from my cot. It took me only a minute to rekindle the wick of my oil lamp. By that time Bekatha was curled up on my cot, sobbing pitifully and holding her stomach. 'It's so sore, Taita. Please make the pain go away.'

I took her tenderly in my arms. 'Where is the bleeding, my little one?'

'It's bleeding between my legs. Please make it stop. I don't want to die.'

I groaned inwardly. So now I had to deal with not one but two little fillies in oestrus.

Colonel Hui might soon have more to worry about other than simply ducking pellets of bread and dates thrown at him across the dinner table.

We lingered at the Miyah Keiv while I waited for Zaras' injuries to heal sufficiently to allow him to commence the last part of the journey to the Land of the Two Rivers and the city of Babylon. This would be the longer and most arduous leg, so I was determined not to take any risks with his health.

It often surprises me how much punishment a young body can accept, and how swiftly it can recover. Despite the sword that only a few days previously the Jackal had driven up into his innards, and the fact that I had gutted him and then sewn him up again, Zaras acted as though he was in training for the annual athletic games that Pharaoh holds during the first week in Epiphi before the temple of Horus in Thebes to celebrate the harvest.

At first these exertions were only a limited and laboured walk along the base of the cliff accompanied by Tehuti. Every fifty paces or so he would be forced to stop and clutch at his stomach, trying not to groan and shrugging off Tehuti's proffered hand.

Despite my warnings and protests, each day he extended his range and increased his speed. Soon he took to wearing full armour and carrying a slab of sandstone on his shoulder.

Each day I ordered him to strip naked while I examined his wounds. They seemed to close and shrivel into pale scars even as I watched. He had a rare ability to ignore and subdue bodily pain. He forced his injured muscles to work when another less courageous person would be crippled and incapacitated for weeks and even longer. In his case this activity seemed to accelerate the healing process, rather than retard it.

However, Zaras' injuries had taken him to the very edge of the void. Even my vast skills had been only just sufficient to save him, and the memories of the other patients that I had treated with mouldy mushrooms were still too fresh in my mind.

Quite apart from the fondness that I had developed for Zaras, and the fact that he had become a symbol and proof of my curative skills, I saw in his debilitated physical condition the perfect opportunity to separate him from Princess Tehuti before the two of them had an opportunity to completely ruin my carefully laid plans to establish an alliance between the Supreme Minos of Crete and my own Pharaoh Tamose, an alliance essential to the survival of Egypt as a sovereign nation.

So it was that on the fifth evening following our return to the striated cliffs I summoned Lord Remrem and Hui to my tent to give them their new orders. I also ordered Zaras to attend the meeting. Naturally I intended that he and Hui would be merely observers and not participants in any of the principal discussions.

The four of us had just settled down to the business in hand, each of us with a goblet of fine wine on the table in front of him to ease the anguish of making the difficult decisions which confronted us, when abruptly I felt a cool draught of evening air on the back of my neck. I turned quickly, expecting to discover an eavesdropper to our deliberations. But to my consternation Princess Tehuti floated through the entrance of the tent on a wave of her particular perfume.

'Do not let me interrupt your deliberations, my lords. Please ignore me entirely. I shall say not a single word. I shall sit so quietly you will soon forget my presence entirely.'

To make herself entirely unobtrusive, she was wearing a splendid dress of rare golden gossamer silk which I had purchased for her at great expense in the souk in Thebes. At the time she had willingly agreed with my stricture not to wear it until we arrived in Crete and she was presented to the Supreme Minos for the first time. Perhaps she had forgotten our pact?

On her feet she wore slippers of silver. At her throat hung the Hathor necklace, and another of sparkling coloured stones, mainly sapphires and emeralds. Her hair was a glossy miracle, exceeded only by her smile.

She was as lovely as I had ever seen her.

With a swirl of the golden skirts she sat at my feet, placed her elbows on her knees and her chin in the cup of her hand so that the diamond ring which I had given her sparkled with lights. Then she cast a sidelong smile at Zaras and tried to appear innocent.

How do women know these things that are so obscure to us lesser mortals of the other gender? I had not informed her of our meeting; in fact I had only summoned the others an hour previously and I had given them no inkling of what I proposed to discuss. She could not possibly have known what was afoot. But here she was dressed for battle and with the determined glint in her eyes that I knew so well.

'Please continue with what you were about to say, Taita darling. I have promised that I shall not interrupt you.'

'Thank you, Your Royal Highness.' I hesitated. Was there any way at all that I could avoid a confrontation? I wondered.

Of course there was. I was the bearer of the pharaonic hawk seal. I spoke with the voice of a king. Nobody would dare defy me, would they? I gathered my courage.

'My lord and gentlemen, I have spoken with Al Namjoo our guide, and with Condos the Head Keeper of the Royal Stables. They have both agreed with me that our party is too numerous to abide here at the Miyah Keiv any longer. I remind you that we have over three hundred horses and camels, quite apart from our men and the royal ladies. At the rate that we are consuming it, within the next few days the water in the cavern will be entirely expended. As you will all agree, this would be disastrous.'

'Of course! No question about it; we have to move on.' As he voiced his agreement Remrem stroked his beard, which I knew was silvery grey but which he dyed bright ginger with henna to conceal his true age. He is a great lord and a cunning and valiant warrior. I love him as if he were my brother, which in many ways he is. However, Remrem does have one failing. He is quite insufferably vain about his appearance.

I nodded my thanks for his support and went on speaking. 'It is not quite as simple as that, my lord. Al Namjoo tells me that the next oasis on our route is called Zaynab, which means 'Precious Jewel'. It is over two hundred leagues ahead of us. It will take ten days to cover that distance. This means that when we reach it, our livestock will be exhausted and suffering grievously from thirst. We will have to rest them at Zaynab for at least two weeks to allow them to recover. However, Zaynab is a small oasis. The water that it contains is insufficient to supply the needs of our entire company for more than a mere few days.' I paused to let Remrem or someone else suggest the logical solution to this quandary. This would enable me to divert some of the blame to the other party when Princess Tehuti cast us all into turmoil and uproar, which she would certainly do as soon as she learned all the ramifications of my plan. There was a heavy silence so I was forced to continue and face the consequences alone.

'The only solution is for us to split our company: to send half our men and animals ahead to Zaynab. The other half will remain here for two weeks to give them a start. We will maintain this separation for the remainder of our journey. We will not reassemble until we reach the Land of the Two Rivers. In this manner we will never be in danger of entirely exhausting the water in any one oasis with our combined numbers.'

There was a silence as they all considered this. 'As ever your plan has much merit, Taita.' Remrem spoke at last in his great rumbling voice. 'And if I know you at all, you will already have decided on the division of our forces.' I smiled and bowed my head slightly in acquiescence.

'You, my Lord Remrem, will take command of the vanguard. This will comprise half the men and all the camels. In addition you will take under your care the royal ladies, Princess Bekatha and Princess Tehuti. Naturally, the Cretan girl Loxias will go with them as their lady-in-waiting.'

'I am obliged to you, Lord Taita. Your confidence in me is most gratifying.' Remrem had the knack of making even these fine sentiments sound pompous.

I drew a deep breath and went on, 'When I follow you two weeks later, I will bring up the horses. I will also keep Captain Zaras and Colonel Hui with me in the second party. I will need Hui to manage the horses.' I looked at him and he nodded. Hui could not bear to be separated from his beloved animals. Then I turned to Zaras, 'Two weeks from now you should be sufficiently recovered from your wounds to travel safely.'

My plan was little short of genius. The princesses would go ahead with Remrem. I would keep Zaras and Hui with me. With a single stroke I had separated the girls from the boys, and arranged that both Zaras and all my livestock arrived in Babylon well watered and in fine fettle. Most importantly I had ensured that my princesses would also arrive intact and untapped.

I did not want to look at Tehuti. I hoped that I had left her with no space in which to manoeuvre, so that she would capitulate gracefully.

'No.' Her voice was soft but distinct. 'I don't think that is a good idea at all, Lord Taita.' Once more I had become Lord Taita, and not darling Taita.

I knew I had been over-optimistic. I reached into my sleeve and took hold of the royal hawk seal which I always carried with me. I needed all the authority I could muster.

'I am so very sorry to hear that, Your Royal Highness. I was certain that you would see the necessity of making these arrangements, as Lord Remrem did so readily.' I produced the hawk seal from my sleeve and rubbed it between my fingers absent-mindedly.

'Oh, are you offering that bauble to me?' Without waiting for my answer she reached up and took it from my hand. I was so surprised that I relinquished it without protest.

'Is it true what they say, Lord Taita?'

'What do they say, Your Highness?'

'They say that whoever holds the hawk seal speaks with the voice of Pharaoh.'

'Yes, Highness. That is true.'

'Look who is holding it now, my lord.'

By now the other three men in the tent were aware that a trial of wills was in progress and they were attempting unsuccessfully to hide their fascination. It was obvious even to me that I was starting to look ridiculous. I felt the frown beginning to crease my forehead and I smoothed it away as I bowed dutifully to Tehuti.

'I wait to hear you speak with the noble voice of Pharaoh!' I attempted a small jest. It was not well received. Tehuti's smile crumbled into tragic ruins, and her lovely eyes flooded with tears.

'Oh, darling Taita,' she whispered and it was almost a sob, 'please don't be so cruel to me. You are the only father I have ever known. Don't send me away, I beg of you. You promised my brother and my mother that you would always take care of me. You are the only man I love and trust.' Her voice choked and she handed the hawk seal back to me. 'Here! Take it. Send me away if you must. I will do whatever you command me.'

Our interested audience stopped smiling. Their expressions became dismayed and horrified. In unison they turned their recriminatory gaze on me. I was suddenly the villain.

Of course none of them were aware of just what a consummate actress she is. She made me appear to be a bully and an utter dastard. In a moment I lost all stomach for the contest.

'Forgive me, Tehuti. Tell me what you want and I will give it to you.'

'Bekatha and I just want to stay with you, our real father. That is all.' She choked back another sob, but that was superfluous. She knew she had won. She had achieved her purpose without once mentioning the name of the man whom we were really squabbling over.

F our days later, in the cool of the late afternoon, Lord Remrem marched with half our company towards the oasis of Zaynab two hundred leagues to the north. I took Tehuti with me and we rode out with Remrem to see him safely launched on the first five leagues of his journey. Then at last we made our farewells and the two of us turned back towards Miyah Keiv. Our bodyguard of twenty Blue Crocodile Guards fell in behind us at a discreet distance, close enough to rush to our rescue if danger threatened, but not close enough to overhear our conversation.

Before we left the Miyah Keiv I had invited Princess Bekatha to ride with us, but to my astonishment she had declined with the excuse that she wished to complete the scroll of hiero-glyphics which I had set as part of her lessons. Bekatha was not usually such a diligent and dedicated pupil. Now I was about to learn who had instigated her sudden interest in writing.

For the first league Tehuti and I rode stirrup to stirrup in companionable silence. Then she asked me suddenly, 'You knew my father very well, didn't you? I know almost nothing about him. You have never spoken of him before. Please tell me about him, Taita.'

'Everybody in Egypt knows your father very well. He was the divine god Pharaoh Mamose: the eighth of that name and line. He was the pillar of the realm, the just, the great, the all-seeing, the all-merciful . . .'

'No, he was not.' She contradicted me flatly. 'Please don't lie to me, darling Taita.' This accusation scattered my wits across the desert, and I turned in the saddle and stared at her in alarm as I gathered them up again.

'It seems I have been misinformed!' I attempted a dismissive laugh, but it sounded flat even to me. 'If it was not Pharaoh, then please tell me who was the person fortunate enough to have you for a daughter. I truly do envy him.'

'My true father was Lord Tanus, and his father was Pianki, Lord Harrab. His mother was a freed Tehenu slave, with the fair hair and blue eyes that I have inherited. They say that she was very beautiful. They say that my father took after her and that he was also very beautiful. They say he was the most beautiful man in Egypt.'

'Who told you all this . . .' I was about to say, '. . . all this arrant nonsense.' But with an effort I was able to check myself.

'My own mother told me. Queen Lostris. Now tell me that she lied to me.'

I was bewildered and as close as I have ever been to complete panic. The throne of Pharaoh and the foundations of my very Egypt were shaking. The firmament was about to fall in upon me. This was the most dangerous utterance I had ever heard.

'Who else have you told?' I gasped at last.

'Nobody; only you.'

'Do you know what will happen if you ever did tell anybody else?'

'Darling Taita, I am not a complete idiot.' She leaned out of the saddle and took my hand, like a mother calming her frightened child.

'Are you certain you have not spoken of this to your brother?' I demanded, my voice rising, shrill in my own ears. 'Does Pharaoh know about this? Bekatha? Have you told her?'

'No.' Her voice was calm, reassuring. 'Bekatha is still a silly little girl. And it would kill Mem if he knew he was not the true Pharaoh.'

'Your mother told you that, as well?' I shook her hand urgently; by now I was terrified. 'She told you everything? Please say that I have misunderstood, please!'

'You understood me perfectly. My mother told me that all three of us are the offspring of Lord Tanus and not those of Pharaoh Mamose. We are three little bastards.'

'Why are you telling me all this now, Tehuti?'

'Because I am soon going to be in a very similar position to that in which my mother was caught up. You saved her . . .' she started and I shook my head in denial.

'Do not shake your head at me, Lord Taita!' She laughed at me. She actually laughed in my face! 'You saved my mother, and now you must do the same for me.'

This much was true. Queen Lostris had been the only true love of my life, but now she was gone and Tehuti had taken her place. I could deny her nothing, but I could at least state my own rules and conditions. She would almost certainly ignore them just as her mother had done, but at least I would have made the effort.

'Tell me exactly what you require of me, Tehuti.'

'My mother was married to a king, but she had the husband of her own choice. She bore his children, not those of the king. She could not have done that on her own. You helped her achieve all that. Isn't that what happened?'

'Yes, that is what happened,' I confessed. It seemed the only course open to me.

'I have lived in my brother's harem most of my life,' Tehuti continued. 'He has two hundred wives, but he only loves one of them. Masara was the first of all of them, and she has given him three sons. If I could have what she has then I would be content. But I have watched the misery of his other wives. Most of them have not been visited by my brother more than once or twice in all the time they have been his wives. Do you know what they do, Taita?' she demanded, and her tone was heavy with disapproval. I shook my head and she went on, 'They play with themselves or with the other women of the harem instead of with a man . . . a man whom they want and love. They have toy penises made from ivory or silver. They push these horrid things up into themselves, or into each other.' She broke off and shuddered. 'It is so sad. I don't want to be like them.'

I saw her face change, become bleak with sorrow. I saw the sudden tears well up in the inner corners of her eyes. Now she was no longer acting.

'I know that you are going to take me to a strange and foreign land. There you will give me to an old man who is all wrinkled and grey; someone with cold hands and a foul breath that will sicken me to the pit of my stomach. He will do ugly things to me . . .' She choked back a sob. 'Just once before that happens I want to have what you gave to my mother. I want to have a man who makes me laugh and makes my heart beat faster. I want a man who truly loves me and whom I truly love.'

210

'You want Zaras.' I spoke softly, and she raised her chin and met my gaze through the tears.

'Yes, I want Zaras. Just once I want to be in love and hold that precious thing to my heart. I want to have Zaras as my husband and to have him deep inside me. If you give me that for just a little space of time, then I will gladly go and do my duty for my Pharaoh, for Egypt and for you, my darling Taita.'

'Will you promise me that, Tehuti? Will you tell no other person ever; not even your own children?'

'My mother . . .' she started, but I cut her protest short.

'There were special circumstances with your mother. They will not be the same in your case. You must promise me truly.'

'I promise you truly,' she agreed, and I could not doubt her.

'You must understand that you will not be able to bear Zaras' children; not ever?'

'I wish it were not so, Taita. I would dearly love to have a little Zaras of my very own. But I know that it has to be the way you say.'

'Every month when the red flower of your womanhood is due to blossom I will give you a draught to drink. The infant will be carried out of your womb on the tide of your blood.'

'I will weep to think on it.'

'When you become the wife of the Supreme Minos you will forsake Zaras for all time. You will abide in the royal harem in Crete. Zaras will return to Egypt. You will never see him again. Do you understand that, Tehuti?' She nodded her head.

'Speak!' I commanded her. 'Say that you understand.'

'I understand.' She spoke up clearly.

'On the night of your wedding to the Minos I will prepare a lamb's bladder of blood for you. It will burst when he takes you to his bed. It will convince him of your virginity and your chastity.'

'I understand,' she whispered.

'You will tell nobody,' I insisted. 'Not even Bekatha; especially not Bekatha.' Her little sister was an inveterate chatterbox and famously unable to keep a secret.

'I will tell nobody,' she agreed, 'not even my little sister.'

'Do you understand what danger you will be in, Tehuti? The Minos will have the power of life and death over you. It is foolhardy to cheat a king. You must take the utmost care never to be discovered.'

'I understand. I know that you are taking the same risk as I am. I love you all the more for that.'

Of course it was madness, but I have done many mad things in my life. My only consolation was that I still had a tiny breathing space in which to make my preparations. Zaras' wounds placed a restraint upon him. He was not yet in a condition to embark upon the wilder excesses of love. However, he was healing swiftly.

T wo days later Zaras came to me and asked permission to speak.

'Since when do you have to ask my permission? Lack of it has never held you back before.' He looked embarrassed.

'Princess Tehuti wants me to teach her the manual of arms, and to instruct her in use of the sword. I told her that I would need to have your permission to do this.'

'That was probably not wise, Zaras. What Her Royal Highness wants; Her Royal Highness usually gets.'

'I meant no disrespect,' he hurried to assure me, and I laughed at his distress.

'The princess is an excellent archer,' I pointed out. 'She is very quick. She has sharp eyes, and good strong arms. So I have little doubt that she will make a good sword fighter. It is a skill that could stand her in good stead at some time in the future. Who knows? It might even save her life one day.' I am not sure why I said that. In the event it turned out to be one of the great understatements of my life. 'Do you have any objection to doing as she requests of you, Zaras?'

'Not the least objection, my lord,' Zaras assured me hurriedly. 'On the contrary, I would consider it to be a great honour and privilege.'

'Then get on with it. I will be very interested to see what you can make of her.' I thought no more of it, which statement is not the literal truth. I thought of very little else. I agonized a great deal over Zaras and Tehuti in the weeks that followed.

Zaras grew stronger every day. If he was hard on his men, he was utterly ruthless with himself.

From sunrise each morning until noon he led his men on a foot race over the roughest terrain. I ran with them. I have been blessed with extraordinary strength and powers of endurance, and I am able to match men half my age, or even younger.

In the beginning I could see how Zaras suffered and was impressed with how he was able to conceal his distress from everybody but me. But within days he was matching me stride for stride, leading his men in the battalion's marching song and laughing freely at my jokes and sallies.

I approved his industry and his constant search for self-improvement. On the other hand there is a limit to all things. Behaviour that is acceptable in the common people is not always suitable to the dignity of the upper strata of our society.

When without consulting me Zaras decided that on the future morning runs every man must carry a bag of sand equal to a quarter of their own body weight, I realized that I had been neglecting other more important duties. Instead of mindlessly charging through the desert trying to compete with a gang of young hooligans, I had to tutor my princesses in the sciences of mathematics and astrology; and I had to write the final chapters of my treatise on the genealogy of the gods. As far as I am concerned, mind must always take precedence over muscle.

While we lingered at Miyah Keiv to allow Lord Remrem and his party to precede us to Zaynab Oasis I had time to read, and plan ahead for our arrival in Babylon. Time passed pleasantly if not swiftly.

For others in our company there were more spectacular and explosive events. Chief amongst these was the termination of the friendship between Bekatha and Colonel Hui.

At Bekatha's insistence Hui was giving her riding lessons each evening. Under his tutelage she was fast becoming an intrepid equestrienne. She had always been fearless, and her balance and her seat in the saddle surpassed that of most of Hui's troopers. These fine gentlemen had always been charioteers by nature, and most of them preferred to be behind a horse rather than on top of it.

On the other hand Bekatha loved to ride high and handsome as I had taught her. She was always able to get the very best out of her mount. She loved to show off her skills and she always performed at her best when she had an audience.

One evening Hui was coaching her in the game of spheres. The sphere was a large and weighty ball composed of strips of woven rawhide. The opposing teams were made up of four riders each, and the object was to carry the sphere between two upright stakes at the end of a marked ground while the opposing team endeavoured to prevent that from happening. It was a rough and raucous contest usually watched and cheered on by a large crowd.

This particular evening Hui was making Bekatha practise leaning out from the saddle to pick up a sphere which was rolling and bouncing over the sandy ground ahead of her horse. As usual there was an audience of some fifty off-duty guardsmen and other loafers lining the field to watch the sport.

Bekatha came down the field at full gallop. She had both hands free of the reins and was guiding her mount with her knees.

Hui was standing on the sideline holding the sphere and waiting for her. As she came up he threw the sphere out ahead of her. She leaned from the saddle to make the pick-up; all her weight was on her near-side stirrup. In my informed and critical judgement I thought it was a most elegant and athletic performance. The crowd roared their encouragement, and I joined in with them.

Bekatha seemed almost elfin on the back of the enormous animal but still she was able to reach down far enough to grasp one of the four leather handles of the rolling sphere. Triumphantly she began to lift her prize.

Then her stirrup leather snapped, and to my consternation Bekatha sailed clear of the saddle. I began to run before she hit the ground. I was sure she was killed or at the least seriously injured. Hui was just as quick and he was closer to her than I was as she was unhorsed.

To my delighted relief Bekatha bounded to her feet again and stood there quivering with mortification and rage. She had landed in a mound of fresh horse manure. This had broken her fall and probably saved her life, but it had done little for her appearance and nothing at all for her dignity.

She was besmeared from the top of her fiery curls downwards with loose green dung. Hui came up short before he reached her, and he stood staring at her. I could see that he had not the faintest idea of what he should do next. Before I could reach him to mollify Bekatha and resolve the crisis, Hui did the one thing most certain to escalate it. He laughed.

Bekatha responded in the only way that was natural to her. She slipped the leash on her famous temper. She was still clutching the sphere in her right hand. She hurled it at his head. Hui was not expecting to be attacked and he was taken off guard. The range was point-blank. The sphere was heavy and the sundried leather was hard as bone. It hit him on the bridge of his prominent nose and the blood spurted in a jet. Even that was insufficient to appease Bekatha's wounded pride.

She stooped and in one swift movement gathered up a double handful of horse dung from the pile in which she was standing; then she charged straight at Hui and slapped both handfuls on to his injured nose.

'If you think that I am funny you should see yourself now, Colonel Hui,' she told him in cold fury. Then she spun around and marched from the field heading for the royal compound. No one else in the crowd of spectators dared to laugh, not even I.

Hui was never again invited to dine at the royal table. He never again enjoyed the distinction of being bombarded with foodstuffs, or of giving riding lessons to royalty.

A few days later I overheard a conversation between Bekatha and Loxias. It was in Minoan and they were in the tent in the royal compound which I had set aside as the girls' classroom. I was standing outside the back of the tent admiring the view of the multi-coloured cliffs above the encampment. Of course I was not deliberately eavesdropping on my pupils, but sometimes when I paused briefly at this particular spot before entering the tent I did inadvertently overhear interesting exchanges between them.

'Have you forgiven Colonel Hui yet?' I heard Loxias ask and Bekatha answered vehemently:

'I shall never forgive him. He is an oaf and a barbarian. When I am Queen of Crete I shall probably have him beheaded.'

'That should be amusing. Will you invite me to watch?'

'I was not jesting, Loxias. I really mean it.'

'But you told me and Tehuti that he was the only man in the world for you?'

'I have changed my mind.' Bekatha's tone was lofty. 'What would I want with an ugly old man with no manners and forty wives just as ugly as he is?'

'He isn't so old, Bekatha, and he is rather handsome. I know for a fact that he has only five wives in Thebes and some of them are quite pretty.'

'He is ancient,' Bekatha replied firmly. 'He is probably even older than Taita. And he does not strike me as rather handsome with a broken nose and horseshit all over his face. His five wives can have him. I don't want anything more to do with him ever again.'

I excused Bekatha's robust choice of words, and her derogatory reference to my age. At least one of my immediate problems had been resolved for me. It was no longer necessary for me to stand guard over Bekatha's virginity in addition to that of her big sister.

I allowed myself be overtaken with a fit of coughing and the voices within the tent stilled. When I stooped in through the opening the two young ladies' heads were bowed over their writing tablets. They were both most laudably absorbed in the task that I had set them of copying a scroll of Egyptian history from the authoritative version which I had written myself some years previously, and translating it into the Cretan language. Bekatha barely glanced up at me when I paused beside her.

'I am very impressed with your industry and the perfection of your hieroglyphics, Your Highness. But why is your sister not with you?'

'Oh, she's too busy out there.' She pointed with her brush. 'She told me that she would come to join us later.' Then she returned her full attention to the scroll she was working on.

I had been aware of the chanting of the guardsmen coming from the improvised drill ground on the edge of our encampment, but this was so commonplace that I had paid no mind to it. Now that Bekatha had piqued my curiosity I left the tent and went out to investigate. There was a swarm of grooms, entertainers, servants, slaves and other non-combatants lining the drill ground. They were so absorbed that I had to prod them with my staff before they opened the way for me to pass through. I reached the edge of the drill ground, and I stood there and looked around for Tehuti but I could not immediately spot her.

Zaras was standing facing the ranks of his men. They were all wearing half-armour. However, the visors of their helmets were raised to reveal their faces. They stood to attention holding their drawn swords at the salute, the naked blades touching their lips.

'Passage of Arms!' Zaras ordered at a bellow. 'The twelve advancing cuts and lunges. One . . .'

'One!' chanted his men, and in perfect unison they lunged low left, and then recovered. The blades glittered like gold in the low sunlight.

Then suddenly my eyes alighted on a smaller figure in the centre of the leading rank. For a moment I doubted what I was seeing. Then I realized that I was not mistaken, and that it was indeed Tehuti. She wore a perfectly fitting guard's uniform. At least three of her Nubian handmaidens were expert needlewomen who could have sewn that together in an evening. Any one of the regimental blacksmiths might have altered the half-armour to fit her slender form. She was brandishing a heavy regulation sword that had been forged for a man half again her size.

Her face was flushed. Her hair was sodden with sweat, as was her tunic. I was appalled. She looked like a peasant girl who had spent the day scything corn or hoeing her husband's fields. She was surrounded by a gang of rough soldiers, and she was behaving as though she felt no shame for her appearance or respect for her rank and exalted station.

Of course I had agreed to her receiving lessons in sword-play from Zaras. I admit that I had even encouraged the plan. However, I had taken it for granted that those lessons would have taken place in private; and well screened from the common horde.

The good gods will readily attest that I am no snob, but there should be limits to royal condescension.

My first impulse was to rush out on to the drill ground, seize Tehuti by the scruff of her neck, drag her back into the privacy of the royal compound and insist in the strongest terms that in future she was more suitably attired and that her behaviour was more seemly when she was under public scrutiny.

Then my good sense prevailed. I knew that she would not hesitate to defy me in front of an entire regiment, and to dilute the respect and awe in which they hold me. While I dithered the opportunity passed me by.

I watched her glide through the Passage of Arms with such consummate skill and grace that she made the hard warriors who surrounded her seem to be lumbering ploughmen. She never missed a step nor lost the rhythm. Smoothly she switched her sword from hand to hand, lunging and cutting as swiftly and accurately with the left as with the right. Her face was a mask of concentration and determination. Her performance was a thing of high skill and great beauty, and there was no mistaking the power in the slender arms that wielded the heavy blade. She made it whisper and sing a song of deadly menace as she moved through the exercises. At the end she stopped as still as an ivory statue, balancing in full extension and holding her sword as though it were made of gossamer, not heavy metal.

'Stand easy!' Zaras ordered. The spectators burst into a chorus of applause, clapping and stamping their feet. Then a single voice called her name, drawing it out into three distinct syllables:

'Te-Hoo-Tee!' Immediately the chant was taken up by the others: 'Te-Hoo-Tee!'

Their adulation was contagious. I was filled with pride and love for my little protégée. I found myself caught up in the fervour of hero worship.

'Te-Hoo-Tee.'

My own dignity was forgotten as I joined in the chanting chorus.

A last a camel rider arrived at Miyah Keiv from the north. He carried a message from Lord Remrem informing me that his advance company was about to march from the oasis at Zaynab where they had been recuperating for the last two weeks.

Remrem assured me that all was well. He had lost no men and only one camel, which had broken its leg in a fight with another bull. He had been forced to slaughter the beast and feed the meat as rations to his men. He urged me to come on to Zaynab at my best speed where I would find the oasis deserted and the surface water fully replenished from its subterranean spring.

I passed the order to Zaras, but it took another two days to break camp and load the pack animals. During that time I summoned Zaras to my quarters and made him strip to enable me to check the healing of his injuries. I found him to be in magnificent physical condition. His surgical scars were difficult to detect, particularly in view of the fact that his dark body hair had grown out profusely to cover them. He assured me that despite the internal laceration inflicted upon it his bowel function was as efficient as it had ever been; and I did not feel that it was necessary to require a demonstration of this claim from him. That very morning I had seen him returning at the front of a ten-league foot race, in full armour and with a large sack of sand balanced on one shoulder.

Our company marched from Miyah Keiv in the late after-noon when the sun had lost its virulent heat. We continued through the night, with a waxing moon to light our way. We went into camp again with the rise of the hot new sun and almost twenty leagues behind us. I was well pleased. I walked through the new encampment to make certain that all was in good order before I took my own rest. It always surprises me how a few kind words from me are treasured by even the lowliest members of our entourage. One often forgets how one is revered by others less talented than oneself.

However, on this occasion my equanimity was shattered by the uproar that greeted me when I returned to the royal compound. In fact I became aware of it while I was still some distance away. The weeping, the wails of despair, the cries of bitter remonstrations all carried clearly on the desert air. I broke into a run, convinced that tragedy and death had struck in our midst.

When I entered the compound I found that the royal hand-maidens and servants were almost witless with terror. They were unable to respond to my urgent questions. I became so impatient with their stupidity that I seized one of the Nubian handmaidens by the shoulders and tried to shake some sense into her. This proved to be unwise. The simple uproar surrounding me became total bedlam.

Hurriedly I released the little lass and reassured her that I was not going to chastise her, and then I headed for the central tent which belonged to Tehuti. When I entered I had to push my way through the throng of loudly lamenting femininity to reach my princess, who was lying on her cot. She was on her stomach with her face buried in her arms. Her entire body was racked with sobs.

As soon as she heard my voice she jumped off the cot and threw herself into my arms.

'What is it, my little one? Has somebody died? What terrible tragedy has overtaken you?'

'My ring! I have lost my ring ... and I am certain that somebody has stolen it.'

'What ring?' For the moment I was mystified.

She held up her left hand with all her fingers extended stiffly. 'My ring is gone. The ring you gave me; the magical diamond ring that you brought me from the fortress at Tamiat.'

'Calm yourself. We will find it for you.' I was relieved at the mild nature of the calamity.

'But what if you can't find it? It's the one thing I love most in the entire world. I will kill myself if it is lost.'

'Firstly get all these women out of here, and then we can talk about it calmly and sensibly.' I used my staff and my most persuasive language to drive the cackling women from the tent. Then I returned to sit beside Tehuti on the cot and take her hand.

'Now, tell me where and when you last saw it,' I invited her. She pondered my question and as I watched her face I realized that despite all the sobbing and lamentation and threats of suicide her lovely eyes were devoid of tears. In fact now that we were alone she appeared to be quite relaxed, even quite enjoying herself. My suspicions were immediately aroused.

'Ah, yes! I have it!' Her face lit up with theatrical relief. 'I remember now. I know where I must have lost it. Just before we left Miyah Keiv yesterday afternoon Loxias, Bekatha and I went for a last swim in the water cavern. I remember that I took the ring off my finger before I entered the water, and I placed it in the same crack in the rock that I always do, so that I would not lose it. I must have left it there.'

'Are you certain? You could not have dropped it elsewhere?' I asked seriously, going along with her fibs and fantasies.

'Yes, I am certain. And no, I could not have dropped it elsewhere,' she assured me just as earnestly.

'Well, that makes it very easy.' I smiled at her. 'Your worries are over, Tehuti. I shall send Colonel Hui back to Miyah Keiv to find it for you. On his fastest horse he should get there and back before tomorrow morning.'

'But . . .' She was taken aback. She wrung her hands with distress. 'No . . . I don't want you to send Hui.'

'Why not?' I asked innocently. 'Hui is a good man.'

'I think . . .' She paused as she tried to find a convincing reason. I gave her time to come up with her next invention.

'It will be difficult to describe to Hui exactly where I left it. Hui is a foreigner. His Egyptian isn't very good.'

I watched her steadily and she could not meet my eyes. 'He may have a foreign accent but his Egyptian is good enough to command a regiment,' I refuted her excuse, but she rallied gamely.

'I don't trust Hui. You know how he humiliated our poor little Bekatha. He will probably steal the ring. I wouldn't put anything past him.'

'In that case perhaps you should rather go back to the cavern to find it yourself.'

'I hadn't thought of that!' she exclaimed enthusiastically, having steered me to the conclusion she wished for all along. 'But you are right, Taita. I will have to go myself.'

'But you cannot go alone. I will have to send somebody with you. Not Hui, of course, because you do not trust foreigners.' I pretended to think it over. 'I would have sent Lord Remrem, but of course he is not here. At any other time I would ride with you, but my back is sore and I must rest it.' I placed both hands in the small of my back and gave a soft grunt of pain.

'My poor Taita! I would never allow you to take the chance of injuring yourself further.' She watched my face anxiously.

'I have it!' I exclaimed. 'I shall have to send Captain Zaras with you!'

She dropped her eyes. She realized that I had been teasing her, and she had the grace to be abashed. She looked up at me and she saw my expression was benign. She gave up her play-acting and giggled endearingly. Then she threw her arms around my neck and hugged me so hard that it hurt.

'I love you,' she whispered. 'I really and truly do.'

I returned her hug, and I whispered back, 'It might be more discreet if you leave that naughty old ring with me, just in case it does truly jump from your finger.'

She reached into her sleeve. When she brought out her hand it was closed into a fist. She held it tantalizingly in front of my face.

'I would trust you with anything else that I have, except this.'

She opened her hand and the famous diamond ring lay in her palm.

'When I return it shall be on my finger, and I shall never remove it again. It will always be the symbol of my love for Zaras. Even if my duty forces me to relinquish him forever, this ring will remain with me to remind me of him.'

She and Zaras left within the hour. They pressed their mounts so urgently towards the south that their bodyguard had fallen back half a league behind them as they disappeared over a distant dune.

I felt only a little guilty at this flagrant dereliction of my duty. However, my guilt was overshadowed by my elation that I felt at having been able to grant this fleeting interlude of happiness to two young people so very dear to me.

I had not expected the two of them to hurry back from Miyah Keiv to rejoin the caravan. They did not disappoint me. We waited at Zaynab Oasis for almost a week before the two of them finally reappeared.

As they dismounted outside my command tent Tehuti whispered to Zaras, 'Wait here. I must speak to him alone.'

They were in bright sunlight so they did not see me watching them from the shadows of the tent. I was able to read Tehuti's lips without her being aware of it.

She ran to the opening of my tent. As I came to meet her, she let out a soft cry of joy and she rushed into my open arms. While we embraced I realized that in the short time since I had last seen her she had been transmuted miraculously from childhood to full womanhood; from dross to royal gold.

'Did you find what you went to seek?' I asked without releasing her.

'Oh, yes I did.' She held up her hand in front of me. The diamond sparkled at me, but not as brightly as her eyes. 'I love this. But I love the other treasure that I found in the cavern much more dearly.'

'I don't think we should discuss that,' I interrupted her hastily, and stepped back from her embrace. 'I don't want to hear about it.'

'But I am going to tell you everything; every tiny detail; because it is the most wonderful thing that has ever happened to me.' She spoke with utter sincerity.

I looked out through the tent opening. Poor Zaras was still standing there with a hangdog aspect; very much like a small boy who had been caught in the orchard stealing apples and was expecting a beating for it. I let the subject pass without belabouring it further.

I was so close in spirit to Tehuti that a little of her ecstatic mood seemed to be transferred to me; and from me to all the others in the company.

The encampment became a happy place filled with smiles and laughter. However, I was pleasantly surprised with how discreet Tehuti and Zaras were in perpetuating their romance. I think that I was probably the only one who knew that it was happening. Even Bekatha, who lets very little pass her by, seemed to be unaware. I was content with and even proud of my decision to be the guardian of their love rather than the

225

impediment to it. I was poignantly reminded how so long ago I had filled the same role for Tehuti's father and mother.

Our stay at Zaynab Oasis was too short for all of us. We had to move on. Week after week we followed the tracks that Remrem and his party had left across the magnificent wilderness. Like no other place in the world the desert has a beauty and grandeur that calms the frantic heart and brings us closer to our gods. This was one of the most memorable and satisfying periods of my life.

But with each march northwards we drew closer to Lord Remrem and his column until finally we caught up with him and joined our forces with his. This was all part of my carefully laid plans, and the reunion took place when we were only forty leagues south of the Euphrates, although there was no indication that such a mighty river lay so close ahead of us. We were still surrounded by barren rock-strewn hills and dusty sun-scorched valleys.

Our one-eyed guide, Al Namjoo, had brought us to the final oasis before we reached the river. This was a place named Khrus. Here there was a cluster of some fifteen wells, all of them delivering good sweet water. This supply supported a populous village and an extensive plantation of date palms and other agriculture. There was sufficient water available to support even the large numbers of men and animals in our caravan for a short time.

No sooner had we encamped than Al Namjoo came to me with an even more lugubrious expression than the one that usually decorated his ugly visage.

'Revered Lord Taita!' He bowed before me. I had learned that since the execution of his treacherous son such obsequious behaviour usually heralded an outrageous request or some particularly unpleasant and pessimistic announcement. 'From here the caravan route to the town of Ur of the Chaldees on the Euphrates River is well travelled, and clearly marked. The river is close by. It would not be possible for you to go astray,' he told me.

'In that case you will have no difficulty in guiding us to Ur, in accordance with our agreement, will you, Al Namjoo?'

'Mighty Lord Taita, I beg your understanding and compassion. I dare not enter the town of Ur. It would be more than my wretched life is worth. I have blood enemies there. These Akkadians are vindictive and dangerous people. I pray you to release me and let me return south to Zuba, there to mourn my eldest son.' He squeezed a tear from his empty eye socket. It was not a pleasing sight to watch.

'Of course you wish me to pay you the full amount for your hire that we agreed upon?' I asked, and he dropped to his knees and plucked tufts of curling hair from his beard.

'You are my father and my master. The choice is yours, but I am a poor man. I have to care for my son Haroun's widow and all her offspring. The fates have been unkind to me.'

I listened to the catalogue of his woes while I considered his request. I could not disregard the fact that he was the father of a treacherous son, and that a son is cast in the same mould as his sire. On the other hand I had forced him to kill his own son. Did that not pay off the debt? I asked myself. Perhaps he had suffered enough?

I am a kind and generous man by nature, but perhaps this is more a fault than a virtue. I shrugged and told him, 'You have done good work for me, Al Namjoo. You may go with my blessing.' I opened my purse and took two silver mem coins from it. These I dropped into his cupped palms. Then I allowed him to kiss my feet and depart.

Four days later I stood on the low hills above Ur of the Chaldees and looked down on the town and on the green Euphrates River for the first time. I was chagrined to realize that the river was wider than our Mother Nile, which until that time I had never doubted was the greatest river in the world.

The Euphrates' banks were heavily forested for as far as I was able to see in both directions. Large fields of agriculture had been hewn out of the forest. After the harsh desert landscape through which we had travelled for so long such an expanse of lush greenery was a delight to my eyes. On the river-bank below where I stood sprawled the city of Ur. At its centre was a large ziggurat, a temple dedicated to the goddess Ishtar, the principal deity of the Sumerian and Akkadian people. This one was a pyramid-shaped building with five terraces of receding size banked one on top of the other. Not only was it a temple, but it served as a refuge for the priests and priestesses when the river burst its banks and inundated the city and its surroundings.

We started down the road into the city. I rode at the head of our column with Lord Remrem and the princesses, and before we reached the foot of the hills a procession of priests and priestesses emerged from the main gate in the city wall of dried red mud-bricks, and came to meet us.

Although Babylon was still 120 leagues further upstream, I had not wanted to arrive in the capital city of King Nimrod immediately after completing the desert crossing. I wanted to impress the Sumerians with our wealth and pomp. In our present travel-worn condition we looked more like desert Bedouin than the representatives of one of the greatest and most prosperous nations on earth.

As the procession approached I recognized Lord Phat Tur walking at the head of it between the high priest and priestess from the temple. Phat Tur was the Egyptian ambassador to Sumeria. He and I had known each other since long before he had left Thebes to take up his present post. He was a diligent and reliable official, so I was confident that the preparations for our arrival in Babylon had been well taken care of. I dismounted to greet him warmly and then as we walked together back to the city gates we chatted together as old friends.

'As you requested, Taita, I have chartered ten large comfortable river barges to carry you, the princesses and the senior members of your delegation upstream to Babylon, as soon as you are ready to travel. Naturally I will accompany you. But in the meantime I respectfully suggest that the greater part of your caravan should travel ahead of you by road to Babylon, to await your arrival there.'

By the time we had settled into the accommodation that Phat Tur had arranged for us in the great ziggurat the sun was setting. I left the princesses and their women to unpack all the finery that they had brought with them from Thebes. At last they were able to begin the primping and preening in preparation for their arrival at the court of King Nimrod in Babylon.

I had explained to the royal ladies just how important it was that they make a grand showing to impress His Majesty King Nimrod as well as the Cretan ambassador, who would report it all to his master, the Supreme Minos in Crete.

I dined that evening with Phat Tur and Remrem. We sat out on the wide terrace of the ziggurat under the panoply of stars, and indulged our appetites on huge golden river perch as long as my arm, which had been netted that morning in the Euphrates. We washed the luscious pink flesh down with several flagons of a pleasant red wine from the vineyards that grew along the river-bank.

Once we had eaten we were able to turn our full attention to my grand plan for prosecuting the war against the Hyksos to its ultimate conclusion.

'As you well know, it is my intention to inveigle both King Nimrod and the Supreme Minos into a military coalition with our beloved Pharaoh. Once we have achieved that, then we will have King Gorrab laid out on the anvil with three great hammers pounding him into annihilation.'

'As always your choice of words is captivating but not particularly edifying, my good Taita. I am not entirely clear as to who is the anvil and who are the hammers that you speak of so eloquently,' Remrem demurred. I sighed inwardly. Sometimes conversation with Remrem is rather like taking a cripple up the mountain. He has to be helped every step of the way.

'You must forgive me. I was using a metaphor. I should have made myself clearer. The Sahara is the anvil, and the armies of Crete, Sumeria and our Egypt are the hammers.'

'Then what you might have said was that we would have Gorrab surrounded,' Remrem lectured me pedantically. 'Your reference to hammers and anvils was somewhat confusing. Plain speech is always preferable, don't you think?'

'Indubitably; and I am grateful to you, my lord, for your scholarly advice,' I replied with such restraint that I surprised even myself. 'However, the point that I was trying to make was that neither Crete nor Sumeria are as committed to the struggle against the Hyksos as we are.' With relief I switched my attention from Remrem to Phat Tur. 'I would very much like to hear your views on King Nimrod's position. Perhaps you might be able to enlighten us further.'

Phat Tur inclined his head in acquiescence. 'I was eagerly waiting for this opportunity to meet you face to face, and to explain matters to you more fully than was ever possible by messages carried on the leg of a pigeon. Of course you know that Nimrod inherited the crown from his father King Marduk who died fourteen years ago.'

'Yes,' I agreed. 'I know all that.'

'The last thirty years of Marduk's reign were spent in rebuilding Babylon, and transforming it into the most beautiful and splendid city in creation.'

'I had indeed heard that Marduk had undertaken some extensive works. However, I doubt that Babylon can ever match the splendour of Thebes.'

'Then I think you have a surprise in store for you.' Phat Tur

230

smiled. 'It is generally believed that King Marduk spent over six hundred lakhs of silver on the project. What is certain is that he stripped the treasury bare in the process of carrying through this obsession of his.'

I stared at him in amazement. It took me some little time before I could frame my reply. 'I was led to believe that Sumeria was as rich, if not richer than Crete?' I shook my head doubtfully.

'Yes. That is what most people think. I have been living in Babylon for the last five years and at first I also believed the myth of the great wealth of Sumeria. It is only very recently that I learned the truth. King Nimrod does not have sufficient funds to pay his own ministers. His civil service is in tatters. His army is crippled by lack of weapons and equipment. His troops are deserting in droves because he cannot pay them. He could not possibly mount an offensive against the Hyksos, even though he is fully aware that by not doing so he places his country in deadly jeopardy.'

Both Remrem and I stared at him speechlessly.

Remrem's expression was stricken. I knew that he was seeing our entire project crumbling to dust. He had been certain that Nimrod of Sumeria would make us a powerful ally. Phat Tur was busily destroying that hope.

On the other hand I was elated. For me the way forward was now clear. Nimrod was insolvent. He was losing his army and his country. He must be desperate. I had almost ten lakhs of silver hidden under the false floorboards of my wagons and in the saddlebags of my camels, and hundreds of lakhs more piled up in Pharaoh's treasury in the Valley of the Kings. King Nimrod and Sumeria belonged to us. I would be able to dictate our own price. Nimrod dared not refuse me.

I had my first hammer in my hand, despite Remrem's quibbling and nitpicking at my choice of words. My other hammer was waiting for me on the island of Crete. The price for it in silver was minimal, but the price in misery and heartbreak might prove extortionate.

The following morning I woke in elated spirits when my head slave, Rustie, brought my breakfast and with it a silver tumbler of my favourite wine. I diluted the wine with rose-water and sipped it as I paced the terrace looking down on the mighty river which has been a focus of history since the beginning of time.

Despite my recently acquired intelligence as to King Nimrod's impecunious state, the magnificent vista of river and distant snow-capped mountains laid out before me and the exquisite wine in my cup, I felt my mood evaporating. I knew that there was something important that I was overlooking, but like a mosquito buzzing around my head it was eluding me and though I tried I could not swat it down.

I took another turn around the terrace and then I stopped in mid-stride with my right foot in the air. Rustie was staring at me in alarm. 'Is there aught amiss, master?' he demanded.

I lowered my foot to the paving. 'Nothing that cannot be dealt with,' I assured him. I went to my writing table and dashed off a few words on a scrap of papyrus. I folded and sealed it and handed it to Rustie. 'Please take this to Her Royal Highness Princess Tehuti at once; and make sure you deliver it into her hand. Then go to the head groom and tell him I want two of his best horses saddled and waiting in the yard. I will be there immediately, if not sooner. I do not want to be kept waiting.' Rustie fled to do my bidding.

What I needed to do could not be done within the ziggurat. I had no doubt that there were hidden rooms built into the stone walls, and secret windows and listening posts manned by minions of King Nimrod or at the very least those of the high priest. I could well imagine with what glee they would report to their masters the fact that I was purveying over-ripe fruit.

I drained the rest of the wine in my cup with much less ceremony than it deserved and hurried to my room to don my riding cloak. Then I went down to the stables in the rear of the ziggurat. Tehuti kept me waiting less than half an hour, but when she came she was gay and laughing. Her lovely face was aglow with happiness and high spirits, and a new and delicate beauty which had never been there before. She ran to embrace me and stood on tiptoe to whisper in my ear.

'Rustie says you have a surprise for me. That's why I was not to tell the other girls that I was going to meet you.' She laughed in my face. 'Tell me! Tell me! You know that I cannot abide secrets, my darling Tata . . .'

'Let us go where we can be alone.' Despite her insistence that she would curl up and die with the suspense, I boosted her into the saddle, and then galloped ahead of her down to the bank of the River Euphrates. When I rode on to the towpath I slowed my mount to a walk and let Tehuti come up alongside me.

'How can you be so cruel? I know you have a gift for me. I swear by my love for Osiris that I cannot bear your torture another moment.'

'This time I have no present for you. All I have is a simple little question. How long is it since you and Zaras returned from the pool of Miyah Keiv?'

'Oh, that is an easy one. It is forty-three days and . . .' She glanced up at the sun to gauge its height. '. . . and about seven hours.'

I nodded without smiling. 'And since then have you missed anything?'

'Oh, no! See! I still have my magical ring.' She held out her hand towards me, and the diamond on her finger sparkled almost as brightly as her eyes.

I did not return her smile but looked into those lovely eyes expressionlessly. After a short period of my silence the joy that suffused her features faded, and was replaced by an expression of confusion, until suddenly she realized exactly where my questions were leading her. She dropped her eyes from mine.

'You forgot to tell me, didn't you, Tehuti?' My tone was remorseless, unforgiving. 'You have missed your red moon by almost a month; and you tried to hide that fact from me; even though you had given me your word.'

'I did not seek to deceive you,' she whispered. 'I just wanted to keep my baby alive inside me for a very little longer. I would have told you, Tata, truly I would have.'

'Yes,' I agreed, 'I am sure you would have told me after it was too late. You put your own life and the throne of Egypt in jeopardy by your thoughtless selfishness.'

'I will never do it again, darling Tata.' Her voice choked, and she turned her face away from me to hide her tears whilst she struck them from her eyes with the back of the hand on which she wore the diamond ring.

'So you say.' I was angry and I did not attempt to hide the fact. 'Come with me now.'

'Where are we going?'

'Back to my apartment in the ziggurat.'

I had prepared the draught before I went down to meet her in the stables. I had boiled the dried bark of the knob-thorn tree which I had brought back with me from the wild land beyond the cataracts of Mother Nile. By the time we reached my apartment the virulent juices had cooled. I led Tehuti into my sleeping chamber and sat her upon the couch. Then I brought the cup to her, and made her drink every last drop of the black brew. I knew that the taste was bitter as gall, but I would not spare her. Thrice she gagged and almost retched, but I was unrelenting.

Only when the cup was empty would I take pity upon her. By then her face was white as a sun-bleached bone and her eyes were bloodshot and swimming in their tears.

'I am so sorry, Tata. It was wicked and stupid of me. I betrayed your trust and I know you can never forgive me.'

I sat down beside her and took her in my arms and rocked her until her sobs quietened. When she fell asleep I covered her with a fur blanket and went down to talk to the other two girls. I explained to them that Tehuti had been struck down by a contagious and pernicious fever and because of the threat of infection to themselves I could not allow them to visit her until she was cured.

I returned to where Tehuti lay and I stayed by her side over the harrowing days and nights that followed. During the days I read to her, played my lute and sang to her all her favourite ballads. During the nights I took her into my bed and nursed her like a sick child until the effects of the sleeping draught that I had given her took effect.

On the third night she woke me with her moans and whimpers of pain. I took her in my arms and rocked her, all the while murmuring endearments and encouragement until I felt the contractions of her womb commence. Then I massaged her stomach to ease the pains and to assist the good gods in voiding the dead thing within her.

When at last it was ejected in a rush of blood and mucus she struggled up on her elbows and pleaded with me, 'Please let me see him. Please let me see my baby.'

Attached to the placenta was such an obscene little homunculus of slime and blood that I knew the sight of it would haunt her for the remainder of her days. I could not accede to her pleas. I scraped the lifeless morsel into my silver wine chalice and as soon as night fell I spirited it down to the stables, and rode with it deep into the forests that grew right up to the bank of the river and I buried it in its tiny silver sarcophagus at the base of a giant plane tree. I knelt beside the unmarked grave and prayed to Isis, the goddess of children, to take care of the tiny soul.

I returned to my bedchamber in the ziggurat. I thought that Tehuti was sleeping but when I slipped into the bed beside her I found she was still weeping. I held her close and I grieved for the pain I had inflicted upon her, and for my own guilt at having snuffed out that precious spark of life which had been struck between a man and woman, both of whom I loved so dearly.

We passed only twelve more nights in the ziggurat at Ur. By that time Tehuti had recovered from her ordeal, and her beauty was unimpaired.

On the last morning I rode out with Lord Remrem through the city gates. Our caravan was camped just outside the walls. The tents had been struck, the pack animals were all loaded and the company was ready to set out on the last short leg of the long journey to Babylon.

Remrem's bodyguard were drawn up to receive him. I bade him a warm farewell. Remrem is a fine soldier and a gentleman but a cubit of his company can stretch a league. An hour with him can feel like a month. I was happy to let him go.

I waited while he took his place at the head of the caravan with his officers surrounding him. He raised his right hand and the horns blared out the order to advance. The drums began to beat and he marched away. I turned my horse's head and rode back to Ur with a light heart.

My princesses with their entourage were waiting on the wharf when I came down to the river. The barges that Phat Tur had commandeered were anchored in midstream. They were decked out with coloured flags and bunting. As soon as I dismounted and embraced my two charges the leading barge slipped its anchor and steered in to the wharf for the loading to begin.

Phat Tur had organized the crews with his usual efficiency. He handed the princesses aboard and led them to the day bed under a sun-awning in the stern of the leading barge. The pageboys served them with honeyed sherbet in gold chalices that were cooled by ice brought down from the peaks of the Zagros Mountains by fast chariots in specially insulated boxes. The girls had never tasted anything so sweet and cold and they squealed with surprise and delight.

There was a fair breeze to fill the sails and relays of oarsmen to speed the barges up the mighty river. On the open deck musicians played, clowns clowned and jugglers juggled. I allowed Bekatha to beat me on the bao board, and Zaras recited his latest poetry for Tehuti's delectation. These verses were not up to the high standard set by his accounts of clashing legions and battles to the death. Instead they dealt with broken hearts and unrequited passion which reduced at least one of member of his royal audience to tears, but left me unmoved and wishing for surcease.

When we were not employed in entertaining the princesses, Phat Tur and I plotted how we could best usurp command of the legions and chariots of King Nimrod. Without Lord Remrem to slow down the proceedings the two of us were able to polish, refine and finalize these plans long before our barge rounded the final bend in the river and we found laid out before us the splendours of Babylon.

F or one of the very few times in my life I was truly struck dumb with astonishment. I realized at once that the descriptions of the city that I had dismissed as wildly exaggerated were rather understated and restrained.

My beloved Thebes, lovely city of a hundred gates, was a humble village when compared to this shining city that was spread out along both banks of the river. I recognized many of the monuments from drawings and sketches I had seen of them. However, depictions of these stupendous works on a papyrus scroll were as ineffectual as attempting to describe the great Middle Sea by displaying a bucket of salt water.

The palace of Marduk dominated the south bank. It was built entirely of gleaming white marble. Phat Tur stood beside me at the prow of the barge confirming for me what my eyes doubted.

'The façade of the palace is half a league long from east to west, and three times as tall as the palace of Pharaoh in Thebes.' He was delighting in my bewilderment. 'Facing it on the northern bank of the river are the Hanging Gardens. Marduk sited them there so that every terrace and window of his palace enjoys a full view of their splendour.'

The gardens comprised a series of open galleries many times higher than the palace facing them. The genius of King Marduk's architects had created the illusion that they were not standing on solid ground, but that they were miraculously suspended from the sky. They were canted at an angle so that an observer in the palace on the opposite bank of the river could have a full view of every single tree and plant that covered the galleries like a forest.

Since Pharaoh gifted me with the estate of Mechir along the bank of the Nile, my fascination with the cultivation of plants has become an obsession. This marvellous garden in the sky made all my own fertile fields seem paltry.

'I love trees and all green things. They gladden my heart and lighten my soul,' I told Phat Tur as we stood together looking up at the aerial gardens.

'King Marduk must have loved plants as much as you do,' Phat Tur remarked drily. 'He impoverished his nation to make his point.'

I thought it prudent to change the subject. The ambassador was unaware that there was a great treasure of silver in the saddlebags of my camel train. An unguarded word from him might alert King Nimrod to its existence, and all rulers are at heart bandits and ravenous for bullion. I had no reason to believe that Nimrod was an exception.

'How do they get water to those trees?' I demanded of Phat Tur.

'King Marduk's engineers designed those water screws.' He pointed across at the bronze columns which rose at an angle from the surface of the river to the highest points on the upper gallery of the gardens. When I studied them with closer attention I saw that the columns were hollow pipes that were rotating ponderously.

'What keeps them turning?' I wanted to know.

'There are windmills on top of them, as you can see. Below the surface of the river there are water vane pumps,' Phat Tur explained. 'The river current spins the screws that are inside the pipes. The revolving screws scoop up the water and lift it to the top of the pipe.' He pointed upwards. 'There! Can you see it?'

I peered upwards and saw the river water cascading from the upper end of the pipes into the gutters that carried it away to every part of the galleries below. Like all beautiful ideas it was so simple. I was mortified that I had not thought of it myself. Implementing the idea would be my major project as soon as I returned to my estates at Mechir. I had quadrupled the production on my fields with the introduction of compost and fertilizer. I could double it again by introducing screws such as these to water my fields. Of course it would not be necessary to tell anybody in Thebes that the invention was not my very own. Everybody in Egypt took my genius for granted. There was no cause for me to disillusion them.

'What is that edifice standing beyond the gardens?' I pointed out the tower of stone that was so tall it seemed to scrape the belly of the scudding clouds coming up from the Persian Gulf.

'It is the Tower of Clouds, sacred to the goddess Ishtar. It also was built by King Marduk, after he had elevated himself to the status of a god. He wished to marry the goddess Ishtar. As you know, Taita, Ishtar is the goddess of love, sex and victory in war. These were the fundamentals most highly prized and sought after by Marduk himself. He ordered the tower to be built to impress Ishtar with his wealth and power; and to tempt her to come down to the top of his tower where he could marry her. Thereafter the two of them would rule all creation as husband and wife. Sadly for both of them Marduk died before the tower reached its projected height of three hundred cubits. Thus Ishtar was able to resist the temptation to descend to earth.' Phat Tur chuckled at the ironies of fate, and I smiled with him.

'What is to become of the tower now that Marduk has no further use for it?' I wanted to know.

'Marduk bequeathed it to his son, the present King Nimrod, whom you are about to meet. Nimrod has neither the wealth nor the will to continue with his father's plan to lure Ishtar down from her divine abode.'

'I have heard men refer to Nimrod as the Great Hunter who has slain in excess of one hundred lions and one hundred great aurochs bulls in the mountains of Zagros,' I remarked. 'If he is such a great hunter is he not also a great lover of woman-kind? Why then does he spurn the opportunity of a dalliance with the goddess?'

'I believe he would enjoy nothing more than entertaining the goddess in his bed. He has the reputation of being a prodi-gious sexual athlete as well as a mighty hunter. It is a great shame that the contents of his treasury do not reach as far as does his genital member.'

I took Phat Tur's arm and led him across to the port side of the vessel from where we had a better view of King Nimrod's palace. The size and grandeur of the building held me captivated for some time, and then my gaze strayed further upstream and lighted on a ziggurat which stood on the river-bank alongside the palace.

This was another vast building, three or four times larger than the ziggurat at Ur of the Chaldees where we had stayed when first we reached the Euphrates. This one was circular in shape, rather than pyramidal. The terrace rose in a continuous spiral around the main building from ground level to the summit.

Phat Tur saw that my attention was now fastened upon it and he told me, 'That is the Temple of Ishtar, not to be confused with the Tower of the Goddess. It is a fascinating place. I cannot describe to you the nature of the ceremonies that take place within its walls. I feel compelled to take you there at the first opportunity and let you watch them for yourself.'

'You have aroused my curiosity, Phat Tur,' I assured him.

'It will give me pleasure to satisfy it.' He smiled mysteriously. Then he pointed ahead at the throng of gaudily dressed humanity that crowded the stone landing place on the river-bank below the palace walls.

'Lord Tuggarta, the grand chamberlain, and other exalted nobility of King Nimrod's court are gathered there to welcome you as the envoy of Pharaoh and the bearer of the hawk seal. This is a show of great respect. His Majesty, in person, will be waiting to receive you in the throne room of the palace.'

I hurried back along the deck to where my two princesses were surrounded by their slaves and serving women. I made a deep obeisance to them for the benefit of the reception committee watching us from the palace landing, but at the same time I reminded the girls in a whisper of the manner in which I expected them to comport themselves, as the representatives of the Pharaonic House of Egypt. Then I took up my position behind them, with Phat Tur at my side.

As the oarsmen brought us in neatly alongside the landing I took the opportunity to study the Sumerian nobility waiting to welcome us.

I saw at once that the women, even the older ones, were more comely and good to look upon than their menfolk, as is the case in every nation with which I am familiar. Their tawny skins were glossy and unblemished. Without exception their hair was black as midnight and their sloe eyes were cunningly painted. They were possessed of an inherent dignity, even the younger ones.

The men were mostly tall with fierce hard features. Their noses were prominent and beaked. Their cheekbones were high. Their dark hair was worn shoulder length, and crimped into tight ringlets. Their long beards hung down in sculptured waves to the level of their waists. The ankle-length gowns of both men and women were made of elaborately patterned wool.

There was no mistaking the fact that these were a noble, warlike and formidable people.

An elaborately decorated gangplank was lowered from the stone wharf to the deck of our vessel and we went ashore, to be greeted by Lord Tuggarta. Phat Tur acted as our translator. I hung back demurely. I did not wish our hosts to be aware of the fact that I was thoroughly conversant with their language. I knew that there were difficult negotiations ahead and I would use any advantage that was available to me.

From the wharf we moved in stately procession, led by Lord Tuggarta, to the throne room of the palace. This was a cavernous room, with a high arched ceiling. The walls were hung with the trophies of the battlefield and of the hunting field. It seemed apparent to me from this display that King Nimrod had slaughtered considerably in excess of the hundred lions and hundred aurochs bulls with which rumour and hearsay credited him. The atmosphere in the throne room was rank with the smell of poorly cured animal skins and skulls, and unwashed and perspiring human bodies. Phat Tur had warned me that the Sumerians looked upon bathing as highly detrimental to health.

When King Nimrod rose from his throne of gold and ivory set on a white marble plinth inlaid with semi-precious stones, I saw that he towered over his tallest subjects. His shoulders were wide, his arms heavily muscled. When he raised his right hand and spread his bejewelled fingers in greeting I thought that his hand was probably large enough to envelop my head. He looked down on my two princesses with a lascivious sparkle in his dark eyes, and I could tell at once that he was not only a mighty hunter, but also a lecher of equivalent status.

Through the medium of our interpreters we spent the next hour exchanging trite and insincere compliments and good wishes. Then King Nimrod retired and we were shown to the quarters which had been allocated to us in the palace precincts for the duration of our stay.

I was pleased to discover that our hosts had recognized my importance and standing, and that they had demonstrated this fact by the accommodations they had set aside for me. These were spacious and airy rooms that overlooked the river and the Temple of Ishtar which stood close alongside the palace. The rooms were decorated with magnificent furniture made from rare wood and exotic materials. The draperies were wool and precious silk. The bed was vast in size and unwelcoming in design. I decided immediately that I would sleep elsewhere.

With the assistance of Phat Tur I managed to induce the palace staff to deliver several large buckets of hot water to the terrace outside my apartment. Then I stripped naked while my own slaves poured the water over my head and body. By the time I had completed my bath the sun was almost on the horizon. However, the heat of the day remained enervating, until a breeze of sweet cool air began to waft down from the snow-capped Zagros Mountains on the eastern horizon.

I dismissed my slaves and lingered on the terrace, still naked from my ablutions. I revelled in the sunset and the play of light upon the surface of the river below me.

Suddenly I became aware of the fact that I was being observed. I turned quickly towards the high temple ziggurat that stood beside the palace. The spiral terrace that rose from ground level to the top of the temple passed so close to where I stood that it seemed I might easily have lobbed a small stone across the gap that separated us.

On the temple terrace opposite me stood a cloaked and hooded figure. I could not see the eyes in the shadow of the hood, but I could feel them focused on my face. I felt perfectly at ease under this scrutiny, but intrigued by the identity of the stranger. I am fully aware that except for the injuries that were inflicted on me so long ago, my body is tall and exceptionally well formed. My musculature is honed by hard riding and exercises at arms. Modesty usually prevents me from employing the word beautiful when describing myself, but honesty requires me to do so in this instance.

Both the stranger and I stood calmly studying each other. Then slowly the cloaked figure raised both hands and lifted the hood off its head and let it drop in folds around its shoulders. Perversely I had presumed that the stranger was a man, but now I was faced with abundant evidence that I had been mistaken.

This was a woman who stood before me, a woman lovely beyond my most extravagant dreams of beauty. Her face was so divine that it caused me exquisite anguish to look upon it. I searched for words to describe it, but all the superlatives of our glorious language paled and were rendered trite and mundane before it. I have never before experienced such soul-rending emotion. Here was all that I have ever hungered for and been denied, everything of value that a cruel fate has placed far beyond my reach for all time. Here was all the glory of femininity embodied.

Slowly I reached out my hand towards her, understanding that it was a forlorn gesture, knowing full well that such magnificence would remain always far beyond my reach, but that it would also remain preserved entire in my memory to haunt me through all eternity.

She smiled at me sadly, an expression of sympathy for my plight and deep regret for having brought it upon me. Then she covered her head with the hood of her cloak, turned from me and glided away into the precincts of the temple, leaving me bereft.

I thought that I might never be able to sleep again, that all my nights from henceforth to the day of my death would be filled with images of the hooded woman. But it was not so.

That same evening as I stretched out in my cot on the palace terrace under the stars I closed my eyes and fell immediately into a deep and dreamless sleep. The very next thing of which I was aware was Phat Tur's hands shaking me and his voice spurring me awake.

I sat up and realized that the sun was above the horizon and a troop of my servants and slaves were lined up behind Phat Tur bearing all my personal trappings and accoutrements that identified me as an envoy of the Pharaonic House of Mamose, and the bearer of the hawk seal.

'Rouse yourself, my lord!' Phat Tur exhorted me. 'King Nimrod is assembling his war council and he invites you to conclave.'

I blinked my eyes in the brilliant early-morning sunlight. I expected to feel jaded and depressed by memories of the strange visitation of the previous evening. Instead I was astonished by how marvellously well I felt.

'If His Majesty is waiting, then tell me why you keep me dawdling here, Phat Tur? Let us get on with the business.' The fact that I was able to jest at such a time was an indication of my light and ebullient mood.

By the time that we reached the council chamber most of the Sumerian military leaders were assembled; all of them in full dress and wearing their decorations and honours. The only one missing was King Nimrod himself. His empty throne at the head of the long table was a warning to me that he intended to stand aloof from the proceedings until I had put forward my proposals for forming an alliance.

After we had observed protocol, I responded to the speeches of welcome; employing Phat Tur as my interpreter. I was still not prepared to let the other side know that I was fluent in their language. Then I opened the negotiations with a titbit to tempt Nimrod to join us at the table.

'Gentlemen, I am of course fully aware that your navy is one of the most formidable on all the seas; your ships the strongest, your officers the most skilled and your sailors the most gallant.' They looked pleased with these compliments, which were extravagant. The Supreme Minos of Crete has a far larger and more powerful fleet. The volume of his sea trade is many times larger than the trade of Sumeria. I went on putting my proposition to them. 'I wish to purchase six of your fine capital ships to deploy them in our struggle with the Hyksos impostor and usurper, Gorrab.'

Admiral Alorus was the commander-in-chief of the Sumerian navy. He was a tall thin man with streaks of white in his carefully curled beard, very dark rings under his eyes, and crooked teeth spotted with decay. He acknowledged my request with a raised eyebrow and a chuckle, not derisive but mildly amused.

'My Lord Taita, I know that King Nimrod applauds your warlike intentions towards our common enemy. I also know that I speak with His Majesty's voice when I remind you of the fact that a single ship of war is a costly item and as for a fleet of that number . . .' He broke off with an expressive shake of his head.

'Nothing worthwhile is ever cheap,' I agreed with him. 'My Pharaoh is as well aware of that as your King Nimrod. Egypt is in an unenviable position. The Hyksos control the Nile River northwards from Akhenaten as far as the Middle Sea. We do not have sea-going ships of war with which to oppose the Hyksos usurper Gorrab. We have only river galleys, and these are locked in the Nile. If we were able to launch a surprise offensive on his fleet in the open sea what havoc we might be able to wreak.'

I took from my sleeve a papyrus scroll and placed it on the table between us. Admiral Alorus glanced at it casually, but when he realized that on it I had listed the names and specifications of six of the major Sumerian battle galleys he snatched up the scroll and studied it avidly. At last he looked up at me over the top of the papyrus.

'Where did you get this information?' he demanded brusquely. 'It is all highly confidential.' It was my turn to shrug and shake my head as though I could not understand the question. Phat Tur's agents had of course prepared the list for us.

'Would you be agreeable to selling those vessels to us?' I spoke quietly and reasonably. 'And if so, what price would King Nimrod consider acceptable.'

'I beg your indulgence.' Alorus stood up and bowed to me. 'Naturally I shall have to consult His Majesty before I can answer those questions.' He hurried from the council chamber, and it was almost an hour by the water clock standing against the facing wall before he returned.

'King Nimrod wishes me to inform you that those particular vessels that you have selected cost one hundred and fifty silver deben each to build and launch. If he were to sell them to you, which is highly unlikely, he could not consider a lesser price than that,' Admiral Alorus announced. I made a quick calculation while Phat Tur was still translating the offer. There are ten thousand deben in a lakh of silver. I had sufficient metal in one saddlebag to purchase forty warships, but my counter offer to Alorus was for seventy-five silver deben a ship. Alorus left the room a second time to speak to the king, and when Nimrod returned with him I knew that he was an eager seller at my price.

His Majesty and I haggled like Arabian horse traders for the remainder of the morning and most of the afternoon. Finally we settled on a price of five hundred deben of silver for all six ships delivered to me at the Sumerian port of Sidon on the eastern coast of the Middle Sea by the end of the month of Phamenoth.

Delighted with what he considered a shrewd deal, King Nimrod invited me and my princesses to a special banquet that evening to celebrate our agreement.

As we left the council chamber Phat Tur was at my side and he murmured just loud enough for me to hear, 'I promised to take you to visit the Temple of Ishtar. The temple never closes so we can go there whenever you wish. We have several hours to pass before the royal banquet this evening.'

I was as well pleased by the acquisition of the warships from Nimrod as he was to sell them to me. I had been prepared to pay double that amount. Consequently I was in such a jovial mood that I responded at once to Phat Tur's suggestion, 'If it is as instructive and interesting as you have suggested then let us visit the temple at once.'

We left the palace and as we walked along the waterfront of the river towards the Temple of Ishtar, Phat Tur reminded me of the history of the temple.

'As I have already told you King Marduk had over one hundred wives and concubines, but his grand passion was for the goddess Ishtar. First he built the temple to win her favour, and when that proved insufficient to tempt her he started work on the great tower on the other bank.' Both of us turned to contemplate the top of the unfinished tower, which showed even above the upper gallery of the magnificent Hanging Gardens. 'I have already described how Marduk died before his passion for the goddess could be consummated. Although Marduk's affections were concentrated on a single object, those of Nimrod his son are much more widely disseminated. It is his boast that before he dies he wishes to have carnal knowledge of every nubile woman in Sumeria: young or old; married or virginal.'

'That is not an entirely unreasonable ambition for a king to entertain,' I remarked with a straight face. 'As with his hunting exploits, it seems that Nimrod is more concerned with numbers than quality. But are not his eyes larger than his other bodily organs?'

'It is a well-known fact that King Nimrod is insatiable.' Phat Tur shook his head. 'So far he is unfaltering in his resolve.'

'But I do not understand how this relates to his father's temple,' I encouraged him.

'Within six months of King Nimrod's ascent to the throne he passed an ordinance which compels every woman in the kingdom to sit in the temple for one day in her life. For a fee no matter how great or how small she must have intercourse with any man who asks her, be he friend, enemy or stranger. No woman may refuse, and no husband may forbid this union.'

'Does that mean that King Nimrod must stand in line with all his subjects to take his pick of the ladies on offer?' I asked. Phat Tur smiled knowingly and shook his head.

'According to the royal ordinance, the women must take up their stations at sunrise but only one man is allowed to enter the temple before noon to make his selections. No doubt you are able to guess who that man might be.' He gave me a conspiratorial grin. 'After the noon hour any other Sumerian citizen may enter to take his pick of the women who remain within.'

By the time that we reached the front entrance of the temple it was late afternoon. There was a line of fifty men, or maybe more, waiting their turn to enter the main gate of the sacred precincts. Some of them were off-duty soldiers or sailors; others wore the white skullcaps that distinguished them as lawyers, or the blood-smeared black robe that was the uniform of the physician. The remainder were a motley crew of both old and young, and of every class in the kingdom from nobleman to labourer.

'The priests and priestesses of the goddess are distinguished by their green robes,' Phat Tur explained. 'That is one of them.' He pointed out the man who had come through the gateway and was hurrying towards us. 'His name is Onyos and I have arranged for him to guide us through the temple, and to explain the mysteries to you.'

Onyos greeted us respectfully and then led us to a barred wicket gate set in the wall to one side of the main gates. At our approach the wicket was opened from within, and we passed through it into the main nave of the temple.

This was so vast that the arched ceiling high above us was shrouded in gloom and shadows. A single ray of sunlight burned down from above and lit the golden statue of the goddess that stood in the centre of the floor.

'There is an enormous bronze mirror on the temple roof.' Phat Tur anticipated my question. 'It is set on wheels and turned by ten slaves to follow the path of the sun from dawn to dusk, and reflect its rays down upon the statue.' The effect was magnificent and from the blazing statue splinters of moving light were thrown on to the walls of the nave.

'Have you taken note of the murals, Lord Taita?' Phat Tur

asked. 'They do say it took two hundred artists twenty years to paint them.'

'They are astonishing,' I conceded reluctantly. 'There is nothing to match these in any other temple I have visited; not even in the funerary temple of Pharaoh Mamose.' I had designed the murals in Mamose's tomb so I was insincere in making such a ridiculous comparison.

'The subjects are fascinating, as I am sure you will agree?' Phat Tur was displaying an almost proprietary pride in the artwork. 'All the ardent passions of the goddess Ishtar are depicted here.' He pointed them out one after the other. 'War . . .'

Armoured legions marched in battle array across the high temple walls. Chariots wheeled and charged in storms of dust. Flights of arrows filled the skies. Cities burned and hordes of refugees fled before the rampaging armies. Weeping women held up their dead children, and pleaded for mercy from the conquerors. Great warships with rams of burnished bronze stove in the sides of lesser craft and hurled their crews into a sea already strewn with floating wreckage and corpses. Above the battlefield the goddess flew, pointing at the victors and condemning the vanquished.

'War, love and sex . . .' Phat Tur turned slowly, pointing to the other walls and then bending backwards to draw my attention to the arched and vaulted ceiling fifty cubits above us. 'No other temple that I have ever heard of contains such a display of erotic and venereal art.'

I followed the sweep of his arms. Wherever I looked were graphic depictions of spurting men and gushing women locked in wanton embrace; or of some god with monstrous genitalia buried deeply in one of the bodily orifices of a goddess. Floating on a sea of steaming sperm and feminine ejaculants, the participants were eternally frozen in their voluptuous contortions.

Over all of them hovered Ishtar on shining white wings, her

lovely head encircled in a nimbus of fire, exhorting them to ever greater abandon.

Phat Tur and I circled the nave slowly, marvelling at the imagination of the apocryphal two hundred artists who had laboured twenty years to conjure up these monumental works.

At intervals along each wall of the nave were large cubicles or booths. I counted fourteen of these adjuncts: seven on each side of the nave. We were unable to see into the doorways of these compartments because they were jammed with humanity, both men and women staring with fascination into the recesses beyond. I knew that Phat Tur was waiting for me to ask the question as to what was taking place within, but I declined to abandon my dignity. At last he spoke to our green-robed guide, and the priest led us to the nearest stall and with his staff fell upon the idlers who were crowded in the entrance, urging them in a loud voice to: 'Make way for the honoured guests of King Nimrod!' With sullen expressions and muttered protests the crowd opened for us and closed behind us again when we reached the front rank. From there we had an uninterrupted view into the interior of the stall.

Placed around the walls of the circular inner room were mattresses covered with woven woollen blankets in bright colours.

'Fourteen compartments each with fourteen women on fourteen beds. Fourteen is the magical number of the goddess Ishtar to whom all this frantic activity is dedicated,' Phat Tur explained gleefully. I knew he was a devotee of the goddess Hathor, and that he had scant respect for any other deity.

I peered into the chamber and counted the women to check his statement. His numbers were correct. However, none of the fourteen females on display were particularly attractive. Most of them were past even middle age, and a few of them were downright repulsive. I remarked on this to Phat Tur, and he agreed readily with my opinion.

'King Nimrod has already made his choice of all the young and pretty ones. He has skimmed the cream from the jug, and picked the ripest cherries from the bough. These sorry creatures that remain are his rejects.'

I switched my attention back to the women in the room. Five of these were sitting cross-legged, each on her own mattress. They were all wearing crowns of red roses on their heads. This was their only clothing; otherwise they were naked. They waited patiently, with downcast eyes.

'The red rose is the flower of the goddess.' Phat Tur explained their head-dresses.

The remaining nine mattresses were occupied by the women who had discarded their floral crowns and were flagrantly coupling with men who were also in various stages of undress. The men grunted as they lunged into them, and the women under them chanted praises to the goddess as they received and reciprocated their devout ardour in full measure.

With mounting distaste I watched one of the men suddenly arch his back in a paroxysm of ecstasy and with a long shuddering cry topple off the female creature under him. His partner immediately rose to her feet, picked up her robe that lay at the head of the mattress, and pulled it over her head. She paused only to throw the small copper coin that the man must have paid her into his face, and then, weeping silently, she pushed her way through the spellbound crowd in the doorway and ran out into the street beyond the temple gates.

Standing behind me was a sailor. He elbowed me to one side and stepped into the stall. He went to one of the crowned women sitting there.

'I call upon you to pay your debt to the goddess,' he challenged her, and he tossed a coin into her lap. She looked up at him dispassionately as he pulled his kilt up above his waist and with his free hand worked his member vigorously into full arousal. His belly was protuberant and covered with a dense carpet of black hair. The woman grimaced as she removed the floral crown from her head and lay back on the mattress, letting her knees fall apart.

I took Phat Tur by the arm and drew him out of the throng of spectators, and then led him firmly towards the temple gates.

The spectacle of sordid little people performing a grotesque parody of something so essentially beautiful inclines me towards melancholy rather than pleasure.

I spent the afternoon of the following day with Nimrod, after he had returned from his morning devotions in the Temple of Ishtar. The king was attended by his military staff and senior advisers during our deliberations.

Lord Remrem and I were trying to persuade them to pursue the campaign against the Hyksos with more determination and vigour. But once a military machine has lost its direction and momentum, it is extremely difficult to get the wheels turning again.

What it all hinged upon was Nimrod's lack of funds. The amount that I had paid him for the flotilla of six warships was insignificant when compared to his needs. Despite the fact that he had bled his citizens white with taxation, Nimrod had not been able to pay his army and navy for almost two years. Their weapons, chariots and other equipment were in ruinous condition. His remaining troops were on the verge of mutiny.

For Pharaoh and our very Egypt the situation was teetering on the brink of catastrophe. If Sumeria failed us then our entire eastern front would be exposed. Somehow I had to find a way to bail King Nimrod out of his predicament. Not for his sake, but for our own national survival.

I had calculated that King Nimrod needed a minimum of thirty lakhs of silver for Sumeria to become once more a military force of any consequence.

The crisis that I had to avert was double-pronged. Nimrod

was the one prong and, although I hated to admit it, my own beloved Pharaoh was the second prong. Nimrod was destitute; while Memnon Tamose was wallowing in an ocean of silver. Nimrod had grown resigned to his state of penury, while Pharaoh was a newly rich skinflint. He was sitting on a fabulous treasure of almost six hundred lakhs of silver. It meant nothing that I alone and almost unaided had won that treasure for him. The treasure was his, but I knew my Mem so very well. I had raised him from early childhood and taught him everything he knew. I had taught him that silver is bitter hard to win and ridiculously easy to spend. Now somehow I had to make him unlearn my lesson. I had to get him to part with thirty lakhs of silver and give it to a man whom he did not know and did not trust. I was not at all certain that I trusted Nimrod myself. However, I knew that we had no choice. We had to trust him if our very Egypt was to survive.

After a challenging day spent in the company of King Nimrod and his staff, I retired to my own quarters early that evening. I dined alone on a single ripe fig and a little cheese and hard bread, for I had no appetite. Of course, I poured myself a few drops of wine, but the first sip tasted like raw vinegar. I pushed the goblet away and concentrated my mind on composing a message to Mem; a message that I must fit on to a scrap of light parchment that a pigeon could carry back to Thebes for me, a message which must convince Pharaoh Tamose to commit an act which he would consider to be abysmal folly.

Many hours later I had discarded my sixth draft of the message, and I was desperate. Bear in mind that I am a man who deals in words, but still I could not find the words which would convince Pharaoh. I knew that I had failed before I had even begun. I straightened my cramped legs and stood up from my writing table. I crossed to the doorway that led out on to the terrace. I looked up at the new moon and saw by its height that it was well past midnight.

While I watched, a cloud no larger than my hand drifted across the moon and plunged the world around me into darkness. I thought that loss of the moonlight must surely intensify my distress. But miraculously it had completely the opposite effect on my mood. I felt a sense of deep calm come over me, displacing the despair which had gripped me the moment before.

Then I heard a voice call my name. It was a quiet voice but clear as the piping of a thrush at the first light of dawn; so clear that I looked around me to find who had spoken. I was alone.

Suddenly the solution to my predicament presented itself to me full-blown. I wondered how I could have hesitated.

I held the hawk seal. I held all the powers of Pharaoh in my one hand. I knew that to rescue my country from disaster and my Pharaoh from ruin I must exert those powers. Even if my actions ran contrary to Pharaoh's will; even if they invoked his fury.

As I made the decision, I wondered from where and from whom guidance had come. The solution was so alien to my deeply ingrained loyalties and creed of behaviour that I realized, with a pious sense of awe, that the decision had not been mine alone.

The little cloud that had shrouded the moon passed on and once again the soft lunar light burst forth to bathe the midnight world. It glowed on the marble walls of Ishtar's temple.

The hooded lady was there on the terrace opposite where I stood, exactly where I had last seen her. As before, the hood of her silver-grey robe covered her face. I knew then from whence my inspiration had come.

I wanted desperately to see her face again. In some miraculous fashion she sensed my need. With a toss of her head she threw the hood back over her shoulders and her features were revealed. Her face was paler than the moonlight that played on it. She was lovelier than I remembered, more beautiful than anything I had ever seen or imagined.

I reached out with both my hands towards her across the deep void that divided us. But her expression became remote and sad. She receded from me. She faded away gradually into the night until she was gone, and the moonlight faded with her.

In the morning when Phat Tur came to my apartment I was fully dressed and waiting for him. My strength and determination had been bolstered, and I felt supremely confident. I walked through the halls and passages of the palace with such a light and eager step that Lord Remrem, Phat Tur and the rest of my entourage had to hurry to keep up with me.

Nimrod's throne was empty when we entered the council chamber. However the room was filled with his councillors and military commanders. They stood to welcome me to the long table, and shortly after we had taken our seats the trumpeters outside the main doors sounded a fanfare.

King Nimrod paced into the room in solemn state. My first thought when I saw him this early in the day was that he had foregone his cream-skimming and cherry-picking in the Temple of Ishtar to be with us.

I was conscious of the respect which he was according to me, and this reinforced my confidence in what I was about to do. We went through the observation of royal protocol and then I came to my feet and addressed the king directly.

'Your Majesty, I have a proposal which is so sensitive and confidential that I would like to restrict it to your royal person and to that of your single most trusted confidant. I give you my assurance that my offer will be very much to our mutual benefit and will go a long way towards resolving the predicament in which we find ourselves at this moment.'

Nimrod was clearly taken aback and for a while he tried to avoid making a decision, but I would not countenance an alternative and at last he yielded to my urgings.

I kept Lord Remrem at my right hand and Phat Tur at my left to translate. Nimrod gestured at Admiral Alorus to remain at the table. Then he dismissed the rest of his staff.

When only the five of us remained in the chamber I removed the hawk seal from the sleeve of my robe and placed it on the table between us.

'I am sure that Your Majesty is aware of the significance of this token.'

'Although this is the first time I have actually laid eyes upon it, I understand that this is the hawk seal which confirms that you speak with the voice and authority of Pharaoh Tamose of Egypt.'

'That is correct, Majesty.'

King Nimrod fastened his cold dark eyes upon me. He said nothing more but waited with the intensity of a leopard at the waterhole sensing the approach of its prey. I regarded him every bit as intently.

'Your Majesty, you and I both are battle-tempered warriors, with the experience and wisdom to know that wars are won not only with a gallant spirit and a keen blade, but also with the weight of silver we are able to hurl against the foe.'

'I have never heard it expressed in those terms before, but they are wise words you speak and infused with the truth.' Nimrod spoke quietly.

'In the name of Pharaoh Tamose of Egypt and by the authority of the hawk seal which I bear I offer you silver to the weight and value of thirty lakhs on the single condition that you enter into a military alliance with Egypt and that you employ this bounty exclusively on the destruction of King Gorrab and his Hyksos horde.'

I heard Remrem draw breath sharply beside me. He knew that I did not have Pharaoh's sanction for this offer; and he realized what a risk I was taking. But I did not deign to glance at him. Nimrod rocked back in his throne and he stared at me in silent disbelief. I saw a rash of tiny sweat drops ooze from the skin of his forehead beneath the rim of his crown.

When at last he spoke his voice was hoarse with incredulity and avarice. 'Does your Pharaoh indeed have a sum of that magnitude to dispose of?'

'I give you my assurance that he does, Your Majesty. I have been commanded by Pharaoh to seal the accord of our two nations by immediately delivering into Your Majesty's hand the sum of three lakhs of silver. This is merely a pledge of what is to follow.'

For a long while Nimrod stared at me in silence. Then suddenly he sprang to his feet and began pacing rapidly back and forth across the floor of the chamber. His face was creased into a murderous scowl and he chewed his lip until a drop of blood dripped from his chin on to his embroidered tunic. He exhibited no sign of pain.

Suddenly he stopped in front of me and glared into my face. 'Three lakhs immediately and twenty-seven more to follow within the year?' he demanded. I waited for Phat Tur to make the translation before I agreed.

'Even as Your Majesty says. However, you must send a regiment of your finest to take delivery of the balance of the treasure in Thebes. Pharaoh will not accept the risk of transporting it with his own men.'

Nimrod spun around and resumed his pacing. His bronze-soled sandals rang on the paving slabs as he stamped up and down the chamber. He began to argue with himself in Sumerian.

'How can I trust this devious and ball-less freak? It is no secret that he is in league with Seth and all the dark devils. There are even those who believe that he himself is one of the darker spirits from beyond the void,' he muttered and then when he realized what he had said he spun around and shouted

259

at Phat Tur, 'Translate my words at your peril! If you do I will throttle you with your own intestines, do you understand?'

Phat Tur paled and dropped his gaze. 'As Your Majesty commands,' he acquiesced. Nimrod resumed his march up and down the chamber, and his argument with himself. Then he stopped in front of me again.

'Tell him I trust him,' he ordered Phat Tur. 'But that I must have a binding covenant with Pharaoh Tamose of Egypt before I can agree to an alliance.' As he stated this condition I saw the flare of lascivious guile in his eyes.

'If it is at all possible, I know that Pharaoh will accede,' I hedged cautiously.

'I wish to unite my own family with the royal family of Egypt,' Nimrod stated. 'I wish to take Pharaoh's two sisters, Tehuti and Bekatha, to be my wives. In that way Pharaoh and I will become brothers-in-law.'

I was amazed at the extent of his greed, gall and randiness. This rogue wanted both the money and the meat. 'It is a great honour you are offering to bestow on Egypt. In any other circumstances I know my Pharaoh would not hesitate a moment before agreeing with your suggestion.' In a reasonable tone of voice I concealed my anger from this obnoxious creature who had heaped insults on me and who now was blatantly lusting after my beloved girls. 'However, Pharaoh has already pledged both his sisters in marriage to the Supreme Minos of Crete to seal the military alliance between our two nations. He dare not renege on this promise. The Minoan would not accept the insult to his honour.'

Nimrod shrugged and muttered something obscene. However, I could tell he was not too seriously irked by my refusal. Both of us knew that it had been an opportunistic attempt on his part to wring the last possible advantage from our agreement. No matter how much some men are offered they will always try for a little more.

Nimrod took another turn around the chamber while he rallied his wits, and then he made the next attempt: 'I would enjoy the sight of the three lakhs of silver you spoke of earlier; by no means because I do not trust you and your Pharaoh to honour your agreement, but merely because I am interested to see how you concealed them until now . . .' Nimrod addressed me directly, hoping, I am sure, to trick me into betraying the fact that I understood Sumerian. I frustrated him once again by looking to Phat Tur for translation. I was beginning to enjoy circumventing Nimrod's snares. It was not dissimilar to playing the bao stones against Lord Aton.

I sent Zaras and Hui to fetch the silver from our regimental camp beyond the city walls. It took two wagons and fifty men to make the transfer. It was an impressive pile of bullion when it was finally heaped on the floor of the council chamber. Nimrod walked around the glittering pile, fondling every ingot, speaking endearments to them as though they were his beloved pets.

That evening we feasted once more at Nimrod's board. I found the wine to be eminently more drinkable than the gut-rot he had served us previously. However, its effect on the manners and behaviour of my host and his minions was less meritorious.

King Nimrod had missed his morning exertions in the Temple of Ishtar. Agreeable or not, we were treated to an exhibition of the Mighty Hunter's insatiability. Half the females in the banquet hall ended the evening in a state of prurient abandon.

I was pleased that I had left my two princesses locked in their apartment with Zaras and a dozen of his men standing guard at their door.

The six war galleys that I had purchased from Nimrod were undergoing a refit in Sidon harbour and would not be ready for me to take command of them until the end of the month of Phamenoth.

I employed this hiatus to work with King Nimrod and his staff in planning and plotting our combined campaign against the Hyksos. I had selected Lord Remrem to remain in Babylon and act as Pharaoh's military attaché.

Reluctantly I had agreed that Colonel Hui would stay with Remrem as his assistant. Under my tutelage Hui had developed into one of the most skilled protagonists of the science of chariot warfare. I knew I would miss him and his expertise sorely when we opened hostilities with the Hyksos hordes in northern Egypt along the coast of the Middle Sea. But Bekatha had made her aversion for him manifest. I knew that she would cause a furore if I took Hui with us to Crete.

Within weeks of Nimrod receiving the silver incentive the workshops of his army were fully employed with the manufacture of new armour and weapons, repairing old chariots and building hundreds more to my own superior design and specifications. The streets of Babylon became crowded with marching columns of recruits, and the souks were tumultuous with haggling buyers and sellers.

Through Phat Tur and his agents I learned that every other city in Sumeria was enjoying this same martial resuscitation. By the thousands the formerly unemployed warriors of Sumeria were flocking back to the royal standard – and the king's silver coin.

The work I had set myself was difficult and complicated enough without me making it worse by pretending not to be fluent in the Sumerian language. I began to speak a halting and childlike Sumerian to my hosts, which daily became more fluent and grammatically correct. Even His Majesty King Nimrod was forced in my presence to cease his insulting remarks about me to his sycophants. Soon I was able to baffle our hosts with my quick banter and my clever puns and play on their own language.

One morning I watched Admiral Alorus on the far side of the chariot drilling ground remark to Nimrod that my rapid acquisition of the Sumerian language was nothing short of miraculous. When I crossed the wide ground to thank him for the compliment Alorus shrank away from me in superstitious awe, and he made the sign against the evil eye. I don't think he had ever heard of lip-reading. But of course he believed in witchcraft, as does every educated and sensible person.

In the cool of the afternoons I took the opportunity to swim in the Euphrates or ride through the southern hills beyond the city limits with my princesses for company. It amused me how often we encountered Zaras on our forays to even the most remote locations. It was almost as though somebody had alerted him to our coming. Of course it could not have been Tehuti. Her astonishment at finding him loitering beside the trail almost superseded my own.

In the evenings there were always invitations to dine with our Sumerian hosts or with my own officers. If King Nimrod were present I insisted that my princesses sat close to me where I could watch over them.

When most of the others had retired I sat alone on the terrace outside my apartment, waiting until long after midnight for the return of the hooded lady. Night after night she disappointed me.

With all this bustling employment the days rolled by swiftly. Then a messenger arrived from the naval base at Sidon with news that the six war galleys I had purchased from Nimrod would be ready for launching twenty days earlier than anticipated. It would take our cumbersome caravan almost half that long to reach Sidon on the coast of the Middle Sea. I ordered

Zaras and Hui to make the final preparations for departure from Babylon to the coast.

That evening, after I had escorted my princesses to their royal quarters in the eastern wing of the palace, I returned to my own apartment before the moon had set. My slaves had left oil lamps burning in my chamber and on the terrace beside my cot. According to my instructions they had mixed the oil in the lamps with herbs whose fumes drove off the mosquitoes and other nocturnal insects, but at the same time induced restful sleep and agreeable dreams.

Rustie was waiting up to see me to bed. He came to take away my worn garments and place a silver chalice of wine beside my cot.

'It's long after midnight, master,' he reprimanded me. 'You have not slept more than a few hours since the beginning of the week.' Rustie has been my slave for so many years that both of us have lost count. Long ago he granted himself licence to treat me as though he were my nursemaid.

With his help I divested myself of my clothing and then went out on to the terrace, and took up the wine chalice. I wet my lips and sighed with contentment. It was a ten-year-old vintage from my own vineyards on the Mechir estate. Then I turned to look across at the terrace of the temple of the goddess. I was disappointed but resigned to find that it was deserted. It was weeks since I last had a glimpse of the hooded lady.

I dismissed Rustie and sent him still grumbling on his way, and then I paced the marble slabs, going over in my mind the salient points of the negotiations that I had held with the king that evening.

Abruptly I paused in mid-stride. The quality of the moon-light had changed, taking on a subtle golden luminosity. I looked up at the moon. I knew at once that there were preternatural forces at play, but I could not immediately ascertain whether they were benign or malignant. I made the sign of Horus with two fingers to avert evil and I waited quietly for the mystic forces to declare themselves.

Gradually I became aware of a subtle and elusive aroma on the warm night air. I had smelled nothing quite like it before, but although I could not place it all my senses were aroused. I felt an unusual but agreeable sensation building up in my neck and shoulders and running down my spine. This alerted me to the powerful presence close behind me.

I turned to face it and I was so startled that I dropped the wine chalice and it rang on the paving. For a moment my heart stilled in my breast, and then began to thump again like the hoof-beats of a runaway horse.

The mysterious lady from the temple stood before me; so close that I could make out her exquisite features in the shadows beneath the hood. If I had reached out I could have touched her but I could not move.

At last I found my voice, but when I spoke it was hushed with veneration. 'Who are you?'

'My name is Inana.'

I was struck to the very quick of my being by both the sound and sense of her reply. It resonated in my ears like celestial music. I knew at once that no sound so beautiful could ever issue from a human mouth. The sense of what she had said was even more striking. Inana was the ancient name from the very beginning of time for the goddess Ishtar.

'My name is Taita.' It was the only reply that I could think of.

'Apart from your name you know very little about yourself, do you? You do not even know the name of your father or your mother.' She smiled in gentle sympathy as she said it.

'No. I never knew them.' I acknowledged the truth of her statement. Compassionately she held out one hand to me, and without hesitation I took it. Immediately I felt the heat and strength from it flowing into me.

'Do not be afraid, Taita. I am your friend, and more than your friend.'

'I am not afraid of you, Inana.' She held out her other hand and when I took that one also I knew that a powerful bond of blood and mind existed between us.

'I know you!' I exclaimed in wonder. 'I feel that I have known you from the very beginning. Tell me who you are.'

'I have not come to tell you about myself. I have come to tell you about yourself. Come with me, Taita.' Still holding both my hands she moved backwards, leading me from the open terrace into my own bedchamber. Her footsteps, if there were any, made no sound. There was only the soft swishing of her skirts. I sensed that under them her feet were not touching the ground, and that she was suspended just above the surface.

The beautiful lantern-lit room that we entered had been my home for all these past weeks and I thought that I knew every inch of it, but now I saw that there was a door in the facing wall that I had never noticed before. As Inana led me towards it the door swung open of its own accord. There was utter darkness beyond the portals. Still holding hands we plunged into the darkness and it engulfed us. We plummeted downwards, but she held my hands and I was unafraid. The wind of our descent blew into my face with such force that I had to slit my eyes against it. We flew in darkness for what seemed an eternity, but I knew time was an illusion. Then I felt solid footing beneath me and we were no longer moving. There was light, at first only a glimmering. I could make out the shape of Inana's head again, and then slowly her bodily form appeared beneath it. I saw that now she was as naked as I was.

I have seen the bodies of many beautiful women during my long life, but Inana far surpassed any of them. Her hips were

266

voluptuous but above them her narrow waist emphasized their elegant contours. Although she was as tall as I am her limbs were so delicately smooth and sculptured that I could not prevent myself reaching out to stroke them. Lightly I ran my fingers up her arms from her wrists to the curve of her shoulders. Her skin was silken but the muscles beneath it were adamantine.

Her hair was piled high, but when she shook her head it came cascading down in a glowing wave over her shoulders, and fell as far as her knees. This rippling curtain did not cover her breasts which thrust their way through it like living creatures. They were perfect rounds, white as mare's milk and tipped with ruby nipples that puckered as my gaze passed over them.

Her body was hairless. Her pudenda were also entirely devoid of hair. The tips of her inner lips protruded shyly from the vertical cleft. The sweet dew of feminine arousal glistened upon them.

The light grew stronger still and I realized that we were standing in the Hanging Gardens high above the city of Babylon. The masses of shrubbery and flowers that surrounded us were wondrously lovely, but they were rendered mundane by Inana's beauty. She took my hands from her shoulders and she kissed them one after the other. I shivered at the sensation that pervaded my whole being.

'What do you want of me, Inana?' It did not sound like my own voice that said it.

'I propose to unite with you.'

'Surely you know that I am not a whole man,' I whispered in my shame. 'I was emasculated a long time ago.'

'Yes.' Her voice was gentle, compassionate. 'I was there when they did that to you. I felt the knife as keenly as you did. I wept for you, Taita. But I rejoiced for myself. Coupling is not the same as uniting. I was speaking not of the brief conjoining of the flesh that ends too soon in a puny muscular spasm, sparse reward for the man who renders up his seed, or for the woman who accepts it into her womb. That is merely nature's expedient for launching another mortal life into a brief and inconsequential existence that too soon is obliterated by death.'

She guided my right hand down from her lips and thrust my fingers deeply into the crevice between her luscious thighs. It was narrow as my two fingers and lubricious. I felt my own loins melting with the heat of hers. 'I was not speaking of this.' With her fingertips she gently caressed the brutal scar between my legs where once my manhood had been: 'Nor of this.'

'What else is there that joins a man and a woman, Inana?'

'There is the uniting of souls rather than bodies. The melding of superior minds. That is the true miracle of existence that can very rarely be consummated.'

She drew me down on to the greensward of the secret garden. It was silken and soft beneath us as the down of the eider duck. She came over me in a swift and sinuous movement and at once our bodies were locked as closely and intimately as the gods had designed them to be. Our legs and our arms were entwined, and our breath was mingling. I could feel her heart beating against my own.

Gradually our two hearts became a single organ that we shared, and they beat as one. Our combined breathing harmonized and sustained both sets of our lungs. It was the most uplifting and fulfilling sensation I had ever experienced. I wanted to be more deeply engulfed by her body, and to engulf her completely in mine so that we might become a single organism.

Then I suffered a fleeting sense of panic and helplessness as I felt her mind taking control of mine. I tried to prevent it, but then I realized that I was usurping her mind even as she did the same to me. As she took my memories from me so I garnered hers. Between us nothing was lost or forgotten. We were sharing an existence that stretched back into the distant past.

'Now I know who my father is,' I whispered, hearing the wonder of it in my own voice.

'Who is he?' she asked. She knew the answer before she formed the question, and I heard her question although she had not spoken.

'He is Meniotos, the god of anger and morality,' I replied in the divine silence that we shared.

'Who then is your mother?' Inana asked and I took the answer from the single mind that we shared.

'My mother was Selias, but she was a human and mortal. She died giving birth to me.'

'You are a demi-god, Taita. You are neither entirely human nor completely divine. Even though you are a long liver, one day you too must die.' She wrapped my soul more tightly and protectively with her own. 'It is a day that is still far off. However, I will be there to shield and sustain you when it happens. After you have gone I will mourn you for a thousand years.'

'Who are you, Inana? Why do I feel so bound to you in both body and spirit? Who is your father?'

'My father is Hyperion, the god of light. He is the brother of Meniotos. So we are of the same divine blood, you and I,' she answered directly.

'I heard your answer before I asked my question,' I told her silently. 'And your mother? Was she a mortal human or a goddess?'

'My mother is Artemis,' Inana replied.

'Artemis is the goddess of the hunt and of all wild animals,' I acknowledged. 'She is also the virgin goddess, and the goddess of maidens. How can she be both a virgin and your natural mother?'

'You must know, Taita, that with those of us who are gods and demi-gods all things are possible. My father Hyperion restored my mother's virginity to her the hour after I was born.' I smiled at the charming practicality of her father's solution, and I felt Inana smile with me before she continued, 'But I am a virgin like my mother, and by the decree of Zeus who is the father of all the gods I must always remain a virgin. That is my punishment for refusing Zeus, who is my grandfather, when he sought to have his incestuous way and copulate with me.'

'That is a cruel punishment for such a trivial offence,' I sympathized with her.

'I think not, Taita. I think it the kindest and sweetest reward; for how otherwise could you and I be lovers through the ages that have passed and those that are yet to come, and still retain our virginity and purity?'

'How could anyone know our destiny, Inana? I had not even been born in the remote time about which you are speaking.'

'I was there when you were born, Taita. I was there when your manhood was ripped from you, and I wept for you then although I knew how richly we both would profit from that terrible deed through the millennia.'

'You speak of millennia. Will you and I be together for that long, Inana?'

She did not reply directly to my question. 'Although you have been unaware of it I have followed you closely since the day of your birth. I knew of everything that befell you: every brief joy and every excruciating agony.'

'Why me, Inana?'

'Because we are one, Taita. We are of one blood and one breath.'

'I can keep nothing from you,' I conceded. 'However, I am not virgin as you are. I have been carnally united with other women in my life.'

Inana shook her head sadly. 'You have known only one woman, Taita. I was there when it happened. I could have warned you against it, for you paid for that transitory pleasure with the blade of the castrating knife.' I felt her breath in my mouth and her sorrow in my own heart as she went on, 'I could have spared you the agony, but if I had done so, if I had warned you of the consequences, then you and I would never have been able to couple as we are doing now, in eternal and divine chastity.'

I thought on what she had said and then I sighed as she sighed within me.

'It all happened so long ago. I do not remember the girl's face. I do not even remember her name,' I admitted.

'That is because I have expunged the memory from your mind,' she whispered. 'If you wish I can replace it, and you can keep it with you for the next five thousand years, but it will bring you no joy. Do you want that?'

'You know that I do not.' I was renouncing that poor lost soul, who had been a slave with me. In our shared misery we had given each other some little comfort. She had given me love. But she had long ago been swallowed up by the abyss of space and time and gone where nobody could follow her; not even an emasculated demi-god.

I surrendered myself to the moment, feasting on the contents of Inana's mind and memory even as she feasted on mine. With our bodies and souls interlocked time was no longer a river rushing breathlessly by. It became a gentle ocean on which we floated together, savouring every moment as though it was a slice of eternity. She bolstered the ramparts of my soul, rendering me immeasurably wiser and invulnerable to evil.

Together we achieved a state of spiritual grace.

After an eternity my soul spoke to hers. 'I don't want this ever to end, Inana. I want to remain with you forever like this.' Then I heard her voice reply from the very depths of my being:

'You are a part of me, Taita, and I am a part of you. But at the same time we are separate and entire, each to ourselves. We have our own distinct existences to which we must return. We have our own destinies which we alone must work out.'

'Please don't leave me,' I implored her.

'I am leaving you now. It is time for me to go.' Her voice was no longer commingled with mine.

'Will you return to me?'

'Yes.'

'Where?' I demanded.

'Wherever you are.'

'When, Inana? When will I see you again?'

'In a day, a year or perhaps in a thousand years.' I felt her body unfold to release me from her embrace and her arms slipped away.

'Stay just a little longer,' I implored her but she was already gone and I sat up. I looked around me in bewilderment. I found myself lying on my cot on the terrace of the palace. I jumped up and ran into the main bedchamber. I stopped in the middle of the large room and stared at the far wall where last I had seen the doorway to the secret garden into which Inana had flown with me. There was no doorway now.

I crossed the floor slowly and began to examine the facing wall minutely, running my fingertips over the surface, seeking the joint between door and jamb. The plasterwork was smooth and uninterrupted. I remembered then what Inana had said to me.

You must know, Taita, that with those of us who are gods and demi-gods all things are possible.

It seemed that many years had passed since I had last stood on this spot. Was there such a dimension as time in that far place to which Inana had transported me? I wondered. Even if there were, perhaps time had remained frozen in this world while I was in the other with her?

While I tried to separate reality from fantasy, and truth from falsehood, my eyes alighted on the floral display of red roses in the huge bronze amphora that stood in the centre of the floor. I crossed to it and examined the blooms on their thorny stems. They were as fresh as when I had last seen them.

'They could have been renewed many times in my absence.'

I spoke aloud. Then I looked down. There was a single red blossom lying on the marble slabs. I remembered that I had snapped it off the main stem the previous afternoon to savour its perfume, and then I had dropped it to the floor for the palace servants to clear away.

I stooped to pick it up and sniffed the bloom. It was as fragrant as when I last smelled it, and when I examined it more closely I found that although it had been without water it was not wilted, but as fresh and crisp as when I had broken it off the stem.

Did Inana and I spend only a single night in that divine embrace and not a lifetime as I imagined? I wondered. It did not seem possible. I stood bemused, brushing the petals of the red rose against my lips.

I heard the doors of the main apartment open and then muted voices speaking in Egyptian. 'Who is that?' I shouted and one of them replied:

'It is I, master.' I recognized the voice of Rustie. Moments later he appeared in the doorway of the bedchamber.

'Where have you been?' I demanded.

'You told me not to awake you until the sun was above the horizon, master,' he protested with ill-concealed indignation.

'When did I tell you that?'

'Last night when you dismissed me.' So I had been away for only a single night. Then again, perhaps it had never happened. Perhaps all of it had only been a dream, but I desperately hoped not. I was already yearning for my next tryst with Inana, if of course she was real and not a phantom of my mind. Would I ever know the answer to that mystery: phantom or reality, what and who was Inana?

'I had forgotten. Please forgive me, Rustie.'

'Of course, master. But it is I who should apologize to you.' Rustie is so easily mollified. He is a lovely man and I am really very fond of him. However, I reminded him sternly:

'Do not forget that we are leaving for Sidon in five days' time. You must be ready to travel again by then.'

'I have already packed most of our possessions into the wagons. I can be ready to march within the hour.'

Every hour of those last five days we spent in Babylon seemed to be filled with frantic activity. There were the last meetings with Nimrod and his council, the signing of accords between our nations, and the arrangements agreed upon for the remainder of the bullion that I had promised him to be collected by Nimrod's minions in Thebes. I was mightily pleased that I would not be present when the promissory bond for twenty-seven lakhs of silver, which I had signed with the hawk seal, was presented to Pharaoh Tamose.

On top of all this, there was the arrival in Babylon of the emissary that the Supreme Minos had sent to Babylon to welcome my mission and travel with us to Crete. He had sailed from Knossos in a flotilla of war galleys with his entourage. He had left the ships in the Sumerian port of Sidon and travelled overland with his entourage to meet me.

His name was Toran, which translated from Minoan as 'the Son of the Bull'. He was a handsome man in the prime of his life and he travelled in such state as befitted the representative of the richest and most powerful monarch on this earth. King Nimrod set aside an entire wing of the palace to accommodate his entourage. Simply to feed and entertain the Cretan visitors Nimrod was obliged to spend much of the three lakhs of silver which I had bestowed upon him. He was eager to see Toran return to his island and did all in his power to hasten his departure.

Notwithstanding his physical beauty and regal manners Toran was one of the shrewdest and most intelligent men I had ever encountered. At our first meeting we formed a strong bond of mutual respect; almost immediately each of us recognized the superior qualities of the other.

One of the many virtues that we shared was a loathing of the Hyksos barbarians and everything even remotely associated with them. I spent almost an hour commiserating with him on the despicable and unprovoked attack they had made on the Minoan fortress of Tamiat, and the atrocities that they had committed upon the Cretan troops that they had captured there. Toran's youngest son was one of the junior officers whom they had beheaded after he had surrendered to them.

However, neither of us mentioned the three great Cretan treasure triremes and the 580 lakhs of silver bullion that the Hyksos had stolen from the Supreme Minos. It was as though that vast treasure had never existed. I for one would readily have sworn before all the gods that I had no knowledge of it.

What finally convinced me of Toran's superior talents and his advanced intellect was his fluent command of the Egyptian language and the fact that he had read and studied much of my own writing on various subjects. He told me that he considered my treatise on naval warfare and tactics to be a work of genius, and that he had translated much of my poetry into the Minoan language.

It was not until the second day of our deliberations that we broached the subject of the proposed alliance between our two mighty nations, and the manner in which we might confirm and consolidate this treaty. These deliberations took another three days during which the two of us tested all our bargaining powers against each other to the utmost; until on the fourth day we were able to sign an accord which I had written out in both Egyptian hieroglyphics and Minoan Linear A script.

I deemed it was now the propitious time to introduce my princesses to Toran. I invited him and his suite to dine with us the following evening.

I personally supervised the selection of the wines and decided on the dishes to be served. My menu was almost as long as the treaty with Crete that I had just signed, but considerably more enthralling. Then I devoted the entire afternoon to preparing my two princesses for the occasion. It was essential for my purpose, not to mention for the benefit of our very Egypt, that Toran should be inveigled into sending a glowing description of all their attributes back to the palace of Knossos.

With extreme care I chose from the huge wardrobe that I had brought from Thebes those materials and colours that best complemented the beauty of my two girls: pink for Bekatha and green for Tehuti.

I sat alongside the two beauticians who were applying their make-up. I would not accept anything less than perfection from either of them. By the time I was satisfied with their efforts I had reduced both of them to tears, but the results were well worth all my persistence. The only beauty I have ever looked upon which exceeded that of my girls on that particular evening was the face of the goddess Inana in the moonlight. I knew that neither Toran nor his master in Crete would be able to resist my two girls; just as I had never been able to do so.

That evening I waited until Toran and the rest of the company were seated at the magnificently decorated table that I had prepared, and all of them had been served with wine, before I gave the signal for the girls to make their entrance.

When they came gliding in side by side through double doors at the end of the hall an immediate and profound silence fell upon the company. The men were held captive with admiration, and the women with envy.

My princesses paused in front of Toran and both of them made a graceful obeisance. They were being followed by Loxias. She also dipped into a curtsey. Of course I had not lavished any of my attention on the Cretan lass. She was wearing a rather drab little dress that exposed her knees. Her face and her knees were quite pretty, but not exceptionally so. It was obvious that she had attended to her own hair and make-up. She was after all a servant and very fortunate to have been allowed by me to attend the banquet.

I glanced sideways at Toran to judge his reaction to this plethora of feminine pulchritude, and I saw he was staring over the heads of my two princesses and that he was smiling. I switched my attention in the same direction as his and saw to my astonishment and chagrin that Loxias was shyly smiling back at him. It was then that I recalled her previous admiration for Lord Remrem. I realized that the child must have a penchant for older men.

Immediately I moderated my inflated opinion of Toran. He might be a suave and erudite statesman with an elevated taste in literature, but when it came to women it was obvious he could not tell a glittering hummingbird from a drab little sparrow.

I gestured at my girls to take their places on each side of Toran. They already had my instructions to dazzle him with their command of the Minoan language. Then with a jerk of my head I banished Loxias to the far end of the hall where she was at liberty to exercise her banal charms on some of my junior officers closer to her own age and station in life.

Over the next several weeks I was obliged to spend a great deal of my time in earnest conclave with Toran, Lord Remrem and the Sumerian high command, planning and coordinating our joint campaign against King Gorrab. The days fled away before us, and it seemed that there was never a moment's respite for me.

Two days before the departure of our caravan from Babylon

to the port of Sidon I could no longer resist the compulsion I felt to make a farewell visit to the Temple of Ishtar. It was my fervent hope that I might find some lingering trace of Inana within that bizarre building, perhaps a cryptic message from her or at the very least an esoteric trace of her presence.

I arranged with Onyos, the green-robed priest of the goddess, for him to allow me access to the temple after it was closed to all other worshippers. I went alone, dressed in a hooded grey robe that resembled the one that Inana always wore. It was an hour after midnight when I reached the wicket door of the temple where Onyos was waiting for me.

'I wish to be alone,' I dismissed him as I placed a silver mem coin in his palm. He backed away from me respectfully, making a deep and sweeping bow, and disappeared into the shadows of the hypostyle nave.

Without the reflection of the great sun mirror in the roof to light it, the temple was a gloomy and eerie place. Except for a very few green-robed priests and priestesses it was deserted. The stalls in which the women waited to perform their obligatory service to the goddess were empty. A few of the more spectacular frescoes were illuminated by oil lamps with polished copper reflectors.

The wavering light danced upon the painted figures, imbuing them with a lurid life of their own. I paused before some of them and wondered at the chasm which separated these images from the true nature of the divine and chaste deity to whom they were dedicated. During the voyage of exploration upon which Inana had taken me I learned that what men believe about the gods is mostly their own wishful imaginings. The idea that a man can bend the immortals to his will with prayer and sacrifice or pious confession is ludicrous. The immortals do only what suits them best, and that is care for their own power and pleasure.

I searched slowly and intently through the cavernous halls

and cloisters, but I could not detect even the most tenuous evidence of Inana's existence in any of them. King Marduk had raised this enormous edifice in an attempt to lure the goddess into it and capture her, but I knew now that the goddess is never the prey; she is the huntress.

I climbed the terrace that spiralled up the exterior walls of the temple. This was where she had so often appeared to me, but now there was nothing of her remaining here. I reached the flat roof and sat there beside the gigantic metal mirror that in the daylight hours reflected the sun's rays down into the nave.

I searched the star-bejewelled vault of the midnight sky above me. But she had left nothing there for me. All I had was my memory of her, and her promise that she would return to me one day.

King Nimrod had ordered the building of a royal pavilion outside the main gates of the city. It was decorated with flags, flowers and palm fronds. On the day that we marched for Sidon His Majesty took up his station high on the saluting podium.

He was surrounded by his Sumerian nobles, his senior military officers and the city dignitaries. Lord Remrem, Colonel Hui and the other Egyptian officers who were to remain in Babylon with him also occupied privileged positions on the dais.

The previous day I had sent all the servants, slaves and other non-combatants ahead of our main force. With them had gone the baggage wagons and the remount herds of horses and camels. So I had with me only the officers and the fighting men when we marched past King Nimrod.

All our chariots, weapons and armour had been repaired, renewed and polished so they glittered in the sunlight. The horses and camels had been fed, rested and groomed until they were in peak condition. Zaras had seen to it that the men had received the same attention and had not been allowed to slack off. We looked like the hard little fighting army that we truly were.

Many of the men had formed relationships within the local population, so there were numerous weeping ladies lining the road that led down to the coast. Some of these were already growing big with child. All this added abundantly to the excitement and drama of the moment.

Toran rode at my left hand, and my two princesses at my right. Loxias had somehow managed to find herself a place close behind the Minoan ambassador. This no longer surprised or perturbed me. I had learned that she no longer slept in the same chamber as my own girls, and that since Toran's arrival in Baghdad she had found new lodgings for herself. I made no further enquiries into the matter.

With the ambassador and my royal princesses riding on each side of me and the regimental band of horns, flutes and drums coming up behind us I led my men out of the city gates. I halted the column when we came level with the royal pavilion. I dismounted and climbed the steps to where King Nimrod stood on the podium.

The band stopped playing and the crowds fell respectfully silent as I went down on one knee before King Nimrod. His Majesty lifted me back on to my feet and embraced me as fondly as my own brother might have done, if I had one. This was only fitting for I had restored his kingdom and his army to him. I had also made him a rich man and replaced a great part of the fortune that his father King Marduk had squandered.

We exchanged vows of eternal friendship which on my side were not entirely sincere. Then we parted.

As I remounted my own stallion I raised my right hand in preparation to give the order to march and the band played the opening bars of the regimental anthem.

In this fraught moment a well-beloved voice at my left hand uttered a cry that reverberated off the massive walls of the city.

'Stop!' cried Princess Bekatha and we all obeyed her command. The music of the band together with the cheers of the crowds faltered into an awkward silence. Every eye, including mine, turned and focused upon her.

'What ails you, my darling?' I asked in placatory tones. I saw that she was on the verge of one of her famous tantrums. Perhaps I am partially responsible for the abandon of Bekatha's temper. I may have been overly lenient with her in the past.

'What does Hui think he is doing up there on the platform, hiding behind Lord Remrem while I am being marched off on my own to some bleak and godless island at the far end of the earth.' Bekatha flung out her right hand and pointed out the person who had given her such dire offence. 'Just look at him skulking there!' Every head in the gathering, including that of King Nimrod, turned towards Hui

'You said you never wanted to see Hui again,' Loxias reminded Bekatha.

Bekatha rounded on her. 'You keep out of this, or you will be very sorry for yourself!'

'Loxias is right. You said you hated Hui.' Tehuti came gallantly to the support of the Cretan girl.

'I never said that. I never used the word hated!'

'Yes, you did.' The other two girls spoke in unison, and Tehuti elaborated a little further:

'You even said you were going to have him beheaded.'

'I never said beheaded.' Bekatha's eyes filled with tears of fury. 'I said punished. I said I would have him punished.'

Those at the back of the crowded podium began to demand information from those in front who could understand a little Egyptian: 'What did she say?'

'She says she is going to have somebody beheaded.' Little children in the crowd began whining petulantly to be lifted on to their parents' shoulders so that they could have a better view of the execution.

'Even I heard you say that Hui is an oaf and a barbarian.' I entered the conversation circumspectly under the cover of the hubbub.

'All I said was that Hui shouldn't have laughed at me.'

'You don't think he is ugly?'

She dropped her eyes and her voice. 'Not really. In fact he is really quite sweet in a funny sort of way.'

'What about his five wives?'

'He promised to send them home to their mothers.'

I blinked. Obviously matters had already advanced far beyond my control. 'Perhaps it would be better if we left him here in Babylon, or if you stick to your promise and have him beheaded,' I suggested.

'Don't be so horrible, Tata.'

'Are you absolutely certain that you want Hui to come with us to Crete?'

She nodded, and her smile was irresistible, to me at least. I stood in the stirrups and shouted over the heads of the crowd.

'Hui! Get your kit packed and fall in. I am not going to wait for you. If you have not rejoined your regiment before sunset I will post you absent without leave.'

I kicked my heels into the flanks of my horse, and we marched for the coast. Out of the corner of my eye I saw Colonel Hui scramble down off the royal podium with indecent haste. Ignoring Lord Remrem's protests, he rushed towards the city gates to retrieve his kit.

I wondered why I felt so pleased with myself. I had just made a difficult position almost totally untenable. There was no profit in it for me, except that I now had the best charioteer in Egypt back under my command and I had made my little Bekatha happy again.

We followed the Euphrates River in a north-westerly direction for the following six days, until we intercepted the King's Highway at the city of Resafa. Then we turned to follow the highway down through the mountains as far as Ash-Sham, the City of Jasmine.

Since leaving the Red Sea we had travelled in an enormous circle which had never brought us closer than seven hundred leagues to the Hyksos-dominated lands around the northern reaches of Mother Nile.

From the City of Jasmine we could at last head directly west for the port of Sidon on the most easterly shores of the Middle Sea. This was the most beautiful and pleasing stage of our long journey. It took us down through the mountains and forests of Lebanon.

The highway was lined with gigantic cedar trees that had never felt the axe. They seemed to be the pillars on which the sky was suspended, reaching up to the veritable home of the gods. At this season of the year their upper branches were decked with hoary garlands of crisp new snow and the air was redolent with the scent of their resin.

As we dropped down towards the coast the weather warmed and we could divest ourselves of the furs and heavy woollen shawls that we had purchased in the City of Jasmine. We emerged from the cedar forests to discover another mountain standing before us. My guides assured me that this was the Rana Mountain, which in the Canaanite language means 'Perfect in Beauty'. It stands upon the shores of the Middle Sea between the Phoenician ports of Tyre and Sidon and separates them by a distance of almost twenty leagues.

The trade road that we were following was split by the

mountain. We took the right-hand fork and as we rounded the flank of Mount Rana we were afforded our first glimpse of the sea. It was a marvellous shade of deep cerulean blue that stretched away to the horizon. Even the bellies of the towering mountains of cloud above it were stained blue by the reflection of the waters below.

The port of Sidon was one of the most prosperous and bustling trade cities on this coast. The harbour was crammed with shipping. Even at this distance I could make out the double-headed axe emblem of Crete on the sails of many of the larger vessels. These were part of the flotilla which had conveyed Toran from Crete to this place. He came to me to bid me farewell and then rode ahead to the port to go aboard his flagship and take command of her. He would sail ahead of us to alert the Supreme Minos to our imminent arrival.

I selected an area of open ground bordering the road half a league outside the stone walls of the port. Here a stream running down from the slopes of Mount Rana would provide us with an adequate water supply. I ordered Zaras to set up our regimental camp on this site. Before the camp was ready for occupation a delegation emerged from the main gates of the city and came down the road towards us.

I saw that the man leading them was dressed in the robes of a high-ranking Sumerian officer. He rode up to where I stood and dismounted.

'I am Naram Sin, the governor of the province of Sidon.' He held his clenched fist against his heart in a gesture of respect. 'Of course I know you are Lord Taita. Your name is already known and revered throughout all of Sumeria. I am strictly commanded by His Majesty King Nimrod to accord unto you all respect and to obey your instructions at once and without question. I am to see to it that you and the royal ladies in your care lack for nothing.'

'Thank you for this friendly welcome. My first request to you is that you supply us with fodder for our animals.'

Naram Sin spun on his heel and rapped out a string of orders for his subordinates. They scurried away to his bidding; and the governor turned back to me. 'Is there any other way in which I can assist you, my lord?'

'Please lead me to the shipyards where my flotilla is being refitted. I am eager to inspect the work.'

The six galleys that I had purchased from Nimrod were at first sight a major disappointment to me. They were standing on stocks so that I was able to examine their hulls beneath the waterline. I made the mistake of comparing them to the great Minoan triremes that I had captured at the fort of Tamiat. These Sumerian ships were almost half the size and I could see from the design of the hulls that they would be much slower and not nearly so handy.

With an effort I thrust aside my disillusionment, and determined to concentrate all my attention on making the best of what was at hand.

Over the next few weeks I spent most of my waking hours in the yards with Zaras and the shipwrights. They were making the best of a bad job, but that was not enough to satisfy me. I always demand perfection.

I inspected every plank and spar. I prised out nails from the hulls at random and inspected them for corrosion. I did the same with the bronze fittings. I dug with the point of my sword into the caulking of the hull to ascertain the quality of the workmanship. I had all the sails unfurled and laid out on the beach so I could go over them minutely, searching for and repairing tears and weak spots in the canvas.

Then I ordered a series of modifications to the hulls. Zaras and I had discussed these in detail during the long journey down from Babylon. When I showed the superintendent of the shipyard my drawings he grumbled and groused and came up with a dozen objections, which I beat down relentlessly.

I wanted to employ these galleys in close support to our land forces that would soon be operating against the Hyksos legions along the northern shores of Egypt. Despite my original misgivings I was now confident that these ships would be capable of moving large contingents of men swiftly from any point in the delta to where they were needed most. However, troops were ineffectual without their chariots and horses.

The yard superintendent finally capitulated to my demands and built loading ramps into the sterns of my galleys. I made him reinforce the decking between the rowing benches so that this could carry twelve chariots with their horses even in heavy seas.

We would be able to reverse these vessels up to any shelving beach or other suitable landing site and deliver a squadron of over seventy fighting chariots with their horse teams in the traces and their men in the cockpit ready to go into action immediately. Once they had achieved their objective they could be recovered from the beach just as expeditiously.

While this work was being carried out Toran received orders from the Supreme Minos to delay his departure so that he could sail in convoy with us. He was to place his large and commodious galleys at my disposal to convey the royal princesses and their entourage in greater comfort than they would enjoy on my much smaller vessels.

It was fortunate that the Cretan ruler had accorded me this courtesy; otherwise Toran would not have had the opportunity to witness the warlike capabilities of my small force.

By the time that the modifications to the hulls of my ships were completed the season of storms came to an end. The gods blessed us with fair weather and moderate seas. But before we set sail for Crete I determined that we must put to the test the seaworthiness of the renovated hulls and the operation of the modifications which I had installed. At the same time I would be able to drill my charioteers in the operation of the stern loading ramps.

We put to sea and sailed up and down the coast for several days landing our chariots on every feasible beach or headland and then recovering them again. I kept the men at it until they and their horses were thoroughly trained and skilled at these manoeuvres. When at last I was satisfied we sailed back to the port of Sidon.

In the early morning, two days before our final departure for Crete, I was walking down from our campsite to the shipyard to supervise the day's work when on the outskirts of the port I was accosted by a one-eyed beggar. I tried to brush him aside and continue my conversation with Zaras and Hui, who were accompanying me. The filthy rascal was importunate. Whining, he clutched at my sleeve. I turned back and raised my staff to beat him off, but he showed no fear and grinned at me impudently.

'Lord Aton challenges you to a game of bao,' he mouthed at me. I lowered my staff and gaped at him. The statement was so incongruous coming from that toothless and odorous maw that for once I was taken completely aback. Before I could recover my wits the fellow thrust a minute roll of papyrus into my hand and then darted away down a crowded alley. Zaras immediately charged after him, but I called him back.

'Let him go, Zaras. He is a friend of a friend.'

Zaras stopped reluctantly and looked back at me. 'Are you sure that he didn't cut your purse? Don't you want me to beat the truth out of him, just in case?'

'Have done!' I told him. 'Let him go! Come back here, Zaras!' He obeyed me, but looking back over his shoulder longingly.

I returned immediately to the camp and sequestered myself in my tent before I unfolded the papyrus. I saw at a glance that it was indeed a message from Aton. His calligraphy is unmistakable. Like his manner, it is pretentious.

On the fifth day of Pachon the Vulture despatched a pack of two hundred jackals east from Zanat to intercept the wounded falcon at the hole in the wall and prevent his flight to the new island nest.

The contents of the message itself confirmed unequivocally the identity of the author. In the private code that Aton and I employed the Vulture was King Gorrab. Two hundred jackals meant that number of Hyksos chariots. Zanat was our code name for the border town of Nello between northern Egypt and Sinai. The Hole in the Wall was Sidon. The new island nest was Crete. Of course, the wounded falcon was my personal hieroglyph.

In plain language Aton was warning me that sixteen days previously Gorrab had despatched a detachment of two hundred chariots along the coastal road from Nello to Sidon to intercept me and prevent me setting sail for Crete.

It was not a great shock or surprise to me that Gorrab and his minions had learned of my mission. In any company as large and diffuse as the one I had led from Thebes to Babylon, and now down to the port of Sidon, there would be somebody with a loud mouth and others with big ears. We had been long enough on the road for the news to have reached Gorrab's lair in Memphis, and for him to react to it. Even though I had taken every precaution possible to cover my tracks I was resigned to the fact that Gorrab knew that I was in command of this mission. My reputation precedes me. He must know also just how formidable an opponent I am.

I did not waste a moment longer pondering how Aton had garnered this information, if it were authentic and how he had delivered it to me. Aton has ways and means of doing things, just as I have. He did not make mistakes, again just like me.

I stuck my head out of the flap of my tent and shouted for

Zaras. He was waiting close at hand and he arrived almost immediately, with Hui on his heels.

'Get the men and chariots loaded back on to the ships at once. I want to sail before noon,' I told them.

'Where to?' Hui asked. 'Is this another exercise?'

'Don't ask idiotic questions.' Zaras rounded on him savagely. 'Just do what Taita orders you, and do it quickly.'

I t was a full hour short of noon when I led my flotilla out of Sidon harbour. At my invitation Toran stood beside me in the stern of my flagship, which I had named the *Outrage*. Outrage had been my initial reaction when I first laid eyes on her.

As soon as we cleared the breakwater I turned on to a southerly heading. The rest of my ships tacked in succession behind me and we ran parallel to the coast in line astern. I had made some rapid calculations based on the succinct information that Aton had given me.

If, as Aton had warned me, the Hyksos raiders had indeed set out from Zanat on the fifth of Shemu, they would have faced a journey of over four hundred leagues to reach Sidon. Laden chariots could cover only about twenty leagues a day over such an extended distance without crippling the horses. Horses have to rest and graze. Thus the journey would take them almost twenty days in all. According to Aton's intelligence they had already been on the road for sixteen days. Therefore they were probably only eighty leagues or so ahead. I anchored our ships as soon as the sun set.

When Toran demanded why I was reluctant to sail on through the hours of darkness I explained to him, 'I can't take the chance of sailing clean past the enemy in darkness. But anchoring will not delay our meeting for too long. The Hyksos chariots will be closing with us at their best speed. We can expect to meet them at about noon on the day after tomorrow.'

When I gave Toran these calculations, he had another acute question for me.

'How will we know when we do come level with them? Surely we will only have occasional glimpses of the coastal road from the deck of this ship.'

'Dust and smoke,' I told him.

'I don't understand.'

'Two hundred chariots will kick up a cloud of dust that we will be able to see from a great distance out at sea.'

Toran nodded but then insisted, 'What about the smoke?'

'It is one of the Hyksos' many appealing habits to burn every village they capture, preferably with the inhabitants barricaded in the buildings. You can be sure their progress will be marked by clouds of dust and pillars of smoke. They truly are an unlovable people.'

As I had predicted, an hour past noon on the second day I spotted smoke rising from beyond a copse of trees not more than a few hundred paces inland of the curling line of low surf that was breaking on the shore.

I climbed to the masthead, from which vantage point I saw that the fires had been very recently lit. I could tell this was so because the column of smoke grew denser and rose higher as I watched it. Then more smoke sprang up from three other separate locations beyond the first column.

'There goes another village and every living creature in it,' I muttered, and at that moment I saw two female figures emerge from the bush and scrub above the beach. Both of them were running with terrified abandon. One of the women was carrying a little child over her shoulder, and she was looking back as she ran. They raced down through the yellow beach sand to the water's edge and then turned to run along the damp verge where the sand was firmer under their feet. They were looking out at our ships and waving frantically to us.

Suddenly a chariot of Hyksos design came dashing down a

rutted track through the scrub above the beach. There were three men in it. All of them were clad in distinctive Hyksos armour with bowl-shaped bronze helmets. The driver reined in his horse before they reached the treacherously soft sands at the edge of the sea. All three of them jumped down from the carriage and started out in pursuit of the running women. They paid very little attention to our vessels. We were too far offshore to offer them any obvious threat. It is strange how landsmen understand so little about ships, and what they are capable of. All their attention was fixed on the women they were pursuing. I knew from bitter experience that, when they had finished with the mother, they would use her infant every bit as brutally.

'Are you going in to rescue those women?' Toran cupped his hands around his mouth to shout up at me from the quarterdeck.

'There is no place to land safely. Better to let those Hyksos swine live now if we can slaughter them and two hundred of their brethren later,' I called down to him, and then gave the order to the helm to lay the ship on an offshore course. Toran remained at the ship's stern rail staring back at the beach, watching how the charioteers treated the women they had captured. I ignored his outraged shouts of horror and fury.

I did not even glance back at what was taking place on the beach. I had seen it all a hundred or more times before, but that in no way made it any easier to watch. Instead I concentrated all my attention on taking my little flotilla well clear of the land and then heading back parallel to the shore, the same way we had come.

A few hours previously we had sailed past a small bay guarded by rocky headlands. This had been gouged out of the mainland by a sizeable river. In this dry season the river itself had been reduced to a trickle. The coastal road crossed it at a ford guarded by steep and rocky banks on each side. These would offer a serious obstacle to the column of chariots coming up along the road towards the port of Sidon. The Hyksos would be forced to manhandle each individual chariot across the ford. Deprived of their manoeuvrability, they would be vulnerable while this was happening.

Earlier in the day as we sailed past this bay I had taken note of a narrow beach of yellow sand, tucked in behind the northernmost headland. This was protected from the main thrust of the sea by the headland itself. The slope was gradual and the sands looked to be firm enough to allow our chariots to pass over them and reach the hard ground beyond.

I headed back along the coast towards this natural site for an ambuscade. As I passed each of my other galleys I steered close enough to shout my orders across to the men on board. One after the other they went about and followed the *Outrage* back to the landing I had chosen. We had all canvas set and the oarsmen had increased the stroke from cruise speed to attack speed. Cruise is the stroke that the men on the oars can maintain for three hours without respite, while attack speed will exhaust them completely in an hour.

The wakes churned white and curling under our sterns as we raced for the landing ground. We were moving so fast that I doubted the oarsmen could keep up the stroke rate. However, their blood was up and they never faltered until we saw the bay open up ahead of our bows.

I studied it eagerly and realized that it was even better suited to my purpose than I had at first imagined. The beach was wide enough to accommodate two of my galleys simultaneously. This would speed up the task of getting my force ashore.

In addition to this benefit, I saw now that the road along which the Hyksos chariot column would be forced to approach the ford was lined with thick and almost impenetrable bush and trees. This would severely hamper the deployment of the rear echelon of their chariots. They would be unable to advance because the ford would be blocked by the leading vehicles being dragged through it. They could not retreat swiftly because the track was too narrow to allow the chariots to manoeuvre handily. If I concealed my archers in the bushes on each side of the track they would be able to shoot their arrows from murderously close range into these stranded vehicles.

I signalled to Hui to bring his galley up alongside me as we approached the bay. I shouted my orders across the narrow gap between our ships. He understood at once what I was asking for and as we came behind the protection of the headland we dropped our sails in unison and used opposing thrust on our banks of oars to spin our ships through a half-circle so that we were stern on to the beach. Our chariots were now facing the stern loading ramp. The horses were in the traces, and the crews were in the cockpits of the chariots, fully armed and armoured.

At the last moment Toran rushed down from the upper deck and demanded to be allowed to ride with me in the leading vehicle. I admired his courage, but he was no warrior. Ashore he would only be a hindrance. He was my contact with the Supreme Minos and I dare not risk having him killed in the impending battle.

'Stay on board, and observe the action so that later you can report to the Supreme Minos!' I dismissed him brusquely. At that moment the ship's stern came up so hard on the hard wet sand that Toran was thrown off his feet, and he rolled into the scuppers. This solved my problem and I left him to fend for himself.

'Go! Go! Go!' I shouted as the stern ramp dropped open with a crash. I whipped up my team and steered them down the ramp. The horses splashed through the water that reached no higher than their hocks. As soon as they lunged up on to the dry sand, my crew and I jumped down from the cockpit and put our combined weight to the frame, helping the horses to drag the chariot up the beach on to hard dry land. Then we immediately jumped back into the cockpit and headed inland at a canter. Chariot after chariot rolled down the ramp and followed mine in quick succession.

Before we reached the coastal road we came suddenly upon a shabby little village that up to this moment had been hidden from my view by a fold in the ground. It consisted of no more than a dozen squalid hovels. As we galloped between them the occupants came rushing out. The women and their brats were squealing with terror. There were ten men with them. All of them were dressed in rags and they were so filthy that their features were barely recognizable as human. But the men had armed themselves with wooden clubs, and they faced us in a pathetic show of defiance.

Without stopping I bellowed at them in Sumerian, 'Take your women and children and run for a safe place in the forest! An army of rapists and killers is coming up the road from the south. They will be here before noon. Run! Get out of here quickly as you can.' I knew that they would have a hideout in the forest not too far away. They would not have survived this long without one. I looked back and saw them already acting on my warning. Carrying the children and a few meagre bundles of their possessions, they had abandoned their huts and were scurrying into the scrub like a pack of terrified wild animals. I paid them no further heed, but headed for the coastal road which I could now see ahead of me.

When I reached it I halted without crossing over. All seventy of my chariots had come ashore safely and were bunched up behind me in close order. I looked out to sea and saw that my flotilla of ships was already half a league down the coast and aiming to round the next headland behind which they would anchor. Of course their oars were shipped, for they had insufficient men to row them. Every man who was not needed to work the sails had taken up arms and come ashore under Zaras' command. They were following my squadron of chariots at the double.

I could only guess at how long it would take the Hyksos column to arrive at the ford, but unless they were delayed by the pleasures of pillage and rape my guess was that it would not be much more than two or three hours, only just sufficient time to make my dispositions to meet them. While I waited impatiently for Zaras to come up with his foot-soldiers, I studied the terrain on both sides of the river carefully.

Beyond the ford the forest was too dense for my chariots. I would send Zaras and his infantry across the river to take advantage of the thick cover there. However, on this side of the river there was open ground from the beach where we had landed right up to the edge of the forest two hundred yards beyond the road along which we were now parked. Here I would have space to deploy my chariots to the greatest advantage.

Once I had decided on my plan of action, I ordered Hui to take his squadron across the dusty road and conceal them along the verge of the forest, there to await my further orders. Hui was a grand master of chariots. I knew I could place my trust in him. I watched as he ordered his drivers to dismount from their vehicles and walk the horses slowly across the road, so as not to raise a dust cloud to alert the Hyksos to our presence.

As soon as each vehicle was safely across the drivers remounted and then trotted over the springy turf to the edge of the forest. Here they dismounted again and reversed the chariot into the cover of the thick undergrowth. Then they went back into the forest to cut leafy branches, which they dragged forward to build a screen in front of the line of chariots. I walked back with Hui to the edge of the road, and we made certain that the chariots were completely hidden.

While all this was taking place Zaras arrived at the road with his archers. In addition to the powerful recurved bow each of them carried, every man had a hank of spare bowstrings draped around his neck and three leather quivers packed with arrows slung over his shoulders, fifty arrows for each man.

I gave them all a few minutes to catch their breath while I pointed out to Zaras where I wanted him to position himself on the far side of the ford. Then I sent them away again, and watched from the high bank as they waded across the stream two hundred yards below the ford.

As each of them reached the far bank they smeared their faces and the backs of their hands with black river mud, before they climbed the far bank. Zaras and Akemi, his trusted lieutenant, were the last two men up the slope, making certain that they had left no sign to alert the Hyksos to their presence.

Once they reached the level ground above the gorge Zaras concealed his men in the dense forest that bordered the road, placing them at intervals of twenty paces down each side of the track. They were hidden even from close range by the dense foliage and their masks of black mud. The Hyksos column would have to pass between these double ranks of deadly skilled archers.

When Zaras' men had taken up their ambush positions I hurried back towards the edge of the forest where my line of chariots waited in ambush.

Once I was satisfied that they were completely hidden, I selected a tall tree which grew close behind where my own chariot stood. Without much difficulty I climbed to its upper branches. From this vantage point I had a good view of the road on both sides of the ford. I was pleased that even from this height I could not make out any trace of Zaras' men on the far side of the river.

I was at last satisfied with our preparations to receive the Hyksos raiders, and I looked out to sea only to find that my flotilla of warships had also completely disappeared behind the rocky promontory to the north of the river mouth. The sea was empty and the forest around me was still and silent, not disturbed by even the rustle of a wild animal or the call of a bird.

I waited on my branch until I judged by the changing height and angle of the sun that another hour had passed as slowly as a cripple without his crutches. Then at the limit of my field of vision I picked out a pale smear of dust rising above the forest far beyond where Zaras waited with his archers.

This cloud of dust gradually drew closer and became more substantial. Suddenly at the base of the cloud I saw a flash of reflected sunlight off a polished metal surface, a helmet or perhaps the blade of a weapon.

Shortly after this I saw the first pair of chariots appear around the distant bend in the road. There was no doubt that they were Hyksos. The high and ungainly design of the carriage and the clumsy wheels with the gleaming knives set into the rims were all distinctive.

The Hyksos column entered that section of the road along which Zaras waited with his archers. When the head of the column reached the bank of the ford the Hyksos officer in the leading chariot raised his gloved fist to signal the squadron coming up behind him to halt.

Then the commander very carefully studied the ford below him and the ground on our side of the river. Even from this distance I could tell that he was a fop. His cloak was dyed a vivid Tyrian blue. Three or four sparkling necklaces hung at his throat. His helmet was of polished bronze, with hinged silver cheek-pieces that were cunningly engraved, and I coveted it.

Satisfied at last that there was nothing untoward waiting for him, the Hyksos officer jumped down from his vehicle and ran down the rocky track to reach the river at the bottom of it. He did not hesitate but with three of his men following him he plunged into the water and waded across to the opposite bank. Satisfied that it was fordable, he turned and climbed back to where he had left his chariot. He mounted up, and with shouts of encouragement to his horses he steered them down the bank.

His horses balked on the verge of the river, but he cracked his whip over their heads and reluctantly they edged forward until the water lapped their bellies. Then suddenly the offside wheel struck a submerged rock and the chariot was thrown over on its side. The horses in the traces were dragged down on to their knees and pinned there by the weight of the capsized vehicle and the pressure of the running water. The driver and his two crewmen were flung overboard and pulled under by the weight of their armour and accoutrements.

Immediately the men in the following vehicles jumped down and waded out to the floundering men and horses. With a hubbub of shouted orders and counter-orders they pulled the men to the surface before they drowned, and then they lifted the chariot back on to its wheels. Once the horses had regained their footing they heaved the vehicle out of the water and up the steep bank on to level ground directly in front of where our own chariots were hidden.

Cautiously the other enemy drivers steered their chariots down the bank into the ford, where the waiting gang shoved and manhandled them across the river. From my perch I had a fine view of the column of enemy chariots backed up behind the ford, waiting their turn to make the crossing. I was able to keep an accurate count of their total number, and I put this at no more than 160 as opposed to the two hundred chariots that Aton had warned me to expect. I knew that the shortfall could be explained by the losses that the Hyksos must have suffered on the long hard drive that they had made up from northern Egypt over the past sixteen days. The design of their vehicles rendered them susceptible to broken axles and shattered wheel rims. There was also the attrition of their horses caused by the long hours of hard driving over torturous terrain and rough roads.

As each chariot made the crossing of the ford and came up the bank to park on the level on this side of the river, the crews hobbled the horses and then turned them loose to graze. Then the men either threw themselves down on the grass to rest and sleep, or they gathered around hastily lit cooking fires to prepare themselves a hot meal.

I was surprised but pleased that their commander allowed such sloppy behaviour and relaxed discipline to prevail while they were in unknown and potentially hostile territory. He posted no sentries or lookouts, and sent no scouts to reconnoitre the road ahead. He even allowed his men to set aside their heavy armour and weapons while they relaxed. Most of them seemed close to exhaustion; and none of them approached the perimeter of the forest in which our chariots were hidden. Even those of them who were forced to answer the call of nature did not wander off too far from their comrades to do their business. Here in this strange and foreign land the Hyksos troops instinctively kept close together for mutual protection.

On the far side of the river the congestion of men, chariots and horses on the road through the forest was gradually relieved. I was counting the chariots as they arrived on this bank. I was anticipating the moment when the enemy had been split into two equal groups and all of them had been completely lulled by the absence of any apparent threat. As the moment drew closer I took the bright yellow silk scarf from my pocket, where I had concealed it, and I unrolled it.

The Hyksos commander in the blue cloak and conspicuous helmet was still standing on the bank above the ford supervising the crossing of his troops. However, I could still see nothing of Zaras or any of his men, although I knew precisely where every one of them was hidden. When he had seen me climb into the tree, Zaras had given me a cheery wave before settling down in his own hide.

The next Hyksos chariot climbed the track out of the river gorge, with the horses lunging against the traces and the men behind it heaving and straining. This was number eighty-five of those who had so far made the river crossing. The Hyksos force was now in the critical position of being divided into two almost equal halves; neither of which was in a position to offer support to the other.

In my tome on the art of war I have written: *An enemy riven is an enemy driven.* This was an opportunity to demonstrate the wisdom of my own teachings.

I stood up slowly, balancing easily on the branch of my tree. I waved the bright yellow scarf three times around my head. Across the river I saw Zaras come to his feet immediately. He raised his clenched fist in my direction, acknowledging my signal. In his other hand he held his war bow, with an arrow nocked and ready.

I waited just long enough to watch the thick undergrowth on both sides of the road come alive with Zaras' men as they rose from cover. As one man they lifted their bows, poised for the order to release their first volley.

Zaras was first to let his arrow fly. It rose high against the backdrop of the distant blue mountains. I knew which target he had chosen even before his arrow began the drop. The Hyksos commander was still standing on the bank with his back turned to Zaras. He was thrown forward by the heavy strike of the arrow, and he tumbled down the steep bank out of my line of sight.

Zaras already had three more arrows in flight. He is very quick; every bit as fast as I am. His men followed his lead and their missiles rose like a quick dark cloud of locusts and then dropped upon the line of stranded Hyksos chariots strung out along the road between the two companies of bowmen.

In the heat most of the Hyksos charioteers had removed their helmets and body armour. Their horses were protected only by the thick felt battle blankets that covered their backs but left their withers and rumps exposed. I could clearly hear the soft 'Whump! Whump!' sound of flint arrowheads striking living flesh, and driving deep.

This was followed immediately by the cries of wounded men and the shrill whinnying of their horses as they also were struck. Pandemonium raged through the closely crowded ranks of our enemies.

Panicking horses reared in their traces and hacked at the men who were trying to lead them with their fore-hooves. Those animals that were struck in the hindquarters lashed out in pain with their back legs, smashing in the bows of the vehicle they were towing and throwing the occupants overboard.

As soon as the drivers lost control of their pain-maddened horses they tried to bolt, but there was no space in which they could manoeuvre. They merely crashed into the chariot which blocked the road ahead of them, and shunted that vehicle into the one ahead of it. Swiftly it developed into a chain reaction that overturned some chariots, tore the wheels off others, maimed horses and drivers and eventually caught those chariots in the front ranks and hurled them down the steep gorge into the river.

Horses, chariots and men slid and rolled down the incline on top of the men and chariots that were already waist deep in the ford, struggling to get across to the far bank. This mass of maddened animals and men, together with the wreckage of their chariots, effectively blocked the ford. There was no escape in that direction.

Each of Zaras' archers carried fifty arrows and at that close range very few of them missed. I saw one man thrown headlong from the footplate of his chariot who managed miraculously to keep on his feet without being trampled or shredded by the wheel knives. He started to run to get clear of the turmoil, but then he stopped abruptly after only a few strides as three arrows pegged simultaneously into his naked back. The razor-sharp flint heads protruded abruptly from his hairy chest. Elegantly as a dancer, he spun in a pirouette before he collapsed and was sucked from my view into this maelstrom of death.

On my side of the river the Hyksos charioteers who had already managed to cross the ford jumped up from where they were lying in the grass or sitting beside their cooking fires. They stared back in helpless horror at the slaughter of their comrades on the far bank.

I watched no longer, but slid down the trunk of my tree and darted to my chariot. One of my team leaned down and grabbed my arm to swing me up into the cockpit. As I gathered up the reins I gave the order, 'Cohort will advance. Walk! Trot! Charge!' My cry was taken up along the line.

In extended line abreast my chariots burst out of the forest at full gallop. Hui and I were in the centre, running wheel to wheel. On both sides of us the squadrons were angled back in arrowhead formation.

Ahead of us most of the Hyksos who had been scattered over the open ground had run back to the bank of the river. Now they crowded there, staring down in helpless horror at the fate that had overtaken their comrades in the ford below them and on the crowded forest road, which was still being flailed by Zaras' arrow storm.

None of the Hyksos chariots on this bank of the river were manned. There were no horses in the traces to draw them. The knee-haltered animals that had been turned loose were scattered across the open grassland. Most of the enemy drivers turned back from the river, and raced after their animals in a futile attempt to recapture them. The horses were startled by the sudden uproar and confusion and they ran wild. Even their leg hobbles could only slow them to the speed of a running man.

I threw my head back and shouted with laughter to relieve my fear and express my jubilation. Even above the rumble of the wheels and the thunder of hooves on the hard ground I heard Hui echo my laughter. We came down upon them in a solid phalanx, running wheel to wheel with no spaces between us through which any of the Hyksos might escape. Yet still they seemed oblivious to our charge. Most of them were not even looking in our direction. Only those who had given up the race to catch their own teams now stood mesmerized with terror and stared back at us dumbly. They knew that they could not out-run our charge. Our bows were raised, and our arrows were nocked.

When we were less than seventy paces from the nearest of them I shouted the order to let our arrows fly. Even from a racing chariot most of my lads could hit a running man from fifty paces. Most of the fugitives went down before they could reach their vehicles.

I saw only one of them who was able to make it back to where he had parked his chariot. He seized his bow from the weapons bin and a handful of arrows from the quiver. Then he turned back to face us. He was a huge hairy beast of a man, strong and maddened with rage like a wild boar standing at bay before the hounds. He raised his bow and got a single arrow away before our arrows began to strike him. His shaft struck the driver of the chariot three down the line from mine. He was one of Lord Kratas' sons. He was a fine lad; brave as his father and fifty times more beautiful. He was one of my favourites, and the arrow killed him instantly.

I shot three arrows into the Hyksos brute before he could nock another of this own. Then every second archer in our line was shooting at him, until he bristled with our arrows like a porcupine with quills. But he stayed on his feet and shot one back at me. It struck high on the forehead of my helmet, and glanced away humming, but the shock almost threw me out of the vehicle.

I never suggested that the Hyksos are cowards. In the end it took seventeen arrows to kill this one. Five of them were mine. I counted them later.

After that it was butchery. I am not averse to a little butchery when the opportunity presents itself, especially in circumstances such as these. However, slave-taking is considerably more lucrative than butchery, so I was the first to call to the fleeing Hyksos in their own language, 'Yield, you whining dogs of Gorrab, or die!'

'Yield or die!' The call was taken up along our line of charging chariots: 'Yield or die!'

Most of the fleeing Hyksos dropped to their knees at my first command and lifted up their empty hands in surrender, but a few of them kept running until my chariot line opened and spread out to encircle them. Then they came up short and panting with exertion and terror. They looked around at the drawn bows which were aimed at them from every direction, and then their terror turned to resignation and one after another they fell to earth with cries of: 'Mercy, in the name of all the gods! Spare us, great Lord Taita. We meant you no harm.' The good god Horus will attest that I am by no means a glory-seeker. However, I am honest enough to admit that I was pleased and flattered to be recognized on the battlefield by my own enemies.

'Put the ropes on these little heroes,' I ordered Hui. 'Sweep the field and bring in all their horses. Allow none of them to escape.'

I put my own horses into a tight half-circle and drove them back to the lip of the gorge above the river crossing. I reined in on the crest, and looked down on the carnage that choked the ford and the road beyond it.

Here also the fighting was over and Zaras' men were taking in their prisoners and gathering the loot. I could see at a quick glance that their casualties had been similar to ours on this side of the river: only light to minimal. I was pleased that Zaras was unhurt and was supervising the work of taking in the prisoners and rounding up the Hyksos horses. These animals were every bit as valuable as the men.

Zaras looked up suddenly and saw me standing on the top of the bank above him. He saluted me and then cupped his hands around his mouth and shouted across the gorge, 'More power to your sword, Lord Taita! Another good day's hunting, indeed. I shall soon be able to afford a wife.'

It was a silly little joke. I had already made Zaras a wealthy man with his share of the bounty we had captured at the Tamiat fort. And his quip about taking a wife was not very subtle. Nevertheless I raised a smile and gave him a wave before I turned away.

I sent a horseman out on to the headland behind which the flotilla was hidden with orders to fly the blue recall flag.

By now my jubilation was swiftly evaporating, for the worst part of the day lay ahead of me. I had to deal with the Hyksos horses, many of which were injured. I have always had a deep affection for these animals. I was the first man in Egypt to break and tame one of these marvellous beasts, which only made my duty towards them now more onerous.

Riding ten of the unwounded horses bareback my grooms and I rounded up those surviving horses which were still able to stand. Swiftly I separated out those animals that were unhurt or only lightly wounded and these I sent northwards along the coastal road back to Sidon, with my grooms to herd them along. These were trained chariot animals and therefore particularly valuable.

Those animals which had been grievously or fatally wounded I had despatched at once to put an end to their suffering. First I placed a peace offering of crushed millet before each of them, and when they lowered their heads and took a good mouthful one of my men swung a heavy bronze-headed club down between their ears to shatter the poll of their skull. Their deaths were mercifully swift.

Once this ghastly work was done I turned my attention to our Hyksos prisoners. My order of precedence was clear-cut. As much as I loved the horses, I hated their owners with a deep and bitter loathing. I moved quickly along the ranks of kneeling men examining each of them in a cursory manner. If they were unwounded or were only lightly injured I sent them down to the beach to await the return of my galleys.

However, there were many prisoners who were too badly injured to be of further use to us, even as slaves. A man with a barbed arrowhead buried deeply in his chest cavity does not have much time left to wield an oar. I ordered these miserable creatures to be laid out in the shade, given a drink of water to keep them alive a little longer and left them to work out their own destinies with their vile god, who I was certain was hovering close by.

I know that I should have alleviated their suffering as I had their wounded horses, with a blow of the club to their heads. But they were Hyksos and I owed them no special favours.

At last I had a moment to think about myself and my two royal charges. I remounted my chariot and drove back to the river crossing, and parked on the high bank. I left the reins in the hands of my driver and I walked to the lip of the gorge. This section of the battlefield was now devoid of a living soul. Although I knew where to search for the body of the enemy commander, I could not pick him out immediately in the litter of wrecked chariots, strewn equipment and corpses on the opposite bank. Then I spotted a distinctive speck of indigo blue much further down the slope than I had expected to find him, almost at the river's edge.

I started down the steep slope, keeping my balance even with loose stones rolling under my feet. When I reached the bottom I jumped down into the water and waded across to the far bank.

I found the Hyksos captain's corpse deeply wedged between two large rocks. He had rolled down the slope almost to the water's edge. Only a fold of his cloak had revealed his resting place to me.

I reached down and grabbed one of his legs by the ankle and heaved him out of the crack in which his body had jammed. There was a copious splash of blood on the cloak, but my servant was an excellent launderer. I folded the cloak and set it aside. Then I searched for the dead man's helmet. I had to work back up the slope to where he had first struck the rocks. There I found it; also providentially hidden under the wreckage of a chariot. The looters who had been here before me had overlooked both the helmet and the corpse.

I sat down with the helmet in my lap and admired the engravings. These were marvellously rendered images of the Egyptian gods: Hathor and Osiris on the cheek-pieces and Horus on the forehead. The Hyksos captain must have taken it from the corpse of one of our high-ranking officers on another battlefield. It was a treasure almost beyond price. It made my own head-dress look shabby and common. It had been badly dented where the Hyksos arrow had struck.

I discarded it without a pang; then almost reverentially I replaced it with the gold and silver masterpiece. The interior was padded with leather, and it fitted me as though it had been crafted especially for me. At that moment I would have given a great deal for a mirror.

I scrambled back down to where I had left the captain's corpse. It was adorned with three necklaces; like the helmet they were all three lovely creations. But one of them was decorated with a rock-crystal carving of the head of Seth. I hurled it into the river. The other two were marvellously carved ivory depictions of elephants and camels. The princesses would adore them, although they had never seen an elephant in their young lives.

I climbed back to where I had left my chariot. And my driver ogled my helmet, struck dumb with awe. I drove back to the beach where most of the men paused in what they were doing to stare at me. I must have been a wondrous sight.

The ships of my flotilla sailed back around the headland into the bay. They ran up on to the beach, stern first, and dropped their loading ramps.

The prisoners I had selected were marched on board, led down to the lowest deck and shackled by both ankles to the rowing benches. They would remain down there with their bare feet in the bilge water until Seth sent his dark angel to free them from their durance.

An hour before sunset we had taken all our own men and chariots back on board, and we were ready to set sail for Sidon. Toran was standing beside me on the quarterdeck. He looked back at the shore and nodded at the Hyksos wounded that I had left above the beach.

'I see that you have spared the lives of the wounded enemy. I have never before heard of such clemency from a victorious general.'

'I am sorry to have disappointed you. But I have left them for others to deal with. Here they come now.'

The inhabitants of the village whom earlier I had sent to hide from the approaching Hyksos chariots had returned. The men were still armed with the wooden spades and hoes with which they had earlier attempted to threaten us.

Now they ignored us completely. We watched as the man who appeared to be the leader of this sorry rabble stood over an injured Hyksos and hefted his spade. Then he swung it down with both hands from high above his head, as though he was chopping a log of firewood. Even from this distance we could hear the victim's skull burst with a sound like an over-ripe melon dropped on a stone floor. Then the man with the spade moved on implacably, leaving the Hyksos warrior's body jerking and twitching in his death throes.

The next wounded man saw him coming and tried to drag himself away on his elbows. The shaft of the arrow that had divided the vertebrae of his spine was still protruding from his back. His paralysed legs slithered after him. He was screeching like a woman in labour. The peasant laughed as he stood over him, and with his spade prodded him into suitable position to receive the mercy stroke.

The slovenly women and their grubby children followed their menfolk closely, swarming over the fresh Hyksos corpses like blow-flies, stripping them of every stitch of their bloodied clothing and any trinkets of possible value. The shrieks of their excited laughter carried clearly to us across the water.

'My lord, it is now apparent that despite appearances you are not a man to be trifled with.' Toran looked at me with renewed respect.

When I steered the *Outrage* into Sidon harbour an hour before noon the next day both my girls were on the jetty, waving and dancing with excitement. It was always a competition between them as to who would be first to greet me whenever I returned from one of my periodic absences. Tehuti was usually the more demure and restrained, but on this occasion she took both me and her sister by surprise. With the training Zaras had given her recently she had developed into an exceptional athlete and swordswoman.

Now she demonstrated some of these new skills. She kicked off her sandals, and flew barefooted over the stone slabs of the jetty and sprang out over the gap that still separated my ship from the shore. This was a distance of fully five yards. Had she fallen short she would have been crushed and drowned between the hull and the jetty before I would have been able to rescue her.

I died a dozen agonizing deaths in the brief period that she was airborne. But when her feet hit the deck my terror turned instantly to the anger of relief. I rushed down the deck, determined to remonstrate with her for such unseemly behaviour.

'You look so dashing in your new cloak and helmet, Taita darling. Where did you find them? They make you look as noble as any king! But have you brought us a present?' All this was uttered in a single breath. My anger collapsed, and I hugged her to my bosom.

'Of course I brought you a gift. But tell me first, have you behaved yourself while I was away?'

'You gave me no option. You took all my temptations away with you.' Her grin was impish, and she looked across at the galley which followed mine into the harbour. Zaras stood on the steering deck, and even at the distance that separated them a look passed between the two of them like a strike of lightning.

It took another four days for us to complete the preparations for the final voyage to Knossos in Crete. Toran invited us to travel on board his flagship. This magnificent trireme was at least twice the size of any of my Sumerian-built galleys.

'You and your charges will be very much more comfortable aboard the *Sacred Bull* than on one of your little luggers.' This was the name of his vessel: rather pretentious, I thought. Moreover I did not particularly like his dismissive reference to my own fighting galleys which had just proved themselves in their first significant victory over the Hyksos. I hesitated.

'If you travel with me we would have the time and opportunity to discuss in more detail what you should expect when we reach Knossos. The politics and protocol of the Court of the Supreme Minos are highly complicated, but they must be strictly observed.' Still I hesitated and he continued persuasively,

'My chef is celebrated as one of the best in the Hellenic world, and I should also mention that I have on board twenty large amphorae of the finest red wines of the Cyclades. I understand that this is but a poor incentive for you to spend two weeks in my company, but I am enamoured of your wit and in awe of your learning and erudition. I beg you to humour me, my lord, and accept my offer of hospitality.' My remaining reservations evaporated in the face of such compelling argument.

'You are extremely gracious, Ambassador,' I accepted, but I did wonder how much it was my company he valued so highly, or was it more that of little Loxias, the Minoan handmaiden to my princesses.

Both Tehuti and Bekatha objected strenuously to these travel arrangements that I had agreed upon with Toran. They came to my cabin in the *Outrage* and presented me with a long list of their objections, each one weaker and less convincing than the one preceding it.

I turned on them my most forbidding expression and listened without interruption until their protestations tapered off, and they looked at me with such distress that I took pity on them.

'So, am I to believe that both of you mistrust Ambassador Toran and believe he is plotting to lure you on board his ship to have you murdered in your sleep?' They squirmed with embarrassment.

'And when did the two of you conceive the notion that the *Sacred Bull* is such a large ship that it is not able to float, and that it will sink and drown all of us?'

Their silence continued, until suddenly Bekatha's tears overflowed her eyelids and streamed down her cheeks. I was appalled. If I had realized the extent of her distress, I would not have teased her so unkindly. I jumped up from my stool to comfort her. She pushed me away, and turned her face from me.

'I will never see him again,' she sobbed. I pretended to be mystified by this statement.

'Whom will you never see again? Are you talking about Ambassador Toran?'

She ignored my question and went on in a welter of words. 'You promised Tehuti that we could all be together at least until we reached Crete. Only then would we have to be sequestered in the seraglio of the Supreme Minos. But you promised that as long as we were discreet, we could go on seeing them until we arrived in Crete. But now we will never be able to see them again. My life is ending.'

'I need clarification, darling Bekatha,' I interrupted her. 'Whom are we discussing here?'

Bekatha turned to face me again, but now her expression was furious. 'You know very well whom we are talking about. We are talking about my Hui.'

'And my Zaras.' Tehuti spoke quietly but just as clearly as her little sister.

It had indeed been my intention to gently and subtly wean the two of them off their perilous liaisons long before we arrived in Crete and took up residence in the palace of the Minos. Now my plan had struck the reef of their intransigence, and was sinking under me.

I tried my best to jolly them along, but at every turn I was immediately rebuffed by the two of them. In the end I capitulated.

Both Zaras and Hui were aboard the *Sacred Bull* when we finally sailed from the harbour of Sidon.

W e were a flotilla of seven ships. The *Sacred Bull* sailed in the centre of this formation. Two of the swiftest galleys, which should have been commanded by Zaras and myself, sailed as the vanguard. However Dilbar and Akemi were now the captains.

My other four galleys acted as our flankers and rearguard

for the flotilla. Each ship maintained visual contact with its immediate neighbours. In this way we could sweep the sea for sixty leagues in every direction. I had drawn up a system of simple flag signals so that on the flagship I would be warned of danger long before it actually materialized.

All these precautions were essential, for this part of the Middle Sea was the hunting ground of the Sea Peoples. These were renegades and outcasts from all the civilized and law-abiding nations. In exile they had banded together into a loose affiliation of pirates. They gave allegiance to no one, called no man master. They were completely without morals, conscience or remorse. They were dangerous as ravening lions or as poisonous snakes and scorpions. They rendered the seas more perilous than any hidden reef or pack of man-eating sharks. In Egypt we referred to them as 'the Sons of Yamm'. Yamm is the god of the sea when it is turbulent and raging. He is not one of the kindly gods.

However this was the most propitious period of the year for sailing on the Great Green, which is our Egyptian name for this part of the Middle Sea. The weather was mild, the winds fair and the sea calm. As passengers on the *Sacred Bull* we were enjoying ourselves.

Zaras continued Tehuti's weapons training. He improvised a floating wooden target for her arrows which he towed behind the ship on a line of variable length.

He had also brought with him wooden practice swords, whose blades were padded with sheepskin, and wooden shields. He and Tehuti sparred on the open deck. Her triumphant cries registered the fact that she had scored another hit. She never held back on the ferocity of her thrusts and cuts. These were always full-blooded and Zaras, that consummate swordsman, seemed to have difficulty avoiding them. Strangely he never was able to lay his blade on her in retaliation.

Bekatha joined in with the archery lessons, but she was not

strong enough to draw the same weight bow as her big sister, so she could not shoot an arrow as far or as accurately. She sulked for a day, and then challenged Tehuti to a single bout with the wooden swords. The bruises she received from her sister took a week to fade.

She retired gracefully from the contest, and diverted all energy into teaching Colonel Hui the game of bao. Hui made a lamentable student. She drubbed him mercilessly. When he at last rebelled at the torment she switched his lessons to singing and dancing and riddling.

To the surprise of us all Hui had a good voice and a light step. He excelled in the first two disciplines, especially as the dancing gave him an excuse to embrace his teacher. However, his great strength was his riddling. Bekatha struggled to keep pace with his devious reasoning.

'Two mothers and three daughters go out riding. How many horses do they need?' He put the question to her.

'Five, of course.'

'Wrong,' he gloated. 'They need only three. They are grand-mother, mother and daughter.'

'Oh, you silly man!' She threw the pomegranate she was eating at his head. Hui caught it and took a bite before he threw it back at her.

Ambassador Toran's chef lived up fully to his master's promises of excellence. He served us with a succession of delicious meals which we ate under a canvas sun-awning on the poop deck to the music of a four-man band of flutes and other wind instruments.

The Cyclades wines that Toran served were a glory on the tongue, and only the conversation sparkled brighter.

They were happy days, and like carefree children we all laughed a great deal and were happy.

Of course, nothing is ever perfect. It seemed that the *Sacred Bull* was infested with rats or some other strange nocturnal creatures. When we had all retired to our bunks I heard them scampering surreptitiously up and down the passageway outside my cabin, or rustling and squeaking in the cabins on either side of mine, where I was sure my innocent girls were fast asleep.

Even the master cabin of Ambassador Toran, across the aisle from mine, was not free from these mysterious disturbances. He did not seem to resent them for at intervals I heard him chuckling and whispering, and the replies he received sounded very much to me like feminine Minoan exhortations to greater endeavour.

W e had been fourteen days at sea, and Toran and I were sitting in the shade cast by the mainsail over the foredeck. We were deep in conversation over a flagon of his excellent wine when we were disturbed by sudden activity on the poop deck.

I glanced up and saw that Captain Hypatos, the Minoan commander of the *Sacred Bull*, was flying signal flags at the masthead. I stood up abruptly, interrupting Toran in the middle of a sentence.

'Something is happening that might be important. Come with me.' We hurried back along the deck to the group of ship's officers gathered on the poop deck. All of them were staring ahead.

'What is it, Hypatos?' Toran demanded of his captain, who pointed over our bows.

'A signal from one of our scouting galleys, sir. But the distance is extreme. I'm sorry, but the message is unclear,' Captain Hypatos apologized.

I glanced at the ship which was hull down on the horizon. It was my own ship, the *Outrage*, now being commanded by Akemi. 'They are reporting that their sister ship is under attack and being boarded by the crew of a strange vessel.' I translated

315

the flag signal to plain language for them. 'Akemi signals that he is going to Dilbar's assistance.'

'How do you deduce all that information, my lord?' Hypatos looked astonished.

'I simply read Akemi's signal,' I explained patiently.

'At that distance?' Toran intervened. 'That seems like witch-craft to me, Taita.'

'The falcon is my personal hieroglyph,' I told him lightly. 'Both that bird and I have sharp eyesight. Please order Hypatos to set all sail and order his rowers to go to attack speed.'

It took us over an hour to catch up with our vanguard galleys. When we did so we discovered that they were hove to, with oars shipped and sails backed. They were locked in battle with an Arabian dhow. It was a larger ship than either of my galleys; with twin lateen sails and a headsail, which were now all aback and in disarray. It was obvious that the fighting was almost over, for the crew of the dhow were throwing down their weapons, and raising their empty hands.

As we closed with the locked vessels I saw that the name of the captured dhow was printed on her bows in Egyptian hiero-glyphs. It was the *Dove*. I smiled at the incongruity of it. She was certainly no bird of peace.

'Lay us alongside the enemy!' I ordered Hypatos. He completed the manoeuvre skilfully; and I clambered down the rope ladder and landed on the deck of the embattled dhow. Zaras followed me closely as a sheepdog. I could sense how disappointed he was to have missed the fighting. Both Dilbar and Akemi came to meet me, sword in hand.

'What have we here?' I asked them as they saluted me. With the bloodied blade of his weapon Dilbar indicated the lines of prisoners kneeling on the deck. Their hands were locked behind their necks, and their foreheads were pressed to the planking.

'These little rascals took it that we were sailing alone,' Dilbar explained. 'They made out that they were floundering and

316

asked for assistance. There were only a few of them on the deck. When we came up alongside those who had been hiding below jumped out, and grappled us with boarding hooks. Then they all came storming over our side.' He looked smug. 'Of course we were ready for them. We kept them busy until Akemi arrived and joined in the revels.'

'How many have you captured?' I demanded.

'I'm afraid we were forced to kill a few of them, before these other motherless bastards had the good sense to surrender,' Akemi apologized. He knew that I preferred slaves to corpses. 'However, we have bagged thirty-eight live ones.'

'Good work, both of you. Share them out between your galleys, and find them employment on the rowing benches.'

As our men began hoisting the captives to their feet and shoving them to their new stations on the slave decks of my galleys, I spotted one of prisoners who was trying to make himself inconspicuous in the rear rank. This was a futile effort. He was obviously the pirate leader, for he was the most richly dressed and, despite his attempt at servility, there was about him a natural air of grace and self-assurance. Nevertheless he was trying to avoid making eye contact with me.

'Nakati!' I accosted him, and he straightened his back and lifted his chin before he looked into my face. Then he gave me a guard's salute, clenched fist held to his chest.

'My lord!' he acknowledged me. 'I prayed never to meet you again.'

'The gods are not always attentive to our pleas,' I commiserated with him.

'Do you know this animal, master?' Dilbar intervened in our conversation.

'He was a captain in the red battalion of Pharaoh's guards. Five or six years ago he knifed his own colonel to death in a drunken squabble over a tavern harlot in Abydos. He disappeared before he could be apprehended and hanged.'

'Shall I kill him now?'

I shook my head. 'Let's delay that pleasure for a little while longer.' There had been a time when Nakati had been a first-rate fighting officer, seemingly destined for higher rank and greater things. 'In the meantime keep him busy at the oars.'

'Should I spare the whip on him?'

'Surely you jest, Dilbar? See to it that he is given his full measure of all the slave rations, including the lash.'

'I recall that you were always beneficent, Lord Taita.' Nakati kept a straight face. I found his sense of humour laudable in the circumstances and he spoke my name with respect. I nodded to the deck officer to take him away with the other prisoners. Then I crossed to the main cargo hatch of the *Dove*.

'Dilbar, have your men knock out the wedges and prise open this hatch.' When the cover of the hatch crashed back on to the deck I peered down into the hold. It was packed with ingots of copper and tin. It was obvious that we were not the first customers to receive the attentions of Nakati and his crew.

'Transfer this hoard into the *Outrage*,' I ordered Dilbar. 'Then put a prize crew into the pirate and bring her along in convoy with us to Crete.' An imaginative plan was already forming in the back of my mind. However, I wanted Nakati to spend sufficient time on the rowing bench to put him in the proper mood to listen to my proposition with his full attention.

I waited until we were only four or five days short of our landfall on the island of Crete; then I ordered him to be ferried across to the *Sacred Bull* and escorted to my cabin.

All his fine feathers had been plucked. He was dressed only in his chains and a brief and filthy loincloth. His arrogant manner had been ameliorated. His back was scored by the lash. His arms were lean and hardened from heaving on the oar. His belly was as concave as that of a starving greyhound. There was no superfluous meat on his frame.

However, I judged that although he had been well whipped, he was not yet beaten. The coals still glowed beneath the ashes of his pride. He had not disappointed me.

'Have you still got a wife in Thebes or has she run off with somebody else?' I asked him and he stared at me. His eyes were hard and bright. His famous sense of humour was restrained.

'Children?' I persisted. 'How many? Boys or girls? Do they ever think of you, I wonder? Do you ever think of them?'

'Why don't you grow yourself another set of genitalia, then go and fuck yourself to death?' he suggested, and I suppressed a smile. I really admired his panache. I ignored his suggestion and went on as though he had not voiced it.

'I suspect that at heart you are still a son of our very Egypt; a civilized man and not a bloody pirate.' He showed no reaction, but I kept on at him. 'You made one mistake, and it cost you everything you ever had of value.' Despite himself he flinched. Unerringly I had hit another raw nerve, and he flared at me:

'What's it to you, you smug bastard?'

'Not much to me,' I agreed. 'But I suspect it means a great deal to your wife and children.'

'It's too late now. Not much anyone can do about it.' His tone changed again, and there was an ocean of regret in his voice.

'I can get you pardoned,' I told him.

He snorted with bitter laughter. 'You are not Pharaoh.'

'No, I am not, but I am the bearer of the hawk seal. My word is as good as that of Pharaoh.' I saw hope dawn in his eyes, and it was a good thing to watch.

'What do you want of me, my lord?' He was begging now; no more defiance.

'I want you to help me free our very Egypt from the Hyksos hordes.'

'You make it sound so simple, but I have spent more than half my life in that forlorn cause.'

'It is apparent to me that since you fled Thebes you have become one of the princes of the Sea Peoples. I am certain many of your comrades are also Egyptian outcasts who would fight for the chance to return to their homeland.'

Nakati inclined his head in assent. 'They would fight even harder for a little silver and a plot of rich black Egyptian soil to plough,' he suggested.

'That is the reward I can promise you, and them,' I assured him. 'Bring me fifty ships such as your *Dove* and the men to serve and fight them, and I shall give you back your pride, your honour and your freedom.'

He thought about what I had said and then at last he shook his head. 'I could never find you fifty ships. But let me have my own *Dove* and her crew and within three months I will return with at least fifteen more ships. My solemn oath on it!'

I went to the door of my cabin and opened it. Zaras and three of his men were waiting there with drawn swords, ready to rush to my rescue.

'Send to the galley and have the cook bring food and wine.'

When Zaras returned I was seated at the table with Nakati opposite me. He had washed his face in my basin and combed his wet hair. He was dressed in the clothing I had provided. Although he was tall and broad-shouldered he was lean, as I am, and my clothes fitted him well.

The cabin boy who followed Zaras set a large bowl of cold salted pork before Nakati and I poured three bumpers of red wine and gestured to Zaras to join us at the table. We started to talk, and we were still talking the next morning when the dawn broke.

Captain Hypatos backed his sails and our prize crew brought the *Dove* alongside. Nakati went down to her deck and resumed command of his dhow, then he sailed her across to the galleys in which I had imprisoned his crew. On each of them he went down to the slave deck and picked out his own men who were chained to the benches. Then he brought them up into the sunlight.

These men were in a sorry state. They wore only loincloths and like Nakati they all bore the marks of the lash. On my orders, Akemi and Dilbar had driven them hard. They had crossed the borderline of despair and resignation. I knew that if anybody could bring them back it would be Nakati. I would not have enjoyed the challenge.

Nakati saluted me from the poop deck of the *Dove*. Then he put the helm over and bore away on a northerly heading. The pirate fleet was out there, lurking in their lairs that were scattered among the myriad uninhabited islands of the Aegean archipelago.

'Will you ever see him again, I wonder?' Zaras asked, and I shrugged. I would not tempt the dark gods by replying affirmatively to the question; however, I had an agreement with Nakati, and I am a good enough judge of men to believe that I could trust him to do his very best to keep to it.

I had already proven to my own satisfaction, and to the chagrin of the enemy, that I could land a large detachment of chariots at any poorly defended spot on the Hyksos-occupied shore, visit death and mayhem on Gorrab's forces, and then take to the ships again before the enemy could retaliate. Of course, my tiny army could never hope to engage in a full-scale campaign against the tyrant, but I could certainly force him to divert a very large number of his main troops from his southern border with our very Egypt to defend his extended northern front.

I had agreed to pay Nakati and his men one thousand silver mem each as a bounty to compensate them for the plunder they would have to forgo when they sailed under me. Then when the campaign against the Hyksos led eventually to the liberation of all of Egypt his men would be pardoned for any offences they may have committed, including piracy and murder. Each of them would be honourably discharged from the navy and granted Egyptian citizenship. In addition they would be rewarded with five hundred kha-ta of fertile and irrigable land on the estate of Lord Taita of Mechir along the River Nile south of the city of Thebes.

As I watched the *Dove* sail away I wondered how much of this largesse I had promised Nakati I could retrieve from the treasury of Pharaoh, and how much I would have to meet from my own coffers. No doubt Pharaoh would be grateful, but as for expressing his gratitude in coin I was less sanguine. My Mem and his silver are not readily parted.

I knew that Captain Hypatos had made this same voyage between Sumeria and Crete on a number of previous occasions. But when I asked him when we might expect to reach Knossos he became evasive.

'Of course, it depends on the winds and the currents that we encounter, but I would wager that within sixteen days we will make our landfall on the sacred island of Crete.'

I was pleased to have this estimate. Our chariot horses had been confined to their stalls long enough. Their general condition was deteriorating. Their coats were staring and they were losing weight and becoming apathetic. Hui was as worried as I was.

At dinner on the fourteenth evening of the promised sixteen, I reminded Hypatos of his declaration and he backed his sails a little.

'Lord Taita, you must understand that all mariners are subject to the will and whim of the great god Poseidon, who rules the seas. Sixteen days was my estimate, and a good one at that.'

One thing that both Hypatos and I were reasonably certain of was that we were no longer in danger of pirate attack. No corsair would risk operating so close to the main harbour of the most powerful fleet in all the seas. So I flew the recall signal for all my galleys. Long before sunset they had taken up a close escort formation around the *Sacred Bull*.

Long before dawn the next morning I left my cabin quietly, went on deck and climbed to the masthead. In the first misty grey light of pre-dawn I swept the horizon ahead of our bows and found it empty; devoid of any sign of land.

I was about to descend the mast and return to my cabin when an albatross appeared out of the mists and hovered above me on wide pinions, turning its head from side to side to peer down at me. I am fascinated by all birdlife and this was the first chance I had ever been given to study one of these most magnificent of all birds from such close range. He seemed equally interested in me, gliding almost close enough for me to touch while he studied me with glittering black eyes. But when I reached out my hand to him, he banked away steeply and disappeared back into the haze from which he had materialized.

I looked down at the deck before I started to descend and was surprised to see that while I had been absorbed by the great bird a couple had come up from below decks and were standing in the bows of the ship gazing out to the horizon just as intently as I had done a few minutes before. I could not be certain who they were, for they were swaddled in heavy clothing against the dawn chill and their faces were turned away from me.

When at last they turned to face each other I was able to recognize that they were Zaras and Tehuti. They glanced around the deck but they did not raise their eyes to the masthead. Satisfied that they were unobserved, Zaras took her in his arms and kissed her. She stood on tiptoe and clung to him with a desperation that was palpable. I felt like a voyeur, intruding on this intimate moment. But before I could avert my gaze Tehuti drew back a little to speak and I could read her lips.

'As always, Taita was right. There is no sign of land. The gods have given us at least one more precious day to be together before they tear us apart forever.' Her expression was tragic.

'You are a princess,' Zaras reminded her, 'and I am a warrior. We both have a sacred duty to perform, no matter what the cost. We will endure.'

'I know that what you say is the truth, but when you go you will take my heart and my will to live with you. You will leave me an empty husk.' She reached up and kissed him again.

I turned my head away. I could not watch the depths of their despair for a moment longer. I also had a sacred duty to perform. We are all mere insects caught in the web that the gods spin for us. There is no way that we can escape it.

I waited until they had left the deck and gone below before I climbed down the mast and went to my cabin.

I had not wept since that long-ago day that Tehuti's mother died. But I wept again now.

The next morning I climbed once again to the masthead, and this time I was not disappointed. In the early light the island of Crete lay low and blue on our starboard horizon. This was not where I had expected to find it, for rather than dead ahead it lay fifty leagues or more to the north of us.

In truth I was not unhappy with this minor setback. I was not in such a desperate hurry to make the acquaintance of the Supreme Minos that in order to do so I was willing to deprive my princesses of these few additional days of their happiness. I determined to make the most of this unexpected opportunity to see more of this kingdom of myths and legends. Already the romance and mystic might of it seemed to be reaching out to me across the waters.

I wanted to enjoy it to the full without the intrusion of others, but it was not to be. From the *Outrage*, which sailed ahead of us, there was sudden commotion and wild cries of 'Land ho!'

Almost at once the deck below me seemed to be swarming with excited humanity. They crowded the starboard rail and climbed into the rigging for a better view of the land.

I was not left alone for long before Ambassador Toran climbed up to join me at the masthead. He was even more elated than I was, and like me he was unconcerned by the additional term of our voyage.

'Hypatos' error in navigation is forgivable, given the long period we had sailed without sight of land; given also the vagaries of wind and current. Navigation at sea is never an exact science. It is more a developed instinct. Indeed Hypatos' miscalculation may be fortuitous.'

I looked at him askance. 'Would you care to elaborate?'

'I am sure you recall that before we sailed from Sidon I explained that by decree of the Supreme Minos, no foreign warships are allowed to enter the harbour of Knossos on the north shore of his kingdom. That is where our own battle galleys are based.'

'Yes indeed, you told me that my ships would have to use the port of Krimad, on the southern coast. In fact, that location will be a great deal more convenient for my galleys. They will not have so far to travel to reach the Hyksos positions in the delta of the Nile.'

Toran directed my attention to the distant land. 'Do you see those white buildings at the base of Mount Ida? Those are the boat yards of Krimad harbour. You should detach your squadron immediately and send them to take up their allotted moorings in the harbour. Captain Hypatos will send one of his officers to act as a pilot for your captains.'

'Excellent!' I approved. 'Does the Supreme Minos wish me to remain with my flotilla in Krimad?'

'No, no, Taita!' he hurried to reassure me. 'The Supreme Minos is fully aware that you are the representative of Pharaoh Tamose, and therefore deserving of the utmost respect. A mansion on the slopes of Mount Ida above the city of Knossos has been set aside for your exclusive use. However . . .' He paused and drooped an eyelid at me in a conspiratorial manner. '. . . there are members of your entourage presently aboard this ship who might best be accommodated in Krimad rather than Knossos.'

'Ah!' I feigned ignorance. 'And who might those persons be?'

'I do not mean to imply improper behaviour by anyone, but there are those who seem rather too familiar with the future brides of the Supreme Minos.'

'Surely you do not mean little Loxias, the royal handmaiden?' Toran dropped his eyes. I had discreetly reminded him that both of us had secrets to hide.

'I leave it to your impeccable judgement.' Toran withdrew gracefully from the discussion.

W hen we descended to the main deck Captain Hypatos was there to meet with me a smile.

'Sixteen days it was, my Lord Taita.'

'I must compliment you on a masterly display of navigation, Hypatos,' I commended him. 'Please signal the captains of my galleys to come on board immediately.'

Hypatos gave the order to back the sails of the flagship and hoist the signal 'All Captains'.

The commanders of my galleys launched their skiffs and had their crews row them across to the *Sacred Bull*. In order of seniority, headed by Dilbar and Akemi, they came on board. I pointed out to them Krimad harbour and explained that it was to be their future base of operations.

Then Zaras and Hui formally resumed command of their own ships, and prepared to leave the flagship. Their servants had packed their luggage, and this was lowered into the skiffs to be taken across to the galleys.

I had deliberately given Zaras and Hui very short notice of their transfer; and I had refrained from informing Tehuti and Bekatha of their imminent departure. At all costs I wanted to avoid a public display of emotion.

However, my girls are not so easily duped. They had realized almost immediately that there was something odd afoot. They left their cabins and came up to the poop deck to investigate. They were in a light and relaxed mood which changed abruptly as they saw Zaras and Hui on the main deck below them, standing at the head of their men.

Surreptitiously I watched my two girls coming to terms with the hard cold fact that the dreaded moment had arrived and that the parting was imminent.

Tehuti's features turned cold and pale as those of a corpse laid out on the slab for burial. Bekatha's lower lip quivered and she blinked her eyelids to hold back her tears.

On the main deck Zaras called his officers to attention and they saluted the poop. I saw Bekatha grope for the hand of her older sister and grip it so fiercely that her knuckles turned frosty white.

Tehuti's lips moved as she whispered to her, 'Be brave, Bekatha. Everybody is watching us.'

Loxias was standing close behind the two of them, but now she stepped up beside Bekatha, and took her other hand.

Zaras addressed Captain Hypatos formally, 'Permission to leave ship, Captain?' And Hypatos replied just as formally.

'Permission granted, Captain!'

Zaras turned to the ship's side and led his contingent down the rope ladder to the waiting skiffs. Hui followed him. Neither was aware of the girls standing on the poop behind them. They did not look back.

As she watched Hui go Bekatha swayed slightly on her feet, and she made a soft choking sound. Then, still holding hands, the three girls turned to the companionway that led down to their cabins. Bekatha stumbled slightly on the first step, but Tehuti unobtrusively steadied her and prevented her from falling.

Toran was standing opposite me on the port side of the deck. As the three girls disappeared below he glanced in my direction and gave me an almost imperceptible nod of approval.

With that simple gesture we had become accomplices. I knew that in future we would be able to trust each other.

Once the skiffs had left the *Sacred Bull* and were heading back to the galleys, Hypatos tacked the flagship and reversed our course, heading back to round the eastern cape of the island.

I looked over the raked transom of the flagship and watched my galleys in line astern heading in directly for Krimad harbour. I was still saddened by witnessing the distress of my girls. I sought distraction by crossing to stand with Toran at the port rail and asking a trite question to which I already knew the answer.

'What is the direct overland distance separating Knossos from Krimad?'

'It is not so much the actual distance that is significant. That is a mere forty leagues or a trifle less,' Toran explained. 'The problem is that the road is steep and treacherous where it passes around the base of Mount Ida and heavy-going the rest of the way. Your horses might need as much as two days to complete the journey. You will kill them if you force them beyond that.'

I knew that I would need to travel that route regularly if I were to keep contact with my ship's officers and also with my girls in the royal seraglio. On the other hand, I could not accept the delays that Toran was estimating. I decided that I would have to set up a chain of relays across the island. With fresh horses waiting at intervals of ten leagues along the route I would be able to drive them hard. I should be able to make the crossing of the island in seven hours or a little less. That would be my first concern just as soon as I had settled my girls in their new home.

I went below for a short while to entice them up on deck, hoping to distract them from their sorrows. But they refused to come with me. Their misery was so profound that they could barely open their mouths to reply to my solicitous questions. They sat on one bunk, clinging to each other for some small comfort. Loxias sat cross-legged on the deck at their feet. Not for the first time I was touched by the Minoan girl's loyalty.

My girls needed time on their own to come to terms with the cruelty of fate and the heartlessness of the gods. The exigencies of life are magnified a hundredfold by youth, but are alleviated to the same extent by the leavening of age. We must all learn to endure.

I left them and returned to the deck. Toran had gone below so I climbed back into the rigging.

These were Hypatos' home waters, and he knew them intimately. At times he skirted the reefs and the headlands so closely that it seemed I could step ashore from the deck without wetting my feet.

I gazed across at the passing landscape with fascination. I had not expected it to be so mountainous, nor to be so lushly forested. I have spent so much of my life in the dry desert places that for me it was exotic and beautiful.

It was past noon when we rounded the most easterly point of the island and changed course to head back along the northern shore towards Knossos. The angle of the sunlight was so altered that the water under our keel was transmuted to a wondrous shade of blue.

The sea ahead of us was dotted with shipping: from tiny anchored fishing boats to the great trading triremes with their churning banks of long oars and their clouds of vivid sails.

As we passed the mouths of the bays and harbours which indented the shoreline I saw that these were also crowded with anchored ships, taking on or discharging cargo. The cargoes they carried were the sinews of trade which generated the wealth that had transformed this small island into a colossus towering over the civilized world.

And yet I knew from my studies that the land itself was rocky and rugged. The soil was poor, devoid of precious minerals and unsuited to cultivation. Although the great forests grew upon it in profusion, their roots offered a further barrier to the rearing of valuable crops.

The Minoans had solved this problem by sending out their ships across the seas to gather up the raw materials produced by other lands. Paying a pittance for these riches, they transported them back to Crete. Here, by the application of their engineering skills and their genius for design and innovation, they transformed them into highly desirable products for which the rest of the world hungered.

They refined the ore which other more primitive peoples had scratched from the earth with sharpened sticks, and they fashioned these metals into swords and knives; helmets and armour for warriors; and hoes and pitchforks and ploughshares for farmers.

They had perfected the firing of silica sands and other minerals to make glass: an extraordinary substance which they fashioned into plates and dishes and utensils that graced the banquet tables of kings; ornaments and jewellery of myriad colours to delight the wives of rich men; and beads which some tribes used as currency. There were some primitive countries in which a string of these glass beads could buy a thoroughbred horse or a beautiful young virgin.

The Minoans traded these products for the hemp and cotton, linen and wool that subsistence farmers in other lands had grown. They worked and wove these into cloth and canvas for garments and tents and ships' sails.

These in turn they sent out to trade; repeating the cycle endlessly until no other nation could match their wealth; not even our very Egypt.

There was a hidden cost to this ceaseless and single-minded pursuit of riches.

From my vantage point high in the rigging of the *Sacred Bull* I looked out across the land and I saw the smoke rising from the myriad forges and furnaces in which the ores were refined, the metals alloyed and the sands transmuted to glass.

On the mountainsides above the towns and factories were wide areas of desolation, the scarred earth where the forests had been put to the axe to provide the timber for the hulls of the Minoan trading ships, or to be burned into charcoal for the furnaces in their mills.

I saw the inshore waters stained and corrupted by the poisonous dyes and corrosive fluids they used in their mills, and which they drained directly into the sea.

As much as any man alive I enjoy the weight and lustre of silver and gold in my hands. But faced by this defloration of pristine nature I wondered at the ultimate price that man is prepared to pay to feed his insatiable greed.

My musings were interrupted by a hail from below and I peered down and saw Ambassador Toran had returned to the deck and was beckoning me to come down to join him. When I reached his side he was apologetic.

'I cannot remain too long aloft,' he explained. 'I find the ship's gyrations to be unpleasantly exaggerated by the height of the mast, and I would not care to part with the excellent breakfast my chef went to such pains to prepare for me.' He took my arm and led me forward. 'The view from the bows will be just as good as from the masthead, and I wanted to be able to point out the sights of interest as we clear Dragonada Island and have a full view of Knossos and Mount Cronus.' We settled ourselves comfortably in the shade of the foresail while the ship tacked around the point of the island and a fresh vista of the northern coast of Crete was spread out before us.

On our port side we had a marvellous view of Mount Ida; which was the complete reverse of that which we had enjoyed from the southern side of the island. From this angle the mountain seemed to be even higher, steeper and more rugged. Below it the city of Knossos and its harbour lay open to us.

The harbour was vast, but its waters seemed barely expansive enough to accommodate the fleet of Minoan war galleys and cargo ships which lay at anchor within. Some of these vessels were large enough to dwarf the *Sacred Bull* on whose deck we reclined.

Above the harbour rose the buildings of the city. I realized at once that it was many times larger in extent than Thebes and Babylon combined. However, compared to Knossos those two smaller cities were pretty, gay and welcoming.

Despite its backdrop of high and majestic mountains and the scope and the grandeur of its architecture, Knossos was a sombre and dark-toned place. My senses are so finely tuned to the subtle undercurrents and hidden nuances of the preter-natural that I knew at once that Knossos had been built upon one of those rare fields of power on which the gods have focused all their energies.

In this enlightened age, it is accepted by educated men that the earth is a living and breathing creature, a gigantic turtle, which swims forever on the black ocean of eternity. The plates that form the carapace that covers the turtle's back are fused along these lines of power. When the earth moves these junctions enable it to flex its body and limbs. These are centres of unimaginable force, some for good but others for evil.

Here was evil; I had the rank taste of it on the back of my tongue and the stench of it in my nostrils.

I shuddered as I tried to come to terms with the enormity of it.

'Are you cold, Taita?' Toran asked solicitously.

Although I shook my head and smiled, I did not trust my face not to reveal my true feelings. I turned away from him and looked directly out to sea. Far from calming my forebodings I found them further agitated by my first close-up view of the twin peaks of Mount Cronus. My perturbation must have been obvious to him, for Toran chuckled and patted my shoulder in an avuncular manner.

'Be of good cheer, Taita! Most people experience the same reaction as you when first they look upon the citadel of Cronus, the father of all the gods. Do you know the history of this place and the story of how all these mysteries came to pass?'

'I know little or nothing about it.' In truth, I was sure that I knew it all much better than Toran himself, but often it is best to plead ignorance. That way you are more likely to learn secrets that might otherwise have been denied you.

Toran took up my instruction with relish. 'As a man of letters and learning you must agree that Cronus is the father of all the gods. Before him there was only Gaia the earth and Uranus the sky. When those two mated Cronus was born of their union.'

'That much I do know,' I conceded carefully. I would not be drawn into an argument, although I knew there were other more plausible explanations of creation. 'But please continue, good Toran.'

'In time Cronus warred against his father Uranus and defeated him. Then he castrated him and made him his slave.

Cronus ruled throughout the golden age of the gods. However, he was aware of the prophecy that one of his children would war against him, as he had done with his own father. So he devoured all his own children at birth to prevent this happening.'

'In the circumstances, eating them was probably a reasonable option. I know of more than one mortal father who wishes he had adopted that expedient,' I bantered with a straight face, but Toran took me seriously and nodded.

'Quite so! However, to continue, when Rhea, who was Cronus' senior wife, gave birth to her sixth child, she named the boy Zeus and hid him from his father in a cave up there on Mount Ida.' He pointed across the bay at the mountain. 'Thus Zeus survived to maturity. Then, as prophesied, he battled with Cronus. When he defeated him he sliced open his father's belly and all his siblings leaped out to freedom.'

'Then Zeus and his brothers and sisters flew to the peak of Mount Olympus where they abide to this day, ruling our lives with a high hand.' I moved the lecture along at an accelerated pace. At times Toran can be a pedant. 'Zeus is now the father of the gods and the lord of the storms. His siblings are Hestia the goddess of home and the hearth; Demeter the goddess of agriculture and bountiful harvest; Hera the goddess of marriage; Hades the lord of the underworld and Poseidon the god of the sea.'

'You said that you were ignorant of their history.' Toran looked mildly aggrieved, but then he hurried on before I could relate the rest of the story. 'Zeus was unable to kill his father by reason of his immortality, so before Zeus departed for Olympus he imprisoned Cronus in the fiery depths of that volcano, which now bears his name.'

Both of us studied the mountain in silence for a while.

'It is the oldest and most powerful volcano in the world.' Toran broke the silence. 'All its power is controlled by Cronus. With it he protects us from the envy of foreign kings and the avarice of less civilized nations. In merely one instance, when the Euboeans sent their fleet to attack us Cronus hurled great fiery rocks upon them from the heights of his mountain, sinking most of their ships and driving the survivors back whence they had come.'

I stared across at the mountain. It was indeed a forbidding sight. There was no evidence of plant or animal life of any kind on the steep, pyramid-shaped ramparts. They fell almost sheer to the water's edge; shining black and glossy red sheets of solidified vitreous lava flow.

From the twin apertures that pierced the summits of the peaks the molten lava still oozed and trickled down, glowing and shimmering with heat, rivers of fire that exploded in clouds of steam when they met the sea that lapped the base of the mountain.

'When Cronus is either very pleased or extremely angry he blows out smoke and fire,' Toran explained. 'The intensity of his anger or pleasure can be judged by the volume and force of his fiery breath. You can see from his gentle exhalations that at present he is sleeping, or in a jovial mood. When he is truly aroused he blows out molten rocks, and clouds of sulphurous smoke that spurt so high into the sky that they mingle with the clouds. Then his bellowing and roaring can be heard in every part of Crete, and his violent shuddering and shaking felt in distant lands far across the sea.'

'What might make him that angry?' I asked Toran.

'He is the mightiest of all the gods. Cronus does not need a reason to be angry, and he certainly is not accountable to us for his whims and fancies. He is angry because he is angry; it is as simple as that.'

I nodded wisely as I listened to Toran extolling the powers and justifying the excesses of his particular god. Of course I did not agree with him. I have studied the history and origin of all the gods. There are hundreds of them. Like the mortals and the demi-gods they differ vastly in their power and temperament, and in their virtue and their iniquity.

What puzzled me was that a superior man such as Toran should pay homage and allegiance to a raging monster in preference to a noble and benevolent deity like Horus.

I trust neither Cronus nor Seth. What is more, I have never been entirely certain of Zeus. How can you trust someone, even a god, who delights in playing shabby tricks on mankind and on his own immediate family?

No, I am a Horus man through and through.

The congestion of shipping in and around the port of Knossos was so great that as we approached the harbour-master sent out a lugger with a message denying the *Sacred Bull* immediate entry, and ordering us to anchor in the roadstead until a berth could be found for us in the inner harbour.

Ambassador Toran went ashore in the harbour-master's lugger to inform the palace of our arrival.

Within an hour of Toran's departure, a cutter came out to our anchorage. She flew the royal ensign of Crete. On the face was the golden bull and on the reverse the double-bladed executioner's axe; signifying the powers of life and death wielded by the Supreme Minos.

I had been warned by Toran before he went ashore that Tehuti and Bekatha, as future royal brides, should be confined to their cabins away from masculine eyes. When they did appear in public their faces must be heavily veiled and even their hands and feet had to be completely covered, until they were securely lodged in the royal seraglio.

When I told them of the Minoan dress code the girls were outraged. They were accustomed to going stark naked when they felt that way inclined. It had taken all my tact and bargaining skills to convince them to pander to Minoan manners and mores; and to behave like members of the Minoan royal family.

With these strictures very much in mind, I was the only non-Minoan on the poop deck of the *Sacred Bull* to greet this deputation from the palace.

Standing in the bows of the approaching cutter with Ambassador Toran were three palace officials. One of these bespoke us as soon as they were within hailing distance. In the name of the Supreme Minos he demanded permission to come on board; a request which Captain Hypatos granted with alacrity.

These three visitors were dressed in full-length black robes, the hems of which swept the deck as they walked down the deck towards me with their deliberate and stately tread. They wore tall brimless hats, which were draped with black ribbons. Their beards were dyed soot-black and had been tightly curled with hot tongs. Their faces were powdered with white chalk, but their eyes were circled with kohl. The contrast was startling. Their expressions were lugubrious.

Ambassador Toran followed them closely, and introduced them to me as they stopped before me. I bowed to each of them in turn as Toran recited their multiple names and elaborate titles.

'Lord Taita!' The senior emissary returned my bow. 'I am ordered by the Supreme Minos to welcome you to the Kingdom of Crete . . .' He went on to assure me that our arrival had been keenly anticipated. However, there had been uncertainty in the palace as to the exact time and date of that happy event. Now they required a further twenty-four hours to prepare a fitting welcome for the royal Egyptian ladies who were betrothed to the Supreme Minos.

'A state barge will come out to this ship at noon tomorrow. It will convey you and the royal brides to the palace where the Supreme Minos will be waiting to welcome them into his family.'

'Your Supreme Minos is extremely gracious!' I acknowledged what was in essence a diplomatically worded royal command rather than an invitation.

'His Majesty has commanded me to assure the royal ladies of his pleasure at their arrival. He has further asked me to present them with these tokens of his royal favour.' He indicated the heavy silver caskets being carried by the black-attired aides that flanked him. They set the gifts down on the deck and then backed away from me with deep bows.

The meeting was at an end. They returned to the cutter which had brought them. I was learning that the Minoans were a serious people who wasted little time on either ceremony or on polite formalities. Ambassador Toran went ashore with them. At least he gave me a brief smile and a discreet wave as he boarded the cutter.

I hoped that the gifts the Supreme Minos had sent might lighten the deep gloom of my princesses. Indeed they proved worthy of the richest monarch on our world. The gold and silver glimmered, and the precious stones lit the cabin with rays of multi-coloured light. Tehuti and Bekatha examined them listlessly before discarding them and returning to their melancholia.

Up until now I had put in place stern strictures that ensured that neither of my girls had ever enjoyed the solace of the grape, but I recognized that the time had come when dire affliction called for strong remedy. I went down to the ship's hold and broached one of Ambassador Toran's amphorae. I half filled three large copper flagons with the luscious red Cyclades wine. Then I topped them up with water, and had the ship's steward carry them up to the cabin in which my girls were languishing.

'You want us to drink that poison?' Tehuti demanded. 'But you told us that it would make us go bald.'

'It will do so only if you drink it when you are very young.

But now you are all grown up,' I explained. 'Look at me. Am I bald?' Reluctantly they conceded that I was not.

'You also told us it would make our teeth fall out,' Bekatha reminded me. In rebuttal I snapped my own perfect set of teeth at her. They considered that in silence for a while.

'It will make you feel more cheerful and happy,' I wheedled.

'I don't want to feel cheerful and happy.' Bekatha spoke firmly. 'I just want to die.'

'At least you will die happy,' I reasoned.

'Perhaps we should make Loxias try it first.' Tehuti regarded the Minoan girl thoughtfully. Bekatha pushed one of the flagons across the table to her. Loxias sighed with resignation. She had long grown accustomed to being assigned the least pleasant and potentially hazardous tasks. She raised the cup to her lips and took a tiny sip; then she straightened up, holding the wine in her mouth.

'Swallow it!' Tehuti ordered her. She obeyed and they watched her carefully; waiting to see if she would shed her hair or her teeth. Loxias smiled.

'It tastes good.' She bowed her head over the flagon again.

'That's enough! You don't have to drink all of it,' Tehuti protested and took the flagon out of her hands. They passed it around their circle, discussing the taste with animation. Bekatha thought it tasted like plums, but Tehuti said that it was definitely ripe pomegranate. Loxias offered no opinion but set about making certain she was not denied her fair share. She was the first one to laugh. The other two stared at her with surprise. Then Bekatha giggled.

Within the hour the three of them had shed all their clothing and decked themselves with the resplendent jewellery that the Supreme Minos had sent them. I was playing one of their favourite dance tunes on my lyre and they were cavorting around the cabin shrieking with laughter. It was after midnight before Bekatha finally collapsed on her bunk, but the other two were not far behind her. I covered them with the bedsheets, kissed each of them goodnight and blew out the lamp. I climbed the companionway to the main deck to savour the night air, feeling well enough pleased with myself.

My princesses were dressed in Minoan style and waiting on the main deck when the royal barge emerged from the harbour at noon the following day and rowed towards the *Sacred Bull*. Until they moved there was nothing to suggest that there was a living creature beneath the layers of black cloth and veils that covered them. Ambassador Toran had sent these costumes and accessories across to us in another vessel earlier that morning. It had taken all my guile and ingenuity to induce the girls to don these outlandish costumes. Loxias had been spared the indignity. Although her dress was long and black and her hat was also tall, conical and decked with black ribbons her face and hands at least were uncovered. She was merely a serving wench, and had she gone bare-breasted I am sure nobody would have remarked the fact.

I led them down into the barge to the solemn beat of the drums played by four of the priests from the temple of Cronus who sat in the stern. Then we were rowed into the inner harbour of the port, and I had the opportunity to study more closely the towering edifices that surrounded the basin and crowded down to the edge of the water.

These were built in their entirety from blocks of dun-grey stone which I later learned were quarried in the mountains. There was little to distinguish any one of these buildings from its neighbours. They were all massively ugly. The rooves were flat. The windows were narrow slits that were covered with opaque grey glass.

The largest building stood directly across from the harbour

340

entrance. It did not need the statue of the golden bull of Crete on its rooftop to indicate to us that this was one of the four great palaces of the Supreme Minos.

With practised precision the oarsmen brought the barge to rest against the quay in front of the palace where a phalanx of dignitaries waited to welcome my small party ashore. Every one of them wore the identical full-length black uniforms and the tall conical hats. All their faces were white with chalk, and their eyes were outlined with kohl. A few of them wore gold and silver chains and other decorations over their coats, denoting their superior rank and status.

Even I was dressed in the full-length black robes which Ambassador Toran had sent out to me. But I wore my magnificent gold helmet with its feathered crest, and my face was devoid of chalk or kohl.

The only persons in the entire assembly who were not wearing solid black were the four lithe and very dark-skinned warriors in bright green tunics with leather cross-straps over their upper bodies and leather helmets covering their heads who came forward smartly to meet my princesses as they stepped ashore. They were armed with short swords and daggers. Two of them carried whips, which I hoped were ceremonial rather than functional. They took up positions on each side of my girls.

There was something strangely feminine about these green-clad bodyguards. Their faces were beardless and smooth. Their features were delicate and finely chiselled, as were their hands. They lacked only the protuberances of feminine breasts. They were as flat-chested as any boy. I decided they were some form of hermaphrodite; just another peculiarity among so many I had already encountered in this peculiar land. I put them out of my mind and followed my girls through the doorway into the cavernous vestibule of the palace.

This was crowded shoulder to shoulder with the black-clad,

chalky-faced multitudes. However, I saw not a single woman in the entire assembly. We Egyptians are proud of our women and we expect them to play a major and highly visible role in the life of our nation. I found this gender-motivated isolationism unnatural and repugnant.

An open lane had been left down the centre of the marble-paved floor just wide enough for my girls and their green-uniformed escorts to pass along it. It ran straight to another set of doors at the far side of the hall. Our little party started down this lane, but I had not covered more than a dozen paces before somebody stepped out of the crowd and fell in beside me. For a moment I did not realize that it was Ambassador Toran because he also was clad entirely in black and his face was deathly white with cadaverous black eye sockets, but he wore a gold chain that I recognized and even though he spoke in sepulchral tones his voice was unmistakable.

'Everything is going precisely as planned. The Supreme Minos and his entire council are waiting for us in the throne room beyond those doors ahead.' He indicated them with a thrust of his chin. 'Even the Queen Mother is with him. That is a rare honour. You will not be expected to take any part in today's proceedings, but from tomorrow onwards you will be working closely with the Lord High Admiral and his war council; planning the campaign against the Hyksos.'

'I am relieved and delighted to hear you say that.' Even though I kept my voice as low as his, it was the truth. It had taken me years of intense planning and even more intense endeavour to reach this point. We were standing on the threshold of success. 'However, when will the marriage ceremony take place?' I asked.

Toran shot me a startled glance through his kohl-ringed eyes, but before he could reply the polished cedar-wood doors with their golden-bull decorations swung soundlessly open ahead of us. To the solemn beat of a single hidden drummer we paced into the throne room, and paused while the doors closed silently behind us.

The interior was so dimly lit. There were no lamps. The few narrow window slits were covered by dark-coloured woollen curtains. The ceiling was so high that it merged into the shadows. However, my eyes adjusted swiftly to their normal acuity so the details of shapes and figures emerged from the gloom.

In the centre of the room was the throne set on a raised podium. A tight knot of men were gathered around the base of the throne. To the left of the throne were gathered the priests of Cronus. They wore long capes and cowls that obscured their features. These garments were a deep russet colour which I learned later from Toran was known as bull's blood red.

On the opposite side of the throne stood another group of courtiers and nobles. Some of these were wearing the traditional long black robes and high hat.

Facing them were the high-ranking military and naval commanders. Their uniforms were as gaudy and colourful as the dress of the nobles was drab.

The throne itself was massive. It was carved from ebony, and inlaid with mother-of-pearl. Even though the seat was wide enough to accommodate five large men in armour, there were only two figures occupying it at present. One of these was the only woman in the throne room, apart from my princesses and Loxias.

I stared at her in incredulity. She was the most ancient woman I have ever laid eyes upon. She seemed as old as time itself. Her scrawny body and limbs were covered with dusty black lace, but her hands were gloveless. Her fingers were twisted into grotesque shapes with arthritis and age. The backs of her skeletal hands were knotted with bunched blue veins.

Her face was yellow and creased like the skin of a windfall apple which had lain at the foot of the tree for a season in the

343

sun. It no longer seemed human. The sparse and greasy strings of her hair were dyed bright red and plastered to her skull or curled around her ears. Her eyes were sunk in their deep sockets. One eye was black and shiny as polished obsidian. The other was opaque and dribbled tears down her withered cheek. The tears dripped on to the black lace that covered her upper body.

In the silence she hawked and coughed up a lump of green and yellow mucus. When she opened her mouth to spit it on the marble tiles I saw that her teeth were black and ragged as the burned-out stumps of the forest after a fire has swept through it.

'Pasiphaë, the Queen Mother,' Toran whispered so softly that only I could hear him.

Beside her towered a gigantic hominoid shape clad in a robe of silver filigree and a breastplate of embossed gold. However, the creature seemed too large to be human. Was it some preternatural beast or being from the Minoan pantheon of the immortals? I wondered.

Its hands were covered by gloves made from furry black skin, which I surmised was wild buffalo. Its lower limbs were covered by high boots of the same material.

The most astonishing feature was the creature's head. It was completely enclosed by a mask of precious metals. This was fashioned in the shape of a wild aurochs bull's head with flaring nostrils and a shaggy mane. The massive horns set in the mask were authentic, taken from the carcass of the same animal. They were long, forward curved and murderously pointed. I had seen almost identical specimens amongst the hunting trophies of King Nimrod in Babylon.

The eyeholes in the mask seemed to be black and empty, until I moved slightly to one side. The masked head turned to follow my movement and in doing so altered the angle of the light from the high windows. I could make out the glint and flickering movement of living eyes deep in the sockets. Were they human, bestial or divine? There was no way of knowing.

The hidden drummer gave a double beat and then fell silent. Nothing and nobody moved in the sudden quiet. Then the masked figure on the throne rose to its feet and spread its arms. It let out a bellow like a wild bull with the smell of oestrus in its nostrils. The sound echoed within the creature's head-mask with such intensity that I realized the Minoan engineers must have devised some means of amplifying it to this extraordinary volume.

In unison the entire congregation including the priests emitted a groan of veneration so deep and intense that it sounded like terror and then they prostrated themselves. The green-clad guards on each side of my girls forced them face-down on the marbled floor.

Ambassador Toran seized my wrist and pulled me down with him. 'Lie still!' he hissed at me. 'On your life don't look up!'

I obeyed him. I had no inkling what was taking place, but I knew that this was no time to argue or object. I lay still; groaning only when the rest of the congregation groaned; knocking my forehead on the paving only when everyone else did so. The tirade from the throne continued unabated, if anything increasing in volume until my head began to throb.

Although I had studied the Minoan language so devotedly I understood not a word of what the Supreme Minos was saying. Either he was haranguing us in an arcane tongue or the amplification had distorted his words beyond my ability to recognize them.

I have a bracelet which I wear on my right wrist on occasions such as this. On a light chain is suspended a small gold disc which I have polished to mirror-like perfection. In the reflection I am able to watch anything or anybody in front or behind me without moving or lifting my head. In this way I have learned many interesting things, and more than once I have avoided death by the same means.

Suddenly in my little mirror I saw a circular black curtain drop silently from amongst the shadows of the ceiling. It was exactly the size of the podium on which the throne stood. It completely encircled and enshrouded both the Supreme Minos and Pasiphaë, his mother.

Then it was drawn up again as swiftly as it had descended; and both the throne and the podium were left empty. The Supreme Minos and his mother had disappeared. It was as neat a stroke of stagecraft as I have ever witnessed.

The hidden drummer began to beat again. At this signal all of us came to our knees and raised our heads. There was a murmur of awe and cries of amazement when we realized that the Supreme Minos and his mother had disappeared. I joined in without needing to be encouraged by Toran. After having fully expressed my astonishment at the miraculous powers of the King of Crete I rose to my feet beside Toran and asked, 'I presume that the Supreme Minos has set a time and date for the marriage ceremony; am I correct?'

'Please forgive me, Lord Taita. I should have explained more fully. I assumed that you understood what was happening.' He looked truly abashed. 'That was the marriage ceremony we have just witnessed.'

I could not remember when last I had been at a loss for anything intelligent or witty to say, but at last I rallied, although I could hear my voice croak as I spoke. 'I don't understand, Toran. I asked about the wedding of my Egyptian princesses.'

'That was the wedding. They are no longer princesses. They are now Minoan queens. You and I have accomplished what we set out to achieve.' He took my arm as though to steady me. I shook off his hand, still staring at him.

'What happens to my girls now?' I insisted.

'The viragoes will take them to the royal seraglio.' He

indicated the green-uniformed bodyguards with an inclination of his head.

'I am not yet ready to accompany them,' I protested. 'First I must pick up my possessions from the *Sacred Bull*.'

'Men are never allowed in the Palace of the Royal Wives. I am really very sorry, my lord.'

'You know full well that I am not a man entire, Toran. I have never been forcibly separated from my girls.'

'In terms of Minoan law you are a man,' he avowed.

'What about these other creatures?' I demanded as I indicated the green-uniformed guards who were lifting my princesses to their feet. 'Aren't they men – even more than I am, Toran?'

'No, Taita. They are women of the Mbelala tribe of western Africa.'

'But they have no breasts!' I protested.

'Those were amputated at puberty so that they are able to wield the sword more skilfully, but down below they are fully women. I shall give you proof of that.' He turned to the captain of the viragoes and spoke sharply. Obediently she lifted the skirt of his green tunic and displayed his perfect cunny.

'You may touch it if you wish, master. But only if you are willing to sacrifice your arm for the privilege.' With her hand on the hilt of her sword the virago smiled, challenging me to make the attempt. I shook my head and turned back to Toran.

'When will I be able to see my girls again?' I heard the pleading tone in my own voice.

'I hate to be the one who must answer that question for you, because the answer is never.' Toran spoke with finality. 'No man other than the Supreme Minos will see their faces again . . . until the day they die.'

Looking back on it later with the wisdom of hindsight I realized the last part of his statement was intended as a covert warning; but I was so distraught in the face of my impending loss that it was lost on me.

The four viragoes lifted my veiled princesses to their feet and led them away. Loxias followed them, but she glanced back at me and whispered too softly for me to hear, although I read her lips, 'I will guard them with my own life.'

I could no longer restrain myself and I started forward to prevent this thing happening, but Toran seized my arm and held me.

'You are unarmed, Taita. Those viragoes are trained killers. They know not mercy.'

I stood and watched them go. I could see that Bekatha was weeping; under the veils her whole body was shaking. In contrast Tehuti stepped out into the unknown like a heroine.

In the wall behind the ebony throne a door opened silently. With an aching despair I watched them disappear through it.

I t was as though my life had ended. They were gone from me forever, those two who for many years had been my main reason for existing.

Ambassador Toran knew how deeply I was attached to my charges and how bitterly I had been wounded by my loss. He proved now how he had become my true friend. He took it upon himself to shepherd me through the weird complexities of Minoan society. He had a carriage waiting for us in the courtyard behind the palace. In it we were driven up the winding road to the large mansion set on the mountainside above the city of Knossos. This was to be the Egyptian Embassy with me as its ambassador.

As we climbed Toran chatted to me lightly to distract me, pointing out the salient features of the city spread below us. These included the naval headquarters and the spreading complex of government buildings by means of which the Supreme Minos ruled his far-flung empire.

'At the head of our government is the State Council, which

348

consists of the ten lords appointed by the Supreme Minos. Their duties and responsibilities cover every facet of our national existence; from the worship of the god Cronus, which is mandatory for all citizens, to the payment of taxes, which is not optional.' Toran chuckled at his little joke. 'The other major ministries are the Admiralty, the Department of Trade, and the Army.'

With an effort I was able to set aside the pain of my loss, and concentrate on this vital information. I was even able to join in the conversation.

'Of course the entire world knows about the Minoan fleet, which surpasses those of all other nations, but I was unaware that you had a significant army.'

'Our army musters almost fifty thousand highly trained men,' Toran told me proudly.

'By Horus, that must be the greater part of your total population,' I exclaimed with astonishment.

'All the senior officers are Minoan but the rank and file are mercenaries. The bulk of our own population are skilled workmen and not soldiers.'

'Now I understand.' I was so fascinated by this information. 'And I am certain that your superb fleet of ships would be able, very swiftly, to transport these fighting men to wherever they are most needed.'

Toran listed for me the names and responsibilities of all the senior military officers. Then he discussed the strengths and weaknesses of each of these men of power. 'Some of them are skilled and far-sighted warriors, but too many of the others see only as far as their own purses, bellies or crotches.'

However, when I tried to question Toran further about the Supreme Minos and the nature of the being behind the golden mask he became as skittish as an unbroken colt and shied away from the subject with a brief warning.

'It is an offence of *lèse-majesté* punishable by death to discuss the person of the Supreme Minos. It is sufficient for you to know that he embodies the spirit of our nation. This time I shall take into consideration the fact that you asked that question in ignorance, but I caution you to take this warning seriously, Taita.'

We both lapsed into awkward silence as we rounded a rocky buttress of the mountain and came suddenly upon the accommodation that had been placed at my disposal. It was a large building, but like all the others I had seen so far it was sombre and ugly. There were no gardens to embellish its stolid grey stonework. Instead it was surrounded with trellised grapevines.

My household servants were lined up in front of the main doors to welcome me, although their welcome was as gloomy as the walls behind them.

'Of course they are slaves,' Toran explained offhandedly. 'All of them have had their tongues and vocal cords removed so you will not be bothered by their idle chatter.'

Neither will I learn anything of interest or importance from them, I thought, although I did not voice my reservation.

'This is Bessus, your major-domo.' He pointed out a sturdy rogue with a pleasant smile. 'He understands Egyptian but for obvious reasons does not speak it. Ask him for whatever you need.'

Toran moved on briskly, leading me on a tour of my new home. The rooms were commodious but austere. My personal effects and spare clothing had been sent up from the harbour ahead of our arrival. They had been unpacked, washed and neatly arranged in my living area. Adjoining my bedroom was a library with a hundred or more large scrolls stacked on the shelves.

'That is the definitive history of the Minoan Empire, a great deal of it written by me. I hope you will perhaps find it instructive,' Toran explained, and then he indicated the low writing table in the centre of the room. 'There are inks and brushes, blank papyrus scrolls of fine quality for your exclusive use. I will be able to arrange delivery of your missives to any destination in the world.'

'You are very kind, good Toran.' I thanked him with a straight face, but I smiled inwardly and qualified his offer silently. *Presumably only after you had made fair copies.* I understood that there was a limit to his friendship and kindness.

'There are fifty amphorae of good wine in the cellars,' he continued. 'They will be replenished as soon as they are empty. Fresh fish and meat will be sent up from the harbour every morning. The two cooks are excellent; I know from personal experience. I chose them for you.'

We went out into the stable yard where the head groom prostrated himself before me. I could see the fresh whip weals across his bare back.

'On your feet, fellow!' I hid my true feelings behind a friendly tone. Once I also had been a slave, and I remembered well enough the kiss of the lash. 'What is your name?' I demanded of him, and with an effort he gurgled his reply. He was a cheerful little fellow, very clearly not Cretan.

'Waaga?' I repeated the sound and he blubbered with laughter. 'Very well, Waaga, show me your horses.' He ran ahead of me to the stables emitting unintelligible but enthusiastic sounds through his empty gullet.

There were eight fine mounts in the small paddock behind the stables. Waaga whistled them up and they came to him at once, whickering with pleasure. He fed each of them with a small baked corn cake from the leather pouch on his hip. If the horses trusted him then I determined to do the same, at least until he proved me wrong. Horses usually show keen judgement.

'One day soon I will need to ride to Krimad on the south shore. I will need a guide to show me the road. Do you know the way?' Waaga nodded emphatically. 'Be ready,' I warned him. 'I will give you very little notice and we will ride hard.' He grinned. It seemed that we were already reaching an accord.

On the following morning I rose before the sun and ate a hurried breakfast before I rode down the mountain to the Admiralty. I spent the entire day there arguing and negotiating with the vice admiral Herakal and his staff, all to very little avail. They offered me eight decrepit biremes which had clearly spent many years as trading ships and had now reached the limit of their useful life. With these they expected me to subdue the Hyksos hordes. I was learning that the Minoans in general were a sullen and difficult people, and extremely hostile towards strangers and foreigners. The only one I had met so far who was an exception to this rule was Ambassador Toran. He was so affable and obliging that he could have been born an Egyptian.

That evening I rode back to my new home, spiritually exhausted and discouraged. I hardly tasted the meal of grilled lamb that the cook had prepared for me. However, a flagon of the delicious wine that Toran had laid down in my cellars gave me the strength to persevere and at dawn the next day I rode down the mountain to the Admiralty once more.

It took all my bargaining skills, and some little assistance from Toran, but by the tenth day I had finally assembled a flotilla of six almost new three-deckers. The vice admiral had reluctantly given me experienced Minoan officers to sail them and hardened mercenaries drawn from amongst the savage tribes of northern Italia to crew them. These people called themselves Latins or Etruscans. Toran assured me that they were excellent sailors and fearsome warriors. With 120 of these savages aboard each of the triremes I was content that we could match any ship in the Hyksos fleet.

I ordered my new captains to sail around the island to the

port of Krimad where Zaras and Hui were anchored with my Sumerian biremes ready for sea. From now onwards this would be our main base of operations; from which we could strike at the enemy who were only six hundred leagues to the south: five days' sailing with favourable winds.

The morning after my squadron of freshly acquired triremes sailed from Knossos, Waaga and I set off in the darkness of pre-dawn to ride to Krimad ahead of the ships. Following my instructions Waaga had saddled two of our horses and we had four others on lead reins. We would be able to change horses as soon as the ones under us showed the first signs of fatigue.

I had been warned by Toran that there were occasionally bands of robbers and outlaws skulking in the forests which covered the mountains of the interior. With this in mind I carried a short sword in its scabbard hanging from my cross-belt, and my long recurved bow slung over my right shoulder.

As a slave Waaga was prohibited from carrying edged weapons, but he was armed with a slingshot and a leather bag of round river stones. I had watched him killing high-flying partridges with this weapon, and I had seen him drop a spotted deer that had been raiding our kitchen garden. I was sure he could crack a bandit's skull just as efficiently.

We started out before sunrise; as soon as it was light enough to descry the rough path. Waaga was a skilful horseman so he was able to keep pace with me. He knew every twist and turn, and every fork in the track. He rode at my right heel, directed me with animal grunts and hand signals.

To begin with we cut obliquely across the lower slopes of Mount Ida, heading to pass to the east of the highest peak, which was still covered with snow even so late in the summer. At this altitude the mature forest trees had been decimated to provide fuel for the forges and furnaces of the factories. The destruction saddened me. The axe-men had left not a single tree standing.

At last we reached the virgin forests at higher altitude and we rode in amongst the magnificent trunks of trees that had stood tall since the time when the gods were young. The upper branches entwined high over our heads, shading the aisles between them with a cool cathedral hush. The hoof-beats of our horses were muffled by the thick banks of green moss. The only sounds were the cries of the birds and small animals. We watered our horses at the streams that ran clear and clean as the mountain air and icy cold from the snow melt.

We paused in a clearing in the forest on the shoulder of the mountain to watch Helios, the god of the sun, thrust his golden head above the eastern horizon.

This was holy ground: where Cronus, the father of all the gods, had been born and his sons and daughters after him. I could sense their presence and smell their perfume in the sweet air and the forest loams. It was an eerie sensation to be so closely in touch with the immortals. Perhaps my heightened sensitivity was due to the kindred blood coursing in my own veins, of which Inana had first made me aware. Then I reminded myself sternly that Inana was almost certainly only a creature of my dreams, and that I was the victim of my own idle superstition. It irked me that her image returned to me so persistently.

I determined to put Inana firmly out of my mind, and as I made the decision I heard the echo of her indulgent laughter. Dream or goddess, I knew she was close and my brave resolution crumbled.

I turned my horse down the steep slope, towards the port of Krimad nestled against the rocky southern shore of Crete. It was still two hours short of noon. We had made excellent time.

Even at a distance of twenty leagues I fancied I could make

out the bare masts of my Sumerian ships huddling in the harbour. When I turned in the saddle and looked back over the way we had come I saw the volcano in which the god Cronus was imprisoned. It dominated the watery northern horizon. A placid stream of creamy-coloured smoke trailed from its twin peaks. I smiled. The god was in an affable mood.

Waaga had taken advantage of this brief pause in our journey to dismount and squat behind the nearest tree. The mere fact that he had done so was an indication that before being taken in slavery he must have been a person of breeding and manners. Only the lowest and commonest classes of men and women spray their water while standing.

Suddenly Waaga leaped to his feet, letting the skirt of his chiton drop around his knees as he pointed at the earth close to where he had been squatting, uttering incoherent snorts and grunts. He was so perturbed that I dismounted and hurried to his side to investigate the cause of his concern.

The soft earth at the base of the tree was so churned and broken that it took me a few moments to pick out the great cloven hoof prints impressed in the dirt. They were many times larger than those left by the milk cows on my own estate at Mechir on the banks of the Nile.

I went down on my knees to measure one of these prints against the full span of my right hand with my fingers and thumb spread to their utmost. My single hand was not large enough. I was forced to spread both my hands over one of the hoof prints to cover it completely.

'In the name of Seth the Malign, what monstrosity left these tracks?' I blurted out my amazement at Waaga. I could make no sense at all of his response. He repeated the same sound in a rising inflexion while hugging himself and shivering in a parody of fear. Then he turned and ran back to his mount and scrambled up into the saddle. He gestured to me to mount up, and at the same time he darted fearful glances into the forest surrounding us. His agitation was infectious and I jumped on to the back of my own horse and urged it forward.

I was trying to find a rational explanation for these gigantic hoof prints. Their size seemed to be fantasy rather than reality – until I remembered the massive skulls and horns of the aurochs that I had seen amongst the hunting trophies of King Nimrod in Babylon. However, the remote Zagros Mountains to the far north-east of the Euphrates River where he had obtained them were half a world away from this tiny, densely populated island.

It seemed highly unlikely that there were wild aurochs still surviving in these lovely forests; unless they were protected by decree of the Supreme Minos. Perhaps he had declared these monstrous creatures royal game as the heraldic symbol of the Minoan nation, and the creature sacred to the god Cronus. The silver mask that the Minos wore gave some credence to that possibility. However, I doubted the wisdom of trying to discuss this with even Toran. He had already warned me not to pry too deeply into the affairs of the Minoan ruler.

I glanced around at Waaga. He was still highly agitated. He was sweating and his lower lip was quivering. He swivelled back and forth in the saddle, darting anxious glances into the undergrowth on either side of the path. He was beginning to annoy me. Even if there were wild aurochs still surviving in these mountains his extravagant behaviour was unwarranted.

Notwithstanding its large size the aurochs was essentially a cow, and cows are placid animals. I was about to take Waaga sharply to task when suddenly he screamed. Coming from his mangled throat and mouth the sound was so unexpected that I was startled and distracted.

His horse shied into mine so violently that if my reaction had not been instantaneous I would have been thrown from the saddle. I recovered my seat and snarled at him. But he was gibbering with terror and pointing into the undergrowth above the path that we were following.

'Calm yourself, idiot!' I yelled at him and then I broke off as I picked out the massive dark shape looming in the thicket above us. At first glance I had thought it was part of the rock formation of the mountain itself. But then it moved and the image jumped into sharp focus.

This was veritably a living animal.

My horse stood sixteen hands tall at the withers, but I found myself forced to lean back in the saddle and *look up* into the eyes of this creature. Those eyes were enormous. They fixed upon mine in a dark and infernal stare. The creature's huge bell-shaped ears were pricked forward, harkening to Waaga's cries. Its back was humped like that of a camel. Its horns were spread wide as the span of both my outstretched arms. They were thick and sharp-pointed as the tusks of an elephant that I had seen in Pharaoh's palace in Thebes.

This was no placid cud-chewing cow. I registered my amazement with a shout that matched Waaga's for volume.

The creature lowered its head, presenting us with those murderously pointed horns, and at the same time it pawed the ground with its front hooves, throwing clods of soft forest loam over its back. Then it launched itself down the slope like an avalanche, crashing through the undergrowth, its eyes still fixed on me.

I was trapped on the narrow pathway, with no escape route and no space in which to turn or manoeuvre. Nor did I have time to draw my sword or string my bow.

Waaga's steed panicked and tried to bolt for safety, and it carried its rider full into the path of the aurochs' charge. But even in face of looming death the little man managed an incredible act of courage. His woollen chlamys was rolled into a ball and strapped to the pommel of his saddle. He ripped it free and with a snap of his wrist spread it like a banner. Then he whipped it over the head of the bull. I will never know if it had been his intention, but the cloak hooked in the lowered horns and wrapped around the bull's head, blindfolding the beast completely.

Even having lost sight of the horse and rider, the bull hooked instinctively at them with its massive rack of horn. I saw the point of one horn enter Waaga's chest below his right armpit, and transfix him completely. It emerged from the opposite side of his body, bursting out through his rib cage.

The bull tossed its head and Waaga's body was hurled high in the air. Still blinded, the bull hooked again and this time he struck the horse, knocking it to its knees.

By now the bull was completely disorientated. It blundered around in the shrubbery, crashing into the tree trunks, trying to rid itself of the cloak which was still wrapped around its head and horns.

Waaga had won me a precious moment of respite in which to kick my feet out of the carved wooden stirrups and drop from the saddle to the ground. My bow was already in my hand and I restrung it in a single movement.

The quiver was still tied to my saddle but I always carried two loose arrows tucked into my belt for just such a situation as this. I nocked one of these and drew, holding for moment against the immense strain of the recurved ash stock.

The bull must have heard or scented me. It switched its great body around, facing towards me. It was still swinging its head from side to side, trying either to place me or throw off the chlamys that was still tangled around its horns. I waited until this movement opened his right shoulder and exposed the front of his chest. Then I released. It was such short range that the arrow generated immense speed and penetration. It disappeared completely into the bull's chest cavity, leaving only a small external wound from which a spurt of bright heart blood pumped.

My second arrow struck a finger higher but on the same line. The bull staggered back on to its hindquarters before wheeling away and crashing blindly into the undergrowth. I listened to it tearing down the steep slope of the mountain. Moments later it went down. I heard its carcass strike the ground with a weighty thump. Then I heard it thrashing about in the bushes, its back legs kicking out spasmodically. At the end it let out a mournful death bellow that echoed off the cliffs.

It took me only a moment to gather my wits and still my shaking hands. Then I went first to where Waaga was lying. At a glance I saw that he had been gutted like a fresh-caught tuna. Blood spurted from the gaping wound, but even as I knelt beside him the flow shrivelled away. His eyes were fixed wide open but the pupils had turned up into his skull, and his mouth had fallen open. He was beyond any help that I could afford him.

His horse was down beside him. The poor beast had been gored in the throat. Through the pierced windpipe the air bubbled from its lungs. In addition I could see that its right foreleg was broken; jagged shards of the cannon bone protruded through the skin. I stood over it and drew my sword. I chopped down between its ears into the brain, killing it instantly.

The string of remounts was still anchored to the saddle of Waaga's dead horse. I led them to the nearest tree and hitched them to it. Then I went to find my own mount and string. They had not gone far and I found them grazing in the nearest clearing in the forest. I led them back to where I had left the others and hitched them to the same tree.

When all was secured, I slipped and slithered down the slope to where the aurochs lay. I circled the mighty carcass, marvelling once more at its size. Now I understood the terror that had overwhelmed Waaga. This was one of the most ferocious animals I had ever imagined. It had attacked us without the slightest provocation.

I could also fully understand why King Nimrod boasted of one hundred kills of this beast, and why the Minoans had chosen it as the heraldic symbol of their nation.

I knelt deferentially beside the carcass, respectful of such a formidable opponent and aware of how near to death it had taken me. I unwrapped Waaga's blood-stained chlamys from the horns, folded it and tucked it under my arm. Then I stood back and saluted the dead bull with a clenched fist before I turned away. It had been an adversary worthy of my arrows.

I climbed back to where the corpse of brave Waaga lay and I wiped the blood from his face and rolled him in his own chlamys. Then I slung him over my shoulder and climbed to the fork of one of the forest trees and wedged him into it; high enough above the ground to keep the carrion-eaters off him until I could arrange for his proper burial.

I sat beside him in the tree and said a short prayer, entrusting him to the care of his particular god, whoever that might be. Then I clambered down to earth again.

As my feet touched the ground it shuddered under me so violently that I almost lost my balance. I grabbed at the trunk of the tree to steady myself. The tree was being wildly agitated; its branches were whipping and waving. As I looked up leaves and twigs showered down into my face. I thought that Waaga's body might be dislodged by the disturbance, but I had wedged it firmly.

Around me the entire forest was being shaken violently. The mountain itself was dancing. There was a rumbling roar and I looked around at the peak of Mount Ida just as a great slab of the granite cliff broke away and came down sliding and tumbling into the valley.

The horses were panicking. They were rearing and shaking their heads as they fought their halters, trying to break free of their tethers. I staggered across to them over the quaking ground. I gentled them and spoke to them soothingly. I have a special way with horses as I do with most birds and animals and I managed to calm them and induce them to lie flat on the ground, preventing them from bolting or falling to injure themselves.

Then I looked back into the north, over the harbour of Knossos and across the open sea to the twin volcanic peaks of Mount Cronus.

The god was furious. He was fighting to be free of the chains with which his son Zeus had bound him. His roars were deafening even at this distance. Smoke, steam and fire billowed from the vents in his mountain dungeon, blotting out the northern horizon. I could see rocks as large as the buildings of the city that he was hurling into the sky.

I felt tiny and helpless in the face of such cataclysmic rage. Even the face of Helios the sun was hidden from us. Dark despair fell over our world. The very earth trembled with fear. The sulphurous stink of it filled the air.

I sat with my horses and buried my face in my folded arms. Even I was afraid. It was a pious and devout terror. There is no place of refuge on this earth wherein you can escape the rage of the gods.

I had slain the monstrous horned creature that was the alter ego of the god. Surely the anger of Cronus was directed at me for such a sacrilegious offence.

For an hour and then another hour the god raged on and then as the sun made its noon it ceased as abruptly as it had begun. The sulphurous clouds rolled away, the mountain stilled and peace returned to the world.

I roused my horses and mounted up, and I led the string of loose animals down the mountain, picking my way through the litter of fallen branches and the small landslides of rocks and loose earth that the god had shaken from the mountain.

Three days previously I had sent a message to Zaras to expect my arrival. Long before I reached the port of Krimad I saw both Zaras and Hui cantering up the path towards me. At a distance they recognized me and with cries of relief they kicked their mounts into a gallop. When they reached me they reined down their mounts and jumped to earth. They almost dragged me from my own saddle, and one after the other they embraced me. I swear on my love for Horus and Hathor that when Zaras released me from his crushing bear hug he actually struck a tear from his eye as he told me, 'We thought for sure that we had got rid of you at last. But even Cronus himself could not do the job for us.' Of course my own eyes were dry, but I was thankful that there was nobody else present to witness such a mawkish display.

'Has the squadron of Minoan warships arrived in Krimad yet?' I attempted to get back on sensible terms.

'No, my lord.' Zaras managed to wipe the grin from his face. He pointed down at the watery horizon. 'As you can see, the sea has been whipped into a fury by the earthquake. Almost certainly they have been driven off course. I expect that they will be delayed for several days.'

'How has our own flotilla ridden out the storm?' While we rode on down the mountain I made certain we discussed naval matters exclusively. I pretended not to notice the hand signals that Hui was sending Zaras, and his equally surreptitious refusals to comply with them. However, when we came in sight of Krimad harbour Hui could restrain himself no longer and, writhing with embarrassment, he blurted out:

'We were wondering if you had brought us any messages, my lord.'

'Messages?' I frowned. 'From whom were you expecting a message?'

'Maybe from the palace . . .' His voice trailed off.

'You were expecting a message from the Supreme Minos?' I feigned ignorance. However, their beseeching gaze was pathetic and against my better judgement I told them, 'No messages; but you have probably heard that the Princesses Tehuti and Bekatha are both married to the Minoan monarch and are safely ensconced in the royal harem. You have both done your duty and are to be highly commended. I will bring all this to the attention of Pharaoh at the very first opportunity. I know he will be grateful.' With the next breath I went on, 'I am sure you are wondering why I have arrived without an escort of any kind. There was an accident in which my servant was killed by a wild animal. At the first opportunity I want you to send a burial party up the mountain to find his remains and give them decent burial.'

I kept talking and issuing orders, giving them no chance to pursue the subject of the princesses. I did not want to admit to them that I had no contact with the girls and had no idea how they were faring in the seraglio.

When we reached the port I was astonished to find that even on this side of the island, which was protected from the volcanic upheavals of Mount Cronus, the sea had been churned into such a furious condition that the waves were breaking over the harbour wall and charging deck-high through the anchorage. However, Zaras and Hui had taken every possible precaution to protect their ships. They had double-lashed them to the stone wharf with the heaviest hawsers the harbour-master was able to provide; and hung them with thick fenders of plaited rope to prevent them from colliding with each other or with the walls of the wharf.

They had left only an anchor watch on board each vessel. The rest of us took shelter in an empty warehouse ashore as guests of the harbour-master. His name was Poimen and he was a typical Minoan, melancholic and pessimistic.

He invited me and my officers to dine with him that first night. I was surprised by this hospitable act. It was only later that I discovered he was not only harbour-master but also a colonel in the Minoan secret police, and that he was drawing up a report on all of us Egyptians for the benefit of his superiors in Knossos.

The food with which his kitchen provided us was over-salted and over-cooked. The wine was thin and sour. The conversation was mundane and pedestrian, centring on the earthquake and the stormy seas that it had engendered. I was sorely in need of diversion, so I demanded of the company at large, 'What is the cause of these earthquakes and volcanic eruptions?'

Nobody was in any doubt that they were inflicted on humanity as a punishment for a crime or an offence committed against the gods.

'What crime would be serious enough to call for such an onerous punishment?' I asked naïvely and was hard put to maintain a sober expression as I listened to the diversity and the absurdity of their replies which covered the full catalogue of human frailty and divine arrogance.

After a while even this palled, so I demanded, 'In what manner can we atone to the gods for our trespasses?'

They all turned their head towards the harbour-master, the senior representative of the Supreme Minos present. He adopted a learned expression and a pontifical tone.

'It is not for us to divine the will of the gods. Only the Supreme Minos, may his name be blessed through all eternity, is capable of such wisdom. However, we can rejoice in the secure knowledge that His Supreme Highness has already fathomed the cause of the divine anger and will make full recompense.' He cocked his head to listen to the sound of the storm beyond the walls of the warehouse. 'Hark! The storm is abating. The anger of the gods has already been appeased.

By this time tomorrow the seas will be quietened and the mountains stilled.'

'How does the Supreme Minos placate the gods so readily?' I pursued the subject relentlessly.

'In the only manner that any god can be appeased,' he replied with a shrug and a superior expression. 'By sacrifice, of course!'

If it had not been for Toran's warning I might have trespassed on to the dangerous ground of the nature of the Supreme Minos, but I curbed my tongue. The harbour-master turned away from me and fell into a lively discussion with his assistants as to what extent the rough seas would affect the fishing.

I was left with the uncomfortable and lingering knowledge that my killing of the aurochs bull and the divine rage of Cronus had followed too closely upon each other to be mere coincidence.

What sacrifice of appeasement had Cronus demanded of the Supreme Minos, I wondered?

B y dawn the following morning the waves were no longer breaking over the protecting walls of Krimad harbour and Zaras and Hui were able to continue their preparations for our naval campaign against the Hyksos.

Four days later the six triremes that had been assigned to me by Vice Admiral Herakal arrived in Krimad. They had been carried far to the east by the heavy seas; almost as far as the island of Cyprus. They were down to their last few barrels of fresh water and their oarsmen were almost totally exhausted.

I rested the Cretan crews for three full days and made certain they were well provided with food, olive oil and wine of reasonable quality. They responded well. When the rest period ended I began joint exercises with the two flotillas.

Language was the main problem we encountered, but I saw to it that every ship had at least two interpreters on board and that the signal flags meant the same thing to the Minoans as they did to our Egyptians.

Both flotillas comprised well-trained and -practised mariners and within the week they were carrying out complicated manoeuvres: sailing in formation and forming line of battle. The Minoans soon learned to land chariots and infantry through the surf, and to recover men, horses and vehicles again after they had carried out their assault.

As they became more adept so the mutual trust and camaraderie between Egyptians and Cretans blossomed. I was welding them into a formidable little fighting force. I knew that very soon I could unleash them upon the Hyksos. Of course my main concern was to decide where they could do the most damage.

Good intelligence wins battles long before the first arrow is shot or the first sword is drawn from its scabbard.

Then without warning a small and almost derelict trading dhow arrived off the entrance to Krimad harbour. Its sail was tattered and stained. Its hull was zebra-striped with excrement which its crew had defecated over the side. Its scruffy crew of eight were bailing frantically to keep it afloat. They seemed more like pariahs than seamen. Their ship was flying no colours and lying low in the water, almost on the point of floundering. No pirate worth his salt was likely to give it a second look; which was probably why it had survived the voyage from wherever it had come.

On the other hand I am not as naïve and arrogant as your average corsair. It was in just too much of an appalling condition to be innocent. I could smell the old fox's scent carried before it on the wind. I ordered Zaras to launch five of our longboats filled with men and bristling with weapons, and to board her immediately.

As soon as our attack boats cleared the harbour entrance the strange dhow dropped her sail and hoisted Egyptian colours.

Zaras towed it into the harbour and tied it to the wharf to delay it from sinking.

The putative captain was frog-marched ashore demanding to speak to Lord Taita. I made my appearance scowling theatrically and ordered him to be given twenty lashes to impress upon him who it was that made the demands in this camp. The wretch fell on his knees, pressing his forehead to the stones of the jetty, and made a recognition sign with his left finger. Aton and I had first used that sign all those years ago when both of us were still slaves.

I countermanded my flogging order and instead had him dragged unceremoniously to my cabin on board my flagship, the *Outrage*. As soon as we reached it I dismissed the guards and ordered my servants to bring hot water for the prisoner to wash in and a fresh chiton to replace his stinky rags.

'What is your name, friend?' I asked him as my cook laid out a meal of shellfish and tuna steaks for us, and I prised the wooden stopper out of an amphora of Etruscan wine.

'*Friend* is as good a name as any other.' He grinned. 'Better by far than the one my mother chose for me.'

'How is our mutual acquaintance?' I asked instead.

'Large,' he replied. 'He sends you greetings and gifts.' He went to the pile of his discarded rags and rummaged in them until he found a scroll of papyrus which was stitched into the hem of one of them. He brought it to me. While I unrolled it I indicated the food. He went to the table and fell to with a will.

I glanced at the papyrus and saw at once that it was the present 'Order of Battle' of the Hyksos fleet. In addition Aton had noted those targets in the Nile Delta which he considered most worthy of my consideration.

Whence Aton had conjured up such a document I could not even hazard a guess. I rerolled it. It deserved my careful attention even though it was probably weeks out of date.

'You spoke of bringing gifts, friend?'

'I have brought you forty-eight messenger pigeons. They are in cages in my ship.' He looked pleased with himself. I unrolled Aton's letter and studied it once more.

'The large man writes of sending me one hundred pigeons.' I spoke mildly. 'What happened to the other fifty-two birds?'

'We ran out of food.'

'You ate my birds?' I was appalled by his gall. He shrugged and grinned unabashed. I shouted for Zaras. When he came I told him, 'Go at once to this rogue's ship. You will find forty-eight pigeons on board. Bring them to me at once; before they disappear mysteriously.' Zaras asked no questions, but hurried away to carry out my orders.

My visitor poured himself another flagon of my precious wine and saluted me with it. 'Good wine. I commend your taste. Our large friend requests that you send him a commensurate gift, to enable the two of you to communicate more regularly.'

I considered the suggestion for only a moment. I knew that Ambassador Toran had a large pigeon coop in Knossos. 'How do you propose I send my birds to him without them also being devoured by jackals and hyenas?'

He never so much as blinked at my calculated insult. 'I shall convey them to him in person; that is if one of your fine ships can take me across and set me ashore in an uninhabited part of the Nile Delta.'

'I can do better than that, friend,' I told him, and he cocked his head enquiringly. 'There is presently a Carthaginian trading dhow here in Krimad harbour. The captain dined with me yesterday evening. Four days from now he plans to return to Carthage via the Hyksos port of Rosetta in the delta. As you are aware the Sultan of Carthage and King Gorrab of the Hyksos are on neutral terms. I can arrange for you to sail with him as far as Rosetta. You will take with you a hundred pigeons that have been hatched in Knossos and which will be eager to return to the coop as soon as they are released. That way the large man and I can be in direct contact within a very short time.'

'I know he will be delighted by that arrangement. The two of you may even use the opportunity to play a few games of bao by pigeon post.'

I found Friend's attempt at humour to be insubordinate, and his intimate knowledge of my personal affairs disconcerting. I am never fully at ease in the company of these clandestine agents. They are a devious and mendacious lot. How can you trust a man who will eat your pigeons?

While I waited for Toran to send my pigeons to me from Knossos I had the derelict dhow in which Friend had crossed the sea from Egypt taken out into deep water and scuttled, before she provoked the curiosity of one of the Hyksos agents that I knew must abound here on Crete. His seven crew members I sent to the rowing benches of the *Outrage*.

Four days later when the Carthaginian trader sailed for Rosetta in the delta, Friend was on board with a hundred healthy and well-fed pigeons from Toran's coop.

Before the Carthaginian disappeared over the southern horizon I released one of Aton's pigeons to wend its way back to him carrying my message thanking him for his gift, informing him of the return gift that Friend was conveying to Rosetta on my behalf. I ended with a notation of my first move of the bao stones: the release of my heron from the west castle. This was a ploy that always made Aton uneasy.

The fact that I had taken umbrage at Friend's levity did not mean that I should reject his very sensible suggestion that I take this rare opportunity of continuing my bao contest with Aton.

The rising sun was on the eastern horizon as I took my leave of Zaras and Hui the next morning and rode back up the slopes of Mount Ida, heading for Knossos along the chain of relay posts that Hui had set up at my orders. He had done a fine job.

His men had marked out the track with bronze distance tags nailed to the trees along the way. So I was never in any doubt of my position, and I never fell below a canter. As I drew nigh to each relay station I blew a blast on my horn to warn the grooms of my approach. As I rode up they had my next horse saddled and waiting. I paused only to gulp down a few mouthfuls of watered wine. Then I was up and away again; munching on the meat and onion sausage that had been thrust into my hand by one of the grooms.

I drew rein beside the fresh mound of earth which marked the grave of the slave who had given his life for mine.

'Sleep well, good Waaga. I know we will meet anon. Then I shall fully express my gratitude to you.' I gave him the clenched-fist salute. Then I kicked my heels into the gelding under me and started down the back end of the mountain towards the harbour of Knossos.

As I rode into the stable yard behind my ambassadorial mansion I glanced up at the afternoon sun and estimated the angle of change since leaving Krimad.

'Under six hours to cross the island!' I told myself with satisfaction. Despite the tiring journey I went directly to the writing table in my library to attend to the pile of papyrus scrolls that were waiting my attention. Most of these were from Ambassador Toran.

I sent one of my slaves down into the city to take my replies to Toran's house near the palace before I ate my dinner alone and then went to my bedchamber.

That night I dreamed of Inana again. She was standing on the terrace outside my chamber and her hood and mantle were aglow with the moonlight. But I could not see her face under the hood. I tried to rise from my couch to go to her, but my limbs were leaden and would not respond to my dictates. I tried to speak to her but my voice faded away before it reached the tip of my tongue. However, I experienced no urgency or concern at my own inability to communicate with her. Rather I felt her benevolence flowing over me, and her divine power covering me like a shield. Trustingly I allowed myself to lapse back into sleep.

I woke again before the dawn and I sprang from my couch feeling wondrously refreshed and alive. I was not prepared for this sense of wellbeing, until suddenly I remembered my dream. Then my joy was tempered with a sweet regret that it had not been reality.

I walked naked from my chamber through the door to the terrace and I filled my lungs with the air that had been cleansed by the passage of a thousand leagues of ocean.

I looked across at Mount Cronus, and the god was in relaxed mood once more. I smiled when he belched a puff of darker smoke. Perhaps he had seen me on the terrace and was wishing me a good day, or he had eaten something for dinner that had given him a touch of flatulence. It was an indication of my good humour that I could indulge myself in such childish nonsense.

However, it was an extravagance I could ill afford. My plan was to launch our first foray on the Hyksos positions along the northern shore of the delta within the next ten days and every hour must be made to count.

I turned determinedly back towards the door to my chamber and as I did so my foot struck something soft. I glanced down to see what it was. Then I stooped and gathered it up and examined it; at first with mild interest and then with mounting wonderment.

It was a flower, or rather a lily. But I had never seen the like, and I am an avid horticulturalist. It was the size of a large wine flagon. Its petals were the colour of freshly cast gold shading down to glowing vermilion in the throat. The stamens were white as carved ivory, and the tips were blue as sapphires.

It was magnificent and so freshly cut that the stem was still bleeding drops of limpid juice. Gently I rolled it between my fingers, and I caught the soft perfume. It was a scent I knew so well that I felt the hair rise on the back of my neck.

It was the smell of the goddess Inana; the perfume of Ishtar, the goddess of flowers whose symbol was the lily.

'It was not a dream,' I whispered. 'She was here.'

I raised the lily to my lips and kissed it. I felt it withering in my hands; the petals crisping and curling. The blazing colours faded to dull and ancient brown like the sunspots on the hands of a very old man. Then the petals crumbled to a fine dust that trickled from between my fingers and floated to the tiles of the terrace. The light dawn breeze scattered them.

The essence of the goddess seemed to have been absorbed from the lily into my own body, bolstering and fortifying me against I knew not what.

I bathed in the leather buckets of hot water that the slaves brought up to the terrace for me. Then I dressed in a blue wool chiton and went through to my library.

The door was closed although I had left it open when I came through to my chamber the previous night.

I pushed it open quietly and then froze with religious dread when I saw the cloaked and hooded feminine figure standing at the window across the room with her back towards me.

'Inana!' I whispered and she turned swiftly and came to kneel at my feet and kiss my hand before I could regain my voice.

'Lord Taita! It is so very good to see you. I missed you. All of us have missed you.' She pushed the hood back on to her shoulders.

'Loxias!' I exclaimed. 'I thought you were somebody else. How did you find me?'

'I asked my good friend, Lord Toran. He told me where you were.'

I lifted her back on to her feet and led her to the couch. When she was seated I rang the brass bell on my writing table and three of my slaves ran up the staircase from the kitchens.

'Bring food and drink,' I ordered.

We sat facing each other while we devoured the large platter of boiled eggs, dried fish, pork sausages and hard bread the slaves laid between us.

'Is it safe for you to be here with me? I thought that you were imprisoned in the royal seraglio with Tehuti and Bekatha.'

'Oh, no!' She shook her curls at me. 'The viragoes see in me only a low-born slave. They allow me to come and go as I wish.'

'The life of a slave obviously suits you very well, Loxias. And you are even prettier than when last I saw you.'

'You are a naughty old flatterer, Taita.' She preened shyly.

'Tell me about my other girls. Are they as happy as you are?'

'They both profess to be dying of boredom. They long for just one of your stories to amuse them.'

'Doesn't their new husband entertain them?' I asked tactfully.

'You mean Old Tin-head, the Supreme Minos?' She purred with laughter. 'That's what we call him, but I suppose he would chop off *our* heads if he heard us. Neither Tehuti nor Bekatha have seen him since the marriage ceremony. None of our new friends in the harem have seen him since their weddings, and some of them have been there for twenty years and more. Certainly nobody has ever seen him without his tin head.'

'I don't understand,' I protested. 'None of his wives have had carnal knowledge of the king? Is that what you are telling me?'

Loxias had been friends with Ambassador Toran long enough

to understand the meaning of the term and she blushed modestly, and dropped her eyes. 'From time to time the Minos sends for certain of his wives to be brought to him by the viragoes. However, once they leave the seraglio they never return.'

'What happens to them?' I was puzzled.

'The viragoes say that they are elevated to the rank of favourites of the gods, and that they ascend to the Higher Temple in the mountains.'

I questioned Loxias minutely, but it was soon apparent that she knew very little about the subject other than what she had just told me, and that she was not particularly interested in the location of this Higher Temple. She attempted to change the subject of our discussion to the whereabouts and the wellbeing of Zaras and Hui. I knew that she was seeking this information at the behest of her royal mistresses.

Repeatedly I had to bring her back to our discussion of the multitudinous brides of the Supreme Minos.

'How many of the other brides have become favourites of the gods since you and the princesses took up residence in the seraglio?' I insisted.

'Forty,' she replied without hesitation. I was surprised by the number and by Loxias' certainty of the exact figure.

'So that is approximately one bride a day since you and the princesses have been resident in the seraglio?'

'No, no, my lord. All forty of them left the seraglio at the same time. They went dancing and singing and with flowers in their hair.'

'The Supreme Minos must have had a busy night.' I could not resist the quip. Loxias struggled to keep a modest expression but there was a sparkle of laughter in her eyes. I went on with my questions: 'None of those forty women have returned to the seraglio, are you sure of that?'

'I am completely sure of that. We know everything that happens in our section of the palace.'

I pondered her replies. I had the uneasy feeling that I was missing something of deep significance.

'Forty brides all left together and none of them have returned,' I mused aloud.

'I have already told you that, Taita.' Her expression was long-suffering. 'Tehuti wants to know where Zaras is now. Is he in Krimad or is he on patrol with his ships? She would like to send him a present. Would you take it to him?' I ignored the question. I was determined not to let myself be sucked into this intrigue.

'When did the brides leave the seraglio?' I laboured my point.

'They left at noon on the day of the earthquake,' Loxias snapped at me impatiently. 'Didn't I already tell you that?'

I stared at her, as my mind raced to keep up with the twists and turns in our conversation. 'Are you telling me that Tin-head had his wicked way with forty virgins in the middle of an earthquake?' I demanded.

'I suppose so.' She giggled. 'If so, I would have loved to watch.' She stood up. 'I must go now or the viragoes will not let me back into the palace. Shall I take the girls a message from you?'

'Tell them I love them more than anything else in the world.'

'What about me?' She pouted dramatically.

'Don't be greedy. You already have one old man who loves you, Loxias.'

'He isn't so old,' she protested. 'He is quite young and very rich. He is going to marry me; just you wait and see.'

After she had gone I sat alone on the terrace thinking over everything she had told me. I could make very little sense of it, and I was left with a feeling of pervading unease, a sense of impending disaster.

I wanted to hurry back to Krimad to immerse myself in the warlike preparations with Zaras and Hui, which I knew would distract me. However, I had to be at Ambassador Toran's pigeon coop when one of the birds that Friend had taken to Aton in Thebes returned.

I was in conference with Lord High Admiral Herakal and his staff when there was a mild commotion at the barred doors of the command room.

'What is it?' Herakal bellowed in a voice that echoed through the cavernous chambers of the Admiralty. 'I ordered no distractions!'

The captain of the guard unlocked the polished cedar-wood doors and came through them bowing and blurting apologies.

'Lord Toran of the Privy Council has sent a message. He says that it is of the utmost importance, and must be delivered to the hand of Lord Taita, the Egyptian, without delay.'

Herakal cast me a lugubrious glance of disapproval and threw up his hands in mock despair. 'Let the knave in! Let them all come in! Go ahead and disobey my orders whenever you take it into your heads to do so.'

Swiftly I came to my feet to protect the fellow who was quailing before Herakal's wrath. 'I must accept full responsibility, Lord High Admiral. I have been expecting a despatch of the utmost importance from my sources in Egypt.'

'We will all wait on your convenience, Lord Taita.' Grumbling to himself, Herakal rose from his stool and stalked to the windows, where he stood staring out at Mount Cronus across the bay. I snatched the despatch from the captain's trembling hand.

It was a tight roll of yellow silk, no larger than the top joint of my little finger and almost weightless. When I unfolded it I saw that it was as long as my arm and densely covered with the coded symbols that Aton and I had devised between us. These were a great advance on any other written language in existence, both in their compactness and in the range and exactitude of meaning that they made available to the writer.

I read through the message swiftly, and glanced up at the lord high admiral before he had time to compose and deliver his next complaint.

'Lord High Admiral, I have wonderful news. We have been presented with the opportunity of striking a blow at the heart of our mutual enemy. Gorrab of the Hyksos has assembled a cavalry force of more than a thousand chariots on the plain of Shur on the western extreme of the Nile Delta.'

'I know that area!' Herakal exclaimed as he turned back from the window; his tone had changed. 'It runs along the shore of the Middle Sea between the cities of Zin and Dhuara.'

'That is correct!' I agreed. 'Over the past year my Pharaoh and Lord Kratas have concentrated their offensive on the westerly bank of the Nile. They have advanced as far north as Lake Moeris, which is only eighty leagues south of Zin.' I spread the yellow silk square on the table, and Herakal and his staff gathered around it. Aton had written his message on one side, but on the reverse side he had drawn a detailed map of northern Egypt which showed the disposition of the armies: both Hyksos and Egyptian.

'My sources report that Gorrab is planning a major flanking manoeuvre, swinging down the eastern border of Egypt to strike our extended line here at Quam.' I touched the silken map. 'It's a cunning plan, but his assembly area at Zin is extremely vulnerable to attack from the sea. It seems that Gorrab is still ignorant of our combined fleet now waiting at Krimad for just such an opportunity.'

'You say Gorrab has a thousand chariots?' Herakal demanded. 'That means he probably has more than three thousand charioteers. You will be heavily outnumbered. If Gorrab becomes aware of your plans you will be annihilated if you attempt to attack them.'

In rebuttal I tapped the scrap of yellow silk. 'Yes, indeed, Gorrab has a thousand chariots concentrated at Zin, but my information is that he has not yet detached his charioteers from his main force facing Pharaoh and Lord Kratas at Lake Moeris. As it stands now he has fewer than five hundred men guarding the chariots.' I read the figures from Aton's silken message. 'Five hundred men and twice as many horses.'

Herakal smoothed his moustaches thoughtfully. 'That is roughly equal in strength to your own force.'

'My flotilla is ready for sea and we can be off Zin in six days from now; before Gorrab is able to bring up the rest of his men. I can beach my chariots in their rear, and attack them before they know we have landed. We will have the advantage of complete surprise which is worth a thousand fully manned chariots.'

'I will tell you straight, Lord Taita, that I don't like it. It all seems too neat and fortuitous. It smells to me like a bear trap. However, the Supreme Minos has given you an independent command. You do not have to have my sanction for this harebrained scheme.'

'Then we have nothing further to discuss, Lord High Admiral. I thank you for your advice and good wishes, and I will take my leave.'

I rode alone over the mountain and I pushed my horses hard. I arrived at Krimad an hour before sunset and found both Zaras and Hui at the stables. They were astonished to see me, but their surprise turned to unholy joy as I told them what I had in mind.

'Get the horses on board while it is still light,' I told Hui. 'Zaras, take as many men as you need and make sure the chariots on all the ships are securely lashed down before we sail.' Bellowing orders at their men they rushed to follow my orders.

I went to the coop which was the new home of Aton's pigeons

which had survived the perilous voyage from Egypt. I selected two of the plumpest and strongest of them and tied the identical message on to each of their legs. Then one at a time I kissed them on the top of their heads and tossed them fluttering into the air. They circled the harbour four times to get their bearings and then headed south-south-east; and disappeared into the gathering dusk. A night run was safest for them. Hawks and falcons do not hunt during the hours of darkness. But I had repeated my message to Aton to make doubly sure.

I had asked him to have guides waiting for us on the beach at Zin in six days' time. They were to meet us when we landed and lead us to where King Gorrab had assembled his chariots.

An hour before midnight my flotilla of six galleys left the harbour. As soon as we had made our offing we turned to the south in line astern, heading for Egypt and the Bay of Zin.

In the darkness of pre-dawn we missed the squadron of twelve fighting galleys led by Nakati, prince of the Sea Peoples, in his own ship, the *Dove*. Nakati was hurrying to Krimad to warn me of the morass of treachery and betrayal into which I was blithely sailing with my little squadron.

Nakati reached the port of Krimad a few hours after sunrise to find me and my ships vanished. However, I had left five of my men who, due to wounds and sickness, were unfit to sail with me. These invalids had been with me on the voyage from Sidon in Sumeria when I captured the *Dove* and chained Nakati to the rowing bench. They had also been present when I unchained him and reinstated him to command of the *Dove*. Thus they knew he was one of us, and so they did not hesitate to tell Nakati where I was headed and the purpose of my sortie to Zin.

Nakati lingered in the port of Krimad just long enough to take on water and provisions from my warehouse. Then almost three hours after sunrise he set off again with his flotilla in pursuit of mine; but I had an eight-hour head start.

Of course at this stage I had no way of knowing that Nakati was following me at his best speed. On the contrary I had heard nothing from him since I turned him free on trust. Now I was inclined to regret that hasty decision. I was starting to believe that he had duped me and returned to his role as prince of the Sea Peoples, and that I would never set eyes upon him again; except over a naked blade.

It was not until much later than the events I am describing here that I learned that Nakati had stood by our agreement. However it had taken him all this time to recruit crews for his ships from amongst the ranks of the pirates and freebooters that made up the tribe of the Sea Peoples.

In retrospect I should have known better, but I had always believed the Sea Peoples to be a disorganized rabble; lacking the organization and structures of a modern navy. I had over-looked the fact that many of the pirate princes were trained and skilled fighting seamen who only by force of circumstances had become renegades. It followed they had at their disposal an extensive and tightly organized intelligence network that was certainly more efficient than that which my old friend Lord Aton was running. Nakati had double agents placed amongst Aton's people, but he also had his spies in the headquarters of the Hyksos in Memphis. I do not doubt that he had even penetrated my own network. Through these sources he was fully aware of the correspondence that Aton and I had exchanged. He knew of my intention to raid the Hyksos chariot depot at Zin, and he knew that the Hyksos were also aware of my intentions. However, Nakati did not have pigeons to send to warn me of what was taking place. He had come in person to save me from disaster, but he had arrived too late.

I n the *Outrage* we made our landfall on the African coast in the half-light an hour before sunrise on the fifth day after leaving Krimad. I had navigated deliberately on a course with slightly westerly deflection. There was no navigator alive who could sail a ship for five days out of sight of land and arrive at a destination as precise as the Bay of Zin. To have made my landfall on the easterly side of the bay would have been dangerous. The coastline closer to the Nile Delta was heavily populated. We would have been spotted as soon as we showed above the horizon. If I could not be certain of sailing directly into the Bay of Zin then it was safer to err to the west. The western shore was the Sahara proper, inhabited sparsely by a few roving Bedouin.

More importantly I was absolutely certain of my headings as soon as I sighted the land. Without hesitation I gave the orders for the flotilla to turn in succession to port and sail in line ahead with the desert close on our starboard side. We sailed for three hours parallel to the shore, before it became clear that I had overdone my deliberate error. This was of great concern to me at the time, but it proved to be fortuitous. It gave Nakati that much extra leeway to close the gap between our two squadrons.

At last we came up level with the mouth of Zin Bay, which I recognized by the prominent headlands that shielded the interior from the northern approaches. I gave the order to tack in succession and we ran in through the entrance to the bay.

The Hyksos were waiting for us. They came at us in a mass as soon as we passed between the headlands of the Bay of Zin. They must have assembled everything that would float for a hundred leagues along the shore and the delta of the Nile. They were too numerous to count. There were craft as small as luggers and as massive as the single trireme which led the attack on our flotilla. The closest vessels blanketed those behind them; the larger ships screened the smaller ones. But at a hasty estimate I judged that there must be at least twenty-five Hyksos vessels opposing our six.

All their decks were thronged with armed men. Their helmets, cuirasses, blades and shields glittered in the blaze of the rising sun. Their war cries and challenges carried clearly across the water as they came to meet us.

The early-morning wind was blowing briskly from the open sea, through the entrance to the bay directly behind our squadron and into the faces of the Hyksos. This prevented me from reversing my course and attempting to escape the way I had come.

On the other hand the Hyksos ships were headed directly into the wind, as close-hauled as their hulls would allow. They were loafing along, barely maintaining steerage. Our six vessels were charging forward with the wind filling our sails and white water foaming under our bows. Within a dozen strokes of our oars we were at full ramming speed.

I could see that the decks of the enemy vessels were so closely packed with men that their archers were hampered by the press of bodies and shields. On the other hand Zaras and Hui, Akemi and Dilbar and my other captains had taken full advantage of our more sparsely manned ships. Even before we passed between the headlands of the bay and ran into the ambush, our archers had been prepared for any eventuality. Their bows were strung and their arrows were laid on the stocks of their bows. As soon as the range between the enemy and our leading ships closed to long arrow shot Zaras gave the order to loose. The wind coming in directly over our stern was our ally: it gave us an advantage of better than a hundred yards. Our archers were able to loose ten volleys before the Hyksos could loft their arrows high enough to reach us.

The dun cloud of our arrows swept over their decks and the slaughter was prodigious. The shrieks of the wounded were counterpointed by the 'Thump! Thump!' of the striking arrows.

The enemy trireme was larger by almost half than any of the ships in my squadron, but in these contrary wind conditions her bulk was much more a liability than an asset. I saw that she was paying off before the wind. The great bronze ram on her bows was no longer pointed at us menacingly. As she yawed she was exposing her tumblehome and her midships where her planking and her treble banks of long oars were most susceptible to our assault.

'Ram her as she turns!' I snapped at Zaras, and he leaped to obey my order. Our drummers increased the beat to attack speed. The men on our rowing benches were fresh and eager. They pulled until their eyes bulged from their sockets. Before the thrust of the wind and the impetus of our oars the *Outrage* hurled herself forward. I prompted Zaras to continually make fine adjustments of our helm so that the bronze spike of our ram was always aimed at the most vulnerable point in the trireme's hull.

We thrust aside the smaller Hyksos luggers and longboats that were between us and our target and at the last moment before we struck the trireme Zaras bellowed the order: 'In oars!' Our rowers shipped their oars neatly and with a rending crash our bronze ram shaped like the beaked head of an eagle smashed through the hull of the trireme and rolled her over on her side. The screams of her men blended with the crackle of rending timbers and splintering oars. Both her masts snapped off at deck level. She rolled past the point of no return. The waters poured in through her open rowing ports. The slaves chained to the benches drowned almost at once, and the fighting men crowded on her top deck were poured into the sea alongside the floundering hulk.

Zaras and I were thrown to the deck of the *Outrage* by the force of the impact. The *Outrage* had been stopped dead in the water, so that by the time we had hauled ourselves to our feet the smaller Hyksos craft had been able to cluster around us and hurl grappling hooks over our sides. Their armed boarders were already scrambling furiously aboard the *Outrage*, howling like a pack of wolves around the carcass of a deer. They were coming over both our gunwales, swinging battle axes and thrusting with swords. We were surrounded.

Zaras and I and the other deck officers formed a circle back to back, facing outwards. We were consummate swordsmen who had fought together on numerous occasions. We outmatched the Hyksos attackers with their wild swings and crude lumbering rushes. But as fast as we cut them down others came swarming over the sides of the *Outrage* to take their places.

Almost at once the deck beneath my feet was slippery with blood and my arms were wet with gore to the elbows; but still the Hyksos barbarians came at us and died. Zaras at my right hand seemed indefatigable; but I was tiring rapidly. My arms were growing heavy and my feet were losing their grace and agility.

I killed another man and as I kicked him off the point of my sword I glanced over the ship's side and saw that all the other vessels of my flotilla were heavily engaged, surrounded by enemy vessels and fighting for survival. Then to my horror I saw that another dozen enemy vessels were entering the bay from the open sea, big fighting galleys filled with cheering men who pulled lustily at their oars. I knew that we were about to be overwhelmed by sheer weight of numbers and we could not survive much longer. I considered for an instant how we might disengage and make a run for the open sea. But I realized that the thought was not only the last resort of the craven spirit, but it was also the fantasy of despair. There was no escape from this bloodbath. We fought on as fresh waves of enemy poured aboard us. At last I was reeling on my feet with exhaustion. Zaras jammed his shield against mine to steady me, but by now even to lift my sword required brutal effort. My face and arms were splattered with the blood of the men I had killed.

Then another bearded enemy face appeared before me and I hacked at it with my blunted blade. By now the cutting edge was dulled and chipped and the point was broken off. My blow was so sloppy and feeble that my new adversary turned it aside with a contemptuous twist of his wrist.

'Taita!' he shouted at me, and I checked my next thrust and stared at him dumbfounded. For a moment I did not recognize him through his beard and the ruddy veil of splattered blood that dulled my vision. But now I realized that he was not another Hyksos brute. His features were noble and familiar.

'Put up your blade, my lord. I am your liege man.' I even recognized his voice.

'Nakati?' I gasped. 'I thought that I had seen the last of you.'

'"The gods are not always attentive to our pleas."' He grinned as he repaid me in my own words. Then he seized my arm to prevent me falling, but I shrugged his hand away. With fresh hope came renewed strength.

'You cut your arrival fine, Nakati. Nonetheless you are welcome.' I pointed over the bows of the *Outrage* to where the surviving Hyksos had abandoned the battle. They were fleeing to the safety of the land; beaching their boats, abandoning them and escaping into the dunes. 'Catch those fine fleet-footed fellows for me. Then we can turn our attention to the destruction of their chariot depot, if we can find it.'

He laughed at my choice of words. 'Neither fine nor fleet-footed enough. The Hyksos cavalry lines are less than a league from where we stand,' he assured me.

'Are you sure of that?' I demanded.

'My informants are not as numerous as yours or Lord Aton's, but they are at least as efficient. They informed me of this ambush that Gorrab's men had prepared for you. I sailed to Krimad to warn you, but when I arrived you had already left. I thank Horus and Isis that I was in time to find you still alive here.'

'I also am grateful for that!' I wiped the sweat and blood from my face with the tail of my chlamys and stooped to pick up an abandoned enemy sword from the deck to replace my own battered weapon. As I straightened up I shouted to Zaras, 'Take us in to the beach. Don't let one of the Hyksos animals escape!'

We ran our own ships aground on the sandy beach. In obedience to my orders Nakati led his men in pursuit of the fugitive Hyksos, while Zaras and Hui unloaded our chariots and put the horses into the traces.

The Bedouin guides that Aton had sent to meet us emerged from where they were hiding in the dunes. Hui and I mounted up and, with half our chariots, followed the guides to the Hyksos cavalry depot.

Zaras joined forces with Nakati's men. In the remainder of the chariots they set off in pursuit of the Hyksos fugitives from the battle who had escaped into the dunes.

The Hyksos guards at the cavalry depot had been too far from the fighting to have been alerted by the tumult and uproar of battle. When Hui and I drove our chariots up to the periphery fence of the depot I called on them in their own language to open the gates. They took us for reinforcements sent from their main army in the south, and they threw the gates open to welcome us.

By the time they realized how mistaken they were our men were amongst them, knocking down their weapons and forcing them to kneel with their hands behind their backs while they were trussed.

In the parking ground of the depot we found 850 newly built chariots drawn up in neat ranks four deep.

Obviously the Hyksos carpenters had copied the design of our Egyptian vehicles. These were a great improvement on the traditional Hyksos machines. The bodywork was woven from Malacca cane and bamboo, much lighter and more flexible than solid pine or cedar. The wheels were spoked rather than solid; making them faster and more durable.

These vehicles had been freshly lacquered and they were so closely packed that their wheel hubs were touching. We anointed them liberally with lamp oil that I had brought with us for this purpose. When we tossed burning torches into them the flames jumped from vehicle to vehicle; reducing them to ashes in the time it takes for a thirsty man to drink a cup of good wine. I was happy to see them burn rather than arrayed against me for they would have made formidable adversaries.

As soon as we had dealt with the Hyksos chariots Aton's guides led us to their cavalry lines. There were almost two thousand chargers being held in the reed-thatched stables.

One thing – perhaps the only thing – I will concede to the Hyksos is their excellence in horse-handling. These animals had clearly been carefully bred and selected, then devotedly groomed and trained to burnished perfection. I love horses in preference to any other animal species, including most human beings. At the very least you can trust a horse.

We drove them down to where our ships lay on the beach of the bay. I was not certain how to dispose of them. Two thousand horses is a great multitude. We did not have room for them in our ships, even with the addition of Nakati's squadron.

When the suggestion was made by one of Nakati's officers that we slaughter these magnificent creatures rather than allow them to be recaptured by the Hyksos I felt every nerve and sinew of my body burn with indignation. I turned on Nakati.

'Are there not fifty men amongst these blackguards of yours that understand and love horses?' I demanded of him.

'There are, my lord.' He could see how infuriated I was.

'Give them to me, Nakati. I will divide the herd between them. Then each of them should attempt independently to drive his animals south into Egyptian territory. They will choose separate routes. I will pay a bounty of a silver deben for each horse they deliver to my estate at Mechir. If any man of them dies in the attempt I will care for his widow and children for life. My oath on it!'

Within less than an hour Nakati had assembled the volunteers. They drew lots for their share of the captured animals and then drove them out into the gathering twilight, splitting up into smaller groups as they went.

Some of them had decided to drive their horses into the Sahara and try to circle to the west around the Hyksos positions to reach our very Egypt. Others were determined to cross the Nile Delta; swimming their horses through the tributaries of the great river to reach the Sinai Peninsula in the east before turning south along the shores of the Red Sea to reach Thebes.

I watched them go and said a devout and fervent prayer to Horus and Inana, begging them to watch over my horses during the perilous journey that lay ahead of them.

N ow I could turn my attention to the prisoners.

With the garrison of the chariot depot and the survivors of the battle in the Bay of Zin we had captured 793 Hyksos charioteers and sailors. Zaras and Nakati had these prisoners kneeling in long lines on the beach above the high waterline. They had been stripped naked and their arms were tied behind their backs. They were resigned and morose as men waiting at the foot of the gallows for the summons from the executioner.

'What should we do with these miserable creatures?' I demanded of Nakati and my officers. None of them showed much interest in the subject. Our ships that had been damaged in the battle had been hastily repaired and relaunched. Those that were beyond repair had been set on fire and were burning on the sands. The battle had been fought and won. Everyone was anxious to go on board and sail away, before fresh Hyksos hordes came howling over the dunes for blood and vengeance.

'Kill them,' suggested Hui off-handedly.

'I agree.' Zaras nodded. 'Kill them all.' He spoke in Hyksosian and loud enough for the nearest prisoners to hear and understand.

'That is good advice.' Nakati gave his opinion. 'If we let them go they will be back tomorrow killing our men and raping our women.' The others growled agreement, but Nakati held up his hand for their attention and went on speaking: 'However, Lord Taita, I know you well enough by now to be certain that you will never agree to our very sensible suggestions. You could never kill in cold blood a man who has surrendered to you.'

'Perhaps you give me too much credit for chivalry.' I shrugged. 'I might surprise you.' But of course he knew my protestation was insincere. He grinned at me.

'Let me make a suggestion,' he proposed. 'Let me show you how we can make certain that these swine never again shoot an arrow or wield a sword against Pharaoh and our very Egypt. Then you can release them to the dictates of your conscience, my lord.'

'How do you propose we achieve that? Will we ask them to give their parole, and place our trust in that?' I was irritated by the futility of this debate. I also was anxious to go on board the *Outrage* and head back to Crete, where my princesses were. I had already made up my mind to release the captives just as soon as we sailed.

'A moment more of your attention, I beg of you.' Nakati nodded to a group of his own Sea People who were standing guard over the kneeling prisoners. They dragged one of the Hyksos charioteers forward and pushed him face down on the sand with his arms still tied behind his back. Nakati stood over him and drew his sword.

'Hold up your thumbs, fellow!' he ordered, and the prisoner obeyed gullibly. With a double flick of his blade Nakati severed the thumbs from both his hands at the second joint. The prisoner screamed with pain and despair as the blood spurted from the stumps and his disjointed parts fell twitching into the sand.

'I will wager that this man will never again wield a sword or draw a bow against Egypt,' Nakati said. We gaped at him in shock and dumb amazement for a few moments before all my men let out whoops of delighted laughter.

Then Zaras stepped forward before I could intervene. With his foot he rolled the naked and maimed prisoner on to his back. He drew his sword and slipped the point of it under the man's flaccid penis. 'And here is the way to make certain he never again rapes an Egyptian woman or one of our new-born infants.' With an upward slash of the blade he severed the member at its juncture with the prisoner's groin. Then he speared it on the point of his sword and flipped it into the surf that lapped the beach.

'An offering to Poseidon, the god of the sea, if he accepts such a foul piece of swine flesh.'

The men around me shouted with approbation; but my voice was louder than any of them.

'Cease that brutality at once, Zaras. Put up your sword. You descend to the same level as any Hyksos animal!'

Zaras ran his blade back into its scabbard, but when he turned to face me his chin was up and his eyes were as fierce as mine. 'My Lord Taita, there is no space in our ships to take them into captivity,' he defied me. 'If you release these animals unharmed how many more of our own people will they slaughter? How many more of our children and women will die?'

Slowly I felt my rage wilting before his stubborn logic. I realized that my own judgement was clouded by the memory of the injuries that had been inflicted on me by the gelding knife. I was reluctant to allow those same brutalities to be visited on another human being, however evil and monstrous. I took a long deep breath to calm myself and then I modulated my voice to exclude the anger from it.

'You make good sense, Zaras. I am going to meet you halfway. We will take their thumbs but leave their pricks for Seth to pick.' I deliberately used the childish euphemism for the penis. I was attempting to de-escalate the tension that had flared between us. Hui and the others guffawed openly and Dilbar grabbed at Akemi's crotch.

'Ain't your prick feeling a peck peckish? You ain't seen a ripe cunny since we sailed from Krimad.' My men were all boys at heart. I forced myself to smile along with them. But when I turned back to Zaras the smile dropped from my lips.

Zaras was glaring at me ferociously. Gradually silence fell over the rest of the men. The only sound was the wind and the whimpering of the wounded prisoner who lay writhing on the sand. When Zaras spoke again his voice was cold and clear. It carried to every one of us, and chilled our hearts.

'My sisters were seven and eight years of age when the Hyksos overran our village. My father was with his regiment. The Hyksos raped my mother first and then both my sisters, taking turns with them for half a day. I was five years old, but I had managed to escape and hide in the fields from where I could see everything. When they had finished with them they threw my mother and sisters into the flames of our cottage while they were still alive and screaming.' Zaras drew a long breath, and then he asked me, 'What would you have me do now?'

There was no answer that I could give him. I shook my head sadly, and said, 'Do your duty to Pharaoh, and to the memory of your family.'

'Thank you, my lord,' Zaras replied. Then he drew his sword and went to join Nakati.

Between them they selected thirty of their best axe-men to perform the amputations. Each of them was given four assistants to pinion the prisoners and drag them forward. The first victims clenched their fists, and refused to present their thumbs for the blade. The axemen wasted no time trying to persuade them to do so. They simply lopped the entire hand off at the wrist. The prisoners that followed were more cooperative.

Then the assistants rolled them on to their backs, and with just as little ceremony their genitalia was hacked away and they were turned loose to stumble into the dunes; moaning and clutching their injuries in an attempt to staunch the bleeding.

The seagulls were attracted by the smell of blood. Raucous flocks of these scavengers gathered to squawk and flap over the growing piles of thumbs and sexual organs. They gulped down these titbits almost as swiftly as the axe-men could hack them loose.

I was sickened by it all. I turned away and went to where our ships were drawn up on the beach. I tried to ignore the screams and supplications of the Hyksos captives. Instead I concentrated on supervising the loading of our chariots and horses, together with the amphorae of water and provisions that we had found in the cavalry depot.

When he had finished the bloody work on the beach Nakati came to take his leave of me. In accordance with our agreement, he intended to continue wreaking havoc on the Hyksos ports and towns along the shores of the Middle Sea.

When at last Zaras clambered on board the deck of the *Outrage* he came to me immediately and went down on one knee before me. 'I disobeyed you, my lord,' he confessed. 'I defied your orders in front of the men. You would be fully justified if you reduced me to the ranks and dismissed me from your command.'

'You did what you knew was right,' I replied. 'No man can ever do better than that. Take command of the ship and set sail for Krimad.'

He rose to his feet. 'Thank you, Taita. I will never disappoint you again.'

As the sun sagged wearily to the western horizon I climbed to the masthead of the *Outrage*, from where I made one last survey of the sea behind us to be absolutely certain that there was no sign of pursuit by a Hyksos squadron. All was clear. The north coast of Egypt was merely a thin strip of blue above the darker blue of the sea. Our flotilla was closed up with stern lanterns lit to enable our navigators to maintain their precise stations in the formation through the hours of darkness.

The leadsman in the bows called, 'No bottom with this line!'

We were in deep water and on course for Crete. I was in my preferred position at the masthead. I heard Zaras dismiss the watch below. The rowers shipped their oars and curled up on the deck to sleep. The wind was fresh on our quarter and all our sails were spread.

Suddenly I was weary to the very depths of my body and soul. The fighting had been gruelling, and my confrontation with Zaras even more so. I considered descending the mast and retiring to my narrow bunk in the stern cabin, but the following breeze was warm and still redolent of the odours of my beloved Egypt. The gentle oscillation of the mainmast lulled me. My body ached dully with the bruises and nicks that I had received in the battle of Zin Bay. My cabin seemed far away. I made certain that the line around my waist was secured to the mast against which my back was pressed, before I closed my eyes and let my chin sag on to my chest.

When I woke again the moon had reached its zenith and its reflection on the surface of the sea was keeping pace with us, casting a pathway of glittering silver over the wavelets. The smell of Africa had been replaced by the salty tingle of the ocean. The only sounds were the susurration of the water under our hull, the regular creaking of the mast in its boot and the whisper of the wind in our rigging.

My aches had dissipated, and my weariness with them. I felt vigorous and alert once more. I was filled with that strange sense of elation which I had come to recognize as a sure sign that the goddess Inana was close. I looked for her eagerly, and felt no surprise when I saw her gliding along the pathway of moonlight to meet our ship. The hood of her mantle was thrown back, and the moonlight played on her face. She was lovely past imagining.

When she came abreast of the *Outrage* she stepped from the surface of the sea on to our deck and looked up at me.

Her expression changed and so did my mood. I was suddenly filled with a sense of dread and foreboding. I knew that Inana had not come to commend me for my victory on the plains of Zin.

She did not speak, but nonetheless I heard her voice echoing softly in my head.

'The god is angry. Cronus demands the ultimate sacrifice.'

'I do not understand.' I tried to speak, but the words stuck in my throat.

'Go to them. They are in mortal danger.' Her voice was silent, but I heard the warning clearly above the sound of the wind and water.

I tried to stir myself to go down to her, but I was unable to move. I wanted her to explain her enigmatic message, but I could not speak.

Then the dark shadows of sleep fell over me like a net, and she was gone. I struggled to retain my senses. I tried to cry out in the darkness: 'Don't go, Inana! Wait for me! I don't understand.' But the darkness overwhelmed me.

I don't know how long I slept the second time, but when I did manage to struggle back out of the darkness the dawn was breaking and the black-winged gulls were dipping and diving across our wake.

I looked down and the deck below me was bustling with activity. The first watch of oarsmen were filing down the companionway to take their turns on the rowing benches.

I untied the rope that secured me to the mast and slid down the backstay to the upper deck. As my feet hit the boards Zaras hurried to meet me. He was smiling and shaking his head.

'My lord, you didn't sleep in the rigging again, did you? Does your bunk no longer please you?' Then he saw my expression and his own smile faded. 'What is it . . .?'

'Jettison all our chariots immediately,' I ordered. 'Transfer all our horses to the other ships of the squadron.'

He gawked at me. 'Why, Taita?'

'Do not question my orders. I don't have time to argue with you again.' I was so impatient that I seized his shoulder and shook it. 'Take a full team of oarsmen from every one of the other ships. I want to be able to change rowers every hour.'

'Every hour?' Zaras blurted.

'I want attack speed all the way to Krimad.'

'Attack speed?' He looked incredulously at me.

'Don't keep repeating everything I say, Seth damn you, Zaras,' I growled at him. 'I want to be in Krimad five days from now, or even sooner if possible.'

'You will kill my men,' he protested.

'Better they die, rather than the royal princesses.'

He stared at me aghast. 'I don't understand . . .'

'Both the princesses are in mortal danger. We may already be too late, but every hour we lose is an hour closer to their certain deaths.'

He spun away from me shouting to the watch officer, 'Fly the signal for "All Captains".'

The other ships came alongside us two at a time, one on our port and one on our starboard side. Each of them put twenty of their best oarsmen on board the *Outrage*, with water and rations for five days. In exchange we gave them the slaves and weaklings from amongst our own crew.

We transferred all our horses across to them, hoisting them on the loading pulleys and swinging them across the gap between our vessels. We used the same equipment to lift our chariots and jettison them overboard. I wanted the *Outrage* to be floating high and light. Even five days to Crete was a tall order.

When it was the turn of Hui's vessel to come alongside, Zaras took him aside and spoke quietly to him, but I read their lips. Hui turned away from him and came striding down the deck to me with a determined expression on his face.

'Very well, Hui,' I forestalled his argument, 'put a good man in command of your ship and come over to us. But be warned you will take your turn on the rowing bench.'

As soon as we had our full complement on board and the first team of rowers in their places on the benches the drummer gave them the beat. He built up gradually from steering speed to attack speed at ten strokes to the minute.

The *Outrage* took wing and we flew through the water. Within the first hour we had left the rest of the flotilla below the horizon behind us.

When I changed teams the men who were relieved fell off their benches, lathered with sweat and choking for breath. Day and night over the next three days our speed never bled off.

Zaras and Hui took their shifts on the benches and even I rowed a full hour in every twelve. When men half my age faltered I never missed the beat. The memory of Inana's unspoken warning sustained me.

Go to them. They are in mortal danger.

*   *   *

396

t was afternoon on the fourth day. I had just relinquished my place on the rowing bench and, still dripping sweat and panting, I went to the ship's bows to scan the sea ahead.

I had no way of calculating how far we had still to go before we raised the island. I was not even certain that we were still on course. I had placed my faith in Inana to guide me. However the sea ahead of us was still empty and the horizon was slick and unbroken.

There was no wind. The sky was cloudless, burnished bright and merciless as the blade of an executioner's axe. The air was heavy and oppressive. It had a faint but unpleasantly sulphurous taste that seared the back of my throat. I coughed and spat over the side, and then I looked back over the stern. The only movement was the undulation of our wake and the stippled whirlpools left by our oar-blades on the polished surface as they rose and fell.

I was about to turn away and go below to try to get a little rest, for I had slept hardly at all since leaving the Bay of Zin, but just then something on the horizon ahead caught my eye. It was a thin undulating dark line. I stood and watched it for a while until I realized that it was a flock of birds flying directly towards us. I am very fond of all the avian species, but I could not recognize these until they came much closer. Then I astonished to see that they were common crows. The Cretan crow is usually a solitary bird, or paired with a mate. Furthermore, crows always stay close to land. It was for all these reasons that I had not identified them from a distance. This was a flock of several hundred of these birds and they were at least a hundred leagues or probably much more from the nearest land. I watched them pass overhead. They were cawing to each other with an urgency that sounded to me like a distress call or at least a warning cry.

When they were gone I looked again to the north and I saw more birds in flight approaching. Some of these were also crows but there were many other species as well. Ibis and herons, kestrels and eagles and other raptors passed over us. Then came the smaller birds: robins and larks, sparrows and doves and shrikes. The sky was filled with birds. Their numbers almost darkened the sun. Their cries were a strident cacophony that was almost deafening. There was a sense of desperation in this feathered exodus.

A tiny yellow canary dropped from the sky and landed on my shoulder. It was clearly exhausted. Its whole body was trembling and it piped pathetically when I took it in my hand and stroked its head.

I looked up again in wonder and still the flocks passed over us in their multitudes. Hui and Zaras came and stood with me, both with their heads thrown back and their faces turned upwards.

'What is happening, Taita?' Hui demanded.

'It seems to be a mass migration. But I have never seen anything quite like it before.'

'It looks more as though they are fleeing from some deadly threat,' Hui suggested.

'Wild animals and especially birds have an instinct for danger,' Zaras agreed, and then looked to me for confirmation. 'Is that not so, my lord?' I ignored the question, not because I did not know the answer but rather because at that moment there was a splash alongside the bows of our ship which was made by some heavy body.

I looked over the side, and the surface of the sea was boiling with life. Great shimmering bodies were tearing under our hull. Another mighty shoal of tuna was following the same direction as the flocks of birds that filled the sky above us. I looked ahead and saw that this shoal stretched out to the northern horizon.

Their silver shapes streamed past us endlessly, and then there were other creatures mingled with them. Glossy black porpoises ripped through the surface with their dagger-sharp dorsal fins, throwing up rooster tails of spray behind them. Whales which were almost as long as our ship blew clouds of steam through the vents atop their heads as they surfaced to breathe. Sharks striped like tigers and with evilly grinning mouths lined with jagged teeth dashed past us, heading southwards.

It seemed that all of creation was in panicked flight from some terrible cataclysm taking place beyond the northern horizon.

As the hours passed so this great agglomeration of flying and swimming creatures gradually thinned out, until there were no more of them.

We were alone in a deserted world; we few mortals and the tiny yellow canary which had stayed with me, sitting on my shoulder and trilling sweetly in my ear.

N ight fell over us, and we rowed on doggedly through the darkness with only the stars to light our way. With the rise of the sun I saw that the sky and the sea were still devoid of all life. The silence and the loneliness seemed ever more ominous and oppressive.

The only sounds seemed to be the creaking of the oars in the rowlocks thrusting us onwards towards Crete, the whisper of the water along our hull and the boom of the drum tolling the beat. None of the men spoke or laughed.

Even my yellow canary had fallen silent, and just before noon he slipped off my shoulder and flopped to the deck. He was dead when I picked him up. I took him to the stern and committed his tiny body to the care of Artemis, the goddess of the birds. I dropped him into the ship's wake. Then I climbed to my station at the masthead.

I scanned the horizon eagerly, but it was empty and my disappointment was difficult to bear. I sat in my perch for an hour and then another; watching and hoping.

The merciless sunlight hurt my eyes and after a while I began to see things that did not exist: phantom ships and illusory islands. I closed my eyes to rest them.

When I opened them again I was astonished to find that my hallucinations had intensified. The watery horizon ahead of our little ship was rising up towards the sky like a range of mountains: solid rather than liquid. Every moment these mighty oceanic Alps grew taller and more menacing. Now they were capped with glistening foam, white as freshly fallen snow.

Then I heard the babble of voices coming up from the deck below. I glanced down and saw that Zaras and Hui and the other deck officers had hurried forward into the bows of the ship. They were huddled there, pointing ahead and arguing with each other. The men on the upper deck benches had ceased rowing and were standing and peering ahead. The ship was losing way and drifting to a halt.

I jumped to the backstay and slid down it to the deck. When I reached it I ran forward, shouting to the men to take up their oars and get the ship under way once more.

The officers in the bows heard my voice and turned to me. Zaras ran back to meet me.

'What is happening? Is the world turning upside down?' He pointed over his shoulder. 'The sea is rising to fill the sky.' He was close to panicking.

'It's a wave.' With an effort I kept my own voice calm and level.

'No.' He shook his head vehemently. 'It's too big. It is coming too fast to be a mere wave.'

'It's a tidal wave.' I spoke with certainty. 'The same as the one that drowned the Empire of Atlantis in antiquity.'

'In the name of all the sweet gods, is there naught we can do to escape it?'

It was unlike Zaras to give up without a fight so I shouted in his face, 'Warn your crew, damn you! Make sure they have the spare oars at hand. When that thing hits us we are going to take damage. It will snap off our oars. We have to maintain steerage and hold true. If it gets us side-on it will roll us over like a log and swamp us completely. Get all the hatches battened down. Ship the masts and lash them down. Rig lifelines along all the rowing benches or else the crew will be washed overboard.'

Zaras responded at once to my peremptory orders and shouted for Hui to join him. I did not interfere any further. I left them to it, and stood in the bows and watched the wave coming.

The closer it came the higher it climbed and the faster it seemed to race towards us. We barely had sufficient time to prepare to receive it before the front slope of the wave caught us.

It lifted our bows so swiftly that my knees buckled under me and my stomach pressed up against my lungs, forcing me to gasp for breath. Up and up we climbed. Our stern dropped and the deck slanted back at such a steep angle that I had to cling to the bulwarks with both hands. The loose gear rolled and clattered down into the stern sheets.

Despite the pandemonium Hui and Zaras kept us head-on to the wave with brisk commands to the men on the rowing benches to 'Heave port!' and 'Avast heaving starboard!'

The men shouted entreaties to their gods and their mothers to save them but they kept rowing.

The higher we climbed the steeper was the slope, until our deck was almost vertical and our bows were pointing to the skies.

For a brief instant I was able to look ahead over the crest of the mighty wave. We were so high that I could see clearly on the distant horizon the southern shore of Crete and above it the tower of smoke billowing up from the vented peak of Mount Cronus on the far side of the island. The sulphur-yellow clouds roiled up upon each other, filling the entire northern sky to the very heavens. Then the creaming crest of the wave curled over us, and buried the *Outrage*'s deck under a fathom of green water.

One of the lifelines snapped under the strain and four of our crew members were swept over the side with it. We never saw them again. The rest of us were smothered by the racing water like rats trapped in an overflowing sewer. The coarse hemp lifeline around my waist was cutting me in half. I was not even able to scream to alleviate my terror. My vision began to black out. I knew that I was drowning.

Then suddenly our bows burst out through the back slope of the tidal wave. I was able to snatch a breath of sweet clean air before we dropped into the void. We fell free for what seemed an eternity. Only the lifelines saved the rest of us from being hurled overboard with all the other loose gear.

Then at last we struck the surface of the sea again with a crash and a shock that threatened to shatter every plank, bulkhead and strake in our hull. Our oars were sheared off at the rowlocks like dry twigs.

I thought we would be driven deep under again. But our gallant little ship shook herself free. We bobbed on the surface, listing heavily, our decks awash. Men and equipment were heaped upon the deck and piled upon each other.

Zaras and Hui raged over them, cursing and kicking them back to their places on the benches. However, some of the crew were gravely injured with broken limbs and crushed rib cages. These were dragged to one side. The spare oars were strapped to the deck beneath the benches. The rowers heaved the shattered stumps of their oars overboard and lifted the new oars into the rowlocks.

Then we all fell to bailing like men possessed. Slowly the *Outrage* rose high and light in the water once more. The drummer picked up the beat. The rowers stumbled back to their seats on the benches, and the blades of the oars bit and sliced through the surface. We sped forward towards Crete. From this low angle it had disappeared below the horizon once more. But now I had the volcano smoke from Mount Cronus to guide me.

A little after noon the wind picked up, and blew half a gale out of the south. The crew raised and restepped the masts and hoisted all our canvas to the following wind. Our speed was almost doubled. The water left behind the tidal wave was choppy and turbulent, strewn with the debris of trees and wreckage of ships and buildings that had been ripped from the island ahead of us. But we barged our way through it, with a team of men in the bows to fend off the more dangerous flotsam.

Within another two hours we raised the silhouette of Crete from the sea once more. It was tiny and insignificant in comparison to the heaven-high column of volcanic smoke that stood above it. Now the rumbling and bellowing of the mad god Cronus swept over us. The uproar was barely muted by the distance, and the surface of the sea itself danced to the fury of the god.

The oarsmen looked back over their shoulders in awe and trepidation as they pulled towards it. The off-duty crews huddled on the deck with the wounded and the dying. All of them were white-faced with terror. But I drove them on remorselessly towards Crete. When they seemed on the verge of mutiny Zaras and Hui unfurled the slave whips and stood over them, ready to use them.

As we drew closer to the land I was awed by the damage that the tidal wave had left in its wake. When we came in sight of the port of Krimad I could barely recognize it. I identified it only by reference to the peak of Mount Ida that stood up behind it.

All the buildings had been carried away by the wave, and even the heavy slabs of the breakwater had been tumbled into the sea like the building blocks of a petulant child.

The forest and cultivated land along the foot of the mountain had been stripped bare. Great trees, the ruins of buildings and the hulls of once mighty ships were mangled together into a mass of rubble.

What perturbed me the most was that the stables were gone. The grooms and horses must have been swallowed up by the wave and washed out to sea. My princesses were on the far side of the island. Without horses it would take days to reach them through the tangled remains of the forest.

I considered trying to circumnavigate the island, but I abandoned the idea. In these perilous conditions it would take many days; and there was no way to tell what we might find if we did succeed in reaching Knossos.

All I could hope for was that a few of the relay stations that I had laid out across the spine of the island were high enough to have escaped the full fury of the tidal wave, and perhaps some of the horses had survived.

We anchored on the edge of the deep water, two cables' length off the ruins of Krimad where the ship was protected by the bulk of the island. Then I called Zaras and Hui to me and told them, 'Each of the relay stations across the mountain has between ten and twenty horses in their stables, if they have survived. With one rider up and two men hanging on the stirrup leathers each animal can carry three men. Pick thirty of your very best men to come ashore with us. They must carry weapons only, no armour to overburden our mounts.'

When the shore party was ready we launched those skiffs which had survived the ravages of the great wave. When we took to the water in these tiny craft they were dangerously overloaded.

I prayed silently to Inana as the waves battered us and the water came sloshing in over the bows. I reminded the goddess that I was simply following her dictates, and she must have been listening. We reached the ruin of the breakwater with only three men swept overboard, and even one of these managed to swim back to the *Outrage*.

The skiffs were pounded to splinters almost as soon as we touched the rocks. However, we were able to scramble on to the remains of the breakwater with linked arms to support each other. We reached firm ground without suffering further loss.

Then Zaras formed the men up into double file and I led them through the remains of the drowned town. It was deserted except for a few swollen corpses, half buried in the rubble. Then we climbed the lower slopes of the mountain which had also been inundated. I was searching for the beginning of the road leading to the first relay station. All trace of it had been obliterated. We might never have found it had we not been guided by the bugling of a hunting horn in the forest above us. Three men of the relay team had watched our arrival from the heights and had come down the path to meet us.

They were terrified, but they had convinced themselves that we had come ashore to rescue them. Their disappointment was pathetic when they realized that was not the case. I led my men up to the relay station at a jog trot that defied the steep gradient. The ground under our feet trembled and shuddered, or rocked and bounced like a small boat in a rip-tide as the temper of the mad god Cronus flared or fell unpredictably.

When we reached the first relay station we found there a total of six men and twenty horses who had survived the devastation. The horses were almost mad with terror as the earth shook under them and the stink of burning brimstone from the mountain across the bay stung their nostrils. It took all my skills to quieten them sufficiently to be able to saddle them.

We tarried there just long enough to check our weapons. I was relieved to find that my recurved bow was still dry in its waxed leather case. I was not so satisfied by the state of my spare bowstrings. I appropriated a wallet of fine dry bowstrings from the captain of the relay station, much to his chagrin. But I held his eyes steadily as he began to protest, and he stammered into silence. Then I ordered him and all his men to remain at the relay station to cover our rear when we were forced to retreat.

I wasted not another minute but shouted at Zaras and Hui to mount up, and I led our little convoy up towards where the pathway crossed the shoulder of Mount Ida.

We had almost reached the crest when there was the thunder of hooves and the snorting and bellowing of a herd of wild beasts coming down the track towards us. I was just in time to lead my men into a dense stand of trees beside the path before a mass of monstrous bodies swept down the pathway towards us.

Of course I recognized them immediately. They were a herd of wild aurochs cattle. They pounded past us with glaring bloodshot eyes. Their backs were humped. Their hides were uniformly brindled black and dark brown. Their tongues lolled from the gaping mouths and the frothy saliva splattered their heaving shoulders. They were driven on by panic and terror, thundering along the pathway that skirted the sheer cliff.

As we watched, another tremor shook the mountain under us. I saw a deep cleft open in the rim of the cliff, full in the track of the aurochs herd. The mountain slope was so steep and the momentum of the herd so irresistible that they were unable to avoid the drop. The entire herd poured over the cliff, the animals behind forcing those in front onwards until every one of them plunged into the void. We heard the massive bodies striking the rocks hundreds of feet below. Afterwards there was silence, until that also was shattered by the next roar of the volcano.

I led my band back on to the pathway and we climbed the last steep slope to the crest. Here we paused again. I looked back to where the tiny shape of the *Outrage* was anchored off the ruins of Krimad. Then I turned in the saddle and looked ahead at the ruins of what had once been the city of Knossos, capital of the mightiest empire on earth.

The great harbour was no more. There was no sign of the lighthouse. It must have been thrown down into the harbour basin. The harbour walls had been carried away, not leaving even their foundations. The wild seas dashed unhindered over the bare rocks on which the great city had stood.

The Supreme Minos' vaunted fleet of ten thousand ships had been hurled up above the tideline and smashed into kindling and splinters. There was no trace of a single floating hull in the whole wide bay. But the waters were thick with floating wreckage and tumultuous with the waves that still hurled themselves against the shore.

The palace in which the Supreme Minos had married my princesses was gone; as was also the Admiralty building and every other stone-built edifice which had lined the waterfront.

Beyond this chaos the twin volcanoes thundered and blew out flame and smoke to fill the heavens.

In disbelief I let my gaze travel over the devastation. The Minoan Empire was no more. It had been obliterated by its own crazed god.

Where are my girls? My heart sobbed more clearly within me than my voice could ever have done. Why did you send me here, Inana? Was it simply to mock and torment me?

As by a force outside myself I felt my eyes directed to the foot of the mountain directly below me where I sat my horse. I saw that the Egyptian Embassy, which had been my home, albeit for so short a period, was still whole and intact. The tidal wave had not reached up that high. It was the only building on the north slope of the island that had survived.

'Come on!' I shouted at Zaras and Hui. 'Follow me!' And I raked my horse's ribs with the spurs. As we started down the hillside through the forest another shock wave from the twin peaks of Mount Cronus swept over us. My stallion shied wildly under me. I fought to control him and although the men hanging on my stirrup leathers were thrown about dangerously they both retained their grip until I had the horse quietened down again and we plunged on downwards.

The embassy seemed completely deserted as I galloped up to the front entrance and jumped from the saddle.

'Zaras and Hui! Go around to the stable yard in the rear and see if any of the horses are still there. We will need more mounts to take us back to Krimad when we find the girls.' I was determined not to surrender to despair. Inana would not have summonsed me if my princesses were no longer alive.

The doors to the embassy were standing wide open. I ran through the building shouting for any survivors. But the echoes mocked me. Every room was deserted, but most of them had been looted. The contents had been thrown about with wild abandon. My servants or the refugees from the city had helped themselves as they fled.

I was uncertain which way to turn next. I felt the first gnawing of despair in my guts. I steeled myself against it and called aloud to the goddess for help. 'Inana! Where are they? Do not desert me now. Lead me to them, I implore you.'

She answered me immediately; her voice echoing down from the upper level of the building. 'Taita! Is that you, my lord?' I heard the patter of her footsteps on the stairway. 'I thought at first it was another gang of robbers seeking plunder,' she cried.

In her hooded gown she raced down the last few steps and threw herself into my arms. I cupped her face in my hands and lifted it. I stared at her for a moment before I found my voice. 'Loxias!' I cried. 'What are you doing here, child! I mistook you for somebody else.'

'My Lord Toran sent me to wait for you here. We knew that you would come. I am to show you the way to the Higher Temple of the god Cronus in the mountains.' She was blubbering so uncontrollably that I had difficulty understanding what she was saying. I hugged her close to quieten her.

'Slow down, my little one! I do not understand any of this. Take a deep breath and speak slowly.'

'At the bidding of the Supreme Minos the priests have taken Tehuti and Bekatha to the Higher Temple. There they will sacrifice them to placate the god Cronus, and to prevent him destroying the Minoan Empire with fire and brimstone.' She drew another deep breath and hurried on, 'They have already sacrificed forty of the virgin wives of the Supreme Minos, but Cronus has rejected them. His rage is unassuaged. He demands the ultimate sacrifice: the virgin princesses of the Pharaonic House of Egypt.'

'Where is Toran now?'

'He has gone to the Higher Temple to try to deter the Supreme Minos from this terrible deed, or at the very least to delay the sacrifice until you arrive. He says that you are the only one who may be able to save Tehuti and Bekatha. Somehow he knew you would come. There was a hooded lady in his dreams who warned him—'

'Do you know the way to this temple?' I interrupted her.

'Yes,' she said. 'It is not too far from here. Toran has told me how to find the secret entrance, and to work my way through the labyrinth.'

I seized her arm and ran with her through the deserted rooms to the front entrance of the embassy. Zaras and Hui were waiting for me there with all their men. Zaras jumped down from the saddle and ran to meet me.

'You have found—' Zaras started, but then he recognized Loxias under the hood. 'Where are the princesses?'

'Enough!' I cut off his questions. 'I will explain all of it to you while we ride. Loxias knows where to find them. She will take us there.'

Hui had found six additional horses in the embassy stables; enough for every one of the men to ride. I seated Loxias on the saddle behind me and she locked her arms around my waist while I whipped up my stallion.

We rode in a tight group. Loxias directed me to the road that ran westwards along the mountainous spine of the island. Within two leagues we reached a fork in the road. The main branch continued straight on, but a lesser track branched off towards the peak of Mount Ida. This route was marked by a monstrous cedar-wood tree; its dead top branches soared upwards towards the backdrop of the billowing volcanic clouds.

'Lord Toran says that this tree is a thousand years old.' Loxias spoke over my shoulder. 'And that is the symbol of the god Cronus.' She pointed to the skull of an enormous aurochs bull that was nailed to the trunk of cedar wood. The horns were almost twice the size of those of the bull which had killed Waaga, the slave. Time and sunlight had bleached them to a dazzling white.

I spent not another moment in contemplating them, but turned our mount on to the track as Loxias directed me. It climbed up through the dense forest, and it was only just wide enough to allow two horses to gallop abreast. It ended abruptly against a high blackstone cliff. Into the foot of this cliff was set a massive brass door. In the centre of this door was a locking wheel of the same metal.

Loxias threw herself out of the saddle behind me and landed catlike on her feet. She ran to the doorway and began to turn the locking wheel, spinning it left and right, counting the revolutions aloud.

Behind her I dismounted and strung my bow, using one of the new dry bowstrings. Then I drew a pair of arrows from my quiver and tucked them into my belt where I could reach them in an instant. I nocked a third arrow and held the stock of my bow in my left hand. Then with my right hand I eased my sword in its scabbard. Zaras and Hui and all their men followed my example, readying their weapons and moving up behind Loxias and me.

Loxias turned the locking wheel one last revolution and the

mechanism clicked loudly. I motioned to Zaras to help her heave on the wheel. At the same time I stepped to one side and drew my arrow to full stretch; aiming over Zaras' shoulder.

The door swung open ponderously. Close behind it stood two of the green-uniformed viragoes from the royal seraglio. Both of them held drawn swords at the ready. They rushed forward to strike at Zaras and Loxias.

Zaras was ready for them, and killed one with a straight thrust into her naked boyish chest. I killed the other with an arrow. At such close range the arrow whipped through her torso and shattered her spinal column as it came out between her shoulder blades. It struck bright sparks from the flint wall of the tunnel behind her. Both the female warriors went down without uttering a sound. We stepped over their corpses. Shoulder to shoulder Zaras and I raced down the tunnel. It was dimly lit by the smoking torches set in brackets on the side walls.

'Toran says to take every turning to the left, or else we will be lost in the maze.' Loxias was close behind me and she called over my shoulder.

I took three left turns in succession. Then I heard very faintly the sound of chanting echoing down the tunnel from ahead. It grew louder as we ran towards it. I made one more turn to the left, and suddenly I saw a glimmer of daylight ahead of us.

I cautioned Loxias and the rest of my men to remain where they were, then I moved forward with Zaras and Hui close on either side of me. The light grew brighter and then we turned one last corner.

There were two more viragoes blocking the tunnel ahead of us, but both of them had their backs turned to us. All their attention was focused ahead, and they were unaware of our presence. We crept up behind them. Zaras and Hui locked hands over their mouths to prevent them crying out, and then there was a quick flash of blades before both the women warriors sagged to the floor. We stepped over their bodies and found ourselves in a viewing balcony which had been hewn out of the living rock.

Twenty cubits or more below us gaped an enormous cavern which was lit by daylight streaming in through a pillared entrance in the facing wall. Through these portals we had another sweeping vista over the ruins of Knossos city and the wide bay to the peaks of Mount Cronus, which filled the horizon.

Directly below us was a spacious semi-circular arena. The floor was covered with fine white sand on which stood an altar fashioned in silver and gold. On the altar stood the golden statue of an aurochs bull that was wreathed with flowers and surrounded with smouldering pots of frankincense.

The arena and the altar were surrounded by tiers of stone benches.

The two lower tiers were filled with rows of black-costumed and high-hatted Minoan nobles. Their faces were powdered with white chalk and their eyes were lined with black kohl in the traditional fashion. All of them were motionless, staring down intently at the empty floor of the arena. Only their mouths moved as they chanted a mournful dirge.

I was astonished by how few of them there were. There had been several thousand in the harbour palace when Tehuti and Bekatha were wedded to the Minos. Gathered here today were fewer than fifty. The eruption and tidal wave must have taken a dire toll of the flower of Minoan society.

Behind these scant survivors rose another tier of seats, which were unoccupied. In the centre of this tier was a tall golden throne. This also was empty.

Directly behind the throne was the entrance to this subterranean temple. It was a cavernous opening which framed the distant prospect of Mount Cronus across the turbid waters of Knossos Bay. The twin volcanoes belched smoke columns which mounted to the skies and almost obliterated the sun, muting it to a dull yellow orb.

The balcony in which we crouched was so high above the floor of the arena that we were well above the eyeline of the audience facing us. We were also partially hidden behind long dark-coloured curtains, which hung from the roof of the cave to just above the sandy floor. Nevertheless I cautioned Zaras and Hui in a whisper to draw back into the shadows and sheathe their swords to prevent reflections of even this diffuse daylight betraying our presence in the temple.

No sooner had I spoken when two lines of priests dressed in their bull's-blood-red robes filed in from each side of the amphitheatre. They took up their positions around the golden throne and their voices joined those of the nobles to fill the temple with mournful lamentation.

Then abruptly all sound was cut off and the heavy silence was more oppressive than the singing. The congregation groaned and as one they sank to their knees and pressed their foreheads to the marble tiles.

I was anticipating the appearance of the Supreme Minos, watching the empty throne with all my attention, expecting another theatrical stratagem. Yet even I was taken by complete surprise.

One moment the throne was empty, and the next the Minoan monarch was seated upon it with the frail and skeletal form of his mother at his side.

She was clad in her widow's weeds, dark and unwholesome. He was resplendent in full regalia, towering over all his subjects, seeming to fill the cavern with his presence. His armour and his hideous bull mask of precious metals shot slivers of brilliant light into the shadows.

Martial music from a hidden orchestra filled the cavern with tumultuous sound, and the congregation cried out in a transport of idolatrous ecstasy.

The Supreme Minos raised his mailed right fist and the silence that gripped the cavern was complete, almost stifling in its intensity. Even the three of us in the balcony high above the arena were intimidated by it.

The Minos made another gesture and the congregation gave voice again. But this was a feral sound, filled with primitive rage. Then the curtains that hung from the roof of the cavern were drawn aside to reveal two barred doorways in the rock wall, one on each side of the amphitheatre. The voice of the congregation rose in a frenzy of anticipation. Even the red-robed priesthood joined in the clamour, but now there was a further element to it. The sound was no longer that of prayer and worship. It became a bellow of salacious arousal, of carnal lust and sadistic rapture.

Through the opening between the curtains marched a phalanx of green-clad viragoes. They wore tall headgear dressed with the brilliant plumage of the flamingo bird. Their raised shields were made from the cured skin of the crocodile, and they overlapped to conceal something in the centre of their formation. They reached the centre of the arena and halted. Then at some pre-arranged signal their ranks opened to reveal my princesses.

Tehuti and Bekatha stood holding hands and looking up at the screaming throng on the tiers above them in utter bewilderment. On their heads they wore wreaths of white roses.

But that was their entire raiment. Their bodies were entirely naked. They seemed very young, tender and almost childlike. The viragoes turned in unison and marched from the arena, leaving Tehuti and Bekatha standing alone.

The thunder of the congregation swept over my two darlings, and they trembled before it. The Supreme Minos rose to his feet and the uproar subsided into silence once more. He turned slowly so his golden mask faced the opening in the rear wall of the temple in which was framed the distant image of Mount Cronus, and his voice soared as he began an invocation to his god. I could not make out a single word of the bellows and animal howling which reverberated from within his helmet.

However, the sense of it was unmistakable, even more so when he drew from the bejewelled scabbard on his belt a massive bronze blade. It was as long as I am tall. He turned towards the two naked children on the sacrificial floor below where he stood.

Now for the first time I discerned the actual words he uttered, although even they were blurred by the mask that covered his head and garbled by the echoes thrown back from the walls of rock.

'Dearly beloved Cronus! Cronus the first of all the gods! I am your son; the fruit of your loins; the flesh of your flesh and the blood of your blood. For a thousand years I have worshipped you. For a thousand years I have loved and obeyed you. Once again I stand before you to renew my vows. I bring you the sacrifice for which your divine soul craves. I bring you royal virgin blood to drink. I bring you royal virgin flesh to devour. Come forth in your earthly guise and partake of the feast I lay before you! Kill! Eat!'

He lifted the sword and stabbed it towards the barred gateway that faced Tehuti and Bekatha.

The double gates swung open but the interior beyond was in darkness. I stared into it but at first I could see nothing beyond the doorposts. Then something moved within: something so enormous and menacing that it defied my imagination.

Bekatha wailed and shrank against her elder sister, her face bleaching with terror. Tehuti placed her arm around her protectively; Bekatha clung to her with both arms. Both of them shrank back from the gateway.

A dense and palpable silence fell over the arena, and the entire world beyond. The rumbling thunder of the volcanoes was cut off abruptly. The earth beneath us was stilled. It seemed that even the great god Cronus was spellbound by the drama being played out in his own temple.

The silence was broken by the angry bovine snorts and the thud of great hooves on the sand-strewn paving. An aurochs bull charged through the gateway into the arena. He came to an abrupt halt as the sudden roar of the congregation struck him, and his front hooves ploughed into the sand and sent up a cloud of dust.

Whereas every other aurochs I had ever seen was brindled black and dark brown, this bull was as gleaming white as the spume on the crest of the tidal wave which had destroyed the city of Knossos. His eyes were as bright as polished rubies. His body seemed to swell even larger with rage as he swung his massive head from side to side, seeking a focus for his rage.

His colossal rack of horn was ivory white. The tips were glistening black and sharp as spearheads. Their spread was twice the span of a man's outspread arms.

Then the creature fixed his gaze on the two naked children standing before it, and it lowered his head. The great hump between his shoulder blades seemed to swell even larger with anger, and it pawed the ground.

I realized suddenly from its colour and its size, as well as from the aura of evil that exuded from it, that this was no creature of forest and mountain, but something that had been sent from the fiery depths of the volcano to accept the sacrifice on behalf of its demonic master.

It snarled at its prey. Its upper lip curled back to expose long canine fangs: the teeth of a carnivore, not those of an herbivore.

'I bring you royal virgin blood to drink. I bring you royal virgin flesh to devour,' the Supreme Minos had urged this creature. 'Kill! Eat!'

I shook off the horror which threatened to paralyse me. 'Zaras! Hui!' I lifted my voice above the deafening clamour of the Minoan congregation. 'We have to get down there to protect them. Use the curtains, but get down there.'

The two of them barged past me, almost knocking me off my feet in their haste. One after the other they dived over the

416

railing of our balcony, and they seized the hanging curtains as they dropped. They used them to break their fall as they slithered down to the floor of the arena. But I saw they were going to be too late to save Tehuti.

The gleaming white bull had focused all its attention on Tehuti and now it launched into its charge, thundering straight at her.

Bekatha screamed. It was a sound that must surely inflame the monster's temper. Zaras and Hui had only just reached the floor, and they still had half the ring to cross before they could intervene.

I drew and shot an arrow. It hit the bull's massive shoulder exactly where I had aimed, but I saw that it had struck bone and been deflected. It whined away and struck one of the noble Minoans in the audience. He dropped out of sight.

The bull was no more than scratched by my arrow. I dared not shoot again, because Bekatha had broken away from her sister. In blind panic she ran directly into the line of the charging bull.

The bull swerved towards her and dropped its monstrous head. It hooked one of the long gleaming horns at her, and the point caught her in the upper arm. I saw bone break and blood fly as she was thrown high over the bull's back. She hit the ground and I think the soft sand broke her fall. The bull turned to follow her.

Tehuti reacted more swiftly than any of us. She raced forward to intercept the bull's charge, screaming shrilly and waving her arms to divert its attention.

She ran under its flaring nostrils from which the steam of its hot and stinking breath spurted in the damp air of the cavern. As she passed she snatched the tiara of roses from her own head and dashed it into the face of the beast.

Taken aback, the great bull checked slightly, giving Tehuti just enough leeway to spin around and race towards where she saw Zaras only halfway down the curtains to the arena floor.

'Zaras!' she screamed. The bull hesitated for only an instant before it turned away from where Bekatha lay and came in pursuit of Tehuti. She was quick as a gazelle, but the bull was faster. It was almost on top of her when she jinked and changed direction, gaining herself a yard before the bull could follow her around.

I saw she would now pass almost directly beneath where I stood against the rail of the balcony. I drew the sword from the scabbard on my belt, lifted it high and hurled it down into the arena. It struck point first and pegged into the sand with its hilt standing upright in front of her.

'Get the sword!' I yelled down to Tehuti.

Once more Tehuti reacted with the speed and strength of a natural athlete. She swerved in her run and as she passed the sword she plucked it from the sand and settled the hilt in her right hand.

The bull was almost on her again. It swung its head and the point of its left horn hissed through the air as it sliced past her shoulder. Tehuti ducked under it and doubled back on the beast, sucking in her belly as the bull brushed past her. Then as the bull tossed up its head to recover its balance Tehuti seized hold of its nearest horn with her free hand, just behind the point.

When the aurochs lifted her on the horn she did not resist. Instead she went with him, jumping in the same direction. She sailed high over the aurochs's humped back and as she dropped she straightened her sword arm and aimed the point of the weapon down into its withers.

Here there was no bone to turn the point. With all her weight behind it Tehuti drove the full length of the blade down between its shoulder blades, transfixing the creature's heart. She released her grip on the hilt and left the blade in the wound.

Then she arched her back as she dropped lightly to her feet behind the stricken bull and pirouetted away, with both arms held high above her own head. She stood poised and watched the monstrous animal pull up short. It spread its front hooves wide apart, and lowered its head until its muzzle almost touched the sand. It opened its mouth wide and bellowed. From its throat shot a torrent of bright blood.

Then it staggered backwards until its back legs collapsed under it and it hit the floor of the arena with a sound like the fall of an axed cedar tree. It rolled on to its side. Its back legs kicked spasmodically, and then at last it lay quiescent. The silence in the cavern persisted for as long as it took me to fill my lungs with air.

Then the great god Cronus in the volcano across the bay gave full rein to his rage. He had been denied his sacrifice. The creature that was his *alter ego* had been slain in the precincts of his own temple.

I raised my head from the spectacle in the temple arena, and I gazed out across the Bay of Knossos and I beheld a wondrous sight.

In the extremity of rage Cronus destroyed his own stronghold. It seemed to happen very slowly. The entire mountain exploded into a thousand massive chunks of rock, some of them as large as Crete itself, and some much larger. They were hurled aloft by the catastrophic forces that were released from the very centre of the volcano that lay thousands of feet below the surface of the sea. The rock had been heated in this deep furnace until it melted and burned with a brilliant white light that seemed to dim the sun and illuminate our entire world. When the rock fell back below the surface, the sea boiled.

The steam from the boiling waters exploded into spinning white clouds that climbed skywards again, obliterating everything. It was all gone: sea and earth and sky. Only the dense wall of steam remained.

All this seemed to happen in silence while the world and every living creature in it held its breath.

Then came the noise of the cataclysm. It had taken that long to cross the waters of the bay. The sound smashed into the island of Crete like a solid object, something almost as substantial as the falling rock itself.

Even though we were partially shielded by the walls of the cavern that surrounded us, we were hurled to the ground by the ferocity and volume of the sound. We lay whimpering and clutching our own deafened ears.

The sound and the quaking of the earth prised great slabs off the roof of the cavern above us. All around me men were crushed screaming and sobbing to death by the falling rock, and the floor leaped and swayed under us like the deck of a ship in a hurricane.

I was amongst the first to gather my senses. But my eyes were still dazzled by the light of the burning mountain; and my hearing was dulled by the thunderous sound. I rolled on to my knees and gazed around the cavern. I was not the only person stirring.

Zaras had crawled to where Tehuti lay beside the carcass of the bull. He was cradling her in his arms. I could see she also was dazed and bewildered.

Hui was kneeling over Bekatha. He seemed afraid to touch her. This was a warrior who had bestridden many a battlefield, but he was terrified by the blood of the woman he loved. She was cradling her broken arm and looking up at Hui like a child seeking comfort from a beloved parent.

I looked beyond them and I saw the Supreme Minos. He was standing in the opening of the cavern facing the clouds of steam which obliterated the place where Mount Cronus had once stood.

The Minos was holding the frail body of his mother in both hands high above his head. I saw that her skull was crushed and her eyes were bulging out of their sockets. She had been struck and killed by the rocks falling from the roof of the cave.

'Why have you done this to us? I am your own son, mighty Cronus,' the Minos bellowed. 'My mother was your lover and your wife. Could you not have accepted the sacrifice I offered you and spared her?'

I knew that I had to kill him before he was able to let loose more evil upon our world. This time I knew he would destroy us all: my princesses, my friends and companions and me.

I threw up my bow and shot the arrow across the cavern. It struck the Minos in the centre of his golden backplate. It transfixed his body, and black blood sprayed from the hole that my arrow had ripped in his armour. The stench of it filled the temple like that of rotting corpses that had lain ten days in the sun.

The force of my striking arrow hurled the Minos bodily through the opening in the cavern wall. He fell from my sight. His mother's corpse lay where he had dropped it, like a pile of old black rags.

I jumped over the balcony wall and slid down the curtains to the floor of the arena. Then as I ran to where Bekatha lay I unhooked the sword scabbard from my belt. I knelt beside her and told Hui, 'Hold her firmly. This will hurt her.'

She whimpered as I straightened the broken bones in her arm, and used the sword sheath as a splint to fix them so. Then I took the wine flask from the pouch on my hip and handed it to Hui.

'Give her as much as she asks for,' I told him. 'But it's a fine Cyclades, and much too good for a ruffian like you.'

Bekatha smiled through her pain and whispered, 'Hui is my man. From now onwards wherever he goes, I go. His home is my home. And the wine I drink is his to share with me.' I was proud of her.

I looked around the temple and saw that the virago guards

from the royal seraglio had fled. I thought that all the Minoan nobles had gone with them, but then I saw Toran standing beside Zaras and Tehuti with his arm around Loxias.

'Will you come with us, my old friend?' I asked him, and Toran paused for a moment before he replied.

'The Minoan Empire has perished here today. It will never rise again. This was prophesied five hundred years ago.' His expression was sombre, but after a moment he went on speaking. 'I have lost my homeland. But Egypt has lost her most powerful ally against the Hyksos scourge.' He sighed. 'Nevertheless Loxias and I will go with you to Thebes and make it our new homeland.'

'I am afraid to ask you, Zaras and Tehuti,' I said as I turned to the two of them. It was no surprise to me that Tehuti spoke for both of them.

'Darling Taita, I love both you and Egypt but I love Zaras more,' she said simply. 'If I return with you to Thebes my brother will seek to marry me to another mad king in some other barbaric land. I have served my Pharaoh and my country to the very limits of my duty. Now I want to be free to live the rest of my life with the man I love.' She took Zaras' hand. 'We will go with Hui and Bekatha, and find another home in the northern lands beyond the Ionian Sea.'

'I wish I could go with you but I cannot,' I told her. 'My duty is with Pharaoh in Thebes. I will tell him that you and Bekatha are dead so that he will never send to search for you.'

'Thank you, darling Tata,' she said, and then she hesitated before she spoke again. 'Perhaps one day, if the gods are kind, you will come to find us again?'

'Perhaps!' I agreed.

'I will name my first son after you,' she promised and I turned away to hide the tears that filled my eyes. Then I climbed the tiers of stone benches which now were empty. I reached the opening of the cavern wall through which my arrow had thrown the body of the Minos.

I stood on the verge of the drop, and looked down three hundred feet to where he lay spreadeagled on the rocks below in a pool of his own congealing blood. My arrow stood out of his silver breastplate. His helmet still covered his head. I could see nothing through the dark eye-holes that seemed to stare up at me.

'What were you?' I pondered the question aloud, but speaking softly. 'Were you man or monster, devil or godling?' Then I shook my head. 'I pray never to know the answer to that question.'

The body of Pasiphaë, the mother of the Minos, lay at my feet. I picked it up and dropped it over the cliff. When I looked down again I saw that they lay together with arms and legs obscenely tangled like those of lovers, rather than mother and son.

I turned away and went down into the arena where my girls waited for me. All of us left the temple and went out through the labyrinth to where the horses waited in the forest. We mounted and rode together as a family for the last time. We climbed the slopes of Mount Ida and we drew rein on the shoulder and looked back across the Bay of Knossos.

Mount Cronus was gone, sucked back into the abysmal depths of the ocean once more. Only the turbid waters of the boiling sea marked its grave.

Then we looked ahead to where the port of Krimad had once stood and we saw all six ships of the flotilla had survived the tidal wave, and were anchored safely offshore. They were waiting to receive us.

All those around me shouted with joy and excitement, urging their horses down the path through the forest. They rode in pairs, Lord Toran with Loxias, Hui cradling Bekatha to his chest to shield her injured arm and Zaras with Tehuti up behind him urging him to greater speed.

I hung back and let them go. 'Let their separate journeys

begin here and end for all of them on the Hills of Happiness,' I whispered aloud, but my pleasure for them was tempered by my melancholia for my own self: poor lonely Taita. Then I heard a voice that might have been only the evening wind in the treetops.

'You will never be alone, Taita, for a noble heart is the lodestone which draws to itself the love of others.'

I looked around me in wild amazement and I thought I saw her coming down to me through the forest in her hood and cloak. But the light was fading and I could have been mistaken.